SEXY AS SIN

THE ACCIDENTAL EXORCIST

JENNIFER CHANCE

Oliver Heber Books

CONTENT NOTE

This dark paranormal romance contains demonic possession and loss of bodily autonomy, body horror, complex consent dynamics, graphic violence, and explicit sexual content. Intended for mature readers (18+) who aren't afraid of the dark. Mostly.

CHAPTER

ONE

Why did demons always go for kids?

And why had I accepted another exorcism job that had taken me two hours out of Chicago, based on nothing but a five-thousand-dollar retainer and a panicked-sounding plea for help?

I tightened my hands on the wheel of Claire Bickwell's cream-colored Lexus and peered at the thick, menacing trees as they loomed over the two-lane road running alongside Starved Rock State Park, seriously beginning to doubt my life choices. *This had better not be some kind of scam.*

It'd sounded legit enough. Barely three days after moving into our new office as Thompson & Associates—a far better business name than Exorcisms-R-Us, Claire had assured me—a woman had emailed us claiming to have heard of our all-inclusive evil eradication service from my most recent—and only—client so far. While I was grateful that Maxwell Graham had told Nanette Simmons we were the real deal, I hadn't quite pinned down how *she* had found *him*. He hadn't wanted to talk about it. Claire had urged me not to care. Nanette had gotten straight to the point.

The Meadowbrook Wellness Recovery Center, drug rehab camp of choice for Chicago's most elite families and their troubled teens, had a problem. A demon problem, they were pretty sure, though they couldn't be certain. Whatever it was, they were willing to pay however much I asked to have me fix it, as long as I came right away.

Claire Bickwell, PharmD, my newly minted part-time office manager at Thompson & Associates and unofficial shadow, should have been working her usual shift today at Reider's, Oak Park's fanciest neighborhood drugstore. Instead, she'd eagerly volunteered to serve as my second-in-demonic-command—as long as I drove. I didn't think I'd need an assistant for this job, but then again, Claire did have a car. She also had a screenshot of the map Nanette had sent with an offhanded warning that cell service was spotty in the preserve.

Sure enough, we'd lost our GPS signal about an hour and a half west of Oak Park, right about when the trees started crowding the road, blocking out the sun. By the time we hit the woods around Meadowbrook, mist was pooling in the forest hollows and the cliffside drop to the Illinois River seemed to slip closer every time we glimpsed it through the fog.

"This is the turn," Claire announced, gesturing with her phone even as I slowed. I'd already seen the small, up-lit sign tucked into the leafy-bowered lane. "And this wellness center, or whatever it is, already feels way nicer than the Grahams' place—like, too nice, you know? Based on Nanette's write-up, the kids here are rich, their parents are powerful, and they all hang out at the same country clubs. I thought demons picked on outcasts. Do they like chummy rich people too?"

"Demons like open doorways." I shrugged. "They pretty much don't care whose door it is."

Chewing my bottom lip, I turned off the winding road, catching a quick glimpse of my hands on the steering wheel. My fingernails were ragged, bitten past the quick. When had I done that? I didn't remember. Couldn't. But I must have—right? I'd been stressed. That was all. Stress.

Meanwhile, Claire leaned closer to the window, trim and professional in her soft pink pantsuit and white silk shell—and, I suspected, far more excited to be here than most of the clients who made this turn.

We fell silent as the lane continued deeper into the forest, and I was grateful for the soothingly spaced lights that guided our way through the gloom. Eventually, the trees broke ranks and we pulled up to the center itself: a gleaming, low-slung building occupying an open space the size of a football field, fronted by a generous, precisely manicured lawn. This definitely wasn't a place you could sneak up on.

Claire leaned forward to drop her phone into the functional but stylish cream-colored leather tote she had apparently found in the exorcist accessories section of Nordstrom. I didn't know what kind of props she'd filled it with, but it looked heavy. "I have two copies in here of that insanely detailed NDA they had us sign, by the way, and one back at the office in case they insist on you signing anything new."

I glanced at her. "You think they'll do that?"

"You didn't hear Nanette on the phone this morning. Something new happened, I think. She was jumpier than a room full of chihuahuas, but she wouldn't tell me anything more than what she said in her email. Which...wasn't a lot, honestly."

"They paid the retainer in full up front, right?" I pointed out. "I guess that's all we need to know."

She snorted. "Yeah, well, you ask us to sign a four-page NDA and drag us two hours out of the city, you're definitely paying up front."

Still, she also didn't make any move to get out of the car. The two of us simply stared at the improbably modern-looking building hunkered down in the middle of nowhere. "You didn't have to come out here, you know," I finally said. "And you absolutely can wait for me here. It may not even be a thing."

"Well, that's just silly." She breathed out again, a little unsteadily. "You're Thompson & Associates. You need an associate who isn't an actual demon. Plus, I'm a doctor."

I squinted at her. "Of pharmacy."

"Which makes me the best *kind* of doctor." She grinned. "Credibility *and* unlimited access to drugs. Plus, I'm a normalizing influence. Without me by your side, you'd scare the crap out of people."

I couldn't help it, I laughed. "So, what's the problem?"

"I don't *know*," she admitted, with a guileless honesty I was beginning to believe was authentic. "I didn't think it would be a big deal when we got in the car. I mean, I was there for your last exorcism, and that has to be creepier than...whatever this is going to be."

"But?"

She sighed. "But then we drove two hours into the middle of the forest primeval to a 'wellness center' that looks like a cross between a Super Max prison and a space station. There's nothing about this place online—it's unsearchable other than the home page of its website, which is password-protected—and this?" She gestured to the building, her words picking up speed. "It isn't at all what it looks like on the website. The building in their promo pics looked like it could have been built by Frank Lloyd Wright. This place seems like Dr. Evil's secret lair. I mean, sure, rich people gonna rich, but—what if something is going on out here that's really wrong?"

I snorted. "You mean, besides a demon possession?"

"*Exactly*," she said, turning to face me in her seat, her shiny blonde hair bouncing earnestly as her blue eyes widened in her fair, pretty face. "What if they're mistreating these kids and getting away with it because no one knows they're out here? What if they're hurting them? What do we do then?"

Her gaze shifted abruptly to the building before I could respond. "We should move. Someone's coming out." Her hand strayed to the necklace at her throat, where the tiny gold cross hung, but actual demons were clearly only part of her concern.

"Moving," I agreed brightly, pushing open the door and stepping out into the sunlight. For all that it was midsummer, I regretted not bringing a sweater. What must this place be like in winter?

"Good morning! Good morning," the woman called out, all smiles and cherry-blossom pink linen dress as she strode out to meet us. The voice tracked with the Nanette who called us, but the age didn't. The woman's face looked a solid ten years younger than it should, with its smooth forehead, plump cheeks, and cupid's-bow lips. "I'm Nanette Simmons. You must be Delia Thompson and Dr. Bickwell, correct? I hope you didn't have any difficulty finding the facility. We're so glad you were able to come so quickly."

She turned and gestured us forward, and I moved with her, grateful for the black linen pants, cream-colored short-sleeved shell, and flats that Claire had handed over to me this morning, instructing me to skip the matching jacket. Nanette Simmons was as polished as the steel and glass installation she led us into, never mind the cheerfully bubbling fountain outside the door and the low-slung, comfortable-looking couches arranged hopefully in the lobby, as if people might actually sit on them.

We weren't going to, clearly, as Nanette continued striding across the bright, open, and scrupulously clean space, her pace too quick for conversation. This close, I picked up the scent of her Chanel perfume, as well as high-key panic, expensive wine drunk too quickly, and hair growing white at the roots. Whatever had happened at Meadowbrook Wellness Recovery Center that had inspired Nanette to call me, it'd happened in a hurry.

"Right this way," she murmured as she keyed open a door with a little plastic card pressed against a reader. The door lock clicked, but Claire stopped, lifting a hand before Nanette could reach forward. My assistant was dressed several notches better than I was, and when she spoke, none of her hesitation from the car was in evidence.

"Ah! Forgive me, I should have requested pass cards already for Delia and me. We'll need those before we go any farther," she said.

Nanette turned, and twin flags of color warmed her cheeks, as soft and rosy as her dress. "You'll have an escort at all times here at Meadowbrook. The group therapy room is just inside—"

"And yet," Claire smiled, flashing a smooth row of teeth. She gestured vaguely back to the conversational seating at the front of the lobby. "We need to be able to exit the premises at will, to ensure the safety of your residents. We can wait there while you get cards."

Nanette blinked, but the woman wasn't an idiot. I could practically see her sorting likely responses and weighing them against the pain of continued delay. The pain won out. "Of course. I fully understand."

She pulled out her phone and made the request, holding Claire's gaze the entire time. When she pocketed the device again, her hands were shaking. "I can explain a bit while we wait, to save time. We've gathered all six current residents in the group room and have a facilitator with them. You'll start in the adjacent observation room, then join the residents when you're ready."

I fought the automatic lip curl. "Do the, um, residents know they're being watched?"

She lifted a brow as carefully shorn as the grass outside. "Of course they do. This facility is not some sort of Victorian sanitarium, Ms. Thompson. We're a caring, collaborative healing center for young people with substance abuse issues, and we boast a remarkable track record. Our residents are here by choice. We're very proud of our ability to work holistically with both our residents and their families to achieve healing of the whole person—ah. Here we are."

Nanette broke off from her PR recitation as a young aide strode up, a dark-haired, dark-eyed man in his early twenties who looked like he could bench press a Buick. Once he handed off the pass cards and we pushed our way through the heavy doors, Nanette visibly relaxed—and kept talking.

"There will be a few additional observers in the viewing room, as per protocol," she said. She shifted her glance to me. "Victoria Ashford is one of our board members. She approved our request to hire you, and she's taken a particular interest in your work, Ms. Thompson. You may remember her son's death a few years ago? She's asked me a great deal of questions about you, and I provided what answers I could. She may wish to have a private conversation with you."

I pressed my lips together. "I'm not a psychic, Ms. Simmons. I can't channel her dead child or bring him back to life."

My words came out a little harsher than I intended, and Nanette's smile showed some strain. "I'm sure she would never ask you to try. I merely wanted to let you know of her interest. Robert Banks will also be in attendance. His son is one of the affected residents."

"One?" I asked sharply. "How many students are 'affected,' exactly?" I'd managed to exorcise six demons at a throw at Maxwell Graham's country estate, but I wasn't looking for a repeat performance.

"We don't *know*," Nanette said, her voice breaking on the last word. "The entire group was doing so well until Mr. Banks' son arrived last week—but since he has, there've been several incidents of the residents acting out, self-harming, attempting to escape. We knew we needed to act quickly."

"And you *started* with an exorcist?" I peered at her, remembering how long it had taken me to face up to my own demon, the one who flowed through my veins like oil and ash, and who'd left an empty hole inside me after I'd evicted him. I'd lasted fifteen years before acknowledging I had a problem, and I'd worked with a guy who did this for a living. "Why not more doctors? Specialists?"

She pulled out her phone again. "Almost immediately after Bobby arrived, the residents began drawing on the walls. I couldn't send you this without the NDA in hand, but I will now. They've been archived, and I don't want them on my phone anymore."

As she poked and slashed at her device, I thought of my own wall drawings, conjuring up the image of another demon in his many shifting forms—a beautiful fallen angel, a grotesque beast of snarling evil...and an impossibly gorgeous hunk of seemingly human male who'd found me in my new office to inform me we were now partners.

Lucian Gray. He'd been MIA for two weeks, but now that we had a case, would he find me again? Did I want him to?

"Here," Nanette said, shoving the phone at me. I took it, but I didn't need to expand the photo much to understand why she'd contacted me. These walls might have been my own, not all that long ago: covered in slurs, demonic symbols, violently drawn images of horned monsters, and denouncements of all that was good and pure in the world.

I showed the image briefly to Claire, who blanched. Then I handed the phone back to Nanette. "Ok, fair. And you think Bobby's the target, here?"

Her anxiety ratcheted down a little. "He's the newest resident, and it was quiet before that—nothing like this has ever happened here. To be fair, Bobby himself hasn't shown any irregular behavior. In fact, he's one of our star residents—expressing genuine remorse, engaging in therapy, working out. He's thrived in this environment. Which is why we…we're just not sure. At this point, the residents have been sensitized to violence, and so when they act out, we don't know if it's causal or if they're mimicking what they've seen." She bit her lip. "You'll see. They can become violent at a moment's notice. You do understand that, yes?" She darted a glance down the hallway and turned away from me as she spoke.

"I do," I said, but she didn't seem to be listening anymore, at least not to me. She led us down the hallway past several doors, and when she reached out to key the final door open, her hand visibly shook. "They're quiet now. That's good. But their energy this morning is bad, Ms. Greene said. She's threatened to quit. I think she's self-medicating."

I glanced at Claire, meeting her startled blue eyes. "She's their therapist?" I asked as the door unlocked.

Nanette sailed inside without answering me. "Good morning, Ms. Ashford, Mr. Banks," she said brightly, as she led us into a shadowed chamber dominated by a large window on one side that opened out onto a space filled with cozy couches and chairs draped with plush-looking throws, thick carpeting, and a half-dozen young adults staring at phones that appeared wired into charging stations. The observation room was dim, deliberately so—the better to hide us from the residents beyond the glass. But it felt less like protection and more like we were the ones in a cage, watching lab rats we couldn't quite control. Awesome. "Ms. Thompson and her associate Dr. Bickwell are—"

Wham!

We all whirled and backed away from the observation

window and the boy who'd suddenly rushed it. I caught a vague impression of a polo shirt and khakis, designer eyeglasses, short dark hair and smooth pale skin, and large hands smacking flat on the window. The boy's mouth stretched too wide, jaw hanging at an angle mouths shouldn't, and his face was slick with sweat that smelled wrong even through the glass—sweet and rotten, like fruit left to die in the sun. *Wham!* He struck again.

"Bobby!" a man's voice called out, shocked, and despite the thick-paned glass that separated the two rooms, Nanette and the two board members scrambled back deeper into the shadows. Claire mewed a soft and primal sound but stood her ground, while I simply stared as the kid swung his head my way. He should have been looking at his own reflection, but somehow, he knew where I stood. He pinned his wide, jittering eyes to me, his mouth still agape in an unhinged grin, his chin dripping.

Our gazes met, the eyes shifted, and just like that, I knew the demon who plagued this soul.

Thank God, I at least knew that.

Mordechai, of course, would've already had a plan for what to do next. Lucian—I couldn't think about him right now. I took a step toward the boy behind the glass and fixed a hard smile on my face.

"Belphegor, you miserable sack of shit," I muttered, and I realized I did know more, at least about the creature himself. I'd been studying every old hoary demon treatise I could get my hands on for the past month, making my way through the Newberry Library's complete catalog of ancient religious texts, so I knew that all demons belonged to one of seven courts, tied to the seven deadly sins. According to those texts, Belphegor was a third-level sloth demon from the Court of Indolence. As a sloth demon, he'd be woefully out of his element in this locked-down facility. I suspected he'd only been inside his host a few weeks, maybe a month. That should make things easier, but he was wound up, almost frantic, and that seemed...off.

As I leaned closer, I sensed the weight of Nanette's panicked gaze on my back, the tension of the other watchers. "You need to go," I told him.

The kid blinked, then he smiled and leaned closer to the window too. As he did, the temperature in the observation room plummeted. My breath fogged in the suddenly frigid air. Bobby couldn't see me, of course, but he knew we were watching. He knew everyone was watching.

"Do I?" he asked, his voice crackling over the speaker.

He stuck out his tongue and licked the one-way mirror in a long, slithering slide of thick, gelatinous bile. The tongue moved wrong, too long, too flexible. It left a trail that should have been yellow-green but shimmered black in the observation room's dim light. Behind the kid, the other residents had gone utterly still.

Then Bobby Banks slammed his forehead into the glass. Blood split the skin above his brow. He reared back, howling with laughter.

Someone gasped behind me. Someone else started shouting. Gripping my pass card in my fist, I whirled and yanked Claire's bag from her unresisting hand, then sprinted for the door.

TWO

I banged into the hallway and made it the twenty feet down to the therapy room door before even drawing a breath. My brain pinballed around my skull with half-remembered prayers, processes, warnings, and words—so many words! Why had I never really listened to all of Mordechai's words?

Slinging the lanyard around my neck, I dumped Claire's bag out on the floor, snatched the Bible and medals—anything blessed would do—and jammed the pass key toward the reader.

The door unlocked and I yanked it open, only to be nearly knocked flat on my ass by Ms. Greene as she rushed through the door and into the hallway. I hadn't even seen her before, and now I got the vague impression of frizzy brown hair, bloodshot eyes, charred rubber panic, and ice baths. "I can't!" she managed and scrambled away. I let her go. She didn't have what I was after.

Instead, I stepped into the room and slammed the door closed behind me.

The kids were back in their chairs, but not for long, I didn't think. And now they all were holding hands with each other, which wasn't creepy *at all*. Had they been holding hands before?

Bobby sat in the center, blood dripping from his forehead, couched between an older teenage girl with long, glossy black hair and a jittery-looking kid who looked to be about fourteen years old.

I'd skimmed the write-up of the students and knew that Bobby Banks was a dedicated jock who balanced his time between the gym and whipping up spinach smoothies at home. How had Belphegor even gotten his claws into this kid? Other than his newly scraped-up forehead, Bobby looked as clean-cut as it got. And the fact that his dad was hyperventilating in the next room meant he had an active, engaged support system. So, how…?

Bobby started trembling, and I reined in my galloping thoughts. "Belphegor," I announced sharply. "Time's up. We both know it."

Though he jolted, the boy didn't lift his gaze to me, so I held up the St. Jude's medal, wincing as it stung my skin. That did the trick, of course. For all their love of darkness and shadow, demons never could resist the bright and the shiny—even when it would hurt them. Focusing on Bobby's shivering shoulders and blood-and-bile-soaked shirt, I moved toward the boy slowly, almost warily, my eyes on the one-time ordinary teenager's face. Where had all the blood come from? "Whoever dwells in the shelter of the Most High will rest in the shadow of the Almighty," I said clearly. "I will say of the Lord, 'He is my refuge and my fortress, my God, in whom I trust. Surely, He will save you from the fowler's snare—'"

Bobby's head snapped up. "But who will save *you*?" he challenged, in a garbled snarl that could only be Belphegor. Then his eyes peeled wide—too wide—flaring red. "What's this?

What's this?" he gasped. "You've touched *Palemerious*? He's returned?"

As Bobby broke off in a wild, insane cackle of unhinged laughter, a stabbing chill ripped through me. That wasn't a name this boy or his demon should associate with me. I'd evicted the evil that had stained me for fifteen years, wrenched it out and set it free.

The fact that said evil had come back to me in the form of a ridiculously gorgeous thirst trap practically dripping with heat and danger—Belphegor shouldn't have picked up on that. No one should have.

This was bad.

As if picking up on my ping-ponging emotions, all the students started laughing now, too loud, too stridently, pounding their feet on the floor, but the girl beside Bobby threw her arms around him and pushed him backward into the couch, squealing with delight. The two collapsed in a wild embrace, then the girl spun away from him, angling toward the wingback chairs.

Bobby slumped over, his elbows dropping heavily to his knees, so I glared at the kid's heaving shoulders. "You have no purpose here, no reason and no power, Belphegor," I said sternly. "You shall not trouble this child of—"

"Get out!" A new shout ripped out from my right. "Go, go, go!"

I jerked my attention to the side as a mop-topped kid of maybe ten erupted out of his chair and barreled straight into my side, scrabbling for any kind of hold on me, climbing me like a tree. He was small and clumsy, his fingers soft and his body slender and frail, or he would have succeeded in wrapping his pale, clammy hands around my neck. He smelled of woodsmoke, worms, and—Belphegor?

I dropped the Bible and medals, wrestling him off me and

grabbing his wrists with my hands. His face came up, his wild eyes met mine—and yup, same demon.

"*Belphegor*," I gritted out, grateful that it sounded like a statement and not a question, but I still couldn't understand what I was seeing. How in the hell—

"Jamie!" Another kid howled as the small boy slumped, dead weight in my hands. A stouter girl suddenly appeared at my side, trying to pull the boy away. She swung toward me, her carefully coiffed blonde hair flowing out in a heavily conditioned wave, then lifted her hands from Jamie to go after me with manicured French-tipped nails curved like claws.

This time I didn't need to look her in the eyes to know, to finally understand. Belphegor was jumping hosts—never mind that he was a sloth demon, given more to couch surfing than body hopping—he was doing it. Mordechai had told me about this, but I'd never seen it, and I was in here alone with these feral kids. Thank God, the therapist had fled, or I'd have to contend with a full-grown woman potentially taking her turn. Claire and the others needed to stay the hell away—or they'd risk possession too.

"Belphegor, your time troubling all these souls is—ended —" I grunted, blocking the girl with an elbow and throwing her off course. Then I swooped down and picked up the Bible, brandishing it like a shield.

The girl stopped short, her eyes wide, as her mouth stretched into a toothy grin made all the more gruesome by the split lip beneath her glistening lip gloss. "You let Pale*merious* go," she giggled, the name of the demon little more than a hiss. "And now he's gone! You should have killed him when you had the chance!"

Killed him? I frowned, but this didn't seem the time to explain that exorcists didn't kill demons.

"You need to go, Belphegor," I snapped instead as new

words flowed through me, words I'd heard a thousand times over, spoken in archaic Hebrew before Rabbi Mordechai settled into English. *"Omar la-Adonai, machsi u-metzudati, Elohai evtach bo."*

"No, I don't," the demon snarled, but I stepped toward the girl he currently squatted in and held her gaze as I repeated more familiar words.

"Oh, yes," I corrected him. "For He shall deliver you from the snare of the fowler and from the deadly pestilence," I murmured softly, almost sensually. "He shall cover you with His feathers, and under His wings shall you find refuge."

The girl opened her mouth to work up a gobbet of spit at me, and her skin went totally white. Around us, I could feel the other kids drawing closer, reaching for her, for us both, but I could also smell the truth about this girl, this poor child that Belphegor now stained with his oily filth. She'd gotten hooked on stimulants trying to stay awake long enough to study—not to be thin, or pretty, or to escape the pressures of an insane sports dream, but just to keep up with the work she would never finish otherwise.

"Belphegor," I chided, feeling more in control again. "Why do you trouble this daughter of the Creator? She has no strength for you to wield. She is trapped in this place of order as you are trapped, and you cannot take her with you. The best you can do is flee this place, never to return."

"I'm trapped," the girl cried, her eyes peeling wide, finally looking terrorized. "I didn't mean to take the pills, I didn't mean—"

"Trapped." Another voice belched out of her, hard and raucous, indicating we were back to Belphegor, but the girl spun away from me, scrabbling back on all fours until she hit Bobby in the shins, then slumped. On cue, Bobby jerked to attention again. Twisting to the left on the couch, he lurched for

the nearest phone plugged into the table beside him. Yanking hard on the device, he drew its cord tight, but the table itself didn't budge. The phones weren't merely charging; they were wired down into stands that'd been bolted to the floor. Nice.

That didn't mean Bobby was without weapons, though. He whipped off his glasses and knuckled the prongs between his fingers, then he charged me. I ducked at the last minute and threw my shoulder into his gut, the two of us going down to the floor. But at least the floor meant easier access to the other holy artifacts I'd hauled in. I rolled their direction, grabbing two oval medals of St. Jude, each the size of my thumb, using the crackling pain that blossomed across my hands to ground myself.

Bobby reached out and snagged my leg, dragging me back, and I used the momentum of his movement to fling my body at him. I knocked him backward on the floor as I scrambled up and sat on his chest. Using a move I'd seen Mordechai pull off with an old man, I slammed my hands over his eyes and pressed in hard, pushing the medals against his eye sockets.

Pain radiated up my arms, blasting my joints and nearly dislocating my shoulders. Since when were exorcisms supposed to *hurt* so much?

"Claire!" I shouted toward the cracked one-way mirror. "Clear us a path!"

I had no idea if Claire or the others heard or understood what I needed, but with Belphegor cowering back from the medals, I leaned down close and began the sacred psalm all over again, chanting it like a mantra while Bobby bucked and writhed beneath me. Glancing up, I caught sight of the others—frozen in place, staring at Bobby and me, once more stone-faced and dead-eyed. Huffing out a grunting breath as I struggled to keep Bobby subdued, I tried a different tack, murmuring to Belphegor about what it would be like to be free, out into the open air, flowing from sunshine to shadow, open and—

"You *lie*," the demon's snarl came again, but there was something behind it now, something desperate and honest in a way I'd heard before from the horde, when Mordechai had trapped them.

"I don't lie," I returned, as evenly as I could, never mind that the boy was now trembling violently beneath me, his breath fetid and rank, like he'd spent so many hours vomiting he didn't know how to eat anymore. "You don't need to trouble this beloved child any longer, Belphegor. You need not twist and hide inside a body that doesn't do what you need. This acolyte was never meant to worship at the altar of sloth and lethargy. He was never real, never good enough for you. In this place of bondage, these children are no longer worthy vessels. You realized that too late, you saw it happening, and now you need to get out. I can help you do that."

"Like you did with Palemerious?" it huffed. "Where is he? He must—"

"Like I do with any demon." I twisted around, eyeing the door, but it still remained steadfastly shut. Where the hell was Claire? I hauled Bobby backward toward the door, my arms hooked beneath his armpits, my hands still over his eyes. He was limp as I dragged him toward the doorway, but he was still shaking, and none of the other kids moved, thank God. I couldn't go through this again.

Plus, sloth demons were never the kind to jump like this, not on purpose—it took way too much energy. Most likely, being trapped in a facility with locks and clocks, rigid schedules, and too-bright lights had proven to be too much for Belphegor. He wasn't jumping to attack, but because he was panicking.

Still, he was really *good* at jumping. I didn't know how long I could keep him trapped.

"*Door*," I growled again, hoping Claire or Nanette could

figure out I needed a clear path to open air to get the demon out of this facility. "All the way out."

I slipped again into a singsong mantra of prayers. Speaking evenly, I freelanced out to Mordechai's second favorite psalm, riffing for the benefit of the demon beneath me. "Why shouldn't you be the one to lie down in green pastures, Belphegor, taking your ease by still waters? Far better there, isn't it, than here in this place of structure and steel, healthy food, and therapy sessions? This isn't the place for you. This was never the place for you."

"They wouldn't let me *out*," the boy sobbed, but Belphegor's plaintive whine came through his broken words. I kept the pressure on the kid's eyes, his weakness. I didn't want the demon exploding an eyeball just because that was the cleanest exit point. "Locks and clocks and smiles and words, but no way out! No way out! So many locks and clocks and smiles and—"

I heard it then, the tell-tale click of the door being released behind me. Keeping my voice low and even, so low even the listeners in the next room couldn't hear, I leaned down. "You are the creation of the Lord most High, His darkness, His spawn, His truth," I whispered to Belphegor. "You exist because He suffers it, and you may leave only because He commands you may. That is the glory and honor and truth and that is the Way, should you choose to follow it. So begone and trouble these children no more, and...stay away from the locks and clocks and smiles and words, Belphegor. Go only to the open air and sunshine, and be free."

"But howwwwww...."

I didn't need to answer that, of course. The answer was right in front of me, because with his broken eyes blocked, the easiest exit out of Bobby was revealed in the burst of fetid air he belched, still trying to expel the toxins he'd shoved into his system all those weeks ago. As I sat three feet from the door, which finally, mercifully, was yanked open by unseen hands, the boy buckled and retched, then projectile vomited more green goo all over my hands, my neck, and my lovely new silk T-shirt.

And in that violent expulsion, I saw it—the demon's true form, a writhing shadow that pulsed with rot and stagnation, of too many limbs moving wrong, sliding out of the boy's mouth like oil and smoke. It belched and gasped, a sound that shouldn't come from anything living, and fled down the hallway in a panic that was almost, almost human.

Then all the other kids started crying, while the vomit-covered Bobby passed out in my arms.

I didn't move for a long moment, simply sat there in the wreckage of broken lives and twisted pathways, trying to catch my breath. Almost without thinking about it, I cast my mind out, looking for...who? Palemerious, the demon I'd learned was apparently a seventh-level commander in the Ravening Court? Or Lucian Gray—a lesser, fourth-level demon now instead of exalted seventh?

Either way, no one responded.

I leaned my head against the wall and sighed, letting my eyes drift shut as shouting adults filled the hallway.

Screw them both. I had a business to run.

It was another hour and fifteen minutes before I sat in a different room off that open lobby, huddled next to Claire in a new long-sleeved T-shirt emblazoned with the Meadowbrook logo, my hair still damp from the complimentary post-exorcism shower the facility provided. Nothing but the best for Meadowbrook friends and family.

Nanette and the female from the observation room sat opposite us now, but while Nanette pressed her hands on two thick folders of paperwork, the woman studied me with keen intensity. Victoria Ashford was maybe fifty years old, dressed in an unstructured black shift with cream piping at the neck and black slingback heels. Her still-red hair was swept back in a stylish blowout, and the tennis bracelet on her wrist could have paid my rent for the next six months before we even started talking about the diamonds at her ears and the rock on her left hand.

She smelled like over-creased sorrow and stale fatigue, lake water and frozen memories.

"Would you like more coffee?" she asked, gesturing to the service that sat on an oversized stainless-steel cart that could double as a gurney. I shook my head but pulled my mug closer, a more effective shield than the Bible had proven to be. I forced myself not to pull down my sleeves further. No one needed to know about the bruises I'd collected in that group therapy room, the fingerprint-sized marks marching from wrist to elbow. Only, they'd been my fingerprints, somehow, perfectly aligned to my fingers. Four on the left bicep, thumb on the inside. Like I'd grabbed myself in the midst of all the fighting. Hard. I had no memory of it. Claire hadn't mentioned it.

In fact, Claire was holding onto her mug with both hands. Had she been injured, too? I doubted it.

She nodded to Nanette and her folders. "While Jeremy finishes his review of the students' rooms, so that we can make sure that we've done our due diligence and everyone is accounted for, I went ahead and asked Nanette to finalize the paperwork for your consultation here. While the students will undergo extensive observation over the next few days, they currently don't appear to have any recollection of the events from today's session."

"They might later," I said frankly. "The behavior that you witnessed today isn't normal for possession, and among the more sensitive children, they may have residual memory or impact. I don't know how long you keep kids in here, but you want to make sure that they are talking about anything that seems off to them, strange dreams, idle thoughts that take a dark turn come with things like that. Most of all, you need to love them."

The words were out before I could stop them, and I fought the blush that crawled up my cheeks. "Sorry," I said, grimacing. "Most of the exorcisms I've helped conduct up to this point were in small, private settings, with families. But it's good advice all the same."

"That's right. Nanette said you worked for several years with the ex-rabbi Mordechai Schneider, is that right?" Ashford asked, leaning forward. "She got your name from one of his most recent clients. I understand Mr. Schneider is no longer with us, but from everything I could find on him, his methods were, shall we say, strikingly non-traditional. He borrowed from both Jewish and Catholic traditions, as well as some that diverged into other religious practices. It appears you follow a similar approach with your work."

I met her gaze, held it. "Rabbi Mordechai died last month, yes. As I explained to Mrs. Simmons, I've only recently begun taking on my own clients, and my methods quite definitely diverge, to use your term, from his. I don't pretend otherwise, and I made it clear that I have no certification or ordination of any sort. She didn't appear to have an issue with that, and she signed the contract indicating her understanding of that fact."

"That's absolutely the truth," Nanette put in, surprising me. The color had never fully faded from her pink cheeks, and her hands trembled as they pressed down on the folders. "Mrs. Ashford, as I explained to you previously, the events that led us to seeking out Ms. Thompson escalated rapidly and we felt it was best to find an expeditious solution as close to home as possible, before exploring more traditional paths. I had the board's full approval, as the cost was a fraction of the damages that we would have sustained under any other circumstances."

"Mm." Victoria Ashford leaned back, picking up her own mug of coffee. "And yet, how do we know if the exorcism we witnessed was real? What happens if the students return to acting erratically in individual and group sessions?"

"You mean is there a money-back guarantee?" Claire's question was so sharp I stiffened, but she studied Mrs. Ashford with the kind of cool superiority that came naturally to someone who usually wore a white coat. "If so, the answer is no, Mrs. Ashford. As was clearly explained to Mrs. Simmons. If and as needed, Delia may choose to return to this facility and continue to assist and/or serve as a liaison to any subsequent practitioners you wish to bring in. But her efforts here this morning have already proven successful, wouldn't you say?"

Ashford swung her gaze to Claire, her expression interested and assessing.

"And you've been her business partner for how long, again?" she asked, her tone equally cool.

The door opened, saving Claire from having to kill the woman in the face, and Mr. Banks bustled in.

"Thank you," he said, rushing up to me and holding out his hand. Surprised, I reached out reflexively, only to have him swallow my hand in both of his. He pumped vigorously, then turned to the other women. "Bobby is fine. He's more than fine. He woke up and recognized me for the first time since the overdose. Truly saw me, which is saying something since he broke his glasses into fourteen pieces in that room."

He swung back to me, his eyes shining with new-sprung tears. "You put medals of Saint Jude over his eyes. The patron saint of lost causes. Why did you do that?"

"I..." I didn't have enough game to give them anything but

an honest answer. "Demons leave through the weakest available portal. All I knew about Bobby was that he played baseball and needed glasses. The easiest point of exit would have been his eyes, but I didn't want him to suffer that. I've already seen what that does." Unbidden, the image of Nikolai Volkov surfaced in my memory. The demon possessing the Eastern European crime lord, trapping him in the back rooms of his own high-end club, had been particularly vicious on his way out. "Bobby had already endured traumatic vomiting episodes in the recent past. I figured that was an easier option."

The man stared at me, something shining in his eyes that made me uncomfortable, and Mrs. Ashford set down her coffee mug with a decided thunk. "Well, I would say, to your point, that it has thus far been a very successful engagement. Probably one of the most successful consulting engagements we've had this year. So thank you, Ms. Thompson, Dr. Bickwell. Nanette will handle the final paperwork and should we need anything else, we'll be in touch."

As Mrs. Ashford stood, Claire's phone buzzed in her pocket, making her jump. We stood as well, and after handshakes all around, she pressed the phone into my hand before moving over to accept the folders from Nanette Simmons.

Surprised, I looked down at the device, then scowled.

The text was from Lucian Gray.

Well done, it said.

Walking into my brand-new office had been weird enough for the last couple of weeks, but it'd gotten progressively weirder after building maintenance had installed the tidy metal placard to the wall beside the door. Though barely the size of a postcard, the sign seemed to flare brightly the moment I topped the staircase leading up from the main floor. With that slim strip of metal, Thompson & Associates now had the sheen of authenticity—a business of competence, consequence, and the vague insinuation of satisfied customers and company cars.

That wasn't why my stomach tightened as we approached the office down the long hallway, though, Claire's high heels clicking loudly along the hardwood floor.

"Somebody's in there," she announced, seeing the same thing I was—the slightly ajar doorway of office 212, light spilling out into the dim hallway. "It's him, isn't it? He's in there."

"*I am,*" Lucian's voice murmured in my ears when I was still fifteen feet away. I shot Claire a glance, but her mouth was still pressed into a grimace that clearly didn't know whether to be excited, nervous, or annoyed.

Join the club.

"Did you hear that?" I asked her abruptly. She glanced at me, confused, and I realized—of course, she hadn't. He was in my head again. All these weeks after the exorcism, he could still slip inside as if he'd never left. The connection felt like spider silk stretched between us—invisible until you walked through it, then clinging, impossible to brush away. My bruises throbbed in warning. "Never mind. He's playing games."

A soft, murmuring chuckle assaulted my ears again, only this time, it slid softly down my neck, curling along my collar-bone. *"At last, sweet Delia, we are beginning to understand each other."*

I glanced past our doorway on down the hallway. It was barely one o'clock in the afternoon, and, as usual, nobody else was in the building at this hour, at least not on our floor. So far, I'd figured out that yoga happened only a few nights a week in the first-floor studio of this charming Oak Park Victorian office building. Either therapy sessions in the other two dozen office suites were also only hosted at night, or the entire place was just a glorified tax write-off for a whole host of small businesses.

Not exactly what I should be hoping for, if I wanted to snag foot traffic from the other on-site practices, or a pop-in from the occasional possessed yogini. But before I could figure out my marketing problems, there was a slight issue of managing my right-hand demon.

I swung into the doorway, sweeping my gaze across the empty reception desk, low couches, and overstuffed chair—stopping short at the door to my inner office. Because that was where Lucian Gray stood against the frame, sucking all the oxygen out of the universe.

In my work with the ex-rabbi Mordechai, I'd helped exorcise my share of demons. While none of them had taken physical form, the ugliness they inflicted on their human hosts was both dramatic and unrelenting.

The demons we'd grappled with hadn't been glittery vampires; they'd been rot wearing human skin—faces smoothed to wax, eyes rolling back to show only yellowed whites, mouths stretched too wide around screams in languages that predated human tongues. They stank of burning sulfur and decay, made their hosts vomit beetles and bile, and left burns, blisters, and broken bones in their wake. They were ancient, patient, and utterly devoid of anything resembling mercy. When they looked at you through someone else's eyes, you felt the weight of every cruelty they'd spawned since the world began.

Lucian Gray, on the other hand, definitely glittered.

Tall, lean, and vibrating with the coiled grace of a predator, he wore a suit of deep indigo, its dark, luxurious fabric like something usually reserved for men who signed treaties or started wars. His hair was the kind of black that caught the light and held it, swept back from a face that promised sins you didn't know you wanted. Chiseled cheekbones, a mouth that quirked at one corner like he was perpetually amused by some private joke, and eyes so dark they were nearly black until the light hit them wrong and you caught a flash of red. Leaning there so casually, he gave the appearance of having all the time in the world...and the urgency of a snake about to strike.

"Hello, Delia," he said easily, and I found myself wondering what poisoned chocolate would taste like. Terrible, I was pretty sure. No, really.

His amused gaze shifted to Claire. "Dr. Bickwell."

"The prodigal assistant returns," Claire harumphed, marching over to the blonde wood reception desk and slinging her exorcist bag on the gray metal table beside it. She dropped into the dove-gray chair and swiveled toward Lucian, kicking off her heels in a move so unconscious, it made me wonder if she normally stood barefoot behind her pharmacy counter.

She folded her arms, glaring from him to me. "He's smirking. Why?"

I blinked at her, then glanced over to Lucian—only this time, he wasn't smirking. His smile was fuller, more genuine, and it hit with a velvet punch low in my belly.

No, this demon didn't drip rats from his jaws. He was beautiful. Dangerous. And entirely too comfortable in his own skin for someone who'd spent a solid fifteen years wearing mine.

He was also a problem. I glanced at Claire, whose eyes had gone a little narrower as her gaze swung between us. "Claire, could you check the bank and make sure the deposit from Meadowbrook landed? Lucian and I need to do some onboarding."

"Onboarding." She snorted. "You need me to stock up on antibiotics for you? My pharmacy shift starts at five."

"About that." Lucian surprised us both by interrupting, his voice a sinuous slide as he refocused on me. "With the successful completion of Thompson & Associates' first assignment, I think you may wish to bring your client manager on full-time, don't you?"

I squinted at him. "After one job?"

Claire leaned forward. "I'm sorry, did your new skin suit come with a lottery win? Because if I'm going to be working with a demon on the regular, I'm getting hazard pay."

He bared his teeth at her. "I assure you, if you worked with me on a regular basis, you'd need far more than antibiotics, Dr. Bickwell. But neither of you should be alone in this office going forward."

"Why not?" I asked sharply, suddenly remembering Belphegor's reaction at the center. He'd known Palemerious, without question. Did he know his new identity? I didn't think so, but...

Lucian turned to Claire. "Why did you choose this building? It seems virtually abandoned."

She bristled. "Because it's pretty, it feels safe, it's got a private parking lot and multiple exit doors, and there are cameras on all four corners of the building as well as trained on all the doors."

I blinked at her response. I hadn't noticed the cameras.

"And it's empty," Lucian pointed out. "That's dangerous."

"It hasn't been so far," she huffed, and I lifted my hands.

"Let me know about the money, Claire, would you? And Lucian?" I gestured him back into my office. He gave Claire another smirk, then turned and slipped through the doorway.

I looked over to see Claire grimacing at me. I didn't have to ask what her slightly panicked expression meant. She could bluster all she wanted to Lucian's face, but she felt the same thing I did...it wasn't the office that was dangerous. It was the guy we planned to work with—the guy whose name had been shouted out multiple times by a demon who shouldn't know it and who certainly shouldn't be connecting it to me. There was a whole lot I didn't know about Lucian Gray, née Palemerious, and it was time I started learning.

Blowing out a steadying breath, I followed him into my interior office.

For the second time in ten minutes, I stopped short at a doorway, staring around. "Um... How long have you been here this morning?"

He chuckled, swiveling his guest chair toward me with a creak of tooled leather. "You're not running a women's retreat here, Delia. I thought I'd help ensure your private space carried a certain level of gravitas."

"Gravitas," I echoed, taking in my newly redecorated office

—all glass, steel, and deep crimson. Expensive. Masculine. Nothing like the cozy space I'd set up. "Where's all the stuff that was in here?"

"Relocated to an empty office on the third floor. Of which there are several." His gaze tracked me as I moved to the desk and took a seat behind it. I didn't miss the fact that the guest chairs he'd chosen were simply a darker mirror of mine, equally as tall and luxurious.

My stomach twisted. He'd been in here—moving furniture, choosing colors, deciding what I needed. It felt invasive, presumptuous. Like he was marking territory that wasn't his.

"Why did you do this?" I sat down surrounded by the smell of leather and spices, but I didn't miss the way the sun from the back window struck Lucian...or how his shadow didn't quite match his body. It wasn't far off—a curve here, an angle there. But its wrongness shimmered at the edge of my awareness, poking and prickling.

Lucian's smile flickered as he watched me. Did he know what I was thinking? "That is a question we don't have time to answer fully," he said. "I wanted you to know that I've found accommodations in the city. You may also want to consider relocating."

I sat back abruptly, aware that he evaded my question but willing to table it for now. He'd found someplace to live? "I'm fine where I am."

"You're living in a duplex with a man you refer to as Deadbeat Steve."

"And I like that." I peered at him more closely. "Where did you move?"

"The Prometheus Building—Lakeshore Drive. Fifteenth floor."

"The..." I stared at him, my lip curling in disbelief. "Like, the *actual* Prometheus building? That's kind of out of the pay grade of your typical exorcist's assistant."

"And yet I have such aspirations of making partner," he said with a wide smile. "It's also the only reasonable accommodations I could secure on short notice, until existing residents in other, more appropriate buildings, choose to leave."

I grimaced. "Lucian...the demon I exorcised this morning was named—is named—Belphegor."

"Mm." He inclined his head. "Third-level demon of the Court of Indolence, a true zealot of sloth and decay. Miserable creature who never shuts up. You didn't kill him, I suppose? That would be too much to hope for?"

"No, I didn't kill him," I snapped. "Exorcists don't kill demons. We exorcise them. You of all people...things...whatever you are, should know that."

His brows drifted up. "I know what Mordechai wanted you to believe, but that's not really the way this works, Delia," he said quietly. "You've been doing your research, so I think you're beginning to suspect that too."

"I'm not suspecting anything," I retorted. I gestured to the still-empty shelves, wincing as the bruises on my arms complained. "Mordechai had, like, a thousand years of history on exorcisms and fifty solid years of practice. You should know, you were hanging out near him for the last fifteen of them. I don't have any of that history, that research. I thought he showed me a fair amount, but the more I check out actual books, the more I realize I don't know shit. I'm going by the barest top level of muscle memory from the exorcisms I watched him perform. The rest is pure, blind intuition. I don't know what I'm doing."

"You knew enough to exorcise Belphegor," Lucian pointed out. His lip curled. "How did he end up locked down in a rehab center?"

"Yeah, well—he didn't want to be. And the interesting part about that? He couldn't get out on his own. He could jump from host to host but not actually leave the building. He kept muttering about locks and clocks and bright lights. Something was keeping him in there, even when he wanted to go. Once I gave him a free pass, he literally jumped at it. Messily, but he went."

Lucian had grown more attentive with my account, and he leaned forward. "Explain that further. What host carried him in?"

"A teenage jock who was in the wrong place at the wrong time—partying somewhere he shouldn't have been. They didn't tell me where."

Lucian tilted his head. "Probably one of Volkov's clubs."

I waved that off. "He's a kid."

"How charming that you think that would matter."

"Well, it doesn't matter. Belphegor *knew* you, Lucian. He said your name—like, your actual name—and he wanted to know what I'd done with you."

Lucian went still. Weirdly still. For five seconds, ten, I watched for the micro-movements that made someone human: a shift of weight, a breath, a blink. Nothing. He was a virtual stone vase, the air freezing in place around him. Then he smiled at me, and the illusion of humanity snapped back into place. For the moment, anyway.

"What you'd *done*," he echoed.

I nodded. "I don't know if he picked up on the residual evidence of your possession in me somehow—"

"Nobody should be aware of that."

"—or if he'd just heard gossip about you getting exorcised, but he said your name, like—I don't know. Like he was surprised to make the connection. He wanted to know where you went."

The complicated-looking phone rang on my desk, jolting me. The first light gleamed along the row of lights at the base of the phone, and the video screen read "Private Caller." Claire's desk phone echoed the ring, and I blinked as I heard her pick up. Did people know my phone number already? Was this the building manager, having discovered Lucian's rehomed furniture?

"You shouldn't be alone in the city," Lucian said. "Not yet. It's not safe."

"Why?" I refocused on him. "Because of Belphegor?"

Claire appeared in the doorway, her eyes wide. She pointed shakily to the button flashing on my phone. "That's—Victoria Ashford. She has another job for you."

CHAPTER

FOUR

"Seriously?"

"Definitely seriously," Claire said, her voice dropping. "And urgently too. Fifty thousand dollars, urgent."

Lucian straightened, his expression shifting from casual threat to razor focus. "Answer it. Put her on video, but don't let her see me. I want to see her."

I narrowed my eyes. "Why?"

"Do you really want to waste the woman's time?" He gestured toward the flashing light. "She chose you. Be chosen."

The words rippled across the room, but he was right. I couldn't get all my questions answered right this second, but I could lock down this next job. I punched the video button and angled the screen so Lucian remained out of frame, then forced my features into an expression that I hoped approached professional.

Victoria Ashford's face materialized—elegant, composed, but with shadows under her eyes that hadn't been there at Meadowbrook. "Ms. Thompson. Thank you for taking my call. I apologize that I wasn't able to speak with you privately earlier, but this is better, perhaps."

"Mrs. Ashford." I kept my voice neutral. "Claire mentioned you have another case?"

"I do." She glanced away from the camera, then back. "If I'm being honest, the Meadowbrook situation was alarming, but I didn't fully believe Nanette's accounts when she contacted me seeking approval to retain you. She can be...a little high-strung."

I snorted. "Well, I'm glad I was able to help."

"I am too. And seeing what you did..." She paused, choosing words carefully. "I believe I may need that kind of intervention for someone very important to our umbrella organization, but I can't be certain. This new case, however, will require discretion beyond a simple NDA. Complete discretion."

Behind me, Lucian moved closer. I could feel him listening, his presence a gravitational pull at my back. A queasy chill rolled through me, a whisper of wrongness I couldn't quite squash down.

"What kind of intervention are you looking for?" I asked.

She blew out a breath. "The CEO of a technology company that I founded and on whose board I still sit, Prometheus Solutions, has been...unwell. Erratic. His behavior has become increasingly concerning." Victoria's voice tightened. "I know this man. I've watched him take a fledgling company, an innovation hub powered by little more than pizza and caffeine, and build it into an empire in a few short years. What's happening to him now—it isn't illness. It isn't stress."

My skin prickled. "And having seen what you saw today, you now think he's possessed?"

"I think," Victoria said carefully, "that he needs help. I'm fully aware that it's unlikely to the extreme that two companies on whose boards I sit would both be plagued by possessions. However, I saw what you did for the children at Meadowbrook. Nanette has kept me apprised throughout the day, and it's as if the troubles of the last few weeks never happened—other than

Ms. Greene, who will need an extended leave of absence to recover from her experience, I suspect."

I grimaced. "Yeah, I can understand that."

"And because of what I saw today, I believe you'll be able to help Kieran Walsh. Before he destroys everything he's built. Before he hurts someone."

"Claire said you were prepared to pay fifty thousand dollars for my work on this assignment," I said flatly. I didn't know where the words came from, but Victoria didn't blink.

"Yes." No hesitation. "Half up front, half upon completion of your work to my satisfaction. When can you begin?"

Dammit. That was more than I'd made in the past two years combined, and I still felt like I was underpricing myself. My instincts screamed warning.

"Where are his offices located?" The question came out before I could stop it.

She blinked. "Well, Lakeshore Drive, of course. The Prometheus building—that's the company he runs." She smiled. "The building is predominantly residential, but the corporation occupies the top three floors. It's quite secure, but I can provide clearance—"

Ice shot through my veins as she pattered on. I turned my head slightly, catching Lucian's reflection in the darkened window. His eyes gleamed red for an instant, and his lips twitched.

He'd moved into the same fucking building as our newest potential client? There was no longer any doubt in my mind. Kieran Walsh was *so* possessed.

"I see." My voice came out strangled. I cleared my throat. "When would you need me to start?"

"As soon as possible. Tomorrow, if you're available. Kieran's condition is deteriorating rapidly." Victoria leaned forward. "Ms. Thompson, I watched you save Bob's only son from something that would have destroyed both the boy and his father, had it continued for much longer. I know what that's like, so please. Let me hire you to do the same for someone else's son."

Bob's only son. I grimaced as I glanced back at Lucian. His expression was carefully neutral, but something danced in those dark eyes. Amusement. Anticipation.

Satisfaction.

He'd known this call was coming. His sudden concern about my security was starting to make a lot more sense. Something sour coated the back of my throat, like breathing in ash and copper.

"You said you know what it's like—what Mr. Banks went through," I said. "Mrs. Ashford, if there's a pattern here—if something connects your experience to Walsh's situation—I need to know."

She pressed her lips together for a moment, then nodded. "I... Yes," she finally said, and I watched her straighten in front of the camera, her hands reaching out to tidy the already-neat stacks of paper on her desk. "My son was the CEO for a time there—of Prometheus Solutions, the company I helped him found. But he was always a designer at heart. In 2019, he found his own replacement in Kieran Walsh, then returned to game development. He passed away in 2020 by accidental drowning. Due to exhaustion, they decided. I don't know what caused him to slip and fall from Navy Pier, but it really doesn't matter. I sometimes think that I may have missed some telltale signs of exhaustion or...I don't know. Something worse. In any event, I don't want to make the same mistake again."

"Understood," I said, my gaze locked on Lucian's. He'd gone still, hyper-expectant, and I knew this was the link he wanted to explore. The question he wanted answered. I just didn't know why he needed the answer so badly.

I refocused on Victoria. "I'll need to assess Mr. Walsh in

person before committing, of course. Standard consultation. If I determine I can help him, we'll discuss any additional terms."

"Of course." Her relief was palpable. "I'll have my assistant send you Kieran's information and schedule. Again, if you could come tomorrow, that would be good. The company is very close to a major escalation, and we need to make sure everything is stable—the stock price, the company, and Kieran himself. Thank you, Ms. Thompson. Truly."

The screen went dark.

For three heartbeats, nobody moved.

Then Claire's voice cut through from the doorway: "Lucian just *happened* to buy a condo in the building where our newest client works? That's...prescient."

"Remarkably prescient." I flashed a look at Lucian. "How did you know we would get this call?"

He shrugged, his grin kicking his mouth up at the corners. "Victoria and I have similar tastes. We also both picked you, you'll notice."

"Cute." I stood, the desk chair rolling backward. "And also bullshit. You need him, why?"

"Information, mostly." He lifted a shoulder, dropped it. "I've been out of the game for fifteen years, unable to track what's happening among the demonic courts. It took very little time to sniff out Kieran Walsh and his...troubles, but I don't know how deep his troubles go."

He moved around the desk to casually retake his guest chair. "I do know that Walsh's company develops artificial intelligence systems, and the system that has been garnering the most recent attention is known as Reflex—traffic management and routing, apparently, but perhaps much more. I know those systems have been learning...interesting things about the people of Chicago. I also know that demons can slip inside many forms, and, like haunted houses, not all of them require flesh. Even machines can be possessed, under the right circumstances."

I stopped. "What?"

He spread his hands in an elegant, all-encompassing gesture. "Everything is connected, Delia. The companies, for sure, but also the families. Victoria Ashford. Robert Banks. Kieran Walsh. Even Nikolai Volkov and the demons he serves so blithely. I don't know what those connections are, but they have deepened in the past fifteen years, intensified, tangled. The city has changed, and we both need to catch up. This case will help us do that."

My jaw clenched. He'd orchestrated this—the timing, the location, probably even Nanette's call to Victoria. He'd set me up like a piece on a chessboard, and I'd slid right into position. The smart move would be to refuse the case, cut him loose, and figure out my own path.

But fifty thousand dollars was fifty thousand dollars. And refusing the case wouldn't change the fact that Walsh was possessed. It also wouldn't stop whatever Lucian had set in motion.

Besides, if I walked away, who would help Walsh? Another exorcist who didn't know the city's demons were connected in a series of infernal courts? Someone Lucian could manipulate even more easily?

I'd walked away prematurely from my last case, and a man had killed himself.

I wasn't going to let that happen again.

Lucian continued as my mind churned, his voice dropping to whiskey-smooth darkness, "I also suspect, though I cannot yet confirm, that Robert Banks' son was at Meadowbrook because of something that happened at a club run by Nikolai Volkov—not one that you've been to, at least not yet, but one that he owns. Victoria Ashford likely has been to it as well. The links are too tight, too intertwined for it all to be mere coincidence."

"But why is everything happening now? This isn't because you're back on the outside, is it? Victoria acted like things have been going screwy for a while now."

"It's not about me. Not directly." He leaned back in his chair, studying me smugly. "That said, my return will undoubtedly stir things up in certain sectors of the city."

"I thought you said no one knew you."

"Did I say that?" His smile was sly. "I said that no one should know the exact nature of our connection. And that remains true. What also remains true is that there are very old, very dangerous creatures in this city, whose power has only grown in the past few hundred years. It will take an exorcist with a certain ability to paint outside the box to combat those creatures."

"And you think that's me." The words tasted like ash. "You think you can manipulate me."

"I prefer to think of it as setting you up for success." He tilted his head. "You need cases and experience in working on your own. I need nothing. And yet, I *want* to assist you in doing what you do best. What we've done—together—for so many years now."

"Why?"

He spread his hands again. "I wish I knew. But it's a compulsion I can't ignore."

"Look, if I take this case—"

"When you take this case," Lucian corrected.

"*If.*" My voice hardened. "*If* I take this case, we do it my way. My rules. You do what I say. You don't interfere with my work. And you *don't* paint outside the box."

For a long moment, Lucian studied me. And in that moment, I saw something flicker behind his eyes—not the predator, not the manipulator. Something almost...uncertain. Like he genuinely didn't know what I'd choose. Like my answer mattered.

Then it was gone, and he smiled. Not the charming smile or the seductive one. This smile was all edges and hunger.

"But we're so good at painting," he murmured.

I jolted, remembering the white-washed walls of my bedroom. The walls he'd helped me paint in lurid and disgusting ways. My fingers traced the scratches on my forearm beneath my sleeve—unconscious, compulsive. Had I started auto-writing again, only this time with my own nails?

Claire's voice, quiet and shaken: "Delia. You don't have to do this."

I turned to her, taking in her wide eyes, the flush in her cheeks. I'd forgotten she was standing there—forgotten everything in the pull of Lucian's gaze. She was scared. So was I.

"Call Victoria's assistant," I said. "Set up the consultation with Walsh for tomorrow afternoon. And dig up everything you can find on Prometheus Solutions."

"Delia—"

"I know." I managed something that might have been a smile. "But we need the money. And..." I glanced back at Lucian. "I can help Kieran Walsh. I know I can."

"You can do more than help." Lucian nodded. "Though I do hope you'll let me play my part. After all..." He moved toward the door. "I'm practically his neighbor now."

He paused in the doorway, turning back with that dangerous smile. "Oh, and Delia? You'll want to bring your Hamsa Hand when you meet with Victoria Ashford and her afflicted CEO. You'll need it."

Then he was gone, leaving only the faint scent of smoke and the echo of footsteps on hardwood.

Claire and I stared at each other, and I studiously avoided

lifting my hand to the amulet I wore around my neck. Since he'd purchased it for me five years ago, Mordechai had spent part of every conversation we'd had urging me to wear it. I'd hated the thing back then, no doubt because I'd had a demon wrapped around my guts. Now I rarely took it off, no matter how much it abraded my skin. My other injuries prickled at that thought, hidden beneath my shirt, running equal parts hot and cold. I pressed my hand against the worst of them, the one along my ribcage. It felt like maybe it had opened while I'd talked to Lucian. What other scratches and bruises would I find when I went home tonight? What damage would I do to myself as I slept?

And why was I still so broken, if Lucian was no longer inside me?

"It's our second case in two days," Claire said finally, finding her smile. "We're going viral."

I huffed a short laugh. "We're going somewhere, that's for sure. Hopefully we'll get back in one piece."

I tried to ignore the voice in my head—my own voice, not Palemerious's—whispering that I'd just agreed to walk straight into a world of darkness I'd never known existed.

With my former possessor demon as a guide.

What could possibly go wrong?

Nothing buzzed around my computer terminal in the Chicago Public Library community health stacks. Nobody spoke, nobody whispered. I couldn't hear anyone breathe.

It was heaven.

I'd spent so much time here in high school, avoiding the reality of needing to go home. I'd come back here to study for my college courses, keeping my head above water in my one-class-per-term schedule. I never understood why more people didn't use this library. It always made me feel safe and grounded. Then again, maybe most people didn't need a library for such things.

One thing was certain, I wasn't feeling all that grounded anymore.

I entered another search query on Prometheus Solutions. So far, everything about the company was coming up roses. Victoria Ashford was, quite legitimately, its founder, and her son served as its first CEO. Kieran Walsh, the CEO since 2019, was a modern-day wunderkind, taking the once street-cred cool video game development company both public and respectable by transforming its game strategy into the real-world application of traffic and infrastructure management. It sounded boring as hell to me, but I supposed that was the point. And it made a certain amount of sense. If you could figure out how to escape a zombie apocalypse, you should be able to help motorists get out of town during a snowstorm.

But the further back I went, the more squirrely the history of Prometheus Solutions got. First, I dug into what had been printed about Finn Ashford, Victoria's son. By all accounts, Finn had been even more successful and certainly more visionary than his successor—right up until the day he dove off Navy Pier and slipped beneath the murky waters of Lake Michigan at age thirty, one year after Walsh had taken over as CEO and Finn had disappeared back into development.

I leaned closer to the screen, resisting the urge to angle it more toward the wall beside me. There were only a handful of other patrons in the library this morning, and none of them cared what I was looking for. But it still felt disquieting to search for the life history of a dead guy.

Finn Ashford had been a star student at Northwestern University before dropping out in 2010 after winning a national fantasy gaming tournament. He'd taken his half-finished computer science and programming degree and bounced around the video game industry for a few years before starting Prometheus Solutions in 2013 along with his mother and a couple of friends,. The friends had since moved on. Everybody had to grow up some time, I supposed. But Finn stuck, probably funded by Victoria's bank account. Then, in 2015, Prometheus Solutions launched Warriors of Darkyn, a massively multi-player online role-playing game which set a new level of sophistication not only in immersive user experience, but in the sophisticated network of escape mechanisms the players were required to master in order to survive the rapidly collapsing realm.

"Warriors of Darkyn," I muttered. I knew I'd heard that name before, which meant my housemate Steve had to have mentioned it. One of the few things Steve loved other than finding a new place to party, was finding a new game and the people who wanted to play it. If he could mix partying with gaming, then so much the better. Warriors of Darkyn, according to all the research I could find, had been shelved after a wildly popular four-year run and replaced with newer games that appealed more to Prometheus's growing mass market audience. Around that time, Emergency Run had also been launched, a public-access traffic management simulation program that was quickly decommissioned and privatized into something called Reflex. After undergoing some notable stress tests, particularly an unexpected test run on the system's capabilities during a bomb scare at the 2020 Chicago Saint Patrick's Day Parade, Reflex started getting interest from Chicago's city planners.

A deeper dive into the bomb scare proved interesting. The alert required the evacuation of some fifty thousand revelers with only a half hour's notice. There'd been absolutely no reported casualties, and Reflex's star was launched. It didn't seem to matter that no bomb had ever been found; the fact that the system was able to move so many people so efficiently had fast-tracked it for implementation in the city's infrastructure and traffic management systems.

Two weeks after the parade, Finn Ashford had taken his own life.

I slumped back in my chair, staring at the screen. Seriously? His company officially hit the big time, and he decided to end it all? Who did that?

I pulled out my phone and texted Steve. *You busy?*

Restocking at Mulligan's. Shift doesn't start till noon. What up?

You remember anything about an old video game called Warriors of Darkyn? And do you still play?

To my surprise, the answer didn't come right away. Then, it was a short, clipped text. *Yeah, on a bootleg server. Why?*

Can you show me?

Steve took so long to respond that I wondered if I'd lost connection. It happened sometimes, but as I was about to text him again, the telltale three dots of a text in progress appeared briefly on the screen. *Hit me up at Mulligan's. Talk there.*

I frowned at the phone, but I could make this work. It was already 10:30 a.m., and I was pretty sure the restaurant opened at 11 a.m. Flush with cash from Meadowbrook Wellness Center, I could even treat Steve to an early lunch.

I packed up the printouts I'd made of all the various articles, thought again about the laptop that Claire was threatening to buy me, and smiled. She had her regular day shift today, but the more I got used to working with her, the less she made any sense as a pharmacist. Who deliberately chose that career anyway? She was a doctor, but not an ordinary doctor, and it had to get tedious to explain that to everyone. Plus, she worked in a drug store, which had to chafe. She was also pushing thirty and nowhere near having an ordinary relationship other than her chat-buddy conversations with Max Graham. I sort of thought she should have a real relationship beyond texting, as a grown-assed woman. Then again: this was Claire.

I was still mulling it over as I exited the library, then stopped cold. Parked in front of the building was a low-slung roadster with an improbably elegant, suit-wearing demon lounging on it.

"I'll drive you," Lucian said.

I didn't move. "How do you even know where I'm going?" I demanded, then my eyes flared wide. "You're still hooked into my mind somehow, aren't you? You know what I'm thinking about. That's how you knew about Belphegor—and how he knew about you."

"You shouldn't say those names so freely."

"Yeah? Then maybe you should start talking."

He spread his arms as I approached his car. "Our connection remains, yes. It's not nearly as strong, and it's fading, but any time your attention turns to a demon, it sharpens. For now, anyway."

Something flickered across his face—regret? Loss? Then it was gone. "You'll barely notice when it's severed completely," he assured me, but though his smile was wry, his words struck me with unexpected force.

"Good." It'd be *fantastic* when no demon could find the slightest hint of him skulking around my psyche. That was exactly what I wanted—what I needed to happen.

Right?

As Lucian popped the passenger door and gestured me inside, I fought the sudden whisper of loss that unexpectedly slipped through me.

"I can walk," I informed him tersely.

"And it will take you an hour. An Uber will take you thirty. I'll get you there in ten."

Leaving the door open, he walked around the front of the car and slid behind the wheel. Scowling, I got in the passenger side—another question occurring to me as I pulled the door closed. "How do you know how to drive, anyway?"

His chuckle did more to ease my nascent anxiety than I wanted to admit. "The short answer is that you know how to drive. The longer answer is I've existed for more than three thousand years. Any human experience that I could sample in that time, I have."

He fired up the car and slipped out into traffic, which allowed me to turn and study him more closely. "So, when exactly did you decide I was thinking about demons today? Because I wasn't."

As he glanced back at me, his eyes caught the light wrong—showing the flat, reflective gleam of a predator's eyes. For a moment, I could have sworn I saw something moving behind his pupils—something with too many edges. Lucian was a demon, I reminded myself for about the fiftieth time today. An entity as old as the world dressed up as a human. I needed to remember that. "Oh?" he challenged. "What were you thinking about, then?"

"Victoria's son, Finn Ashford, and the work he did to launch Prometheus Solutions." I eyed him. "What do you know about that? Was her son possessed?"

"Perhaps." He slanted me another glance, and his voice dropped a full octave to something not quite natural and wholly unnerving. "You have...so many questions, Delia. You'll need to be careful with that."

I fought the full-body shiver. "And you're living four floors beneath Prometheus Solutions, your first apartment since hanging out in my spleen. That's not a coincidence."

"It's not," he agreed. For a long second I didn't think he was going to say anything more, but much like Steve, he couldn't seem to help talking when there was too much silence around.

"When Max and Nanette Simmons spoke your name, I heard it."

"Because of our connection."

"Because I have ears," he corrected. "Any time there are whispers of you, I'll know. Then Nanette reached out to Victoria, and the web widened. I could tell she had suffered a loss; I could tell the Court of Ruin was involved."

I waited for more, but as usual, Lucian parceled out information like a miser counting coins.

"And?" I prompted. "You heard my name, so you just...

signed a lease at the Prometheus building and moved in? You realize that's not normal human behavior."

"Then how fortunate I'm neither human nor normal." He glanced my way again, a sly smile curving his elegant lips, a telltale red nimbus of flame flaring around his inky black pupils. "And, sweet Delia, you know if you want our connection to remain strong, you have only to ask."

"I'll pass," I said automatically. Too automatically, if his smirk was any indication. I forced myself to stop staring at his mouth and glared at the passing buildings instead.

"Court of Ruin, you said. But those are demons aligned with the sin of wrath, right? You're a Ravening Court demon." I couldn't bring myself to mention the deadly sin he represented, but it sang through my blood anyway. *Lust.* Of course it had to be lust. Why couldn't he have been sloth—or gluttony? Why couldn't one thing be easy in my life? "Why would you care about wrath demons?"

"I care about any demon who has influence in this city— and so should you." Lucian practically purred now, and I grimaced. Clearly, our connection hadn't faded all that much. "Beyond that, lust and wrath can be surprisingly aligned, wouldn't you say?"

"I wouldn't know."

"Would you like to?"

This time, the invitation was accompanied by the slightest push in my mind—not the brutal shot of pain or fear that I'd experienced when he'd possessed me, but a caress, a whisper. A hint of dark and twisting passageways I should never wander down. Not if I wanted to find my way back again.

When I didn't respond, he flicked a lazy hand—and I felt a corresponding brush along my cheek, though he didn't touch me. "In this case, I knew that the demons of wrath had taken a distinct interest in the digital architecture of the city. The technology. Like any other structure, technology can be both manipulated and occupied."

"Uh huh." I eyed him, happy for something concrete to focus on. "You're telling me my phone is possessed?"

"Are you surprised?"

Not waiting for my response, he continued. "Not just your phone. The city's entire digital network has served as an open conduit for demonic activity since the 1970s. The Court of Ruin, in particular, has an undue influence over the technology infrastructure of Chicago."

"Of the whole city," I said, thinking back to Reflex, the initiative Prometheus Solutions used to hit the big time. "Including the traffic management systems?"

"That I don't know specifically, but there would be no reason why not, if it was something she took an interest in."

"She?"

He ignored that question. "Reflex Online Navigation Systems is currently testing its 2.0 version, now in beta. That version is due to roll out in the next few weeks, very quietly, with no fanfare. Once it's in place, it won't only be the emergency systems of Chicago that Prometheus Solutions will have access to. All Internet-dependent communication systems will fall under their purview."

I scowled at him. "Does the city know they're doing that? Is that even legal?"

"Unlikely," he shrugged. "But this is Chicago."

I snorted. "Point taken. And—who exactly is *she*?"

He hesitated a moment, then seemed to come to a decision. "You have a tendency to speak the names of demons like they have no power. They do. When I say them, it's like the drip of dew from a petal—but a human? A demon's name on your tongue is like a roaring tide. So be careful with names, Delia. Especially this one: Asmodaea. She's a seventh-level commander in the Court of Ruin, Samael's right hand. If she is the one making Kieran Walsh dance, then you are in for a particularly nasty fight."

"Fair enough." I sat back in my seat, relishing my victory and not wanting to push more. Not yet. Lucian hadn't wanted to tell me about Asmodaea, and I didn't miss the fact that this demon was seventh level, like him. Had he known her, back before he'd slipped inside me for an extended vacation? Had they worked together?

Another thought spun up inside me, raw and seductive: would he tell me anything I wanted to know if I asked? Would he do anything I demanded?

Exactly how 'bound' to me was my unholy demon?

Beside me, Lucian released the softest, most sensual sigh. Then words flowed through my mind that I wasn't sure came from him...or me.

"*You have only to ask, sweet Delia.*"

Heat pooled low in my stomach for one sharp pulse—then something deep and primal in my bones registered anew exactly what sat beside me. The heat curdled, my blood chilled. My bruises throbbed in warning. Every scratch on my skin began to burn as if something beneath was trying to claw its way out, away from danger, away from him. My body was clocking what my mind kept forgetting: I was prey to this creature, never mind its elegant suit and beautiful face. I was entertainment. I was meat.

I stared out the window and tried not to scream.

It took us only a few more minutes to reach Mulligans, and we entered the dark Irish pub after Lucian improbably found parking less than half a block down from the building.

"Let me guess," I began drily, as Lucian slid the car in the open space. "You have your own first-level traffic demon running interference for you."

"Let's just say I retain the influence of my former station, if not the appearance."

Something about that sent me down another rabbit hole of questions I wanted answered, but my curiosity on that score would have to wait. Steve, his dark, curly hair buzzed to a square-cut cap today, and his long, trim form relaxed in jeans and a loose tee, waved us over when we entered the pub. He glanced at Lucian but didn't ask for an introduction. Apparently, he didn't need one, as the two exchanged brief nods.

I opened my mouth to ask him when he cut me off. "I pulled up the game while I was waiting. It's your basic multitiered dungeon scenario, but each dungeon shifts parameters depending on the campaign. You enter the building with a team, fight your way through various traps and attacks, and win when you find the treasure hidden somewhere—usually in the basement. It's got a couple of really cool features, one of which is architect power. That means you've hit the top level of the game, and you can find an exit no matter how complicated the way through or how many ratfuck demons they throw at you."

His gaze slid to Lucian. "No offense."

That was enough of an opening for me. "Okay, out with it. How do you two know each other? And please don't let it be anything weird about me."

Lucian smiled, giving Steve an almost sympathetic glance. "Steve has had the unusual experience of surviving an attempted demon assault," he said. "While you were able to remove him from harm's way, it affected him."

"That's one way of putting it," Steve muttered.

Lucian inclined his head. "As a result, he has a certain awareness when it comes to demons and a definite barrier to them causing him any further harm."

That made him perk up. "No shit?" he asked. "You guys can't fuck with me anymore?"

"Not without your permission," Lucian said. "And I mean that in the most straightforward way possible."

Steve frowned. "That still seems kind of slippery."

Lucian smiled, all teeth. It was the scariest thing I'd seen in days, including Belphegor. "Only if you want it to be."

"Back on track," I ordered, not wanting to think about the implications of what Lucian was suggesting, not yet. And especially not wanting to think about where I fell in that matrix of accessibility. "Have you ever achieved this architect power, Steve? Moving people through the maze faster?" It sounded a whole lot like what I'd learned about Reflex.

"A couple of times, yeah." He nodded, his gaze back on his screen. "But you can only use it once before you have to earn it again, and every time you use it, it takes a lot of strength out of you. You sort of have to ascend to God status in the game to be able to direct people at that level."

"Makes sense," I said, once more thinking about Reflex. "What do you know about Finn Ashford?"

"In-like-Flynn?" Steve's face lit up with a smile. "He was a legend. Up until he died in 2020, he was totally the man when it came to game design. Rumor had it he was working on a new game after they decommissioned Warriors of Darkyn, but nothing ever came of it. And then bam, he was gone."

"Was there ever any chatter about his death?"

Steve sent me a veiled glance. "What kind of chatter are you talking about?"

"Anything hinky. Seems like he was at the top of his game, pardon the pun. So why would he take his own life? Did somebody take it for him? Did he just, like, disappear?"

"There are about four subreddits dedicated to exactly that question, and it's a favorite topic for any Chicago pod dedicated to the supernatural." Steve laughed a little grimly. "But nothing's been proven, and over time the chatter died down. It only picks up again when some new deprecation happens to the server."

I frowned at him. "What do you mean, deprecation?"

"You know, like, something goes crazy with the game, something that's not supposed to happen." He waved a hand at the screen. "Usually it's with the architect's power. Doors open that were never there, walls get thrown up where they weren't before, that kind of thing. A glitch, you know? But one of the cool things about Warriors of Darkyn is that it didn't have any glitches, not in its original form. So, you know, people talk."

"And in the game you're currently playing...does your, uh, character currently have this architect ability?"

He grinned a little slyly. "I mean...maybe?"

"Show me."

Steve angled his computer a little bit closer to him so he could take over the controls again. As I watched, the game shifted, his view panning up until he hovered over a squad of trolls, humans, and what looked like skinny Pikachus bobbing up and down.

"You gotta use it on your team, right?" he said as he worked the keyboard. "Like, you can't just, like, invoke it for no good goddamn reason. And it's a testament to how much I love you that I'm even doing this. I told the gang that I was gonna test it out when you texted me, so they're on standby. But, we need to make it count, since it's use it and lose it."

"You can't get it back? That seems sort of dumb."

He grinned. "I mean, sure, you can. But it's a total pain in the ass, is what I'm saying. You gotta find so much wizard weed and deal with the Darkyn sprites. It's a lot."

I rolled my eyes. "Uh huh. I think you can handle it."

"I'm doing it, all right?" he protested. "I'm doing it."

Steve hit the architect icon, and instantly, his character levitated over the dungeon, the entire structure suddenly transparent, all tunnels color-coded and visible.

"God's eye view," he said with deep satisfaction.

As he leaned into his keyboard, I stared, but not at the screen. Deadbeat Steve had transformed—body taut, face intent, coordinating his people like he was running a military operation. He guided his team through corridors and chutes, warned of incoming attacks, rerouted demons. Seamless. Efficient.

I looked up to see Lucian eyeing me. "You can see why Chicago transit was interested," he offered.

"Oh, yeah." I grimaced. "They select who they want to move through the system, they get them out without a single casualty —and they can do it at scale, no matter if it's snowing or there's a fire or a nuclear bomb's gonna hit the city? Yeah, I can see how that would be worth a few billion dollars."

"Boom! We're through!" Steve crowed, even as my phone buzzed in my pocket. I ignored it. I wasn't quite ready to talk to Victoria again, and who else would be texting me?

I focused on Steve. "You got the...whatever you were looking for?"

"We got the gold and escaped with nobody dead," he confirmed, his eyes still on the screen where a jubilant team of noble warriors hooted and hollered. One of them broke into a strange kind of shimmy dance.

"Well, that's great." I pulled out my phone and glanced down at it, then stopped. The text was from an unknown number.

I've been tracking your research on me this morning. You won. Good job. I'll see you tomorrow at 2 p.m.

Kieran Walsh, I thought. Had to be. And if I had any doubt, the phone dropped several degrees in my hand, like I was holding a chunk of ice. My fingertips went numb where they touched the screen. When I bobbled the phone to my other hand, there were condensation marks on the glass—like breath on a mirror.

"Cancel the meeting," Lucian said abruptly, surprising me. I looked up to meet his eyes, and they flared red. "It's a trap."

"*It's a trap*," Steve echoed in a voice that sounded like he'd swallowed a frog. He remained focused on his game—apparently unaware his band of warriors was being tracked by an entirely different architect.

"I know it's a trap," I told Lucian, putting the phone back in my pocket without answering. "I expected a trap, okay? And if you're honest, you did too. I'm taking the meeting."

Lucian stared at me, a slight smile tugging the corner of his mouth. He nodded.

"Then I'm coming too."

"*It's a trap!*" Steve chortled again, but there was no going back now.

SIX

LUCIAN

The wraparound views of the Prometheus Building lived up to the descriptions he'd been given by the breathless, sweaty real estate rep. But Lucian Gray wasn't surveying either the sun-swept whitecaps of Lake Michigan or the buzz of humanity rushing along the city's streets.

Instead, he stood inside the windowless interior bunker billed as the multi-million-dollar loft's media room, his glance sweeping from screen to screen as he watched every feed from Prometheus Tower's security cameras, from the gracious lobby to the penultimate apartment before the sprawling tech company took over the top of the building. Wiring into the system hadn't been easy, but it had been depressingly predictable. After all, anything touched by a demon could be appropriated by another one, up to a certain level.

And given his age and familiarity with every major business organization in the city—not to mention the demons who infested them—Lucian's access level was pretty high. None of

Belial's agents would sense his touch, and Asmodaea wouldn't care, he didn't think. Not yet. Her domain was Prometheus Solutions proper, not the paths to and from it.

At five minutes to noon, the doors to the building slid open and the man he'd been waiting for strode through. Lucian studied him intently, but there was no obvious tell that Kieran Walsh had been consumed by one of Asmodaea's minions. He didn't walk unnaturally, twitch, or glance around. Then again, he didn't look around at all, at least not with his own eyes.

"Screen four, zoom in. Focus on the face, identify glasses."

"Ray-Ban 476, modeled after Meta-AI-enabled prototype glasses but augmented by Prometheus technology," the computer responded in a sultry female voice. "Prometheus Solutions embarked on a collaboration with Meta AI technology in 20—"

"Understood," he said, cutting off the computer as his eyes narrowed. "Is that Mirr in there? Is that who Asmodaea got to do her dirty work?"

"I'm unable to confirm," the computer crooned, and his lips curled in annoyance. It *was* Mirr, which meant a change of plans. Mirr would know him in a blink—and Lucian couldn't tip his hand too soon.

So far, Asmodaea's plan to infiltrate the city's infrastructure had been proceeding with remarkable restraint. If Lucian hadn't been so unceremoniously unhoused from Delia's body, he might never have noticed. He certainly hadn't picked up on it while he'd held Delia in his thrall. His world had become far more circumscribed than he'd realized, buried as he'd been. He'd given himself permission to forget all that had come before and simply revel in her raw humanity. That and Mordechai's exorcisms had become their own sort of drugs, and he never would have broken the addiction on his own. Not even when—especially when—Delia had begun to wake up to her own abilities.

At the time, he'd simply assumed the influence she had over demons was the same power that any human possessed if they dug deep enough, especially the females of the species. But in these past few weeks, and with the benefit of distance, he'd begun wondering otherwise. There had been a reason why the "retired" but highly successful exorcist Mordechai had chosen her as his assistant, and it had gone beyond simply being curious about the demon he'd watched slip inside the poor girl. Mordechai had wanted to keep Delia close for a very specific use. And how interesting that Lucian had never bothered to think about what that use might be until now?

Just what had the old man been up to, that morning they'd both met Delia for the first time?

"Approaching restricted zone," the computer purred, and Lucian refocused on the screen. Sure enough, the image portrayed Kieran Walsh ascending with two other suited men in the express elevator—the only one with access to the Prometheus Solutions complex at the top of the building. The man still stood easily, appearing relaxed, and he continued to sport the Ray-Bans. What was he looking at behind those mirrored lenses? What was Mirr whispering in his ear?

Lucian leaned forward. "You're next, you glittering tool," he murmured. "And then we'll take out your dear commander once and for all."

As soon as the words were out of his mouth, his lips twisted. *We.*

He still needed Delia for this.

"Delia Thompson, elevator three," murmured the computer. Lucian turned to another screen, this one also tracking the graciously appointed lobby, in time to see Delia enter one in the main bank of elevators.

"Sleep mode. Not a sound until I return," Lucian ordered. The computers winked off, the lights following suit as he exited the media room into the palatial living area. The door snicked shut behind him. Given the views, the condo was big on open concept decorating, so he paused to lounge on the back of a chair as the entry elevator doors slid open to reveal a slightly dismayed Delia.

Something in the borrowed flesh responded—the organ humans called a heart, beating faster in its cage of ribs—as he took in every detail. The still-pale skin, the dark brown hair that brushed her shoulders, the slender fingers with unpolished nails that gripped her shoulder bag. The tightly held jaw and grim compression of her full lips almost made him smile. As she stepped into the living room, she swept the space with keen attention, no doubt checking for exits.

Once again, he fought the smirk. Delia's entire body was coiled tight in fight or flight mode, and her throat worked above the open collar of the stylish white button-down she wore beneath a black linen pantsuit—the same pantsuit she'd worn yesterday, this time with a jacket.

Claire Bickwell was going to regret having chosen that outfit for her. Delia Thompson was a creature of habit. Now that she had experienced some success wearing the comfortable and stylish garment, she would swap out shirts every day until it fell apart.

"Welcome," he said as she stepped out of the elevator, spreading his arms and pitching his voice to the level of amused sarcasm that he knew irritated her so much. "Did Claire drop you off? Or did you steal her car again?"

"I Ubered, not that it matters. There's no reason to have a car in this city. If I wanted to, I could have taken the train." As she spoke, she ventured a little farther into the room, unshouldering her sleek leather bag and dropping it into the chair nearest to the couch. Then she angled behind the couch, keeping it between them. She remained a good ten feet away, but he savored the flare of her scent: the brine of nerves and questions, the sweet-smelling cocktail of Steve's vape, and underneath, *her*. The scent he had worn for fifteen years.

The urge to step closer to her was almost unbearable, but he held himself fast. His fingers curled involuntarily, and he felt the nails of his shedim form—growing sharp for just a moment—bite into his palms. Pain. Good. It reminded him what he was pretending to be. He had occupied her body, stolen her childhood, eavesdropped on her every memory. She hadn't even begun to process that violation yet, and he sure as hell didn't want to steer her down that path. Not yet, anyway.

Instead, he lifted a brow. "The train. No. Not with that bag."

She glanced down at it, appearing startled that she'd pulled it from her shoulder. "Why? What's wrong with the bag?"

"Exactly where does Claire Bickwell get her money, if not from you?" he countered. "Or is Max Graham still funding your startup?"

"I..." she paused, genuinely flummoxed, and when her teeth pressed down on her lip, worrying it in a way that he knew so intimately it was like a caress, he steeled himself anew. "Meadowbrook already wired the money to our account. Claire has a company card. She got this, I don't know, somewhere downtown. It's nice."

"It's a $7,500 Hermès messenger bag. It should be nice." He waved off her startled glance. "It's also appropriate for this particular client, but not for the train. Would you like the tour? This place isn't as homey as your duplex, but it tries."

"Yeah..." She turned to take it in; her fingers trailed along the back of the couch. Suddenly, she jerked her hand back. As if touching his things felt too intimate.

He let his mouth curve into a slow smile as she shot him a nervous glance. "Uncomfortable?" he asked.

"No." The lie came too fast, but she followed it up with a small shrug. "I've never been to any place like this before. I mean, I knew they existed but...Jesus."

He winced against the familiar pain that any sacred word evoked, even one used so casually. The name burned through him like acid on exposed nerve endings, a reminder that some things would always hurt. He didn't correct her though. Pain was life, and life was something he valued more than he used to.

He turned a little abruptly to indicate the windows. "The designers of this place were justifiably enthralled with the view, but they didn't want to limit the preferences of the eventual residents. You can have a city view or water view—or both, as it happens." He leaned down and picked up a remote, unable to help himself. This feature of the apartment had captivated him from the first moment he'd seen it demonstrated. With the click of a button, the blinds over the windows facing the city dropped in a solid whirr.

Delia froze as they did, because these weren't ordinary blinds; they were mirrors. And at this time of day, they reflected the wide-open expanse of Lake Michigan with perfect clarity, as well as anyone who happened to be standing in front of them.

Now, in the mirror's reflection, the two of them appeared to stand closer together. Close enough that Lucian could feel Delia's heat. Close enough to touch. He watched her throat work again as she swallowed, her pupils dilating. *Yes.* She was remembering, of course she was remembering—he could tell by the hitch in her breath—when she'd stood naked in front of another mirror, her hand moving between her thighs. She'd been exploring her pleasure that night, teasing and tempting, rising and falling, pushing herself to ever greater heights but also luring *him* into the open, drawing him out so she could see him—truly see him with all the shadows ripped away. She'd carried him for fifteen years, but she hadn't really *known* him before that night.

Did she now?

Her eyes met his in the reflection, and the recognition there —part fury, part want—drove a spike of need straight through him, quick and hot. He, too, flashed back to that carnal reflection of her, her lips parted, her eyes huge, her breath ragged and—

"Okay! Right. Cool trick. And your reflection is tracking a little better now. Good job on that." Delia shook herself, her voice loud in the quiet apartment, and resolutely pulled her gaze away from the mirror to focus on the furniture, tables, countertops. She pointed to the kitchen in the distance, all stainless steel and marble. "So...you actually eat?"

His reflection? Annoyance spiked within him at the betrayal of his mask, but he schooled his own expression back to something approaching civilized. "I can, yes. I don't if there's no reason to. But this body can do whatever it needs to fit in among humans. Why, are you hungry?"

"Not at all." She walked forward then, drifting her hands along the edge of the couch, the curve of a stool, the line of the kitchen countertop. Her gaze drifted out over the view of Lake Michigan, then back toward the mirrored blinds. "It's a little disorienting, don't you think? How do you know what direction you're looking at? How do you know what's real?"

She grimaced at her own curiosity, waving him quiet before he could answer. "Never mind, it doesn't matter. What else have you learned about Walsh? I can't imagine you wanted me to come over simply to show off your condo, which just happens to be four floors below our newest client. Claire's right, by the way. It's completely creepy that you live here now."

"It was a confluence of fortunate events," he corrected. "But as it happens, the location suits me. To answer your unspoken question, I've decided that I won't be changing residences after this client engagement, assuming this one is successful—which, of course, it must be."

Something in his voice gave him away, and she straightened, turning to him. "What do you mean?" she asked. "Why?"

"There's something you need to see," he said, pitching his tone a little brusque to distract her and striding purposefully for the media room.

It worked. She followed him without asking anything more.

When they stepped into the media room, however, she drew in a short breath as the lights flickered on. The screens remained quiet, but the far wall held more than its share of interest.

"You created a *possession* board?" She didn't wait for him to answer but strode forward, her gaze scanning the wall. In the center hung a photo of Kieran Walsh, along with a series of printed documents and news articles. Surrounding that initial image were several other photos, the Prometheus Solutions organizational chart, Reflex's implementation timeline, articles about the 2020 Saint Patrick's Day bomb scare, Finn Ashford's death notice, an obituary, and city infrastructure maps. Each of those were linked with arrows to Kieran's photo on the whiteboard.

"This is so cool," she breathed. "We've got no room to do this at the office but *damn*. It's way more powerful than seeing it on a laptop."

"I suspect we won't need this level of investigation with most of our clients. After all, Mordechai had only a shed in his backyard to work out of, and he seemed to attract plenty of traffic."

"Yeah," she said, a little grimly, then glanced at the side, where a conspicuously empty section remained. "What was here?"

"Suppositions that haven't yet merited our attention," he lied, seeing in his mind's eye the hierarchy of demons that he'd traced from the lowest level spawn to Asmodaea to Samael—and from the scrabbling demons beneath him to himself to Belial, the general of the Ravening Court. He knew Delia had already learned some of the internal structure of the demonic courts, but there was much she still didn't understand. Much he wasn't ready to share, he finally decided.

There would be a time and a place for those revelations, and it wasn't yet.

Instead, he watched as her attention returned to Kieran. "So, what are we working with here? I haven't met the guy in person; I don't know if he's possessed or not. But you do, right? Like, you've got some sort of demon radar?"

He nodded. This, at least, he could tell her. "Based on my observation of his activities, and the success that Prometheus Solutions has had with a particular type of infrastructure manipulation, yes. My belief is that he is possessed by a demon known as Mirr. A demon of reflection and distortion, both of which are very dangerous, given the focus of Walsh's business."

"And?" she asked. "What aren't you telling me?"

He blinked at her, surprised, but she still stared at the board. "You said yesterday that some demons aren't in the game to possess a human, they're in it to possess structures," she said. "So this Mirr isn't just affecting Walsh, it's affecting his computers and the AI that drives him. That makes him kind of a big deal, right?"

Lucian made a face. "Mirr is a minor demon. Barely fifth level."

"Well, maybe he's minor to you, but he won't be to me." She turned, squaring her shoulders to finally look at him. Lucian felt the weight of her gaze like a physical blow. "You weren't there with Belphegor, but he knew your name anyway. Why? Is there some splinter of you I can't get rid of, that's helping me still take on these cases?"

He stared at her, her human chatter not nearly as important as the piece she glossed over. She'd mentioned this before, but he'd been distracted. He wasn't now.

"He said my name?"

"I told you that," she said, exasperated. "We were pretty far gone in the process, so it didn't become a problem, but now I'm going to go in there and face another demon, and I don't particularly want to have a sidebar conversation about you if I can avoid it. Will it sense your affiliation with me?"

He stared at her, genuinely dismayed. His heart tightened in his chest, which shouldn't be a thing because he shouldn't have a heart. The muscle contracted anyway, traitor flesh responding to a fear he shouldn't be capable of feeling.

"Mirr will know who I am—who I was," he acknowledged. "But if I'm not with you, he might not make the connection as readily. We can't give up that advantage until we're ready to strike, which I don't think is going to be today. Today, you're simply going to see Walsh's possessor up close and personal. So, yes, you should go alone. Because *you* are the exorcist, Delia—you always have been. I may know the enemy, I may even be able to strike the enemy down when the time comes, but I can't release the enemy from a human. No demon can. That is all you, and it always has been."

"Mm." She stepped closer to the board, which meant stepping closer to him. Not touching him, not yet, but he felt her like an irrevocable pull, like gravity. "Okay, so, again... What aren't you telling me? Because there's something else here, isn't there? Something more."

Just like that, his tight hold on himself faltered, and his

research on Prometheus Solutions scattered like smoke. Now, all he saw was Delia—all he wanted was right here, close enough to touch. "So much more," he murmured, watching her, savoring the tremor his soft words evoked along her spine. "Would you like a list? Or shall I trace it on your skin?"

She jolted a little, then held herself very still. "We're not doing that again, Lucian. Not that."

"As you say." He tilted his head. "But it's not going away, is it? This energy between us. It's not fading, sweet Delia."

She turned then, finally meeting his eyes. Now she was only inches away, and her heat shimmered between them, whispery silver and gold. "I shouldn't feel this way," she whispered. "*You* shouldn't make me feel anything at all. I evicted you."

"I know." He nodded slightly. "Believe me, Delia. I know."

The air between them snapped tight, electric. She should step back, now. She needed to.

She didn't.

So he did, ignoring the roaring in his mind, his gut. He stepped back and allowed the space to swell between them again like mist over a waterfall, giving Delia room to grasp what she was rejecting, what she could still have.

What they *would* have together, and soon, he thought. Body to body, heat to heat.

Because she wouldn't step back. And he was only so strong.

"You should get going," he murmured.

"Yes."

A red haze swam before Lucian's eyes as he turned and led her back to the elevator, but it cleared by the time he pressed the button. "You'll need to go up to the eighteenth floor," he told her. "That's another common area. You can access the elevator to the nineteenth floor and Prometheus Solutions from there. I assume Victoria gave you the code?"

She nodded. They still stood too close together, her scent

wrapping around him, her heartbeat thrumming in his ears. Her breathing was careful, controlled, and he inhaled her scent, unable to help himself. "Your pulse is elevated," he murmured.

She shot him a murderous glance. "And you're standing too close to me."

"Am I?" He leaned in—not touching, but close enough that heat flared again. Close enough that his traitorous body wanted to reach out and claw her to him. "You're still afraid of me, aren't you?"

She met his gaze, and in her stormy eyes, he could see the reflection of his own red-rimmed pupils. "Should I be?"

"Yes. Always." When he spoke next, his voice was little more than a growl. "I *know* you, Delia. I know every way you break. Every way you bend." He lifted one hand—slowly, giving her time to move. She didn't, and his fingers hovered a breath away from her jaw. Not touching, barely quivering. "I know what you taste like when you come."

Heat scored her cheeks as she went rigid, fury and want chasing over her fair skin. "Then you know that I won't break easily."

"No." His hand fell away, curling into a fist at his side. If she looked down, she'd see that it was white-knuckled with a restraint he could barely maintain. But of course, she didn't look down. She held his gaze with hazel eyes gone soft with need. "You won't."

He leaned toward her and once more, she didn't step back. Their mouths were an inch apart—

The elevator chimed.

Delia swung away the moment the doors opened and stepped inside the carriage, lifting her chin to glare at him.

"When you meet Walsh, watch his eyes," he told her. "Make sure he doesn't have his glasses on. Mirr can't resist checking reflections, and he will want to see his in your eyes. Don't give him the satisfaction."

"Uh-huh. And he's a minor demon?"

"Barely fifth level." He shrugged with a small smile. "Not useless, but…nothing like me."

The doors slid shut but not before he could hear her last muttered comment. "Fucking great."

He stood there a moment longer, hand pressed flat against the metal, breathing like he'd been in a fight. His other hand was still clenched in a fist, knuckles white. If he opened it, his nails would be black and curved, too long for the human husk he wore. He kept it closed.

He'd been a breath away from sinking his claws into her. From crowding her against that elevator wall and showing her exactly what she had unleashed that night in front of the mirror, and how foolish she'd been to allow him physical form.

But she wasn't ready. And for all his millennia in Belial's court, he wasn't sure he was ready, either—not for what it would mean to touch her, fingers shaking with need, drunk on her scent and sweat, the heat of her body wrapped around him. Not for the moment when she'd look at him with that same fury/want in her eyes and realize she could choose to let him in.

Or choose to shut him out forever.

That all the power was hers…and then *his* for the taking, the moment she faltered.

He pressed his forehead against the cool metal.

"One step at a time," he murmured.

It would have to be enough.

SEVEN

As promised, the journey up to Prometheus Solutions was simple and efficient. I took Lucian's elevator up to the eighteenth floor, which, as it turned out, was the entryway to a spa accessible by most of the upper floors of the building. It was a simple matter to cross the lobby to the discreet placard announcing the private elevator to Prometheus.

Despite my outward calm, inside I was churning. There were so many things about this job that felt wrong, off. Too much I didn't understand. Lucian knew way too much about Kieran Walsh, for one thing, especially for a demon who'd been cooped up inside of me for the past fifteen years. Yes, he'd been out for nearly six weeks now, but why the focus on this random company? What did he know about this Mirr demon—and what did Mirr know about him?

The doors opened on a wonderland of chrome, steel, and glass. My eyes popped wide as I looked around, surprised that I wasn't flinching back from the painfully bright white decor, but it was lit in such a way that it drew the gaze forward, instead of propelling it back. And, much like in Lucian's apartment, this lobby was open on three sides to commanding views of the lakeshore and the bustling city that sprawled out in all directions.

It also smelled wrong. The air was metallic, like licking a battery. Copper and burnt sugar.

Yeah. There were demons here, I thought. Maybe more than one.

I grimaced. Exactly how screwed up *was* Chicago these days?

An efficient-looking woman looked up from the reception desk, its mirror-bright surfaces seeming to make her float in space. "Good morning," she said pleasantly, her voice a smooth but surprisingly strong contralto. "You must be Ms. Thompson. I've alerted Mrs. Ashford of your arrival. She'll be right—"

"Ms. Thompson." My most recent client and apparently new number-one fan, Mrs. Ashford, called out my name before she even fully emerged from the corridor beside the reception desk. She looked decidedly more professional today than she had on Monday, and she'd been no slouch then. Her suit was iron gray with a cream-colored silk shell, and her gray slingback heels leaned more toward comfortable than fashionable. She also seemed older in the sharply bright atmosphere of Prometheus Solutions...but that could've been all the steel.

She gestured me to follow her, striking up a slightly over-loud conversation as we walked. "We've got all the materials ready, as requested. With the upcoming announcement, we want to make as much information available to you as needed for you to fully support our senior team, particularly Mr. Walsh. He's been under such tremendous stress, yet you would never know it to speak with him."

"Of course," I said brightly as she handed me a sleek folder and leaned close.

"He's expecting you. Even before I broached the possibility

of this meeting, it seemed he already knew. He's been different this morning, amped up, excited. I'm hoping you're able to reach your conclusion quickly about what…resources he needs."

I grimaced, appreciating the fact that she didn't want to come straight out and say the word *possessed* when she doubtless was being overheard. As we proceeded deeper into the building, I clocked the entrance and exit points. It didn't look good. Prometheus Solutions appeared to be set up on a grid, with offices lining the exterior walls to take advantage of the view, and a network of access corridors bisecting the center, doubtless home to a rabbit warren of server rooms and workstations bristling with tech. If I got lost in here, it wasn't going to be pretty.

We reached Walsh's office without incident. It was a corner suite, of course, with windows on two sides and multiple screens lining every available wall or table. Once again, mirrored surfaces seemed to be a design motif, but there were too many of them for it to feel quite right. Was this why Lucian believed that Mirr was the demon inhabiting Walsh? Was he simply making an educated guess as opposed to knowing something deep and true?

Victoria scanned the room, frowning. "He said he was—"

"Ah! Victoria, we were just talking about you."

I blinked as someone who was definitely not Kieran Walsh strode into the room from an inner sanctum. This woman was a tall, willowy blonde wrapped in a black bandage dress that could have doubled as a slinky. The sun struck her and seemed to break around her, giving her skin a bright sheen. I blinked, and she looked normal again. She smelled of pink wine and knives.

Beside me, Victoria straightened so sharply I was surprised her spine didn't crack.

"Ms. Reeves." Victoria turned to me, her face now shuttered. "Kieran's events manager."

"That's *right*," the blonde said, her tone sharp enough to cut glass. "Which is why I was so *delighted* to learn you hired a 'wellness coordinator' without involving me. That seems a bit shortsighted given our timeline, don't you think?"

"Jillian, I told you it was fine."

Walsh himself emerged from a side room, a phone to his ear, moving fast and easily, with palpable self-assurance. From my research, I knew he was thirty-two years old, blond and handsome, and now I knew he smelled like biohacks and power lattes. At this distance, I couldn't see anything in his eyes, but I was glad to note that at least he wasn't wearing sunglasses.

"Now, if you'll excuse us, Jillian—"

He held up a finger as someone on the phone apparently spoke to him, but Jillian merely crossed her arms, her gimlet eyes hard on Walsh as he strode over to the window. Without turning our way, she spoke low enough for us to hear, but not so loud as to disturb the call. "Victoria, you do realize that the board cannot continue trying to micromanage Kieran if you expect us to be ready for our unveiling next week or the launch in two. And I can personally assure you he's as well as anyone in this building, no coordinator required."

"I'm sure you can also appreciate the stance of the investors I represent, Ms. Reeves," Victoria said, and I blinked at the steel in her tone. "Ms. Thompson stays."

"She absolutely stays."

We all turned into the brilliance of Walsh's smile, and the man's charisma hit me like a physical blow. Now that he was off the phone, I realized something definitely wasn't right about Walsh. There was an energy inside him that made you want to watch, to listen, and to draw his attention to you even as you prayed you would be found worthy. An energy not quite human, and yet close—perilously close.

I curled my lip as he swung his attention to Victoria ever so briefly, then back to me. "Victoria, punctual as usual, and you must be Ms. Thompson. I'm delighted to meet you."

"Of course," I murmured, as Kieran gestured us to the collection of chairs in front of his desk. We all started forward, only for him to speak again.

"Thank you, Victoria and Jillian, that will be all. Victoria, you may return to escort Ms. Thompson when I buzz you. Jillian, I'll see you at our four o'clock."

"But Kieran—" she began.

"That will be all," he said again, and both women flinched back as if struck. Nonplussed, I continued to the seating area as Victoria murmured something cheerful I couldn't quite process, then she was out the door, Jillian on her heels. No hesitation, no protest. Just the quiet click of the door as it snicked shut behind them.

I was alone.

I looked up and caught my mirror reflection in the far wall, instantly tracking a problem, but not quite sure what it was for a moment—then I saw it. Beside my exact reflection stood Kieran's…only just like Lucian's, his wasn't right. It was too fuzzy at the edges, jittering and buzzing, like static. It hurt to look at.

The man who created that reflection looked stable enough, and he strolled to the chair opposite me but didn't sit. I understood the power play, as well as a second reason why the mirror didn't make sense. When we moved, our actions weren't being matched exactly to my body—or to Walsh's. They were off by a half second. Could that be possible? Was it a deliberate attempt to disorient me, or a trick of the light?

"So, Ms. Thompson, why are you here?"

Walsh's tone was bright and cheerful, but his energy was

intense, almost looming. Ignoring his reflection, I focused on him without looking directly in his eyes and launched into my rehearsed script. "Victoria mentioned you've been experiencing increased stress, particularly given the upcoming events and success milestones of Prometheus Solutions. I simply wish—"

"Have we met before?" His interruption cut across my too-quick recitation, and I blinked.

"No, I don't think so."

He tilted his head. The movement was ever so slightly exaggerated, almost like the twitch of a bird. His voice also changed —becoming sharper, more metallic. "And yet you seem so familiar."

He wasn't looking at me either, not directly, and I felt a chill roll along my skin. *Oh, yeah.* Something had its hooks into Walsh. Something that definitely wasn't a minor demon. Had Lucian let me walk into a trap?

"I have one of those faces, I guess." I smiled, staring at the blond hair that brushed his ear. "Victoria mentioned that you were looking specifically for resources to support you for your upcoming announcement."

Walsh slipped back into his regular intonation, his face clearing enough that he seemed normal again. "Yes, the global launch." He smiled. "In a week, we'll begin the final installation. In two, we'll go live. In one month, Prometheus Solutions will change the world. And if you live in Chicago—which I assume you do—you'll be there to see it, though you may not even notice it happening at first. At least, not if we do our jobs correctly. And we're well equipped to do our jobs correctly. You too, yes?"

"I—"

I blinked, but in what seemed like a second, Walsh had turned and stepped several feet away from me, standing still in the center of the room, staring out the window toward the city.

"Who did the deed, Ms. Thompson?" he asked, but his voice was higher now, sharper, like the glittering cut glass statues on his shelves.

I stood as well, no longer comfortable remaining seated. "What deed?"

"Your release from Palemerious." He said the words with a shiver of pure, sensual delight. I gaped at him, but he didn't wait for me to generate a response—which was good, because all my words seemed buried deep in my throat.

"Your exorcism must have been a *masterpiece* to witness—and from one of the chief commanders of the realm. You should be proud that you're still standing. Palemerious always did like to play dirty."

Despite my every effort to remain cool, my hands clenched at my sides. "I don't know what you're talking about, Mr. Walsh."

He laughed and turned back to me, his eyes still not tracking to mine, but shining now in a decidedly unsettling way. "Don't insult us both. You *reek* of him. Fifteen years, he's been gone. Has he been inside you all this time? And where is he now? Because apparently, he's disappeared again—for good, if you listen to the chattering horde. Vanquished by the cattle he controlled."

Rage laced with the gritty aftertaste of violation pierced through my shock, but even as my mind cleared, the dozen or so screens in the office flickered simultaneously, and the mirrors shifted too—showing movement, shadows, deep within them. I stiffened only partially due to my surprise... because the temperature had also dropped at least twenty degrees.

Suddenly, I felt like laughing. *Okay, demon boy*, I thought. *We can play this your way.* Because I knew this game, and I knew demons. I didn't know if Mirr was the name of the asshole inside Walsh, but it was as good a place to start as any.

Still, there was a difference here between this possession and nearly every other one I'd encountered while working with Mordechai. Walsh, if anything, apparently understood he was possessed...and seemed to be totally on board with it. He and his demon seemed to be in perfect sync. Together, they smelled like champagne and platinum, money and power, all of it over-laying the stink of brimstone and rot. And Walsh *reveled* in it.

That was new.

"Are you feeling all right, Mr. Walsh?" I tried.

Another bright smile. "I think you know I am."

"Do you know why I'm here?"

"He doesn't," came the high, sharp voice out of his mouth. "I do."

Walsh shifted again toward one of the screens, but the movement wasn't right. It was too fluid, almost boneless, his face smoothing like he'd just come off a seriously bad Botox and his features turning almost generic. Still attractive, sure, but flat, uncanny, like early edition AI. And, of course, his eyes now glittered like mirrors.

"You amuse me, Ms. Thompson, and it's been a while since anything has amused me," the voice inside Walsh said. "But you should know where you fit in the hierarchy of our organization here at Prometheus Solutions. It's...fairly low, I'm afraid." He gestured to the screen, where a complicated organizational chart appeared, first looking like any other mind-numbing PowerPoint deck but quickly developing flourishes, dashes, and strikethroughs, like someone was elegantly rearranging the power structure on the fly.

My name was there at the bottom, Thompson & Associates, with a dotted line connection to Victoria Ashford, but I quickly leapt to the name topping the chart in blood red script that started out in stiff corporate lettering and devolved into an elegant script. *Samael.*

I made a face. If that wasn't a demon name, I didn't know what was, and I recognized it as the high command of the Court of Ruin. Worse than that, right beside Samael was a second burst of names, a second hierarchy, topped by the name Belial. Ravening Court, reporting for duty. More names bled down the screen, but only one of them stood out to me in stark relief... because it was struck through. *Palemerious.*

What was this?

I tried to focus on the other names beneath Samael, especially as roles appeared beneath them. *Asmodaea—Commander, North Territory. Mirr—Regional Deputy.* But my gaze kept returning to the second hierarchy and Palemerious until his role flashed into place: *Commander, East Territory, dec.*

Had Lucian known I would see this? Had he sent me in blind on purpose?

"Lovely, isn't it?" the demon voice mused, as if he were talking about a work of art. "Samael and Belial have joined their courts together seamlessly for millennia, and their work is finally building toward real accomplishment. Asmodaea spent centuries perfecting the architecture, the systems. Palemerious never could keep up—though he had his uses. Such a pity he's no longer with us."

My gaze leapt to the facing mirror beside the screen, allowing me to look at Walsh without him fully seeing me. There was definitely something powerful inside the guy, I thought. A glittery, jittery demon with so much agency handed over to him by his human that no one would know who was Mirr—and who was Walsh.

Except Walsh wasn't some ordinary Joe holed up in his parents' basement writing curse words on the wall. He was a billionaire CEO about to control the infrastructure of one of the biggest cities in North America.

"What is it you plan to do with Reflex, once it's installed, Mr. Walsh?" I asked abruptly. "It's focused on traffic management, isn't it?"

And just like that, Walsh was back.

"To start, yes." He smiled, finally turning to look at me directly. His eyes glittered too bright for me to look deeply within them, but he otherwise seemed fully human. "But of course, that's only the beginning. Today's traffic light is tomorrow's signage, and tomorrow's signage is next week's computer system. Slowly, subtly, Reflex's architecture will be infused into any system that seeks to direct someone through it, ensuring that the user experience is seamless, flawless, and ordered. What we're introducing here is a complete transformation of how people will interact with each other—and it will have global implications. In fact—"

Walsh broke off and tilted his head again, too far for ordinary human ease. His voice shifted too. "You know what's fascinating? You still smell like him. I didn't expect that. But then again, Palemerious was always known for his ability to excite the senses. Do you feel him still?"

I jerked back several steps, not realizing he'd gotten so close. He smirked at me, then continued on in the sharp, cutting tones of his demon. "Fifteen years of possession, and now he's gone. But not *quite* gone, is he? You're marked, Delia Thompson. You'll never be free of what you were." He leaned in a little closer. "That's why holy objects don't feel quite comfortable in your hand, am I right? Even when you do the work of angels, you're tainted."

I stared back at him, the rightness of his words digging at me. The medal *had* burned my palm at Meadowbrook, the Bible had stung. I pressed my tongue against my teeth to keep from confirming what he already knew—that I was tainted, wrong, broken in ways I couldn't fix.

Instead, I gave him my best corporate smile.

"As charming as this line of conversation is, I don't think it's particularly helpful." Walsh blinked, my tone apparently bringing the human back to the fore. I might be screaming on the inside, but this demon wasn't going to get the better of me. I remembered some of the corporate speak that Victoria had tutored me on.

"Should we discuss the cadence of our engagement? With barely a month before your big announcement, we need to make sure that you're as prepared as possible. You're doing a great thing, Mr. Walsh."

The screens glitched and jittered, the organizational chart shifting, my name flashing up, higher in the hierarchy, now equal with Walsh, but still below Mirr. Below the scratched-out name of Palemerious, another name flashed on the screen for a moment and then off again, too quickly for me to see it. Had it started with an E? An F?

"You're quite right, of course." Walsh's voice sounded so genuine, I jolted my gaze to him, realizing belatedly that all the screens had gone dark. My bruises flared hot beneath my clothes, like something was trying to claw its way to the surface, but now Walsh looked at me with absolutely human good cheer. "I can make myself available to you as much as you need, as long as you can get past Jillian—she's a terror with my schedule."

He checked his watch, frowned. "For now, though, I'm afraid I must cut our time short. My apologies." He reached for my hand, and I let him take it, surprised to feel it warm, vital. Definitely human. "Victoria has arranged your payment, yes? She's very detailed about such things."

"Of course," I murmured. He nodded, then released my

hand to pull his phone out of his trouser pocket again. He tapped a few lines, then smiled at me. "She'll be right up. Do you have any other questions?"

"I'd like to schedule our next visit," I said, and Walsh laughed, waving me off as he returned to his desk.

"I have people who tell me where to go and how to be for ten hours out of every fifteen in my day—Jillian most of all. You'll need to talk to them about my schedule. But I have an idea that I need to work out…"

He sat down at his computer and immediately began swiping and poking at the screen, something I couldn't see, as if I'd suddenly ceased to exist. I swung away, not breaking stride until I reached the door. When I opened it, Victoria was waiting outside.

She stared at me with huge searching eyes. *How did it go?* she mouthed.

This time, I was the one who gestured her forward. I didn't want to stay one more minute in this building. There was too much to process, too much to understand, too many questions I needed answered.

"It was very productive," I assured her, grateful that she fell into stride alongside me. "Walsh has given me permission to fit as many sessions as I need into his schedule, and I think those sessions should be held here. Ideally in a room without mirrors though, if such a thing exists."

"Oh! Well yes, of course. We have multiple meditation rooms on the twenty-first floor. One of those should work well."

"Do I need to work through Jillian?"

Predictably, she stiffened. What was going on with those two? "You do not," she said firmly. "I'll handle logistics. You… help Kieran."

A few minutes later, I took the Prometheus Solutions elevator straight to the ground level. Was Lucian watching me leave? Was he skulking around my brain the way he apparently still stained my body? I didn't feel him there, but what did that mean, really, when every other demon on the goddamned planet could pick him up just by seeing me? How deep had I fallen into the sea of demon suck?

My index finger ached, and when I glanced down, I saw I'd bitten its nail bloody again without noticing. *Shit.*

I got to the sidewalk, drew in a breath and pulled out my phone.

A text notification appeared at the right of my screen. I ignored it. Instead, I opened my messaging app and keyed in a different set of digits.

We need to talk, now if possible. Where are you?

The response came back less than thirty seconds later, which should've surprised me, but somehow didn't. I made a face when I recognized the location and responded my confirmation.

You're buying.

Fortunately, in this section of Chicago, Uber drivers flocked like pigeons at every street corner. Almost before I'd finished programming a ride, one zipped up to the curb.

I got in, still shaking, and prepared to meet the closest thing to a mafia crime lord I'd ever encountered in the Windy City.

I'd pulled a demon out of Nikolai Volkov six weeks ago. And now it was time for payback.

EIGHT

I was angry enough that I held off on reading Lucian's text for six blocks, but I finally clicked on the icon, my heart twisting at the one-word statement.

Apologies.

If anything, that actually made me feel worse. Because Lucian wasn't sorry. He was trying on human emotions like he tried on his new fancy suits, seeing which ones he preferred, then making adjustments to generate the response he most wanted from his audience. My skin prickled in remembered trauma, my bruises seeming to sink deeper into my bones.

Scowling, I pocketed the phone as the Uber slid to the curb in front of a nondescript gray-brick building on Halsted. Chewing my lower lip, I glanced at the buildings to either side. If I hadn't known better, I'd have thought it was a boutique office or a minimalist spa. The only marker was a small brass plate with the street number—apparently, the Alinea bistro didn't need a sign.

I stepped out, grateful for my black pantsuit as I shouldered Claire's expensive bag. I wouldn't be turned away at the door, at least. Still, as the car pulled off, I felt a little queasy, knowing what I was about to step into. Never mind the fancy new clothes and the high-ticket work, some part of me knew I should be sneaking in through the service entrance of a place like this, not walking through the front door.

The air smelled faintly of rain and exhaust as I hitched my shoulder bag higher and crossed to the entrance. The moment I stepped inside, however, the city sounds vanished. The restaurant's lighting was low, golden, and the air carried the faintest whiff of citrus and something rich and earthy. The hostess glanced up and gave me a subtle nod. Her scent was equally rich, redolent of vanilla candles and soft sheets, her baby safely tucked to sleep while a nanny cooed from a rocking chair. Flustered at that unexpected detail, I gave the woman my name even though she clearly didn't need it. Because that was what you did when you weren't part of the club.

She smiled at me a little sympathetically, then led me through the narrow dining room without another word. My heels clicked softly against polished wood, the rhythm echoing just enough to make me feel too loud. Around us, conversations murmured like secrets, and dishes gleamed like art installations. Then she opened a door to a private room: one table, white linen, two neatly set places, ornate mirror on the far wall. There was a closed doorway in the back corner of the room, promising of deeper secrets—or simply a private entry to the bathrooms? Kind of a toss-up.

I sat. Sparkling water arrived through that secondary doorway, a slice of lemon floating like gold. The server whisked away, leaving the door ajar. I lifted the glass, grateful for something familiar—then barely managed not to choke on the burn. Vodka.

"I was hoping you'd contact me."

I glanced up to see Nikolai Volkov regarding me from the doorway and didn't even bother hiding the jolt. Granted, the last time I'd seen the man, he'd not exactly been at his best, but how had I missed the dangerous grace that seemed to spin out from him like a faint cologne?

Plunking down my glass on the table, I stayed seated as he strode toward me, scrambling to process the sensory explosion. His left eye was covered by a black silken patch—somehow completely not pirate-like—but otherwise, he was absolute perfection in a man. Tall, lean, and elegant in an inky black suit with a slate-gray silk shirt beneath, open at the collar. He moved with the grace of a jaguar, and he reached out a hand to me as he approached. Lamely, I held mine up, then focused on keeping my eyes from crossing as he leaned over it, his lips grazing my knuckles.

He held on to my hand as he sat, his soft smile telling me he could feel my pulse spike. This close, he smelled of velvet, old gold and polished brass knuckles, and I tried to remember what my name was.

Just that quickly, something deep in my bones recoiled, seeing the threat my eyes didn't register. The scratches along my ribs throbbed in warning—the same warning I'd felt around Lucian. Volkov may be free of his demon now, but it had left marks. I could smell the faint char underneath the expensive cologne.

With a final squeeze, he released my hand as a staffer in a black suit sailed through the doorway with a carafe and second drink. He set both out for us, then Volkov slanted a glance at me. "You trust me?"

My lips quirked. "To feed me here? Yes. But I've heard about this place, and I don't have time for complicated. So the drink is fine."

His smile warmed me even more than the vodka. "We couldn't disappoint the chef, and it is early enough that he'll indulge me," he said cheerfully, then glanced at the server.

"Truffle and mushroom tart, with the pumpernickel and gruyere—and all at once. I have seen the presentation already, and it's not necessary here. I will pay him for the affront."

The server bowed and was off in a whisper of stiff cotton, while Volkov pinned me with his one-eyed gaze.

"I expected you sooner."

"I've been a little busy."

"And yet, so silent. Pithius—who never once shut up— didn't even howl your name when he left, so I was left with no information at all. I'm not used to being ignored."

I blinked at him. "You knew the demon I exorcised from you by name? You guys were that chummy?"

He smiled a little grimly. "Not exactly. I owed Pithius a debt, which I paid in full. But he refused to leave."

"Yeah. They do that."

"Given the nature of my agreement with him, I couldn't force him out or conspire to ensure his eviction. But you removed him with an almost offhanded effort. I owe you my life, quite sincerely." He spread his hands. "How can I help you? And—before you begin—you can speak freely here. This room is warded."

"Oh. Of course." *Warded?*

Volkov merely smiled, so I blew out a long breath and sat back. "I don't even know if you can, if I'm being honest. But when I stumbled into that back room in your club and I saw what was going on, even with the demon inside you, you seemed to be the guy in control. And after everything went down, you helped me get Steve out."

He tilted his head slightly. "Steve?"

I squinted at him. "Black guy, maybe six-two, all arms and legs—the ones your little puff pieces were exsanguinating over in the corner?"

"Ah!" He smiled. "Of course. You forget that once you

released Pithius from me, my focus narrowed totally on you. But, of course, you were carrying someone. I took him from you —helped you both outside."

He spoke this as if he were trying to remember a dream, and I grimaced. "You did. But that whole scene in those back rooms seemed, I don't know. Extremely *established*. Like an entire society that no one really knows about, just out of sight. And with my newest job, I'm maybe running up against that society in a big way. And I know absolutely nothing about it."

"Ah." He inclined his head. "But you're an exorcist, and quite a gifted one, it would seem, for all that I've never heard of you."

"Of course you haven't." I waved a hand, exasperated. "I've never done this work on my own. That was kind of an accident. I apprenticed under Mordechai Schneider, the ex-rabbi, and—"

Nikolai narrowed his gaze on me, his expression intent. "Rabbi Mordechai? Him, I have heard of, of course. He trapped many a demon in his day."

Trapped? No. That wasn't how Mordechai worked. He released demons.

Clearly unaware of my inner objections, Volkov continued. "But how could he not have trained you on the hierarchies, the territories? He was in the center of all of it."

I returned his gaze steadily. "The center of what? I don't know anything about hierarchies or territories. Up until a very short time ago, I didn't know anything about a systemic demon problem in Chicago, either, but it seems like that's what we're dealing with. And now, I've been asked to take out a demon named Mirr, who apparently works for someone named Asmodaea, who may or may not be a minion of Samael and all a sudden, my dance card is feeling a little full."

By now Nikolai was staring. "Of all people, Mordechai should have trained you better than this. He was good. He was also responsible for taking out one of the most powerful demons in this city, Palemerious. We'd thought he was dead, possibly destroyed by an executioner while he was restrained, but he's been sensed recently, felt. Still, for Mordechai to have imprisoned him for so long—it's impressive. The old man's crowning achievement, really."

I went cold. "Who?" I asked carefully. "And what do you mean, imprisoning? That's not how Mordechai worked."

"Well, considering how little he told you of the courts, I suppose it's not surprising that he didn't share his most signature accomplishment with you. And it was a long time ago—fifteen years or more. Palemerious was one of Belial's top commanders—brutal, diabolical, enduring. And then he was gone, by the grace of Mordechai. It was a blow to Belial's hold in the city, and slowly and surely, Asmodaea of the Court of Ruin has risen to take his place."

"Right." I grimaced, my brain practically shorting out with all the new information. *Gone by the grace of Mordechai?* "Does um, she have someone named Mirr working for her? I haven't had time to check the hierarchies."

"Mirr?" Nikolai made a face. "He's a tricky sneak, and yes. He has long been a lieutenant of Belial's, and I would not be surprised if Asmodaea has commandeered him for her own uses. You should know, she has Chicago tight in her grasp. If you are squaring off against her, she will not suffer you interrupting her plans well."

I frowned. "You think I might be squaring off against her?"

He quirked a languorous smile at me, his deep-set eyes the color of antique leather. "I do, as it happens. And I relish the idea."

We paused as the server brought in a tray with four small plates, a presentation that was absolutely anathema to the Michelin-starred restaurant, which was known for its highly orchestrated meal flights. But it looked at least reasonably satiating, and it resembled food—not always the case here.

We waited for our server to retreat again, and Volkov picked up his fork with his left hand, his knife with his right. Despite the European affectation, I didn't feel a hundred percent happy with him palming any sort of blade in his dominant hand.

He waited until I took a bite before continuing, while I tried not to moan at the texture and flavor of the miniature truffle tart he'd probably spent $80 for me to scarf down in about ten seconds.

"Asmodaea is one of the seven commanders beneath Samael, head of the Court of Ruin. Everything that spawns from him has the traits of fury, lies, and destruction. Asmodaea takes that molten rage and uses it to strengthen structures, networks, connections. In the ancient world, she wove her influence of rage and lies through temples and tongues, convincing priests that order itself was holiness. In the modern one, she's traded marble for microchips. Her cathedrals are server farms; her psalms, the pulse of data. She doesn't lie outright—she refines the truth until it gleams, until it blinds."

"So she's like a demon of the database."

"In the modern world, yes. She builds not to shelter, but to ensnare. To make the system so seamless, no one remembers what it was like to live without her. Belial's illusions are chaos, but Asmodaea's are comfort."

I didn't want to ask. I wouldn't ask.

I asked.

"And Palemerious? How does—did—he fit in?"

"Since ancient times, Palemerious has served as her mirror, but in Belial's court. Lust and Wrath often worked very well together. Where Asmodaea wove systems, he wove souls. He understood people—how they fractured, what they craved, what they'd trade to stop feeling empty. If she built the cage,

Palemerious convinced you it was home. He could thread devotion through a crowd like silk, uttering one word, and they'd kneel. In the old days, he whispered to kings. I don't know much about him—it was before my time. But together, he and Asmodaea were perfection—her machinery, his magnetism. She commanded the current. He commanded the flesh that touched the switch."

"Neat," I said, grimacing. "And now it's just Asmodaea, and through this demon, Mirr, she's about to use Kieran Walsh's new tool to, what, run Chicago?"

"She could," he agreed, picking up his glass again. "Prometheus Solutions isn't the only company she has her hooks in, but it's the one that can take her the furthest, right now. Among other benefits, the Reflex system will give her instant control over the imports and exports that flow through this city, both legitimately and otherwise."

"Oh, really." I joined him in another sip of vodka soda. "That would hurt you, wouldn't it?"

"Without a doubt." He shrugged. "But where one door closes, another opens. The more challenging issue is whether Asmodaea's star is growing bright enough that Samael or the other generals will take notice. If she draws attention here, other demons will follow, and Chicago will become a battleground, instead of merely a den of iniquity."

"A battleground." I grimaced. "And why do I think demons won't be the only casualty?"

"He lifted a glass, rolling the liquor around in it. "Because they won't be."

"And you don't think it will cause a hit to your business?"

"Not at all. It will simply morph into another form. Someone has to feed the hunger of the darkness." Nikolai drank the contents of his glass in a single draft. "Where sin flows, money follows. But you, Delia Thompson, should be more careful. You're swimming in deeper waters now, playing with bigger fish. You go in and confront Mirr, even exorcise him, and that also could attract Samael's attention."

"Maybe, maybe not." I sipped my own drink, grateful for its heat. "Mordechai seemed to fly under the radar pretty well."

Nikolai pursed his lips. "As we've established, there's more to Mordechai Schneider's work than he fully shared with you. You should be careful."

The rear door to the private room opened, and a server reappeared with two fresh glasses of vodka. We both remained silent until we were alone again—though clearly we weren't quite alone, with service like that.

I narrowed my eyes as he studied me. "Are you trying to scare me off?"

"Not at all. I'm trying to keep you alive."

"Mm. And why would that be? You've already been rescued."

His smile lit a fire in places I hadn't realized had gone cold— only to once again feel wrong, too hot, too quick. Fever-bright, in fact, like infection spreading. My bruises pulsed in time with my heartbeat, and I realized my hands were trembling. Who was this guy?

"Yes, well," he said, watching me. "That rescue bonds me to you, whether I want to be or not. I can help you with information, safety, and access to the tools you will need to succeed in this new world you are setting foot in."

I stiffened. *Bonds.* There was a lot of that going around, it seemed. "I don't need props, Mr. Volkov. Mordechai didn't, and he's the one who trained me."

"Didn't he, though?" Nikolai tilted his glass at me. "Perhaps this is yet another piece of information he chose not to share."

I didn't like thinking about this, but Nikolai wasn't done. "The demonic world has rules, hierarchies, strengths, and weaknesses your mentor never taught you. I know this world well. I could teach you. Show you. Make you strong."

The invitation that hung in the air was palpable, and I offered him a weak smile. "And would that erase your debt to me?"

"Perhaps...or perhaps it would entwine me to you further." He paused a beat. "Would you like that?"

The moment stretched out between us, and he caught my gaze with his one working eye, held it. I had to force myself not to look away first. "I think we will have a great deal to teach each other, Delia Thompson."

And deep in my twice-damned soul, I knew he was right.

I stood to leave, glancing up to catch my reflection in the ornate mirror on the far wall—and a chill skated through me. For a moment, I could have sworn I saw Lucian standing behind me. But when I turned, there was nothing there.

CHAPTER

NINE

I could smell the pizza from the top of the stairs, a savory counterpoint to the aromas of patchouli and cloves wafting up from the yoga studio below. It'd been a solid five hours since my nothing lunch at Alinea, and I'd spent most of it back at the library researching demons. You would've thought I'd have done this years ago, but I guess I could be excused, given that I'd had a lord of the underworld as my back-seat driver the whole freaking time who'd been handed through the door by *my own mentor*.

Now the smell of pizza drew me forward instinctively, never mind that I knew—knew!—that same lord of the underworld was the man—demon—whatever he was, behind it. I didn't care. I reeked of coffee and adrenaline, and my footfalls on the hardwood flooring sounded more like a zombie shuffle than the clickety-clack of a confident, super-together exorcist. Whatever. It'd been a long day.

I lifted my chin as I swung through the door, then blinked at the almost cozy and definitely surreal setup in front of me. Even though we rarely saw anyone on this floor, we were definitely going to need to start going closed-door as a general policy.

The couch and comfortable chair had been replaced by a couple of soft chairs and a center table by the door, allowing room for a second desk to be wedged against the bookcases—still in the soft, vanilla-flavored wood favored by the establishment, but currently bristling with three monitors, a muscular charging dock, and multiple laptops that Steve was manning. Notebooks that looked like they dated back twenty years sat stacked around him in worn-cover disarray. The small table and chairs—now protected by a tarp that could have doubled as a murder accessory—were stacked with open pizza boxes.

Lucian sat at Claire's desk with his feet up on the surface, a plate of pizza ignored by him as his attention focused solely on me, while Claire leaned over one of Steve's monitors. She jumped a little as I entered, twin flags of color in her cheeks indicating her tension.

"He brought equipment—and food," she said quickly. "I couldn't exactly complain." Her hand strayed to her necklace and gave it a tug, but before I could wave off her concern, Steve turned too, speaking around a mouthful of pizza.

"He brought the *good* food. And also, like, highly illegal corporate source code."

I blinked, then swiveled my gaze to Lucian. "Source code from Prometheus?"

"You've been gone a long time," he observed, watching me with hooded eyes. "Busy day?"

"Productive, yes." I unshouldered my bag and held it up toward Claire. "Wherever you found this, I approve. It gave me all the clout I needed."

"Clothes don't make the woman, but they sure don't hurt," she chirped, relief palpable in her voice. "Steve's right, though —this source code seems to be legit."

My gaze met Lucian's again, and I grimaced. "Speaking of source, do I want to know?"

He smiled. "You wanted to understand what we were dealing with, and now you can."

"So you stole it. How?"

"I appropriated it, yes. An earlier version than the current construct, but it should serve. You disappeared after your meeting with Walsh."

"Oh, that's right." I cocked a finger at him, as if spontaneously remembering a critical detail. "You can't track me unless I'm hanging out with a demon. As it happens, I spent some quality time with Nikolai Volkov. It proved enlightening."

"Volkov?" Steve swallowed and turned toward me. "From the Descent? He's kind of scary."

"He's also kind of connected. And he knows a lot about a lot."

Lucian scowled as Claire stabbed at the screen. "That's it, isn't it?" she asked excitedly. "That's the same, like, words and stuff you were looking for?"

Steve swiveled back. "Looks like we have a winner," he said as he dropped his pizza and pulled a handwipe out of the tube on the desk, cleaning off his fingers before he hunched over his keyboard again. I blinked, then realized there were three such tubs arranged around him. Apparently, Claire wasn't going to let him destroy the equipment on the first day.

I smiled, wanting to preserve this moment, this image—but even as I glanced around, something in my chest tightened—not my heart, but deeper, the sense of wrongness twisting inside me. I suddenly felt *occupied*, though I knew I was alone in my own skin now. I refused to look at Lucian, but anger spiked within me. When would this be *over*? When would I be *normal* again?

And what would that even feel like? I'd been living a screwed-up life for so long, what did normal even mean?

"Lucian said the game and traffic system had to be related,

which you know, makes sense, right?" Steve said, reclaiming my focus. "With the God's Eye view and the Architect power? But I couldn't imagine it'd be anywhere close. Except it totally is. Check it out."

He zipped through lines of Reflex code that looked more like the ancient sigils and unknown languages I'd pored over at the library than straight math—and also seemed way above his pay grade. "Since when did you learn code?"

"Yo, I went to college before AI made it obsolete—and I gamed on bootleg servers. You want to keep the game going after the corporate assholes turned the lights off, you had to learn some stuff. But this is what's weird, right?" He pointed at the screen. "There's a shit-ton of non-functional code in here. Characters that don't compile, executables that don't, you know, execute. And it doesn't seem to matter for shit."

I tilted my head, feeling Lucian's stare still hard on me. "So why are they there?"

"Ask him," Steve said, cocking his thumb over his shoulder. "He thought you might know, but I've got nothing."

"I..." I grimaced, peering at the screen, acutely aware of the moment Lucian stood and began moving with a predator's grace around the table toward us. He stopped, too close, and I tried to keep my breathing even. He didn't smell like pizza. He smelled like heat, cinnamon, and entanglements I didn't need.

He chuckled softly, leaning toward the computer, and I gritted my teeth as he brushed my arm. "Those are binding marks," he said in his lazy drawl. "Containment symbols. Asmodaea didn't merely write this code, she consecrated it."

Steve continued scrolling through. "I mean, it does put a whole new spin on virus protection. And if Warriors of Darkyn has some of the same sigils in it as this stuff does, that means she was working on this shit way before Prometheus blew up. Like, we're talking vintage Finn Ashford at this point, not

Kieran. No disrespect to Kieran, of course, but this is some next-level shit."

My brows went up. "Finn? He was working with demons to get his game coded?"

Steve barked out a laugh, the sound remarkably joyful. "I mean, how cool is that, right? At least in theory. But not at first, I don't think. Otherwise, yo, my team would never have been able to get a foothold on the server and keep playing the game when it was decommissioned." He looked up with a grin. "There's only one way to find out, though, if you really want to know. This is Reflex code, but a new version of Warriors of Darkyn is, like, buried inside it, for no apparent reason. Which means we could totally play it and see what gives. You just need to say go."

"Steve..." Claire rubbed her hand over her face, while Lucian straightened, folding his arms as I gaped at them all.

"What? What are you talking about?"

"I mean Anya, Rook, and Mei Zhao." He swiveled toward me. "You remember me talking about them, yeah? I crashed at Rook's apartment when..." he waved his hand at Lucian. "You know. Things got a little jacked up."

"I..." I frowned. "I don't think you ever told me where you went."

He snorted. "Yeah, fair. I probably didn't. No offense." He gave me a smile. "You were a little scary. But they're here online, and they're game, so with your approval..."

"I mean..." I glanced at Lucian. "Is it safe?"

He smiled. "You're asking me about safety?"

Something in his words wrapped around me too tightly, a question, a possibility. A danger I didn't want to explore too deeply.

"Fine, go," I blurted, unreasonably nettled.

Steve didn't give me a chance to change my mind. He

opened a Discord channel and ordered speakers on, and a chorus of three voices chimed in, their names flashing across the screen. Anya Gaines, Rook Washington, Mei Zhao.

"Okay, here we go. Game always lags to start, blah-blah-blah, dungeon-dungeon-dungeon."

Steve kept up a monologue while I drifted over to the pizza boxes, reaching down to grab a fistful of napkins—Claire's work, undoubtedly—and then score my first slice of all-you-could-meat heaven. I groaned in absolute bliss as I swallowed my first bite. Alinea was great and all, but nothing would ever beat pizza in my world.

Lucian had stepped back far enough from the monitors that I nearly bumped into him when I turned around. He lifted a lazy hand to tuck my hair behind my ear. "It'll get in your pizza."

"You want a bite?" I offered my slice, and his eyes glittered.

"I'll eat later."

The slinky promise in that line curled through me, and I covered my unwanted reaction by nearly asphyxiating myself with my next bite of pizza. As I struggled not to cough, however, Lucian leaned closer. "Volkov never gives anything for nothing. Remember that. You think he owes you, but the scale never balances evenly with him. He wants something. He always does."

"Mm." I finally managed. "At least he's honest about what he wants—and I gotta say, he made a good offer."

"Oh, I bet he did."

"I'm serious." I finished the slice, then tossed the napkins away. "He offered to teach me everything I should already know. What Mordechai should have."

"Mordechai..." Lucian sighed, but whatever he was going to say next was cut off by a startled shout from the speakers.

The player named Anya was bristling with annoyance. "Whoa, whoa, whoa," she snapped. "Are you seeing this here?

These demons aren't native to the game. They're new. They're wrong."

"They're assholes," Mei Zhao agreed, her tone tight. "And this one just called me by my real name. Not my character name. That's some bullshit right there."

"We've got more demons coming in on our six." Rook's voice rolled out over the speaker next, cool and fluid, but also layered with concern. "And Mei-Tai, I got the same name check. That is not cool."

"You geared up to hit architect mode, Cube?" Anya asked. Claire and I exchanged a startled glance, but Steve responded smoothly.

"Trying to, but check it. That door flashes on when I hit the tile to activate. I don't activate, but that goddamned door…"

"Let's go," Mei ordered, and on the screen the three characters raced toward the flashing door. "Keep it flashing long enough—"

They burst through the door into a room that looked like nothing more than the lobby of Prometheus, all bright silver and blinding light. In the center, a man turned, his arms flinging wide. Coils of energy spooled from his helmet, and his face was hidden beneath giant black goggles and some kind of breathing unit.

"Demons right behind us—whoa!" Rook cut off, as the screen morphed into a maze of mirrors, their reflections bouncing back at the characters as they bounded forward. "Break through the glass," Mei commanded, and they all hefted their battle hammers.

With each crash, a new voice shouted over the cacophony— not any of theirs. "Five years…boxed and locked…she's everywhere…"

"What the hell is this?" Steve gritted out, the glass rebuilding itself as soon as they struck it down.

"That's not the game talking," Claire said suddenly, her hands gripping the back of Steve's chair. "That's someone in the game. Someone's *trapped* in there."

"Whoa," Rook's voice whispered as all three players froze. "Finn?"

The screen flashed then went to black, with new copy scrolling across the top. UNAUTHORIZED ACCESS DETECTED. INITIATING QUARANTINE.

"Get out, get out, get out!" Steve suddenly yelled, lunging for the power dock. The outlet sparked and he flinched away, even as a new line of text appeared on the screen, a list of names. STEVE MORRISON. CLAIRE BICKWELL. DELIA THOMPSON. MEI ZHAO. ROOK WASHINGTON. ANYA GAINES.

Lucian darted forward and, ignoring the sparking tower, yanked it free from the power cord. The screens went instantly dark, and the nervous chatter and shouts on the speakers went silent. But not everything was dead.

My phone chirped in my pocket, and I yanked it out, seeing the text icon flash on.

One incoming message.

I didn't stab it. "She's in everything, isn't she?" I muttered.

"Not yet. But she will be when Reflex 2.0 launches." Lucian gestured to the phone. "You won't be able to ignore that when you see it, but at least talk to me about it."

Startled, I met his gaze. "Yeah?"

"Yes. It's time."

Steve's phone rang, making us all jump. He stabbed it on. "On speaker," he announced. "Everyone report with seeker word. This is Optimus."

"Donkey." Mei's voice was clear and steady, and Rook followed her. "Belle."

"Cartman," Anya closed the loop. "How is everyone?"

"Bailed in time, then ran a system backup, and nothing

seems fucked," Rook put in. "Totally want to go in again, though."

"There was someone in there, right?" Mei asked. "We all saw the same thing? I mean..."

"It's gotta be Finn," Anya agreed. "It was always bullshit that he jumped off Navy Pier. Nobody believed that. I was on his beta squad. I definitely didn't believe it. I still don't. But that suit..."

She trailed off, and Lucian caught my eye. We moved off slightly as Claire stepped closer to Steve, entering their conversation.

"Show it to me," he said. "You shouldn't look at it alone."

I pulled the phone out of my pocket and stabbed it on again, scrolling to the text app. Only now, there was nothing there.

I turned the device toward him. "Deleted."

He hissed and I pocketed the device again. "I'm going to have to go back to Prometheus, Lucian."

"Not if she knows who you are." He scowled. "Which she clearly does."

"Yeah, but she still thinks you're dead." I gave him a smile that showed I fully understood how insane all this was, and he chuckled. Instinctively, almost without conscious thought, we swayed toward each other, only to stop with Claire's squeak.

We turned back to the screen, which Steve still hadn't powered on again, but which flickered with an otherworldly light all the same.

Only a single word illuminated it.

WATCHING.

The computer went dead.

"Random glitch?" Steve asked. "Or is someone fucking with us?"

"Probably both." Lucian stepped toward the screen, suddenly all business. "Nothing that's happened here is all that surprising. The names of Claire and Delia were on the invoice sheet for the equipment, plus, Thompson & Associates visited Prometheus Solutions this morning. Your players were identifiable through the game. The only name the AI didn't have access to was mine, and you'll note, it didn't use it. So 'watching' is perhaps an overstatement."

"It's still creepy as hell," Steve put in.

"Agreed!" chimed in Mei Zhao.

We spent the next few minutes cleaning up, but when I went for my bag, Claire roused herself. "Oh! There was a delivery for you earlier, like about thirty boxes. I put them in your office. They seemed official and I didn't want to open them." Her hand drifted to her necklace. "They're from Mordechai's nephew."

My pulse spiked, and something shimmered through my nerves. Mordechai—the guy who'd supposedly imprisoned one of the commanders of the demon world...except the only place Palemerious had been was inside *me*. Would there be something in those boxes that explained that cluster of fuckery?

There damned well better be.

"Oh, good." I smiled with an optimism I didn't feel. "You guys go ahead and take off. I'll look at them, then head out."

"We'll both look at them, then I'll take you back to your apartment, Delia," Lucian said.

Claire met my gaze, and I could see the relief in her eyes, so I turned to him, my smile still firmly plastered on my face, even though my heart had begun to thud, my palms to sweat. "Great —yeah. We'll do that."

"You guys want the pizza?" Steve asked hopefully.

CHAPTER

TEN

"Dear God," I whispered as I stared around the inner office. Claire hadn't been kidding. There were boxes stacked floor-to-ceiling, two deep on one side of my office, and lining the floor beneath the window along the back. The guest chairs were stacked high as well. "How could his nephew have let all of this go? I mean...what is all this stuff?"

Lucian leaned against the doorway, for once not imposing on my personal space. If anything, he watched me with something approaching hesitation. "You're tired, Delia," he said quietly. "Maybe this isn't the best time to attempt this."

"No." I blew out a breath, straightening. "No—I mean, I'm in so far above my head I've forgotten what it's like to break the surface. I have to get my hands around this." I glanced up at him, feeling a strange rush of gratitude. After all, he'd never lied about being a powerful demon, at least. Better than Mordechai not mentioning that he'd used me as a paddy wagon to stow away his prisoner until he figured out what to do with him.

And had Mordechai even done that? I still didn't know

enough to make any judgments. Nikolai Volkov wasn't exactly a Boy Scout, and if he was trying to twist me up…

There was so much more I needed to learn, to understand. And maybe it was stuffed into these musty boxes, maybe not, but it was a start. "Thanks for being here, Lucian," I said quietly. "I hope you're prepared to explain anything I don't understand."

He inclined his head slightly and I moved to the desk, where a single box stood, about the size of a case of copy paper. It had the number "one" on it in the lower right-hand corner, and I blinked, then looked around at the other boxes. "Are any of the other ones numbered?"

Lucian stepped into the room. "They don't appear to be, no."

"Well, I guess he gave me a starting place, anyway." I walked around the desk, grateful that there weren't any boxes behind me here, only shelves. I suddenly didn't think I'd have any trouble filling them. Taking a pair of scissors from the desk drawer, I leaned over the box and sliced through the tape, my nose wrinkling at the scent that wafted up. Tomato soup, I thought, and then my gaze got a little blurry.

The box held a moss-green layer of crocheted yarn. "His— shawl," I managed on a half-laugh, pulling the garment out. "He'd always keep the office cold, but he had that on the chair, on the—oh, geez." I forcibly dropped the shawl on the back of my own chair, struggling to retain focus. Directly beneath it was a stack of files, topped by a single letter in a sealed envelope.

"Mordechai's nephew was certainly one for dramatics," Lucian said, his voice dripping into a sneer, but with a quick slice of the scissors again, I was opening the letter, scanning it.

"Yeah—well, if this is right, he didn't have a choice.

Mordechai had instructions in his will...his nephew wasn't even supposed to look at this stuff."

I handed the letter over to Lucian, then pulled the first stack of files out, slipping off the rubber band which crumbled to dust. I made a face and opened the file folder. Mordechai's handwriting confronted me, neat inscriptions down a page—but written in a language I had no hope of deciphering. "What is this, Hebrew?" I muttered.

"All materials herein to be delivered to Delia Thompson upon my death," Lucian read from the letter. "None may be omitted. There's a note here at the bottom with the nephew's number, should you wish to use it."

"I don't," I said grimly. "He had no idea what Mordechai was up to...hell, I didn't even know what Mordechai was up to. Volkov mentioned that he knew a hell of a lot about the Court system in Chicago. Did you know that?"

I peered up at him suddenly, only to find him staring at me, for once not wearing his habitual sneer. "You did know, didn't you? God! How could I have been so blind?"

I turned back to the box and pulled out more files—one with pages on pages of hierarchies that I only recognized because of Walsh's computer screens, others filled with maps. Then, about five files down, came the case files.

"Oh, my God. No," I muttered, suddenly feeling the weight of all those people in need, all those calls. The prayers and supplications, the tears.

"Delia," Lucian murmured, and he was suddenly at my side. Not to humor me or to placate, but merely to take the files from my hands and start stacking them on the shelves. "You'll want to go through these, eventually. Maybe have Claire digitize them."

I snorted. "She'll love that." But with my hands free, I could dip into the box again—and then the next one, and the next. To my surprise, there weren't as many case files as I expected...and very few of them had names I recalled. All too quickly, we came to books, each more ancient than the last.

"What is all this?" I murmured, as I opened up the fifth one, surprised to see—like the others—they were all handwritten.

"Case files from a world that still believed in order," Lucian said, pointing to a symbol halfway down the page. "Here. This demon actually worked for Asmodaea. See this sigil? You've seen it before, haven't you?"

"The logo from Warriors of Darkyn," I said, blinking up from the book to meet his dark eyes. "They worked that sigil into the actual logo of the *game*?"

"Like I said, it's a containment mark." He flipped through the pages, then turned the book toward me again. "This family was targeted by Samael's network for three generations. There were accounts in that blue book you passed by of binding rituals that predate Christianity."

"But...what *is* this?" I sliced open another box—and another, only to be confronted with yet more books. "What the hell was he doing with all these records? Shouldn't they be somewhere, like, sacred? Like some sort of church?"

When Lucian didn't respond, I lifted my hands to my eye sockets, pressing hard as if I could somehow unsee all this. "He didn't tell me jack shit! Even when he was slowing down, getting sick, even when he knew what I was going to face, he told me nothing! Why? Why would he have done this?"

Lucian still said nothing, merely put the books on the shelves. I couldn't explore them now—not all of them. There were too many. "I don't understand any of this, Lucian—do you? Do you know what he was thinking?"

He finally stopped, his hand on the last book—a gorgeous blue volume that looked like it was edged in gold. "I had ample opportunity to observe Mordechai, but only through your eyes, Delia."

"Well, what about before that? I mean, you were around before you crawled into me, right? And how the hell did that even…"

My voice died in my throat as I unearthed the next file, a thick pile of paper in an accordion folder, labeled in Mordechai's careful hand. "PALEMERIOUS."

I looked up to see Lucian staring at me. "Delia," he murmured.

"Don't. Don't say anything, but…" I swallowed. "Don't leave, either, okay? Just don't…"

I pulled out the stack of paper before I said anything else I'd regret. The first page made me press my lips together. "Jesus Christ, he started recording this when I was ten—ten!" I blinked hard, my eyes blurring. "He knew I was already possessed from the moment I met him."

Lucian made a noise deep in his throat. "Not exactly," he began, but I couldn't hear him—couldn't hear anything except the pounding of my blood in my ears.

~10 years, 4 months. Recovering, curious, already showing increased intuition, sensitivity. Able to identify demons by name. P? No. Could do it that first day. But P assisted?

I paged forward, stopping abruptly.

~17 years, 6 months. Death of S. Thompson. D withdrawn but not outwardly projecting grief. P? Protection or deflection?

A shaky laugh bubbled out of me, emerging from somewhere near my toes. "He never did understand why I couldn't grieve properly," I managed, my voice sounding strange in my own ears, shaky and weak. But I kept reading voraciously, needfully, as the notations grew more strident, concerned. When I was aged twenty, twenty-two, my abilities increasing right along with my symptoms of withdrawal, my nightmares—he knew about my nightmares—described in vivid detail. How had he known about those? I hadn't told him all that, had I?

"How did he know?" I whispered. "And why didn't he *do* anything?"

"You would talk," Lucian said abruptly. "In the adrenaline release after an exorcism, as you drove back, you would drift off and then you would talk. You'd tell him what you dreamed of, how you handled it, how you felt. Apparently, he listened."

I stared at him. "And...I mean, you let me do that?"

"Delia." The word seemed wrenched out of him like a confession. "You were—are—stronger than you realize. I couldn't keep you from doing what you wanted to do."

"But why did you stay, then?" I suddenly exploded. "If I was so fucking strong, why couldn't I push you out? Why couldn't Mordechai pull you out? Why didn't he *do* anything?"

Lucian didn't respond right away and I whirled on him, not wanting to know those answers. Those answers were too difficult, too fraught.

"Tell me everything," I said instead. "All of it. Who you are, what you want. Volkov said—"

"Volkov doesn't know half of what he thinks he does," Lucian snapped. His gaze trained on mine, fierce and furious. "And he talks entirely too much."

"He said you were a commander for—"

"Do *not* speak his name." Lucian cut me off. "You, above all people, know that names have power. And you're a human. Demons love nothing more than to hear their names on the lips of humans. I was bound to serve Belial for centuries, and yes, I was his commander. In Belial's hierarchy, you ruled or you licked bootheels, and I was not going to do that. I was given territory, power, and autonomy. But there were limits to that autonomy, and eventually I didn't want those limits anymore. I began to explore exit strategies, and any exit strategy involved hiding. I got quite good at hiding. But Belial still knew who I was, could summon me with the crook of his finger if he wanted. Until finally, he simply didn't want to. When you're a demon, playing the long game takes on an entirely different meaning."

I blew out a shaky breath. "But why me?" I finally asked. "Why did you choose me?"

"I didn't," he said succinctly. "I chose the child before you. The child whose exorcism you interrupted while walking some old lady's dogs."

The outrage, the indignation that welled up in me was almost too much to bear, but fortunately, Lucian didn't give me the chance to process all of it. "When you did finally exorcise me, you unraveled a binding that should never have been broken. It shouldn't have worked. When you summoned me back, asking my help, I agreed to take that binding on again. But don't think for one minute it was because we're friends, Delia. I will do anything to break Belial's hold on me, even if it breaks you in the process."

I stared at him. "You're using me. You need me to get close to what's her fuck because she won't suspect that I evicted you."

His lips twisted. "Asmodaea wouldn't suspect you had anything close to that ability, no. You forget we were far beyond her territory when you exorcised the demons from the Graham estate. And then you summoned me back so any casual observer would have thought I still was exactly where they thought I was. And then the rabbi came and you returned home. To anyone looking..."

I stared at him. "They think Rabbi Ethan exorcised you? I didn't even get credit for *that*?"

His lips twisted. "Are you seeking the approbation of the horde?"

"That's not the point!" I stood, suddenly too edgy, too constricted in the little room. He didn't move from his position by the bookcase, and when I shoved past him, his scent rolled over me, all caramelized sugar and smoked whiskey. "You using me makes a certain amount of sense—but Mordechai? Why would he do that? And how much of what's happening now did you manipulate? I mean, for fuck's sake, you're living in Walsh's building! How long have you been planning to go after him—or after this Asmo—"

"Don't say it."

"I'm going to say it! I don't give a shit about demons hearing me. And if you cared at all for me, if Mordechai did, neither one of you would have absolutely fucking ruined my life for the last fifteen years while you used me to...to..."

I turned on him with wide eyes. "To *hide*. To hide from your enemies until you could attack them on your own terms. You used me from the very beginning!"

"Delia..." Lucian began, and he stepped toward me then, only there was nowhere for me to go. I knew I should flee, I should back up, but suddenly his scent was everywhere. Smoke, spice, and something darker I couldn't name. His gaze flicked to my neck, where I knew my pulse jumped, but I didn't care about that. I couldn't care about—think about—anything but him stepping closer to me.

"You still feel it, don't you," I challenged. "The connection between us. But you can't track me the way you want to, not unless I'm with a demon."

"We have a residual bond, yes. It's fading, but it's present—and when you're in danger of a demonic nature, yes. It strengthens."

I stared at him. "You experience what I experience?"

"Echoes." He shook his head. "Nothing more. And it's

fading. I no longer see what you see. I no longer feel what you feel."

"What about this? You feel this?" Still not thinking clearly, still reeling from a truth I'd grasped and lost in the space of seconds, I lifted my hand sharply, intending to strike. But just as quickly Lucian lifted his, grabbing mine, holding it. Turning it over in his long fingers.

His eyes boring into mine, he dipped his head, drifted his lips over my knuckles. "He kissed you here," he murmured.

I huffed a small breath, but I wasn't going to deny it. "He did. I'm not your property anymore."

"You never were." He lowered his head again, his lips pressing, probing, then he turned my hand so that they dropped to my wrist.

The touch should have repulsed me—this was the creature who'd lived inside my skin, who knew every secret shame. My bruises flared hot, the scratches along my ribs burning. But the heat that pooled low in my belly wasn't revulsion. It was worse.

Desire shot through me, liquid hot, and with a move that surprised even me with its speed, I gripped his hand with mine, then snaked my other hand up to the back of his head, twining in his hair, pulling his head toward my mouth until I crushed his lips to mine.

My brain exploded.

Heat flooded through me as Lucian met my kiss fire for fire, need for need. He tasted like sin and lies and fifteen years of knowing every secret I'd ever kept. His hands found my waist, pulling me closer, and I went willingly, desperately. For one heart-stopping moment, I felt occupied again—that phantom sensation of something inside me, coiled around my spine, whispering in places that shouldn't exist. Only it wasn't some nameless something inside me—it was *Lucian*. I tasted smoke and ash beneath the heat, fear and need, and my body couldn't decide if it was pulling him closer or trying to claw free.

This wasn't tender. This was war declared with lips and teeth and the scrape of his jaw against mine. I bit his lower lip, and he growled deep in his throat, the sound vibrating through my chest. His fingers tightened on my hips, anchoring me, possessive and careful all at once, like he was afraid I'd vanish if he held too tight or not tight enough. I couldn't breathe. Didn't want to breathe. I wanted to drown in this, in him, in the terrifying realization that some part of me had been waiting for way too many years to do exactly *this*.

The outer office door banged open. "Delia?" Claire called out.

I jerked back from Lucian, breathing hard, wheeling around as Claire strode across the outer office. My hands stung, and when I glanced down, blood welled from beneath my fingernails where I'd dug them into my palms. I hadn't felt that happen, but I didn't slow down. I'd almost made it to my desk when she appeared in the doorway—and froze.

"Oh," she managed, her wide eyes moving between us. "Um, the more I thought about it, the more I didn't want to leave you guys alone with all this mess. I told Steve I'd come back to help and...um...I'll be out here if you, ah, need me!"

She reached her hand for the door and pulled it shut.

Lucian and I stared at each other. My hands were shaking, my *bones* were shaking, but he didn't look like he had a hair out of place.

"That didn't mean anything," I said. My lips still burned where his had been—not like a normal kiss, but like I'd pressed them against the mouth of a searing furnace.

His lips twisted. "I know."

"I don't trust you. I'm exhausted and upset and I feel betrayed."

He nodded. "You have every right to feel all those things."

"But I need to work with you now. We're in this now. I want to save Kieran Walsh; I want to understand what happened to Finn Ashford. I want to—I want to understand all of this." I flapped my hand at the books and files. "About why he did what he did. Why you did too."

I expected him to have some smartass response to that. He didn't. Instead, his scent curled around me again, as intimate as a touch. "When you discover that, sweet Delia," he murmured. "Be sure to tell me too."

ELEVEN

The file folder read CHICAGO SIGHTINGS – 1995–2005, and it was easily fifty pages thick—but there was nothing new here. I tossed it down on the stack I'd assigned to demonalia. Mordechai's sharply defined, efficient handwriting had long since faded from being a pleasantly nostalgic memory to more of an indictment of the man who'd kept so much from me.

So far, I'd sketched a demonic infrastructure that was at least five layers deep, from the territory commanders at the level of Asmodaea and Palemerious down to the lieutenants like Mirr and Pithius, to an enforcement level that seemed to be as elusive as dust. The lower tiers of demons were almost not worth talking about, the equivalent of meth heads and ravers in a gang structure that seemed to place a surprisingly high value on control and precision once you got past all the evil possession tricks.

The demons of Chicago were organized, efficient, and thorough. And I hadn't known a damned thing about them after fifteen years of working with Mordechai...except that, for some reason, he'd pulled Palemerious out of one innocent little girl and then watched him jump into me without so much as giving me an ice cream cone to apologize for the inconvenience.

Who did that? And why?

So far, I wasn't finding any answers.

I turned a page and felt a sharp sting as I shifted, then blinked at the blood speckling my nails. I lifted my hand, and more blood caught the corner of my eye.

Scowling, I pulled my shirt away from my neck, trying to see without the benefit of a mirror. Blood welled from four parallel scratches on my collarbone—fresh, deep enough to bleed. I touched the marks, wincing. The spacing matched my nails exactly.

When had I done this? I tried to remember. Couldn't. There was a gap, a blank space where time should be. Five minutes? Ten? I'd been reading and then...nothing. And now I was bleeding. I pulled my collar up to hide the marks.

My back complaining as I straightened, I pushed away from my desk and officially pulled the blinds down against the last rays of sunshine, knowing that my office would be easily visible from the rear parking lot in another few minutes. Everywhere I went outside this building, I felt like I was being watched. I didn't want to feel that way in here.

Turning toward the low hum of conversation in the outer office, I poked my head out to see Claire and Steve hunkered down at their respective desks. Coffee cups and takeout containers were piled on the side table, but we'd eaten hours ago, and my stomach growled at the possibility of another interruption to the endless ordeal of boxes that awaited me.

"Yo, I'm going to head out for more coffee," I said. "You guys want anything?"

"Always," Steve said without looking up. "Mocha for me."

"I'll go with you." Claire stood up and flashed a card at me. "We're already on their frequent flyer system. At this rate, we'll be able to sponsor an espresso machine by the end of the month."

She waited until we hit the stairs before she slanted a glance my way. "So... Have you heard from Lucian?"

"Should I have?"

"Well, yeah. It's been three days. If we're going into the belly of the beast tomorrow to confront a possessed CEO who lives in his building, I think he should maybe be on hand to help guide the process. He knows what's going on in this city, we don't."

I shrugged. "His information is a little out of date. Maybe he's getting caught up as well."

"He wasn't able to keep up to date while he was hanging out inside you? I mean, no disrespect, but how exciting could it be to occupy the brain of a ten-year-old girl being neglected by her mother? Or a flat broke loser of a teenager, or a jittery twenty-something who was coming into her own as an exorcist-in-training?"

I grimaced. I'd been wondering the same thing myself—when I wasn't deliberately trying not to think about Lucian at all, since the kiss that could've been a terrible mistake but somehow wasn't. We stepped into the warm evening and headed for the corner coffee shop, the journey already an automatic routine. "Maybe he was learning how to be human?"

"From *you*?" she snorted. "What did he do with the other twenty-three hours of the day?"

"I mean—dude, I seriously don't understand any of this." I didn't want to tell her about Mordechai's betrayal, not yet. I kept hoping that I'd run across something—anything—that made sense, that didn't paint him as the asshole he clearly seemed to be. "Lucian was a different demon when he was inside me. He was horrible. The stuff of nightmares. A constant soundtrack of crazy dreams and dread punctuated by moments of awesome when Mordechai and I went out on an exorcism task, and then the horror aftermath when I returned home."

"Yeah..." We broke off the conversation as we ordered and collected our drinks, but she picked it up again as soon as we stepped outside. "Maybe he was so mean to you after an exorcism because he didn't want to go back into his Delia box." She snickered a little. "Though he seemed pretty interested in your box the other night."

"Don't even start with me."

"Oh, I'm *so* going to start." She laughed. "You totally kissed him! And he's hot and dangerous and was *inside you* for like your entire teenage years, and you have to tell me everything about that! Was it weird? Was it good? Was it—"

"Remember, the version of him who was inside me was Palemerious, not Lucian," I pointed out. "He's a different person now. Demon. Whatever he is."

"Bullshit," she protested, eyes wide. "Nobody changes that much. I don't care how infernal you are. Some part of him remembers all the hell he put you through, and some part of that demon is lurking in the background, waiting to show his face again. He wasn't always hot, right?"

I winced, remembering the ghoulish images I'd painted so many times on my walls, the epithets and slurs and disgusting proclamations I'd have to whitewash later, horrified by my own sick depravity. I'd thought *I* was having those thoughts, those dreams. That I put those words in my brain, so desperate to leak out onto the walls. I hadn't known until the very end that I'd been carrying around an entirely separate *creature*. "He wasn't, no. He was pretty gross."

"And now?" She juggled her tray of coffee as we re-entered the front door, the scent of vanilla and cloves warring with the aroma of dark mocha. "Do you want more of what you had the other night? Or less? Because there's no wrong answer to that, as long as you're doing the choosing, right? You're allowed to want what you want."

I mulled that idea over as we climbed the stairs, but any thought of continuing the conversation was dashed as we re-entered the office to find Steve pacing around the space.

"Okay. Okay. So hear me out," he announced before we could say anything. He pointed toward his large screen which he'd helpfully turned outward so we both could easily see it. "Okay, check that. First, give me my mocha, and then, hear me out."

He set down his laptop and grabbed a drink before scrolling through screen after screen of online conversations. "My group with Rook, Anya, and Mei is our own thing, right? But we're not the only people who were fans of Warriors of Darkyn. It's like, there's a whole subculture out there with a bunch of fanatics who went absolutely bonkers over Finn Ashford, who's listed as Overflow. That was his handle. The guy was treated as a legend up until he died in 2020, and the community was split between those who thought he'd gone too soon and those who thought he'd never left at all. It didn't help that Darkyn was essentially a dungeon escape game, where the whole concept was to get out as quickly as possible with minimal casualties before the demon hordes descended on you. That's why the architect power was so important. Once you achieved that ability, it was sort of a get out of the dungeon free card. But you could only use it once, and then you had to build up your power again. I told you all that before, but here's where it gets a little hinky."

"I think you already hit the hinky part seven lines back," Claire put in helpfully, but Steve continued as if she hadn't spoken.

"So, I told you I played this game on a bootleg server, and that server was completely locked down. Like, full on, nobody could get in without me knowing it. And yet this last time that I was in there, I started looking at it a lot more closely, and there were differences. Changes in the dungeon layouts, like that. Nothing extreme, but little things here and there that weren't there before. Easter eggs appearing in the code about previous iterations of the game that had gotten long since been changed out."

I frowned. "Isn't that kind of common in video games, though? Like, I would think that easter eggs would be something programmers deliberately put into the code for long-time players."

"Yeah, but these easter eggs have eyes. I didn't notice it, but honestly, I haven't played the game in a minute. Neither had the others on my team. Life gets in the way. But going out to these other forums, there are all these reports of players feeling watched. At first they thought it was cool, that maybe Overflow was in there kind of haunting the game and checking in on his old friends. But what if he's not haunting it? What if he really is actually trapped inside somehow? Like, he can't get out, but he should be able to get out, right? His game code became the basis for a Reflex AI which is entirely designed to get people out of shitty situations. He's in the shittiest of all situations, but he can't get out of there."

"Do you think he's trying to get out?"

Steve waved his hands. "I mean, wouldn't you? Especially if there's a demon now apparently controlling Kieran Walsh? Maybe Finn jumped off that pier because he was on the run from that same demon. Or maybe he tried to shut the whole thing down and got trapped inside instead of killed. Like, right, wouldn't that make sense? Finn was being watched, and he was in the game, and then we went into the game yesterday and maybe probably heard him and *then* we got a message—a straight up message!—that we are being watched! So, could be Walsh isn't the only victim we should be thinking about, right? Maybe we should be trying to rescue Finn as well."

He paused and took a deep drink of his mocha, clearly satisfied with his analysis. "And wouldn't that be fucking cool, yeah? I mean, seriously."

"I guess…" My words broke off as the intercom buzzed. Claire quickly popped around to her computer screen, then blinked. "There's a very large man downstairs who just, um, pushed our button. And for the record, I'm definitely on board with him pushing mine some more."

Steve snorted and I gaped at her. "What?"

In response, she picked up her phone. "Thompson & Associates," she said, in a voice that sounded several octaves lower than her usual chirp. "May I help you?"

She paused, and her eyes rounded as she glanced back at us, giving an enthusiastic thumbs up. "Of course she is. Please come on up to our office, Mr. Barbu—we're on the second floor, 212."

Hanging up, she immediately flounced her hair, then scanned the room. "Steve, stow the food boxes in Delia's office, would you? Delia—brace for an incoming Sergei, special delivery from Nikolai Volkov."

"What are you talking about?" I demanded, my gaze going toward the door as the sound of heavy boots on the stairs arrested my attention.

"Jesus, you're not kidding," Steve muttered as he scooped up the remains of our dinner and carried them into the inner office. "What the hell's with all these boxes?" he called out. "You need help putting this stuff on actual shelves?"

All thoughts of Steve vanished though, as a man's bulky frame filled the doorway. "Ms. Thompson," he said abruptly. "Good. You're here."

"I…am," I agreed. Sergei Barbu, if that was his name, definitely lived up to Claire's description of him. He stood easily six-foot-four and was built like he tossed around ponies for fun. He smelled like blood and steel, but in this case, that could have been his aftershave. Probably in his late twenties with Slavic features and an expensive suit stretched tight over muscles that had muscles, he slanted a glance sharply at Steve as the latter emerged from the inner office and stopped short.

"Whoa," Steve managed, never one without a response. "Who called the Russian mob?"

"Romanian, actually," Sergei said, with a voice that sounded entirely too smooth to be coming out of such a large man. Beside me, I could practically smell Claire going a little woozy.

Sergei glanced toward me. "Mr. Volkov has asked me to check in on you. He has followed rumors circulating about your business here and he is concerned. You have attracted attention within the underworld, and that kind of attention, ah, it is not so good."

I frowned. "And what exactly did he want you to do after checking in on me?"

"To protect you," he said as if it were obvious.

"Oh, well I appreciate it, but—"

"We accept," Claire announced.

I swung my gaze to her, and she met it steadily. "You could have died at the Graham estate, and Walsh and whatever is jacking up his systems has already threatened you. Our office is in a building that is way more empty than not, and we need backup. Plus, I bet Sergei here is pretty good against demons."

To my surprise, Sergei simply held up his hands. "Nobody is good against demons, but you have to fight, eh?"

I grimaced. "Look, we're just getting started here, I hardly need to hire security—"

"There is no charge," Sergei said. "I start immediately and

will work with your technology expert to set up security upgrades." He glanced from Claire to Steve. "Which of you?"

Claire huffed, visibly upset. "Well, that would be Steve."

"Ah," Sergei said, but he didn't look away from her right away. "Then perhaps you can show me the building."

"I..." her eyes rounded again, and I jumped on my opportunity. "Yes. Yes, that's a great idea. Go show him now, Claire—all the doors, all the floors. We're shutting down here shortly anyway."

The moment they left, Steve turned toward me, leaning against his desk as he folded his arms over his chest. "Seriously? We've got the Romanian mob as backup now? What the hell, Delia?"

"You tell me," I said, running my hands through my hair. "What exactly do you know about Nikolai Volkov? I mean, other than you almost died in his club?"

He made a face. "Well, I've been looking into that, and he's the real deal. Word on the street is he's running all sorts of businesses through Chicago, and most of his enforcers are built like Sergei here. But if we start getting known for rubbing elbows with Volkov, I mean, that opens up an entirely different box of problems. There's a lot of dark dealings laid at his door."

"Ordinary-people dark or demon dark?"

"Funny you should ask." Steve scowled. "I need to go back and check my notes, but I started a file on mentions of demons in the area, kind of as an aside. I wasn't really thinking about it because our focus is on Prometheus Solutions and you know, just one guy, but now that you bring Volkov into the mix, and he's definitely in the mix if he's sending his own enforcers over, I need to go back. There was some chatter, if I recall. Maybe a podcaster that got all excited about him and demon sightings? Something like that."

"A podcaster." I stared at him. "About demons in Chicago. Please tell me you're joking."

"I mean…"

As Steve retreated to his desk, Claire's phone rang. Without thinking, I grabbed for it. It had only been a couple of minutes! Was she okay?

I picked it up. "Hello?" I asked, belatedly offering in my best Claire chirp. "You've reached Thompson & Associates. Can I help you?"

"Ah, Ms. Thompson," Nikolai Volkov's voice came across the phone, smooth like butter. "I tried your phone, and when you didn't answer, I grew concerned."

I made a face at Steve across the room. "Well, I appreciate that, Mr. Volkov, but you've already done more than enough. We've met your associate. He's checking the, um, status of the building."

"Good. Sergei is yours for as long as you need him, however you need him." He paused just long enough that I met Steve's eyes again, but Volkov wasn't finished. "As am I."

CHAPTER

TWELVE

LUCIAN

The soft tone drew his attention from the commanding view of the lake, and Lucian shifted his gaze to the forty-inch screen that was currently plugged into the building's security monitors.

"Amplify sound," he murmured as he watched Delia lift the phone to her ear, adjusting her clearly overloaded black messenger bag.

"Right, yes. Tomorrow at three is fine," she said clearly over the speakers. "Ah—not only me this time. I'll have one or two assistants, and yes, they'll be in the room with me. I know I didn't have Claire before—no, I'm afraid that's not possible. It's this way, or it doesn't happen, Victoria."

His lips quirked. Had she always been this self-assured, and he hadn't noticed? As soon as he thought the words, he rejected them. No. While he'd been wound through her system, Delia had been buried under layers of emotional protection and fear, living a life of pure action and reaction, strike and consequence. She hadn't been able to establish herself as anything other than

Mordechai's tool, and he hadn't allowed her to think too far beyond the next demon, the next exorcism, the next opportunity for him to act through her for another taste of the demon he had been for millennia. He might as well have been trapped inside Delia as neatly as if she'd chained him with iron and steel, and he'd always assumed it was by his choice.

Now...he wasn't so sure.

Memories were coming back, reactions. Feelings and sensations he'd buried from that day fifteen years ago—barely a blink in the lifespan of a demon and yet he had *forgotten* what had happened that day. There were blank spaces instead of the moment of his release from the young, sick girl, his possession of the richly intricate mind of Delia. He'd been delighted with his choice, but...

Had it been his choice?

Or had Mordechai simply made him believe that? Simply acted like he wasn't strong enough to remove him when he clearly had just done so from another little girl.

Why *had* Mordechai allowed a demon to remain inside an innocent child for fifteen *years* before finally attempting a new exorcism?

Why?

His gaze flicked to the secondary screens, each on a curated loop of the past seventy-two hours. The first camera, focused on the exterior of the building, showed Volkov's muscle honoring his master's directive to ensure no one got into the place unseen. The second showed Claire and Steve morphing into an unexpectedly effective team, with Steve on research and Claire on everything else required to make the business run.

But the third screen held his attention the most. Split between a wide-angle view of Delia's inner office and a close-up of her desk, it showed him the exact moment she'd found his elegant card with its single word. *Props.* He'd expected her surprise, seeing it there; they hadn't spoken since he'd left her with Claire, the touch of her lips still burning his.

He hadn't expected the slow, languorous drift of her fingers over the inscribed letters, tracing the ink now stained deep into the heavy stationery, her nostrils flaring as she picked up a constellation of scents, emotions, needs. What had she extracted from that card, besides its terse instruction? What had she sampled of his own fractured need, heady with guilt and excitement and—yes—lust.

Always that.

His smile curved, then hardened. She would have been hurt when she'd gathered the tools he'd requested, her still-healing hands damaged anew. She'd followed them anyway. Not for his sake, either, he knew that too. For her own. To get stronger, despite the pain. To stand in the face of evil and destroy it.

Like she might one day destroy him.

He tightened his jaw. *One piece at a time, one move at a time.*

Delia disappeared into the elevator, and he murmured his command for the monitor to go dark. There were things she needed to know, and his ability to manipulate technology was part of that—but no human was comfortable being watched.

The doors opened as he returned to the main room of his apartment, and Delia strode into the space, her fingers still locked on the handle of her messenger bag. "We're set with Prometheus Solutions tomorrow, 3:00 p.m. Victoria wasn't happy with the setup, but she's going to have to get over it," Delia announced all in one breath. She was nervous as she approached him. Uneasy.

Good.

Her gaze snapped to the side of the room, faltered. "What's with the piano?"

He savored the cocktail of her confusion and curiosity.

There had never been any music in Delia's life. He'd made sure of that, without ever questioning why.

There would be now. Not yet. But soon.

"I was bored," he offered.

"Right." He could smell the energy coming off her, sparking and bright, and he forced himself to let her come closer, to travel across the room until she reached the broad marble countertop that separated the kitchen from the rest of the living space. "How'd you get into the office without Sergei seeing you?" she asked as she set her bag on the countertop.

"He blinks."

That earned him a snort, and he watched her, hungrily, as she pressed her palms onto the cool stone surface of the countertop. He could feel their heat cool, the pain ease, and his pulse quickened even as his gut twisted a bit. So much pain he could cause her.

So much pleasure too.

"You clearly were successful in your hunting expedition," he said, chasing those thoughts away.

She grimaced. "You'd be amazed at what you can find at Goodwill. They had a little something for everyone."

She toppled the bag to spill its contents on the counter. A crucifix clattered out, then a rosary, then a tarnished Mezuzah case. A statue of Ganesh the size of Delia's fist rolled halfway across the expanse of marble, then a chipped prayer wheel. More items followed, medals and icons, but he wasn't looking at the religious detritus. He was looking at her hands.

"You didn't wear gloves," he murmured, reaching out.

She pulled her hand away before he could touch her, suddenly smelling of charred pomegranates and open sky, Persephone in flight. "I've managed without them up until now, and I'm going to continue that way. Mordechai always wanted me to avoid touching anything, and I never understood why—

now I do. It's because of you. It's still because of you, and you're not even inside me anymore."

The admission cost her, and she slid her still-red and scraped hand through her hair. "You have water or something?"

"Of course," he said, and he moved away from her, feeling her tension ease and then wind up again as he returned. She'd arranged the icons in a neat row, apparently ignoring how her skin flared red every time she got her fingers near the pieces.

It wasn't her only injury, he suddenly realized. Her entire body practically hummed with pain.

Because of him?

He twisted his lips. *Who else?*

He set the water down beside her, and she wrapped her right hand around the glass, gesturing him to sit at the counter as well, two stools away from her.

"I've gone through Mordechai's books, but it's too much, Lucian," she said. "I need a crash course on the demons we're dealing with here, especially Mirr. I'm missing something, and I don't know what.

"First, drink." A strange thrill skated through him as she picked up the glass, and he could almost feel the cool water flow down his own throat. Her gaze shot to his, but she took a long drink, setting the glass down with a thunk.

"What'd you put in that? It's not just water."

"Painkillers," he said succinctly. "You'll need them."

As she blinked, he pulled his phone out of his jacket and punched out a command. "I'm sending you a report you can study at your leisure, everything I've been able to find thus far without betraying my presence."

She scowled as her phone beeped in her pocket but didn't move for it. "That's what you've spent the last three days doing?"

His lips twisted. "Partly, yes." She didn't need to know about the watching. The needing.

"Give me the headlines."

He nodded. "Asmodaea's infrastructure has expanded quite a bit since the last time I looked closely at it. She was making moves behind my back, building her empire, drawing in lesser players from other Courts to set up miniature pockets of power, beachheads in the sand. It was an impressive assemblage, all without Belial noticing—or me. Though, to be fair, I'd long since stopped focusing on the subtleties of her power plays. I wanted out."

"That was fifteen years ago." Delia watched him, her cool gaze an unexpected balm to his abraded nerves.

"Actually, a bit longer than that. It took Mordechai a year to be summoned to that little house where you found him that morning, found me. I'd planned on leaving with the family within the next six months, but the child fell ill—through no fault of mine, I assure you."

"Right." She tightened her lips. "Then you crawled into me, and while all that was going on, the city developed a demon problem."

"Chicago has always had a demon problem. It's merely grown more pronounced in the last few decades. Standard operating procedure when a shift is happening in the courts, and what I would have done as well had I remained in the city functioning as Belial's chief commander."

"Why though? Why the interest in Chicago?"

"For all the usual reasons: concentration of the population, easy access to imports and exports, a great deal of money, power, and influence flowing through the city. And this city is tucked away enough, here in the middle of the country that it's not going to draw the attention of the other high-placed members of the horde. Belial is one of seven princes of darkness, and a minor one by all accounts. He has long held power here—I made sure of it, until I didn't."

"About that." She held up a heat-seared finger. "Were you ever going to get around to telling me you were a seventh-level commander of darkness? Did I really need to learn about that from Volkov and Mordechai's journals?"

Yes. He didn't say the word out loud, merely shrugged. But she had needed to. Because he had needed to see her face when she'd read those words, inscribed by another's hands. To see the heat claw up her cheeks, her eyes flaring with equal parts interest and dismay. He had watched the world for so long from her eyes...now he could watch her.

He continued on without answering her. "Asmodaea serves Samael, Mirr serves Asmodaea, and at this point, neither of them worries too much about competition—especially with me out of the frame. For demons, the primary focus is—and must always remain—the top of the food chain. They serve Samael, both separately and together."

"Got it." She frowned at him. "So what you're saying is, Mirr could act in opposition to As—" she broke off as he lifted a finger and rolled her eyes. But when she began again, she was more discreet. "Okay, so what you're saying is Baby Demon could freelance on his own if he if he thought his actions would serve the Big Bad Demon better. Even if Evil Mama wanted Baby Demon to do something different."

"Correct. Which begs the following question: is the work at Prometheus Solutions directed by Asmodaea, or is Mirr going out on his own, after all this time influencing Walsh? My strong suspicion is that Asmodaea is behind it, given the level of potential glory in claiming the infrastructure of the city. Either way, she's using him as her proxy, which makes sense given his focus on reflection and distortion. He's a natural for work in the surveillance industry and would be predisposed to ferreting out secrets in the city's corporate, political, and criminal sectors. Nevertheless, he has weaknesses we can exploit."

She gestured to the artifacts. "Hence all the bright shiny," she said, and he nodded.

"But we're not just looking at Mirr with this, we're fighting an entire network of demons. They could be in other companies, they could be in other sectors—entertainment, finance, all of it. And the sam way that we are looking for weaknesses, they are as well."

He nodded to the mess on the table. "You need to handle these without destroying your hands."

"I'm fine."

"Mmm." He picked up a crucifix, turned it around in his hand. His skin remained smooth, unblemished. Pain sizzled through him, but his palm didn't react to it.

Delia set her jaw then reached for the item nearest to her, a rosary. She hissed and dropped it just as quickly. "Catholic shit is always the worst," she muttered.

"You're going to carry these items into Walsh's penthouse tomorrow. If your hands are blistered, Mirr will know you're vulnerable. Let me help."

"Fine," she grumbled, and he didn't know whether to wince or smile. So fierce. So determined. And yet he was the one who had damaged her this way. He was the reason that even the very tools of her profession still caused her pain.

Standing abruptly, he moved behind her, not missing how she tensed at his closeness. Slowly, almost cautiously, as if she were a wild animal about to startle, he laid a hand on her forearm. He fought the urge to close his eyes, to linger there. Instead, he moved his hand down her arm until it reached her poor, damaged fingers. He spread his own fingers wide, interlacing them with hers, and turned her hand over, exposing her palm.

Then he traced a sigil into that palm, an ancient symbol that flared white against her reddened skin, then disappeared.

"What was that?" she asked, but the demand had no sharpness to it. Already her fingers were lightening in color, the redness disappearing. He traced a second symbol on her bared wrist, wondering if she noticed how much his hands were shaking. Probably not, as her eyes had drifted shut and her breath now came fitfully between her lips. She smelled of caution and courage and something else, something needful and strong that made him fight the moan building in the back of his throat. He repeated the process on her other hand and wrist. By the time he was done, she was listing toward him, heat rising up from her like liquid sin.

"Now," he said. "Pick up the statue of Ganesh."

"Ganesh?" She frowned. "I already know that one doesn't hurt as much."

"I know. That's why we're starting there."

She reached out and, despite her assurances of not being concerned, hesitated slightly, her fingers trembling. Then her hand closed around the small figurine and she hefted it, her lips parting in surprise.

"Okay!" She glanced up at him. "That's not really anything."

"Good." He nodded. "Now the rosary."

As if she was afraid she was going to lose her nerve, Delia rolled Ganesh to the side, then grabbed the rosary in one smooth motion. She stiffened. "It still hurts," she admitted. "But you can't tell. My hand isn't turning red."

He nodded. "The pain won't go away until—later. When your hands heal completely. But you can feel it less, hide its effects. And that's the game to keeping other demons from taking advantage."

"I'll take it," she said, and then her lips quirked as she rotated her shoulder. "Where were you when I was getting ducks hurled at me in that lake house? Those things hurt too."

"I know," he said, his gaze drifting along her arm, her shoulder, the skin he couldn't see but could remember, inch by hallowed inch. "Every scar on you is because of me, Delia. Don't think I'm not aware of it."

"Well, you weren't to blame for all of them," she began. Then she stopped herself and shrugged. "Okay, maybe you were."

He couldn't help himself. He laughed, the sound foreign to his ears, jarring, for all that she didn't seem to notice.

He watched her then with a sudden, slippery need he could neither quench nor bank entirely. She seemed completely at ease around him, though she shouldn't be. In truth, she should be more cautious than ever, as the familiarity of him eased into comfort, even solidarity. Demons didn't only destroy those who weren't strong enough to withstand their darkness. They could equally devastate with the softest, most familiar touch.

At that moment, she glanced up at him, and their eyes met. Something of what he was thinking must have translated to her, because she straightened and stood back.

"What did you see?" he asked, as casually as he could. He expected her to lie.

She didn't. She swallowed. "Two of you," she said, her voice rough. Both of you occupying the same space, yet—separate. One like I see you now, the other, like before."

"Before."

She shrugged. "Shadows and smeared blood. Talons. Then it snapped back and—you were just you. The way you want me to see you."

He turned so she couldn't see the snarl on his face, but she wasn't finished.

"Why does it even hurt at all since you're no longer inside me?" she asked quietly.

He exhaled, low and steady. "I don't know. Perhaps because of your work with Mordechai, perhaps because you still wish to be punished."

She snorted. "Guess again."

He fought the need to reach for her, to claw her essence to him, defiling and scattering her light. "Well. When it doesn't hurt at all, you'll know you're officially over me. But be careful, you may find that you like being a monster."

Her phone buzzed, and she reached for her bag a little too quickly, apparently eager for the distraction.

"It's Steve," she said. "I had him run a search on some of the online gaming communities based in Chicago. He says now that he knows what to look for, it's getting weirder and weirder. NPCs in the game seem to know personal details that are not part of the gamer's online personas. They whip this information out to throw the gamers off their...well, game, especially during battle. Some of the gamers are creeped out, some of them think it's cool, but they're all intrigued by it, and none of them are leaving because of it. People are weird."

"People have a need to be seen. Demons understand that perhaps better than most."

"Well, that wins for the creepiest comment of the day," she said dryly. "So, is that how this is working? Mirr has figured out how to get the AI to read these gamers minds?"

"No. This isn't mind reading. This is pattern recognition combined with a demonic presence. The predictability of humans has been an asset to those who would harm them since the dawn of time. Now they simply have more tools."

"If they're that powerful though why does Mirr even need Walsh's body? Why bother possessing him if you can program this into the AI?"

"Because demons are vain, Delia. Asmodaea wants a visible empire, not merely code. She also wants credit, she or Mirr, if he's doing this on his own. Although I don't remember him having anywhere near the skill set for that. He's dangerous, even cunning, but he never impressed me as being that smart."

That made her glance up. "You knew him well?"

He shrugged. "Passably. When you evict him, you'll understand. He doesn't really have the sophistication for this. However, it's also possible that he simply punched up. Prometheus Solutions already had the code in place to control the city's infrastructure—all Mirr had to do was control Walsh."

"Victoria said the next demonstration was in three days. They go live in another week. That doesn't give us a lot of time."

"We're already behind schedule," he corrected her. "Mirr knows what you're here for, and he thinks you're no threat. The moment you go back into his office prepared to do battle, he'll think differently."

"Right." She stood, and still with a vague air of surprise, slid the holy objects back into her bag. "So, we finish this tomorrow. I've already seen Mirr once. I know his name. The rest—I mean, the rest I can do, and I will do, but..."

She blew out a breath and turned toward him, and he blinked. She looked—older, somehow, more certain, more *defined* than he remembered from fifteen years of glances in the mirrors, reflections in windows. She looked human. Frail and fierce and real.

"I want you there, Lucian."

He went still, his heart lurched hard in his chest, need clawing up his throat. "What?"

She tightened her hold on the bag. "Not if it's going to mess you up, not if Mirr will recognize you," she amended quickly. "But if it won't and he won't...I want you there. I've read so much over these past few days that my head is spinning over how lucky I was in that wellness center—even at the Graham's."

"Not luck," he said automatically, but she rejected that with a hard shake of her head.

"Enough luck. My exorcism with Belphegor could've gone sideways in a hurry, and Claire's not trained. Frankly, I don't want her to be trained. Not like this. Not if there's so much more to this demon problem in Chicago than I realized. I had fifteen years to get ready, and I'm still lost. But—"

"I'll be there," he said, and his chest felt wrong again as he saw her shoulders come down. Her mouth softened, then firmed into a tight smile.

"Good," she said, nodding. "Good. Um—thanks. I gotta go." And she turned on her heel and practically fled the room.

He didn't move for several minutes after the elevator doors had slid shut.

CHAPTER

THIRTEEN

"Explain to me how this is going to work if Kieran knows you're going to smack his demon right out of him?" Claire asked as we entered the Prometheus Solutions elevator. "Like, why in the world would he ever agree to get anywhere near us?"

"He doesn't know." I shrugged. "He thinks we're joining him for a group meditation session. You are a certified Reiki practitioner—"

"Wait, I am?"

"And Lucian here is a yogi." I side-eyed him as Claire gaped at me. "You do know yoga, don't you?"

"Please," he scoffed. "I first began my practice with the Indus Valley Civilization in northern India, in accordance with the Rigveda. I assure you, if Mr. Walsh is interested in sharing his practice with us, I will be more than happy to see the god within him. In a manner of speaking."

"But how am I supposed to know Reiki?" Claire demanded.

"I know you've already tried Reiki in our building," I said. "There's like six different practitioners who've left their flyers."

"Well, I mean, yeah, but, like, all I know is that they lay their hands on me and I try not to fall asleep. That isn't a lot to go on."

"Actually, that reminds me." I pointed at her. "According to Victoria, Kieran has an entire arsenal of meds that he likes to use when he meditates. So, nobody drink anything, nobody eat anything, and be prepared for him to shoot up while we're there."

"Shoot up with what?" Claire protested with a squeak. "Are you seriously kidding me right now?"

Any response I might have wanted to give was cut off as the elevator doors slid open, revealing an obviously stressed Victoria Ashford. She breathed out a sigh of relief as she took us all in. We looked about as far from threatening as possible, as I'd instructed both Claire and Lucian to dress in high-end athleisure, while I wore a long swishy pantsuit in some fabric I couldn't spell.

Apparently, we passed muster. "Excellent, you look excellent. Thank you so much. Kieran spoke before the board this morning, and he was adamant that we accept a new timetable for the rollout of Reflex. The board agreed over my objections, which means if the stress test demonstration scheduled for Thursday is successful, rollout will begin as planned next week."

"Seriously?" I squinted at her. "Doesn't Chicago have protocols that you need to follow before making that kind of a decision?"

"You forget, the decision was made six years ago when Reflex was first implemented within the transit system infrastructure. There have been some small pilot programs that have run in the background—with plenty of fail-safes—and they have performed like a champ at every turn. What we're looking at here is merely a leveling up of existing technology.

Most users and systems technicians won't even notice that something's changed. It's an emergency response mechanism and hopefully will never get activated except for in drills. I'm afraid the barrier for acceptance and implementation is pretty low. Ordinarily, I would be elated with this turn of events, but there's nothing normal about Kieran's behavior right now. He holds it together when giving his impassioned speeches before the board or cool commentary to the media, but behind closed doors...well, you'll see. He's devolved significantly since you saw him last week."

This time she took us beyond Kieran's corner office, another five minutes down twisting corridors until we reached a door marked 'Studio.' "He's already in his pre-meditative process, and he's requested that you join him. He has instructed me further to not interfere. Given that I've hired you as his wellness consultants, I'm forced to honor his wishes, but—"

"No, this is good, this is good," I said, clutching my bag, which now seemed too heavy.

"Can I ask what a pre-meditative process is?" Claire asked, and Victoria smiled.

"Kieran is a huge advocate for biohacking. If there is a tincture, elixir, supplement, or powder that might be snake oil or might be the key to eternal life, he's interested, and he typically injects himself prior to meditation. He was this way before Finn died, and it's only gotten more pronounced since."

She glanced at me. "You've warned them?"

"No sharing needles," I agreed.

She gave me a final grim nod, then stepped toward the door. "I have security nearby, but not alerted. I didn't want to do anything that might be recognized as out of the ordinary." Then she opened the door and gave us all a big smile.

"Thank you so much," she said brightly. "I'll be back in an hour to escort you out at the close of your session."

Without another word, we entered the studio. I was expecting more floor-to-ceiling windows, but instead, the studio's four walls were illuminated with a moving image that depicted a flowing hillside overcome with mist. In the center of the room, toward the back, Kieran Walsh sat on a flat cushion, his hands resting on his crossed knees, his eyes closed. Beside him, a jet-black case lay open, and two neat rows of glass vials glinted in the shifting light. Whatever party Kieran was planning for himself was already well underway.

As we approached, the scene projected onto the walls shifted, becoming shards of glass that flashed and glinted in bright light, capturing fragmented images of us as we approached. If I hadn't seen the other view, I would have assumed we were in a hall of mirrors, but the precision with which it captured our reflections was unnervingly uncanny.

I felt a chill snake over me. Mirr was doing this, I was sure. He'd somehow infiltrated the projection system and was playing games. Or no, I pushed that thought away. Mirr was in Walsh. No demon could be in two places at once. If we got rid of the entity possessing Walsh, the computer systems at Prometheus Solutions would return to normal. Any troublesome code could simply be deleted or shut off.

Unbidden, I thought of the demonic hierarchy Walsh had shown me in his office, and what I'd heard from Volkov and read in Mordechai's journals. So many demons—and, if Lucian was to be believed, all of them converging on Chicago.

"Please join me," Kieran said in a loose, dreamy voice. "I wish to talk with you while I explore the vistas of my mind."

Obligingly, we moved forward. Lucian sat on the floor opposite Kieran. I drifted up closer to him, and Claire edged toward the open case. I could see her mouth purse with concern as she catalogued the contents of his party box, and she made a face at me that clearly indicated Kieran was probably in the early stages of a trip.

This would be the place to do it too. Around us, the walls flickered again, and instead of just the four of us, it suddenly appeared as if there were six—twelve—twenty yoga practitioners, all filling the space before Kieran in the images on the walls...but not in reality. The result was an unhinged dichotomy that gave a whole new meaning to the phrase uncanny valley.

Worse, the temperature had already dropped about ten degrees since we'd arrived, and my gaze sharpened on Walsh's face. As I stared, it became smooth, and when he opened his eyes, they shone like mirrors.

Here we go.

I spread my arms wide as Kieran turned to me, but kept my tone conversational. "We're not alone here anymore, are we, Kieran?"

"The ghost is here." He smiled, the expression turning a little manic. "The ghost who haunts my dreams and sings in my blood, who whispers to me of all that will be, across the city, across the world. It is all so close, as close to me as you are right now."

He turned as if seeing Claire for the first time. "Who are you?" he demanded. "What would you teach me?"

Caught off guard, Claire immediately dropped to a seated position beside him. "Good afternoon, Mr. Walsh. I can begin your treatment now."

"Yes..." Walsh's throat worked as he tossed his head back, and to my surprise, he uncrossed his legs and lay back, his body now arched over his flat pillow. I glanced back toward Lucian, but his gaze was pinned to Walsh, his body still in his lotus position but managing to look coiled to strike.

I approached Walsh on the other side of his body from Claire, who was gamely holding her hands over Walsh in her best "Reiki-light" mode, as she murmured words beneath her breath. I waited until I got all the way up to him, then dropped easily into a squat.

"So tell me, Mirr, why do you bother this son of the Creator?" I pulled my hand out of my pocket and pressed the rosary I'd palmed into Kieran's forehead.

Kieran erupted into a snarl, his eyes flashing open and meeting mine directly. "Get out," I ordered Mirr. Instead, Walsh merely grinned with maniacal energy.

"We are one," he cried gleefully as across the room, the cover of my messenger bag flipped open and the half dozen religious articles I'd brought soared into the air. They whipped around the room in a frenzy, knocking into walls, into Claire, neatly clipping her on the chin before she lurched away. They rushed toward me, veering away at the last second, and I began the Psalm of Psalms, the words coming up in Hebrew to spill out into the room.

"*No,*" Kieran shouted, except it wasn't Kieran's voice anymore. Instead, it was high-pitched, outraged, and more than a little insane. The walls shifted again, and in the glittering mirror-like surface, there was an endless parade of Kieran Walshes laughing, crying, shouting, sleeping. All the various forms captured and recorded God only knew when.

"I don't need him anymore," Mirr sneered from Kieran's mouth. "The shift has already begun."

Kieran abruptly rolled to the side, grabbed something out of the biohack box, and lurched for Claire.

Lucian didn't hesitate. He managed to go from full Lotus to springing across the room, shouldering into Kieran as Claire fell away, the contents of the box spilling out. With Lucian pinning him, I dropped to one knee, forcing his face around so that I could see deep into his eyes. And I saw him there, Mirr, gaping out at me with a chittering laugh. "Begone, Mirr," I ordered. "You have no more power here."

"Delia!" Claire shouted, and I turned in time to see all the syringes that had scattered across the room leap up and point toward me. In the space of a breath, they struck.

But Claire was faster. She burst by me, and I caught the gleam of silver as she jabbed a different syringe into Kieran's chest and depressed the plunger.

Kieran jerked, and all the syringes dropped to the ground. His body contorted, joints bending the wrong way, as his mouth foamed with bile and blood. I grabbed the Hamza Hand from around my neck, ripped the chain free, and placed it on his forehead. Heat seared through my palm as metal met flesh. "Begone!" I roared again.

The projections stopped and the walls went back to dead white, illuminated only by the overhead lights. The site of Claire's injection puckered and split, and a substance that looked like liquid silver geysered out of Walsh. An unholy shriek filled the room, reverberating against the walls, and the plume of silver shot up...up...until it splashed against the ceiling projector, and was sucked inside.

"He got away!" Claire squeaked, but Lucian was on the move, grabbing the empty box and hurling it up. It smashed into the projector, nearly knocking it completely off the ceiling.

Beside us, Walsh collapsed into a boneless slump.

"What did you stick him with?" I demanded, and she flushed.

"Ketamine," she said with a wince. "It was the only label out of that box of horrors that I recognized, and the syringe was small enough that I had to take the risk. But if push comes to shove, maybe you could have been the one to stick him out of self-defense, okay? Since I sort of just blew up my own license by doing that?"

"Deal," I said, only now becoming aware of the ratatat of knocking at the door.

"Mr. Walsh?" A thick male voice came through the door. "Are you okay, sir? Is everyone okay?"

I headed across the room, but I hadn't gotten more than a few steps when the walls shifted. The projector still sagged from its mount in the ceiling, and there was no discernible source for the images we saw. Yet the walls were once again turned into mirrors—only now the mirrors were cracked, spider web breaks stretching across them, and the three of us along with Walsh's supine form were refracted back at crazy angles. The door clicked open and the security guards rushed in, but they stopped abruptly at the scene before them. Lucian, in his Lotus pose, Claire kneeling beside Walsh, one hand over his forehead where I'd burned the shit out of him with the Hamsa Hand. And then there was me, standing in a sea of shattered syringes.

Victoria Ashford slid past the security guards. Taking in the scene with a satisfied nod. "Not the worst we've seen, eh, George?" she said with a smile. "He'll sleep now, at least."

"Very well, ma'am," the security guard said. The two of them shifted abruptly to the side as Jillian Reeves rushed into the room.

"Mr. Walsh!" she gasped, but there was none of the breathy sensuality in her voice that had been there the last time I'd heard her murmur his name. Now she was dressed in a crisp suit, handing off her tablet to Victoria before she strode across the detritus of the room, paying no attention to the smashed syringes and scattered artifacts. She dropped to her knees, checked Walsh's vitals, and turned halfway around to the security guard.

"George, I'm so glad you're here," she said brightly. "It appears that Mr. Walsh is going to need assistance back to his on-site quarters. Probably a gurney would be best. If he wakes up, so much the better, but I'd like to make sure that he remains comfortable. Can you assist?"

"Of course, ma'am. He really hasn't gotten much sleep recently."

"That he has not," Jillian said. She stood and surveyed the mess around her. "Please also contact his personal physician to see what he might need to have restocked. I assume no one was injured? Mr. Walsh has been under extreme stress of late and he has been experimenting with various types of therapy, some of which include throwing things."

She gave me a smile that could etch steel. "Typically, of course, he doesn't have guests with him for those sessions. Please note, this is all included under your NDA."

She glanced at Claire and me briefly, then turned to include Lucian in her circle of authority—and jolted. Her lips parted, her posture loosened, and her voice dropped to an intimate register. "I don't believe we've met, Mr....?"

Claire's gaze jumped to mine, her irritation undoubtedly reflected in my own face. But before we could collectively respond, Victoria's phone and Jillian's tablet both issued a staccato alarm.

Victoria juggled the devices until she could scan her own. "Jillian," she snapped. "What's this about a stress test at Chicago General? That wasn't on the docket, not even in our updated timeline. What's this about?"

"It absolutely was not on the docket," she agreed. And with the last, lingering look at Lucian, she shrugged back into her fully professional demeanor and took the tablet from Victoria. "The good news is it seems to have gone very well. Apparently, there was a crash of a major life support system at Chicago General, and Reflex is installed onsite there as a backup system. But it hasn't been engaged since—"

"Since 2022," Victoria snapped. "And why is it being covered by the media? Everyone, we need to get back to Kieran's office—even Ms. Thompson and her associates. I need full coverage of what's going on. I've got a feeling it's definitely going to impact Kieran's sense of well-being. Let's go."

Her phone blaring with an incoming call, she turned on her heel and left the room.

FOURTEEN

Walsh's office looked much like it had the first time I'd visited, except the window shades were up and the only monitors in view were the ones on the same wall as the door. By the time we entered, a half-dozen other men and women in suits were convened, all of them scanning the local feeds that were playing on the screens. A few minutes after we arrived, Walsh was wheeled in, looking like a fairy tale prince tucked into his rolling bed as he was swept into a side room with a door that remained open.

"It's not just Chicago General," a young man said, his eyes rapidly moving from the monitors to his tablet. "In fact, no one seems to care about the hospital, which is insane because that's the far more complicated failsafe."

"Yeah, but O'Hare means air traffic control and that means the eyes of the world," another woman put in. "We've also got emergency services dispatch systems going on the blink, and a network of overhead lights in downtown Chicago cutting out simultaneously. Only nobody knows about those either. The only publicly visible issue was O'Hare, and that's because the alarms went off, backup generators came on and failed, and only then did Reflex step in. Still, we're talking a matter of seconds, not minutes."

"So how is it that—I mean, Jesus, will you look at this?" An older man squinted at the screens filled with social media listings, his face etched with disbelief. "Check your Reflexes? A new infrastructure system proves its worth in unplanned stress tests?" He made a face, then turned to Victoria. "Did you see any of this copy before it went out?"

She shook her head, her own gaze glued to her phone. "Apparently, the system was wired to provide a full report to local news media so that they could be informed in the event of a real catastrophe. It was a switch we'd flipped on in testing that hadn't been flipped off because the system wasn't officially live. And now we've got Kieran out for the count, the mayor on the phone, and I would like someone to take that call. Gaurav?"

"On it." A well-dressed Indian man in his mid-thirties strode over to Kieran's desk, straightening his tie. "Good thing I had a funeral to attend this morning, or this might have been embarrassing."

He slid into Kieran's seat, his dark eyes alert, his smile calm and professional. He hit the button and the video conferencing unit flared to life. "Good morning, Mr. Mayor," he said. "My name is Gaurav Das, and I've been authorized to answer any questions you have. How can we help?"

As that conversation went on, the woman who'd first spoken started muttering to herself. "It's too quick—there's too much." She glanced up at me, and, not recognizing me swept her gaze more broadly. "Can someone explain to me why we have yoga instructors in here?"

"Because they were with Kieran when the system blew," Jillian said crisply as she walked through the door. She didn't stop, but headed straight back to the antechamber where Kieran now rested.

"Didn't exactly blow, though, did it?" another man put in, this one seated at Kieran's conference table. "But Sarah's right. Unless we're dealing with the Rapture here, this shouldn't have gone down this fast. We had no less than five moderate-to-critical system failures that occurred in the blink of an eye, and then righted themselves within sixty seconds. Reflex stepped in and did its job, but there's no way that this should have been a job it had to do."

"Terrorist attack?" someone asked. "Brown-out? Hack?"

"Hack, most likely," the woman named Sarah said. "And a damned well-planned one. We've kept the lid on Reflex's roll-outs across the city. No one would guess how thoroughly we've blanketed the systems."

"They're going to guess now," the man at the desk said. "We issued a fucking press release."

"Not only to the press, either." All eyes switched to Gaurav as he stood at Kieran's desk. With his funeral-ready suit, golden-brown skin, and flashing eyes, he made as compelling a talking head for the company as Kieran did, with the added bonus that he was conscious. "According to the mayor, every governmental office down to dogcatcher was informed about the breakdown, Reflex's response, and process. The city planner and the chief of police received simultaneous alerts to their phones, computers, personal lines, and their *admin's* personal lines. And get this—out of all the systems that failed, want to guess which one he was alerted to?"

"O'Hare," Victoria said, turning to him. "The only one that extended for longer than a few seconds."

"O'Hare," he agreed.

"But what does that mean?" Sarah blustered. "Reflex wasn't

built to create problems and then solve them. It sure as hell shouldn't have known how to choose which one merited public service announcements. And can we please shut down *that* piece of code while we're at it?"

The room exploded into rapid-fire conversation, and I scanned it, not surprised to see Jillian emerging from Kieran Walsh's room. What did surprise me was the way her gaze swept the room, taking in the excited conversation, the stress, with something approaching real pleasure in her expression. She turned my way and caught me watching, but she didn't flinch. If anything, her interest seemed to intensify. She strolled over to me, sliding a glance toward Lucian that was positively predatory before refocusing on my face.

"You're hiding in plain sight, aren't you?" she said with a low, throaty laugh, her voice pitched to a level that seemed like it should be too quiet to hear in all the chaos, yet was strangely crystal clear. "I should have noticed you first, but your friend's darkness was so much closer to the surface. Yours is more interesting, though. Who are you?"

I curled my lip as Lucian chuckled. She—or the demon who so clearly was squatting inside her—didn't recognize Lucian. That was good.

What was bad, though, was the demon I only now saw whispering in her eyes. She was as possessed as Kieran had been, I now understood with sudden, crackling clarity. Low-ranking, sure. Maybe third level? More mischief than maniac... but still there. *Alaria.* "Ms. Reeves, I didn't realize the situation when you and I met before, but I can help you. I know what you're suffering, and I can stop it."

"Why would I ever want you to do that?" she asked, a smile tugging at her lips as she turned to me. "I've spent a good twenty years being invisible, the straight-A student, the efficient assistant, the quiet middle manager, background noise. Then when Mr. Walsh came to the company, something changed. I felt something, *saw* something. Now, when I walk into rooms filled with powerful men and women and their secret monsters, I see them. And what's even better, they see me."

"Monsters," I said, my mind scrambling. This was not a person in distress. Like Kieran, this was a person reveling in the creature lurking inside her.

"All *sorts* of monsters," she said, her voice going a little sultry. "Darkness in all its varied forms. You have it too. It used to be stronger, richer; it threaded through every inch of you, but no longer. That's a pity, isn't it?" My skin prickled, phantom sensations crawling where nothing should be able to reach anymore, but Jillian kept going.

"And yet there is so much there that still remains. If you ever want to explore what that kind of power can get for you, to let it flower into full form...well," she smiled. "I can show you a *very* good time. In the meantime, be sure to give your associate my number, okay?"

She fluttered her lashes at Lucian, but she still spoke to me. "He wears his darkness much closer to the surface. Just the way I like it."

She turned away before I could respond to that, and the chaos of the room returned.

Through all of the cross conversations and the reports coming in, it was clear that a major crisis had beset the city, only to be resolved within sixty seconds, and the barest minimum of the damage had been broadcast for everyone to see. Prometheus Solutions and Reflex were the star of the hour. With a twenty-four-hour news cycle, they likely wouldn't remain that way, but for the people who mattered, the people who made decisions—such as the decision in less than seventy-two hours regarding Reflex's impending rollout—the system had absolutely stuck the landing.

Not thirty seconds after, Mirr had fled Kieran Walsh's body for more hospitable accommodation.

What had I done?

"Ms. Thompson? I can escort you and your team out. Mr. Walsh is now sleeping comfortably."

Victoria spoke a little too loudly, and I quickly got the memo that this was a conversation she *absolutely* wanted to be over-heard. Everyone around us side-eyed our group, some shuffling a little closer for good measure.

"Active therapy isn't normally that active," I admitted with a collegial smile. "When he began using his box of supplements for fastball practice, I didn't react quickly enough."

"On the contrary, you're not at all to blame," Victoria said brightly. "And we were very lucky. It appears Kieran was exposed to one of his higher-dose sedatives, biohacked to his unique chemical makeup. Nothing to be concerned with, thank heavens. We expect him to revive without further intervention within the hour. I'm sure he'll be grateful you were there to help facilitate the experience."

"Of course."

She shuttled us into the elevator with a promise of a follow-up call, but her gaze shifted up to the camera trained on us from the front desk. Were there cameras in the elevators too? And microphones? Either way, it proved to be a very quiet ride down to the eighteenth floor.

"Recap in my apartment?" Lucian murmured, and I nodded.

The moment we got in the residential elevator, though, I let out a long breath.

You're hiding in plain sight, aren't you?

"What's wrong?" Lucian's voice was quiet beside me, and even Claire turned.

"I didn't see it." I didn't look at him. "Jillian. I should have known she was possessed the moment I met her, but I didn't. Not until she told me herself. And she recognized you were a demon, straight off."

He lifted a hand. "Not a demon, I think; merely possessed."

"Well, that's bad enough," I snapped. "And I didn't clock her at all."

"Delia, you've had a lot going on," Claire began, but I shook my head.

"No—you're wrong," I told her. "It's literally the only thing I've ever been good at. Identifying demons. I've been doing it since I was ten. Mordechai kept me around because I could do that." My voice cracked slightly. "And I just...missed her. Completely. Maybe I really am losing it."

"Delia." Lucian's hand lifted, then dropped, as if he'd thought better of touching me. "Willing hosts are different. They mask themselves as part of the compact between demon and human. Alaria wanted to hide, so she hid. From *both* of us."

I looked up sharply at the name. "You didn't see it either?"

"Not until you did, no." Something flickered in his expression as the elevators snicked open—relief? Gratification? "Which means we're still connected. You can take comfort in that."

I snorted as we stepped out of the elevators, then blinked as Claire gave a little gasp.

"This is where you *live*?" she demanded, turning in a tight circle. "Like really and for real, you *bought* this place?"

Lucian and I watched her as she practically floated across the room, her eyes on the lakeside view. But he didn't let her get too far. "I did purchase this, Ms. Bickwell, and I have found it to be extremely comfortable. But perhaps not as comfortable as you were wielding that syringe. Or pocketing the additional supplements that you purloined from Mr. Walsh's kit. I trust you found something interesting?"

"What?" I asked, turning to Claire, who'd jolted to a stop. "I didn't know you were a thief."

"I'm not a thief!" she said, twin stripes of color darkening her cheekbones. "I'm a *doctor* of *pharmacy*, and giving shots is part of the job. I didn't expect to jab him quite so hard, and I definitely didn't expect him to turn into a fountain of demon spew as a result of it, but that part of the afternoon wasn't even the craziest."

She dug in her pocket and pulled out several vials. "I've never even heard of these names, and let me assure you, I've heard of just about every medical concoction that's on the market. What's more, these are brand-name vials from pharmaceutical companies that cross every T and dot every I. So the fact that Kieran Walsh has go juice from these people frankly scares the shit out of me. Because they wouldn't be private labeling something solely for one person's benefit."

I stared at her. "What are you saying? That Kieran Walsh's secret stash of biohacking medicine is being used by the rich and connected across the country? Because that wouldn't surprise me."

"It wouldn't surprise me either, in a *movie*," Claire said, exasperated. "Do you know how long it takes to get FDA approval on medications and supplements like these? I'll tell you. A long time. Too long, frankly. But creating a fancy label that somebody could put on a drug that makes it *look* legitimate but isn't, well...that's a hell of a lot easier. Believe me when I say to you, people see what they want to see and accept what they want to accept. If you tell them that a particular elixir is going to make them smarter or stronger or live a better life, they're all in. Most of the time, of course, those claims are fraudulent. The other end of the spectrum, however, is worse. If these companies are actually creating drugs that have been approved for distribution even to a very tiny percentage of the population, and they've been used by a man who's been possessed by a demon..."

She broke off, waving her hands at us. "What am I even saying? How is this even happening?"

"Dr. Bickwell...does have a point," Lucian said quietly. "A point completely separate from this case, yet one that we would do well to track."

"So now you're going to tell me that demons are pharmacology experts as well?" I protested. "Because I really don't have room on my bingo card for that."

I turned to Claire. "What are you going to do with those vials? Is there any way for you to analyze what those substances really are?"

"Yeah," she said rubbing a hand through her hair. "I mean, yeah, I've got some contacts. But it's going to take a minute. And we've got to hope that Kieran doesn't realize that some of his go juice has taken a walk. Everything was pretty well smashed up there, and I did my best to shatter anything that wasn't, but if he decides to put the puzzle pieces back together, he's going to know that some of the vials are missing."

"Agreed. But I have a feeling he's going to be entirely too busy to be paying attention to that for the time being. Meanwhile, Lucian, can you track anything happening up there?"

He smiled. "Until they sweep for the surveillance nodes I positioned today, yes. I'll keep you apprised." He narrowed his eyes at both of us. "You are both, of course, welcome to stay here. There are multiple bedrooms."

"Don't let Jillian know that," Claire snorted, and I shook my head.

"No. I don't want anyone tracking us here, or doing

anything unusual—we're not supposed to know anything, right? And Kieran—or Mirr..." I narrowed my gaze at Lucian. "He didn't recognize you."

He shrugged. "I told you, he's barely fifth level. I was concerned, admittedly, but once I saw him...what can I say?"

His smile was low, slow, and dangerous. "It's good to be back in the game."

CHAPTER

FIFTEEN

By the time Claire finally dropped me off at home, the sun was setting low over the houses, the shadows lengthening down the short sidewalk to the duplex. The light was on inside, with the kind of flickering cadence that told me Steve was gaming in the main room. I smiled, thinking of it, glad for the lights, sound, and chaos that always accompanied my housemate.

"Hey, Steve," I announced when I turned the key in my lock and pushed the door open. He shouted something incoherent, then broke off into a rant against dwarves. I wasn't hungry, but I opened the freezer anyway, selecting something that promised cheese and salt. There were few things in life that cheese and salt couldn't cure.

"You want any food?" I called and pulled out a second random box at his assent. I glanced around the kitchen as I prepared the simple meal, noting everything in its place. I kept it clean. I had to keep it clean, like I had to keep my walls white and my mother's room tidy, and anywhere Steve lived at least halfway presentable until the next time he blew through. Tidiness meant order, meant control. I'd had to live my life with so much control...

The microwave bleated, startling me with its plaintive alert. When had I put the food in? I frowned, then saw the containers still sitting on the stove, unopened.

"Focus," I muttered, though it was nice, honestly, not having to focus for once. Now, when I came home to the duplex I shared with Steve, it didn't need to serve as a refuge, a retreat. Now, it was simply a house with a fridge full of frozen food and cheap alcohol, a living room full of furniture I hadn't bought and didn't care about, and a white-painted room that had probably shrunk by two inches all around from the layers of paint I'd applied over the last fifteen years.

The microwave bleated again.

I stared at the containers on the stove.

"You know, I've heard that things cook faster when you put them inside the little box with the door," Steve called helpfully from the living room.

"Yeah, yeah." This time, I managed to get his food cooked and on a plate and started mine before turning away from the microwave. I walked into the living room and felt a pang. He sat on the couch, leaning toward the TV, manipulating his gaming console like he was going to save the universe.

I bit my lip, unsure of whether he really *was* saving the universe, but he threw me a glance. "You're good. After all the Darkyn craziness, we decided to revisit some old games. Rook's roommate is getting married, Mei just broke up with her girlfriend, and Anya apparently is getting a promotion to be some sort of head bean counter, so everyone needed a break."

"I'm not a bean counter!" huffed Anya over the speaker. I laughed and left the steaming container on its plate, then went back to nuke my own food. It took another three dings, and when I returned to the living room, Steve eyed me over a forkful of pasta, the controllers set to the side.

"You good?" he asked, tracking me as I picked my way toward the couch. "Because you don't look good. Claire called me and filled me in on the Reflex situation, and I mean—you did the job, right? You got the evil bad out of Walsh?"

"I mean, I guess?" I returned, propping my feet up on the coffee table as I settled into the couch. "Except for now it's in the actual computer system, I think—which is sort of like a house possession on steroids. How do you get a demon out of a computer? Seriously, I don't think you can."

"You got them out of the lake house, though, right?" Steve frowned, his heavy brows furrowing as he looked around the room. "You know, I never thought about that. All this time you had Lucian hanging out in your brain, but he didn't, you know, haunt this place. You had the problem with painting your room every other week, which I totally thought was a sniffing habit, not gonna lie, but otherwise, like—I mean, this is a pretty nice place."

I snorted. "It's really not, Steve. But the rent is cheap enough, and no, so far as I know, it's not haunted." I glanced around. "I don't think it's haunted. I think we would have figured that out by now, yeah?"

"Maybe." Steve shrugged. He pushed his food away and grabbed the controls again. "Then again, I didn't know you were possessed, and you didn't know I was getting my blood sucked out of me in clubs downtown. So maybe we aren't the best at making those kinds of discoveries, yeah?"

"You in, Cube?" Rook's voice sounded over the speakers, and Steve was gone again, immersed in the world served up to him on the thirty-inch screen.

I watched him for longer than I expected I would, but finally dragged myself up to my room, reaching out to flip on the light before I fully opened the door, still subconsciously bracing myself for carnage that simply didn't happen anymore. Ever since I'd managed to get Palemerious out of my system and into his own human-ish body, I hadn't had a single need for night-time autodrawing. My walls had been untouched for so long they'd actually stopped smelling like paint. Maybe I could even paint them a color sometime, instead of miles of flat white.

I snorted as I crawled into bed. Maybe.

The dream started almost as soon as I fell asleep. My body still felt tired. Edgy. But I wasn't in my room anymore. I was in the Prometheus Building, only not Lucian's apartment, but Walsh's command center. The screens had been raised so that the view of the city and the lake was clear and unimpeded, and lights twinkled for miles in one direction and danced in tiny sparks atop far-off boats in another.

But that wasn't where the real action was.

I stared as Jillian Reeves emerged from the inner office that I now knew led to Walsh's sleeping room. She was dressed in a long, silky dress—not at all what she had on today and not even remotely something I could see myself wearing, but it looked good on her, all deep crimson and flowing lines. Her blonde hair was loose too, and it seemed like there was more of it than there should be, tumbling over her shoulders and cascading down her back. She had made it to the front of Kieran's desk when the shadows moved in front of her, and I froze.

Lucian was there. He materialized out of the shadows as if he was waiting for her, and he didn't back away as she shifted toward him, more like turned, so the two of them were circling each other. I could see the demon within her, somehow, glowing directly beneath her skin, and I realized—I hadn't looked all that deeply into her eyes today, in this same office. I was right there, knew there was something wrong, something off within her that I could exorcise, and I hadn't finished the job.

She hadn't wanted me to, sure, but that didn't make up for the fact that I hadn't even tried. Why hadn't I tried?

My mind shied away from the question. In front of me, Lucian and Jillian stopped circling, and Jillian reached out, her fingers trembling as she drew them down Lucian's face. My stomach twisted, and I watched with growing horror as he reached for her hand, grasped it, then drew it toward his mouth, bending over it as Jillian looked over at me—directly at me, as if I was sitting on one of Walsh's overstuffed couches prim and precise and cold and not touching Lucian.

Jillian smiled, and her laughter sounded in my brain. "Darkness to darkness, Delia. Like to like. What did you expect?"

I turned away, only I was no longer in the penthouse, no longer surrounded by the comfort of shadows. Instead, I was in my room—my own room, only every light was on and the walls were no longer white. They were closing in on me, covered in my own shaky scrawl, with all the usual epithets gone, replaced by words just as damning. HOLLOW. EMPTY. PRETENDING. ALONE. MARKED. TAINTED. WEAK. FRIGHTENED. ABANDONED. DEAD—

Another turn, and Jillian and Lucian were there again, wrapped in each other's arms now in Kieran's office, clothes on the floor, her back arching beneath his mouth, his hands. They danced in some sort of macabre, soundless flow, impossibly slow and achingly tender, and her words filled my head again, twisting and raw. "Darkness to darkness," she sneered. "Like to like."

"No!" I screamed the word, but I had done this so many times for so many years, waking up terrified and driven, thrashing and crazed, that I didn't make a sound. The softest gasp barely breached my throat, and I fought against my sheets, my throat constricted, my heart racing, barely managing not to fall out of bed completely.

I couldn't make a sound! I couldn't fall, I couldn't jump! Not if I didn't want to wake Mom, to wake Steve, to wake the Soos next door who could never know what I did in this room with their cans of craft paint, who could never know the horrors racing through my head, who could never know—

I gasped for air, eyes flying open. I was in my room. My bed. The dream was over.

"Delia."

The word, so softly spoken, ripped through my mind like a thundercrack, and I rammed back against my pillow-cushioned headboard so hard I nearly knocked myself unconscious. I grabbed up piles of sheets, fistfuls of them, and twisted around to stare hard at the chair beside my window, the empty chair that I used to hang the sheets from the hooks around the ceilings so I could cover, so I could cover—

The chair wasn't empty now.

Someone sat in it. A long, elegant shadow of a man, dressed in a suit, smelling of cloves and cinnamon, honey and vanilla—and sex.

No. Not sex. But the rest of it, yes. I was nearly sure—

"Delia," Lucian said again, his voice so soft, so certain, I had to be dreaming it. But I had already been dreaming and now I was awake, right?

Right?

"What are you—" my voice sounded wrong in my throat, scratchy and false, and I drew in an uneasy breath and tried again. "What are you doing here? How did you get in?"

His lips quirked. "Which answer would you like first, what or how?"

I pulled the sheets closer to me. I was wearing a T-shirt and gym shorts, my usual nighttime garb, and Lucian was sitting in my bedroom as a real, live, flesh-and-blood person. Not a creature in my thoughts, a nightmare buried in the back of my mind. He was here. He was real.

Or was this simply a new part of the same dream? Would Jillian Reeves come sailing out of my closet or roll out from under my bed next, wearing fishnets and a bustier?

"You need to breathe, Delia. Your heart always pumps too fast, your mouth goes too dry."

"How do you know that?" I asked, my voice sounding incredibly thin.

He chuckled. "We've been doing this a long time. When you dream—no matter what you dream—you call me. And always, I am here."

"What?" I jerked back against my headboard again, my mind finally clearing enough for me to pray that Steve couldn't hear the thump all the way downstairs. "How did you get in?"

"I used your key."

I gaped at him, and he chuckled again, leaning forward on the chair to place his elbows on his knees. "Delia, there are some secrets you can choose to hide from me, but I saw with your eyes these past fifteen years. I touched with your hands. You have hidden a spare key beneath the frog by the hydrangea bush ever since your mother locked you out of the house when you were sixteen and she thought you wanted her boyfriend."

I wrinkled my nose. "I didn't."

"I know you didn't. I couldn't say the same for him."

I blinked then, rapidly, and struggled to remember that summer—it had been so long ago, a year before my mother had died, and the man, the guy—try as I might, I couldn't remember his face, his features. Couldn't remember anything about him except for the smell of leather and cigarettes. "He didn't last all that long."

"You don't say," Lucian said, his voice like silk. He paused a moment, shifted. "Why did you call me tonight, Delia? I don't know your dreams. I never knew your dreams, only that you had them."

"Oh." My mind cleared enough for me to realize the potential for mortification here. "But you heard me and you, what, zipped over here in your car and stole my key from under JoJo Bullfrog so you could check on me?"

His teeth flashed in the moonlight. "I couldn't help myself. It was easier before, but the call was...just as pronounced. Worse, in some ways. Because I wasn't with you."

"Yeah." I swallowed, willing my heart to slow, my hands to stop shaking. "Yeah, well—you're not, and I guess I was wondering who you were with. Specifically, whether you were with Walsh's assistant. Jillian Reeves."

Across the room, Lucian went still. "What do you mean?"

I made a face, looking down at my hands. Why had I said that part out loud? But the name was there now, hanging between us, and as stupid as this was and as foolish as I felt—

"She's possessed, Lucian. Jillian. She has some weird demonette inside her that seeks out darkness in others, and she likes it. I told her I could help her get rid of it and she was all 'why would I want to get rid of it?'—Like it gave her an identity or something. It was creepier than it should have been."

"Alaria." He nodded. His lips twitched. "Second-level mischief demon of the House of Ruin. I don't think demonettes were mentioned in the hierarchy I showed you."

"Look, I don't know *what* it was," I protested. "But it's in her and it makes her drawn to darkness or whatever, and darkness means you."

"Mm..." he said, and he leaned a little closer. Just a little, but suddenly it seemed as if there was no longer any distance between us at all.

"Only me?" he purred.

SIXTEEN

Lucian stood, turning from the window to prowl away from my bed, around the perimeter of the room. Nothing blocked him, because nothing sat against the walls. I'd never wanted anything to obstruct me when I'd attacked the empty, vacant space, filling it full of vile profanities.

"You've painted this room how many times?" Lucian asked. "Fifty? A hundred?"

I pulled the sheets a little tighter around me, watching him like he might lash out. "I lost count."

He lifted one of his elegant hands and traced it over the wall. I felt the touch on the layers of paint like a physical assault, scraping along my skin, setting my nerves on edge. "They're still here," he murmured. "All the words. All the images. Layers upon layers. Covered over so that you could forget them, but they never really left, did they? They cut too deep, stained for too long."

"Not anymore," I said, my voice sounding unusually strong. "I got rid of you. I threw you out. You're no longer inside of me. You're gone."

"Am I?" He turned to me then, and the light from the lamp outside cut across his face, heightening the harsh beauty of his jaw, his cheekbones, the dark, glinting fire of his eyes. "Then why do you still taste my name on your tongue when you're afraid? Why do you hear my voice when you're alone?"

"Oh, please." Now I did roll my eyes, because I could roll my eyes. Because I wasn't a child alone in the dark whispering to somebody who wasn't there, begging for him to leave me alone. "I'm probably going to hear your voice for the rest of my life, unless and until I make so much money that I can finally afford the therapy I so desperately need. God knows, there are about half a dozen practitioners in our building who would hook me up, if they ever actually showed up to their offices. But that doesn't change the fact that you're now talking outside of me instead of inside of me, Lucian. And that makes all the difference."

He turned again, glancing out the window. "Why do you stay here?"

The question made me blink. "It's home."

"No." He barked a short, harsh laugh, an indictment of the lifetime I'd spent in this place. "It *was* home, maybe. Once upon a time. Now, it's a trap. Your mother's ghost couldn't leave it soon enough. My graffiti lies under every coat of paint. You're living in a museum of your own suffering, and you won't do anything about it."

I scowled at him. "Why should I leave? I know this house, it's in a relatively safe neighborhood, and I can afford it. Where else would I go?"

"Anywhere, everywhere. You have money now, Delia. Max has paid your office rent for six months, never mind that he's already drifting back to normalcy—the normal life of an ordinary survivor. A track you might want to follow, at least long enough to get out of here. You've received two lucrative commissions this week alone. The whispers are starting around the city. The murmurs, the suggestions. More people will be coming to your door. Needing you, wanting you, and able to pay for you. You could leave tomorrow if you wanted."

I hunched into my sheets again. "Steve needs—"

"Steve would find his own place within a week, and you know it. He has family, parents who care for him, money when he decides to go get it. You can sublet this place to his gamer friends if you can't let go of it. But stop using him as an excuse to chain yourself to these walls, this paint. There's only one full-length mirror in this entire house, and you only looked into it once. Are you seriously going to go on living that way?"

"Why do you care?" Anger finally bubbled over. "What's it to you either way? You've got your beautiful condo now on the lake, you're living a few floors down from Succubus Prime, you've got a brand-new identity that can take you anywhere you want in the world, and apparently, access to money whenever you want it. Why are you still hanging out here?"

He blinked at me, as if I'd asked him a question he'd never considered before. "I don't know," he said finally, glancing around. "And you're right. If I decided to remain, I should want you weak, tethered to your trauma, easy to influence."

"Right." My lips twisted as I glanced down at my fingers, still clutching my sheets too tightly. The pain from my ragged fingernails and torn cuticles grounded me, and I twisted them into the cheap material. "I'm not as easy to influence as all that, buddy. I'm the one who shook you off."

"Well, it took you long enough," he said with a smirk, and my head came up with a snap. He held my gaze. "What did you dream about, Delia? Before you drew me to your side with the walls and the words, before you reminded me that I should be here? What did you see? What did you want?"

I scowled but suddenly felt awkward with him looming

over me. I threw the sheets off and scrubbed my hands through my hair, never mind my ridiculous outfit. I was suddenly hot, too hot, and I sprang off the bed and stalked by him, opening the window. The air outside was stagnant and humid, and gave me no relief. Neither did the creature behind me.

"Why are you so injured?" he snapped.

"Because you suck!" I snapped, turning sharply toward him. "Because my body has figured out that there's something completely fucked up with you, even if my eyes and mouth and the deep dark part of me that clearly has a death wish wants to let you pound me into the floorboards. I smell you, and half the time I want to choke on the scent, half the time I dissolve into a puddle. I loathe you, and I shiver every time you're near! You disgust me—horrify me—and I can't stop thinking about you. So yeah, I've been chewing my nails a little bit."

He folded his arms. "And the bruises on your arms? The scratches on your back? How do you even reach that far to cause such damage?"

"How did I when you were inside me?" I retorted. "I seem to recall quite a few double-jointed moments during my painting fugues. You didn't worry too much about the damage you were doing me then. What's changed?" He didn't answer that, but merely smirked. "So much anger," he purred, and the push-pull of need tempered with horror spun up inside me again. "You saw me with her in your dream, didn't you? This Jillian Reeves. You saw us together."

"Well, you certainly seemed pretty comfortable with each other. But I guess that makes sense, right? You're both demons, and that's what demons apparently do." *Especially demons from the Court of Lust*, I couldn't help adding to myself.

I could hear the smile in his voice again. "You were jealous," he challenged.

"Oh, please." I folded my arms beneath my chest.

"You were. You are. You hate that Jillian Reeves has embraced what she is, what she has accepted into her, while you fight it. You hate that she offered herself to me while you pretend that you don't want what I am..." His voice dropped to a subtle hush. "Who I am."

"It was a dream," I said tightly.

He leaned down to me, so close, impossibly close. "What is life, if not a dream, sweet Delia? What is this world in which we find ourselves, if not the place of hope and madness? What are we if not the creatures whose magic fills—"

I couldn't help myself. I didn't want to help myself. His words were pulling at me like a current rushing away from the shore, promising me the pleasures of the deep blue ocean, when I knew I was going to end up drowning. But I didn't care anymore. I just wanted to fill the hole that had opened up within me, begging to be noticed, begging to be seen.

I turned to him—and his face was right there, beautiful and perfect in the streetlight, eyes glinting red. I pulled him to me and kissed him hard, angry, overwhelming my terror with the endless aching howl of need that rang in my ears.

Lucian didn't hesitate. His hands moved up, his fingers threading in my hair, pulling me closer, tight to him—as if he were the needy one, the one who had spent all those nights alone, first simply abandoned in my own household, then later, genuinely terrified for my life, aware of the entity within me, but unable to put my fears into words, unable to ask for help, unwilling to ask for it, if help meant that I would be left alone again, if treatment meant I would lose the only thing that had ever wanted to stay...

For a heartbeat I felt it again—that sensation of being filled, occupied, something coiled in places that shouldn't exist. My scratches burned like they were opening fresh, and I tasted smoke and ash beneath his mouth. But I didn't pull away. I couldn't.

"Delia," Lucian cursed as his hands slid down my body, his nimble fingers slipping over my clothes. The simple T-shirt, the thin shorts. He fisted his hands in the cotton, pulling at it, lifting it high on my rib cage until his large hands palmed my waist, and he hauled me close against him. I felt the line of his muscular legs, the heaviness of his cock thickening between us, and my sudden, fragmented gasp seemed to break through the haze he'd woven around us.

"*Yes...*" I practically moaned.

Lucian straightened abruptly, holding me away from him but not letting me flee, pinning me in place as I shivered.

"Did I...misread the room?" I finally managed. And he did let me go then, his laughter flowing over me as he glanced around in the half-darkness.

"The room is the problem. We're not doing this here. Not in this bed, not in this house. Not where you painted over my words a thousand times trying to forget I existed."

I straightened, gathering my own wits about me again. "Well, in my defense, those were pretty nasty words. And there were a lot of them."

"Then all the more reason for you to find someplace else, if you really want to welcome me back inside of you, Delia." The taunt struck me as an affront, which was what he intended. But try as I might, I couldn't bring myself to back down. Not with Jillian Reeves' sly, sultry words ringing in my ear, *darkness to darkness, like to like.*

"I mean, I guess." I shrugged. "Or maybe I'll find some other demon who's not as much of a pain in my ass."

I knew almost before the words were out of my mouth that these were the wrong words to say. Wrong and right at the same time, as the heat in the room soared, and Lucian's breath turned into a hiss between his teeth.

"That would be...a very unwise choice," he murmured.

He turned to me then, and it was his hand that moved first, his fingers that reached out and drifted along my chin, tilting it up. He stared down at me with eyes of obsidian and fire, and he leaned close. For the first time, I smelled the heat of him, burning like banked embers on a fall day, the fire tracing every scratch and stain on my skin, burning it like acid while I leaned into the pain.

"You need to decide, Delia," he whispered, his breath skating over my lips. "Do you want to keep living in the past? Painting over the same walls, sleeping in the same bed, pretending you're the same child your mother left behind? Or do you want to become the woman you were meant to be?"

"You stole who I was meant to be," I said, the words cutting more harshly than I intended, but he didn't flinch.

"Maybe for a while." He tilted his head. "Maybe I wasn't the one who did the stealing. But either way you fought and clawed free your independence, and you achieved it. So, what are you going to do now?"

"I don't know," I whispered, tracking the flickering red sparks in his eyes. "I don't know where to begin."

That earned me another chuckle, the sound of it low, sweet, and warm. "Well, you've already begun, now, haven't you? You've set up your own business; you've attracted the attention of criminals and business scions alike. You've drawn people to you like a moth to the flame."

"You as well?" I asked.

"Me as well," he agreed, leaning forward to nuzzle my lips with his. "Darkness to darkness, like to like."

My eyes drifted shut on the heady perfume of his body, hot, sweet, and crackling fire...

. . .

SOMETHING SKITTERED ACROSS MY CONSCIOUSNESS—MY name, hissed and chittered like insects scurrying over plaster. I felt it crawl across the painted walls, across my skin, wrongness clamoring at the edges of my awareness. Too light. Too distant. I couldn't surface, couldn't wake, drowning in heat and the promise of—

I jolted back to consciousness what seemed like three seconds later, in time to hear a curious whoosh! somewhere in the vicinity of my closet. A moment later, thick, acrid smoke began pouring out through the ceiling light.

"Steve!" I screamed, then realized the air was thick all around me, the room hazy and far too hot. Somewhere, an alarm was squealing in protest, shrill and high. I stumbled out of bed, my lungs already burning as my feet hit the floor. I lurched across the bedroom and yanked open the door to see the hallway filled with smoke, an orange glow coming from down the stairs.

"Steve," I gasped again, and thought enough to drop to my knees, crawling toward the stairway. My eyes were streaming, a wracking cough cutting off sharply as the sound of splintering wood jerked my gaze down the stairs. I was almost to the living room when something massive hit the front door, knocking it completely off its hinges. I gaped as Sergei crashed through the door, a one-man freight train, his face covered by a wet cloth.

"Out! Now!" he ordered, as I wheeled around to see Steve stumbling upright in the living room. He was clearly disoriented, coughing and surrounded by flames, the couch and Mom's afghan blazing. The cheap carpet was already a pool of chemicals. I got a vague impression of a blasted-out wall when Sergei reached me, grabbing my forearm and practically flinging me toward the front door. I went only because he went after Steve next, shouldering him over his back before wheeling around.

"I said, out!" he roared.

I was through the door and down the sidewalk in seconds, then jogged right, spinning back to the other side of the house. "The Soos!" I cried, staring at the duplex. You could see fire on the first floor of my side, but my bedroom window was in the back, and nothing seemed to be disturbed on the Soo's side yet. "Sergei, you have to get the Soos out! My neighbors!"

He cursed and peered back toward the house, as if assessing the likelihood that the fire could blast two homes with one shot. He shoved Steve toward me and bounded off.

I staggered back under Steve's dead weight and half-fell with him to the ground, dimly aware of another discordant sound that broke through the night sky—sirens.

I rolled off Steve and checked his pulse. He was breathing, thank God, but my attention fractured again when the second siren joined the first, and then a third. Fully three trucks roared up less than ninety seconds later, red lights strobing. How the hell was that possible? There could have been a fire marshal parade the next street over and trucks wouldn't have responded that quickly.

I could only stare as men leapt from the truck, hoses deploying, all of them moving with practiced efficiency. Meanwhile, Sergei appeared on the far end of the lot, carrying Mrs. Soo over one shoulder. Behind him, Mr. Soo stumbled out along with two little kids. Jesus Christ, they'd had their *grandchildren* over tonight.

The first responders swarmed them, bristling with reflective blankets and medical gear, and Sergei left them almost immediately and returned to me.

"I'm fine!" I yelled at another EMT who started heading our way. "Help the kids!"

Sergei didn't speak until he came right up to me, but he grabbed my face and stared hard into my eyes. "Breathe," he ordered. "Deeply."

I tried, and he nodded grimly as I coughed and spit out thick gray phlegm. "Keep doing that."

"How did you—" I gasped. "Why were you?"

"Volkov sent me. To watch." He grimaced as he looked at the duplex. "Good thing."

I frowned too. Had he seen Lucian earlier? Had Lucian known what was happening here?

Or had that really been a dream?

My thoughts a chaotic jumble, I stared as the firefighters covered the house with water, blasting through shattered windows, sending steam billowing high into the air. Steve eventually sat up as well, and somehow Sergei scored blankets for us. But I couldn't move, could only stare as I finally saw flames visible through the upstairs window, my mom's room, and watch as the roof began to sag.

"Goddammit," Steve finally spoke, his voice hoarse. "I just broke in that new console. You know how hard it is to get comfortable with your gear? What a pain in the ass."

I burst out laughing. "How are you even still alive?" I asked, staring at him with his dark hair turned gray with soot, his face streaked with smoke residue. His clothes looked singed at the edges, but he was fine. He wasn't even a little charred.

He grinned back at me. "I ask myself that a lot these days," he said ruefully. "Usually after hanging out with you."

"Managed to save a lot of it!" One of the firefighters announced to me as he jogged by. "Lot of damage, but not a total loss."

"Thank you," I called back, the idea of thanking anyone for what happened tonight surreal, and turned back to the scene before us, painted with red, white, and blue emergency lights. Off to the side, I saw Sergei again, his phone to his ear.

Reporting to Volkov.

A long sleek car caught my attention, though how, I didn't know, given the chaos all around. Still, I knew who it was. I just didn't know if this was his first visit of the evening.

I nudged Steve, who clutched the blanket and stared wildly toward the car, shock finally setting in. "Guess we're doing a sleepover at Lucian's tonight."

He grinned back at me, hair standing on end, finally looking a little crazed. "He better have pizza."

SEVENTEEN

The next time I jerked awake, I was lying in a bed the size of Rhode Island with a floor-to-ceiling view of open water. I stared out, disoriented, then frowned down at the silk pajama T-shirt I could see above the pulled-up covers.

"What the hell?" I muttered, trying to decide if I was stuck inside another dream.

But no, my hair was still damp, my clothes from the night before still visible in a pile on the floor of the ensuite bathroom of Lucian's guestroom. The door to the bedroom was closed—and locked, I suspected. And I wasn't alone here. I could hear Steve's voice outside, excitedly chattering.

Steve was here.

That more than anything convinced me it was safe to throw off the covers and hit the floor, wobbling a little.

I scowled down at my body, cataloguing every bruise and cut. I'd washed the soot away, but I looked like I'd been dragged across pavement—my bruises had bruises, and a dozen half-healed gashes wept blood down my arms. Everything hurt.

Just another day in paradise.

I plucked the silky gray PJs as I squinted around the room. There were no other clothes here. How had Lucian even had PJs that fit my size to begin with?

Mystery of the universe in hand, I opened the door and dared re-emerge into polite society.

"Delia! Jeez, it's about time. You've gotta check this gear." He held up the devices. "Lucian said it was delivered to the office early this morning, so he had Claire send it over."

"To the office?" I squinted at Steve, then noticed Lucian in the marble and steel kitchen. Today he was dressed in an open-collared blue shirt that looked like it had been spun from dolphin dreams, his dark hair swept off his forehead and... longer, somehow, than I remembered it. Long enough that I wanted to tangle my fingers in it again, draw him close.

"That was fast," I choked out, not looking directly at Lucian anymore—but still acutely aware that I was in pajamas he'd procured for me.

"Wasn't it, though?" Lucian said with a smile, moving across the kitchen with a coffee mug. He set it on the counter as I sat down, and I smelled the rich cream. Of course, he knew how I took my coffee, though this was admittedly several rungs above the fast-food fare I usually scored. "I had Claire verify with Victoria that it was a legitimate delivery from Prometheus, but she apparently wasn't the one who authorized it. No one seems to know who did."

"Well, I'm not complaining," Steve said from the couch. He wore sweatpants and a T-shirt—his version of new pajamas. "And you know, if Reflex pulsed the power grid to blow up the duplex, I mean, it's legit the least they could do."

"Right." I poked at my phone. Steve, Lucian, and I had hashed this out at length last night, and it was the only possibility that made sense. Reflex had created a problem; Reflex had solved it. Message delivered. "When can we get back into the duplex?"

"Like for our stuff? A couple of days, the fire guy said. But to live there?" Steve scoffed a laugh. "That's gonna be a minute. I can crash with Rook for however long, though. He's critically under-roommated right now, with his buddy getting married. But I don't know what all's gonna be left from the house, or if you'll even want to go back."

He glanced up at me, wincing. "Sorry, Delia. I mean, shit. It's your home."

"Yeah." I waved a silk-jacketed arm at Lucian. "Thanks for the clothes, but I need to get back in the house sooner rather than later. And, you know. Figure out somewhere to live."

"You can stay here as long as you would like," he said, then gestured to the far wall. "I took the liberty of asking Claire to bring over several outfits and supplies."

"Jesus, how long was I asleep?" I squinted at my phone, startled to see it was nearly noon. "I never sleep this late."

"Well, you're the boss, so you're allowed to take the day—score!" Steve called out gleefully. "Yo, Lucian, whatcha got to eat around here?"

"Whatever can be delivered."

"My kind of place."

With that, Steve went back to his machine while I focused on my phone as Lucian ordered enough food with his to feed a football team. He didn't ask me what I wanted to eat. Once again, he knew what I ate. He knew everything about me.

I grimaced. This was getting more creepy, not less.

A story about a kid getting struck by a car while jogging popped up on my feed and I swiped to zoom by it—then froze. I knew that face, I thought. I knew that kid. But when I clicked on the story, it didn't go anywhere real, just to an ad for a travel site.

Reversing back to the news, the article was gone. I scrolled up and back...nothing there. But as I was about to flash away, a second story popped up. One of the girls at Meadowbrook, dead from an overdose.

"What the hell?" I muttered, and Lucian turned to me.

"What's wrong?"

I handed him my phone, then grabbed my coffee mug. When I glanced at Lucian, he flickered—only for a second, his face overlaid with something else. Sharp edges. Too many teeth. Then he was himself again, watching me with those dark eyes.

I blew out a shaky breath. "Every other article is about kids —and not random kids, but the ones I saw in Meadowbrook. Not their names, but their faces, their images—are you seeing that?"

He shrugged. "I am, but it's not landing the same way. I didn't see their faces. To me, it looks like another day in Chicago."

"Check that." Steve parked his console and hauled himself up off the couch, then moved over beside me. He squinted at the phone. "I see kids too—you're not imagining that. But I'm with Lucian. That's not weird to me. What is weird? It's not just you."

He pulled his own phone out and waved it at me. "*I'm* seeing people who look like Mei, Rook, and Anya, like—every-where. Showing up in ads, featured in articles like the kids you're seeing. I look, I freak, I look back—the image is differ-ent. They're seeing it too. There's even some buzz growing online, but mostly among the super intense conspiracy subreddits, the Dark Streets podcast, nothing really main-stream. But something's kind of fucked up, no question. Someone's dicking with people all of a sudden, and it's not cool."

"Yeah, well..." I frowned at him as Lucian's phone

announced the first wave of food arriving. "Keep your head on a swivel. I don't have a good feeling about this."

It was another two hours before we finally made it to the office, me in my store-bought everything and Steve still rocking his sweats and T-shirt. On the drive from Lucian's apartment, I'd clocked three different digital ads featuring the Meadowbrook kids, and Steve had narrowly missed being able to screencap a photo of Anya on another one. Now we were both at our desks zipping through websites, shouting out whenever one of us saw another faked picture.

Claire showed up a few minutes later, but—weirdly enough—she didn't agree with me that the images I was seeing were the Meadowbrook kids. And she, of course, would be the only one who would know.

"I mean, they're close," she said when I showed her yet another picture. She bit her lip at my clear frustration. "Seriously, Delia, they are. But you've got to cut yourself a break here. I did an entire section in school on post-traumatic stress responses and medication, and you definitely would qualify. What you're experiencing is totally normal."

I stiffened. "I'm not imagining this."

"I'm not saying you are," she agreed gently. "But trauma can make us see patterns that aren't there. Maybe you should see one of the therapists in the building, assuming they ever show up?"

"Yeah, no. I'm good."

"Mm. I'm just saying—"

"Yo!" Steve shouted from the outer office. "Dude, you guys, you gotta see this!"

I felt Lucian's eyes on me as I followed Claire to where Steve was hunched over his laptop. "Okay, so I opened up WoD and clicked into God mode, right? The Architect button? Which was like right there and available to me from the go on this version of the game. And there I am, up I go...Rook, Anya, Mei, you seeing this?"

The trio responded over the speakers, and we watched Steve zip through the scene, hovering above the dungeon passages as if he were moving through rock itself. The demons converged, but instead of running from them, Steve levitated up another floor, scooted sideways, popped a trap door in the floor, and dropped into a new chamber.

Then we saw him.

"What the hell is that?" Claire squeaked. A man lay stretched out in a glass tube hooked up to computer consoles, his face visible through the glass.

"That," Steve said with emphasis, "is Finn Ashford. And listen to this. Like, I mean it, listen."

He leaned forward and turned the speakers up, so high that a wave of static flowed out into the room. Then, beneath that static, I heard a whisper that sent the hair on my arms standing straight up.

"*Mom...*" the voice came. "*Trapped.*" And then, after a long pause: "*The mirrors have eyes.*"

"Anya heard it first, running down the hallway on the other side of this wall." Steve gestured. "That's all he says, but he's repeated it at least a dozen times so far. And I've gone out and come back in—there's no change to him."

"But what is he doing in there?" Claire asked. "He's like... plugged into the game? And that's not really him, right? It's some sort of avatar?"

"It's him," Steve said. "We can't be imagining it."

"It's possible," Lucian said quietly. "But not in the game, I don't think. Not even demons have that kind of power. But could he be held somewhere on life support, his brain wired into the system, put to use to serve Asmodaea's needs? Yes. It's possible."

Claire swiveled toward him, gaping. "For five *years*?"

"When Kieran Walsh joined Prometheus Solutions, his impact was instantaneous. I've looked at the old footage," Steve said. "Even he didn't know how the code was falling into place so quickly. He called it magic and gave all the credit to the developers, but those developers quietly left shortly thereafter. Not one of them still works in anything to do with Reflex or infrastructure code. As far as I can tell, they're not even in the city. So something had to keep the systems going. And who better than the man who put it all together in the first place? The man whose heart and soul lived in that code. Hell, maybe Finn did it on purpose."

"Wait, what?" I said abruptly as a chill snaked down my spine. "Say that again. What do you mean by that?"

"Dude, I don't know what I mean," Steve said, backtracking quickly as his gaze remained focused on the screen. "I'm just saying, if the game and the AI of Reflex share a back-end architect and Finn is stuck in the game, maybe he's not stuck at all. Maybe he came in here on purpose, but, like, it didn't work out the way he thought it would. He keeps saying that the mirrors have eyes. Well, Reflex is a bunch of cameras, right? And cameras kind of look like mirrors. Hell, Mirr *sounds* like 'mirror.' So, you know? Maybe there's something to all of that. Maybe he's trying to tell us something, but I mean, shit. Five years stuck inside anything would probably feel like a lifetime."

He winced and glanced up at me. "No offense."

I waved that off. "Can we get him out?"

Lucian tilted his head, staring at the frozen image on the screen. "That depends on whether there's anything left worth saving," he said.

My phone buzzed, and I looked down at it and blinked. "Well, our luck seems to be improving," I said. "That's from the landlord. The fire inspector has cleared us to return to the house tomorrow morning, to get whatever we want out of it before they start full-scale cleanup."

"What can you even get out of there?" Claire protested. "Fire damage is the worst."

"I..." I didn't know how to answer that. I didn't know what to think about anything anymore. The idea of seeing my mom's house, her *things*, damaged beyond repair...

"Whoa, whoa, whoa," Steve announced, drawing our attention again. "You guys, check it. This is the God's-eye view of the dungeon and—I mean, shit, this isn't good."

He slid to the side to give us a better view, and we saw it. "That looks a lot like other demon hordes on the horizon, heading for your dungeon," I said. "Is that what's supposed to be happening in this game?"

"Not any version I've ever played," Steve said, his eyes wide. "And I've been playing this since I was in high school. This is new."

"Totally new!" Anya's voice chimed in from the speakers.

"Fully and unequivocally new," Rook confirmed. "And to make it even crazier—these aren't even the same demon sects that exist in the game. This group is from some other game entirely—I've seen them before, I think, but not in a Prometheus game. They're what? World of Terror, maybe? Out of Turkey?"

"Romania," Mei corrected. "And we're not the only ones seeing it. Discord's blowing up with other teams seeing them coming. Apparently, we're not the only gamers who got special delivery consoles today, and of course, we all had to hook in as soon as we found a locked-down line. Gotta be some sort of promo push, but there's been nothing out of Prometheus to counter it. Of course, Warriors has been out of their lineup for five years, so—shit, what if this is a hack?"

"Best hack ever, if so," Anya said. "Like, seriously? A whole new division of the horde? That's insane! Kill points alone will be epic."

Claire and I exchanged a wary glance, pointedly refusing to look at Lucian. "You don't have to keep at this all night, though, do you?" I asked.

"Hell yes, we do!" Steve said before anyone else could. "I mean, there's a bathroom here, right? I'll be fine."

"I'll feed him," Claire said, making a face. "I'm not spending the night here, but Sergei can babysit him. I'll make sure there's food for both of them."

"Sweet." Steve grinned, leaning into his computer controls. "Get my go-bag tomorrow, Delia, yeah? If you're going to the house? It's by the couch, or whatever's left of the couch."

I winced. "Right."

He let out a long, satisfied hiss then spoke to his screen. "Gang, we need to build up strength points and maybe expand the team. Based on how fast they're moving, those demons will be here in the next forty-eight hours...we better be ready."

EIGHTEEN

Lucian and I didn't talk that night, and we didn't eat. He really didn't need to, and I could barely keep my eyes open. *Trauma*, I told myself. *Fear*, his smirk corrected.

Either way, I burrowed into thousand-thread-count sheets in my borrowed pajamas that night, my door closed but not locked. And I listened to the music from his piano flowing through the open space as I stared out the window toward the endless darkness punctuated by tiny lights on the vast lake. Eventually, I slept, but tonight, I didn't dream. If Lucian sought out the attentions of Jillian Reeves, he did it on his own time.

So I woke up feeling...restless. Needy. And his smile told me he knew it.

The morning found us cruising back to my old neighborhood in Lucian's sleek sedan, the tight confines of the vehicle forcing us together in an intimacy I didn't want to crave as much as I did. He'd provided coffee, which I'd devoured, and light, fluffy baked goods, which I'd ignored—and this last part apparently elevated his concern over me to the point of worry.

"You should eat," he said conversationally, as we navigated

the mid-morning welter of vehicles. "Demons prey on weakness."

"I'm not hungry," I countered. "And we're not going to hook up with any demons today. It's not like they're going to be standing around the duplex, rating their work. We don't even know if there are any demons in on this other than Mirr."

He scoffed at that. "It's definitely more than Mirr. He may be loose in Prometheus's infrastructure now, or he may have already found his way out. But this has Asmodaea's hand all over it—it's too complete, too cutting. She struck surgically at the one location that could cause you the most damage."

"Not the most." I didn't know why I was in such an argumentative mood, but it felt good to dig in, to object. To not accept Lucian's words as anything other than one possibility in an entire demon underworld full of options. "She could have hurt Steve or Claire."

The words hung between us like an indictment, and I immediately wished I could call them back. Did Asmodaea have ears? Had I just sentenced my friends to torment?

To my surprise, though, Lucian discounted the idea immediately. "Not likely. Demons have been playing this game for a very long time, Delia. The trick with humans is to break them down bit by bit, not to devastate or outrage them. Harming one of your own—a spouse, a child, a sibling, a parent, even a friend —that spurs a human to anger, and anger leads to action. That's not the playground of demons. We prefer our prey to be isolated, demoralized, despairing. And thus, your childhood home."

I curled my lip as we entered my neighborhood, feeling a chill despite my tailored, long-sleeved blouse. I'm sure Claire would think the summery blue suited me. I cared more that the sleeves were long and the collar modest enough to keep most of my skin covered. "Which shows you how much she knows me."

"And you should remember that." Lucian nodded. "Much like the computer systems she's currently controlling, Asmodaea relies on pattern recognition more so than actual intuitive thought. Still, going solely on ordinary human responses and patterns, she made a fairly good guess."

We fell silent as we turned the final corner and pulled up across the street from the duplex. A lone utility truck remained on the scene, but no more firefighters were tromping around, and the building didn't look as bad as I expected it to. Unlivable on my side, maybe, but not the hollowed-out shell I'd imagined when I'd allowed myself to think about it at all.

The landlord stood in the driveway in a small cluster of men, talking animatedly on his phone. He waved at me as we walked by, but he seemed in surprisingly good spirits, which made sense as his words reached me on the sidewalk. "Yes, that's what I said. Chicago Gas & Electric's paying for everything—the check's already been cut. I understand that, Bob, which is why I need you to move on this work like yesterday. I don't want them to realize they've made a mistake. They can ask for the money back, but they're not going to tear down a wall we've already installed. You can use the same plans we had for the duplex on Orchard and just..."

I glanced at Lucian as we mounted the stoop, the smell of wet, singed wood stronger here. "The utility company's paying for it that fast? How has the check already been cut?"

He grimaced. "You begin to understand how dangerous this situation is. I would wager that CG&E woke up this morning to the situation already resolved, with hand-wringing executives from Prometheus Solutions apologizing for the system acting without authorization to address the power surge versus waiting for the utility company to make a move. CG&E looks like a hero despite the surge; Prometheus Solutions saved lives, and the money will get funded out of who cares where. You can expect a joint press release about it once Asmodaea decides you're not going to be a problem anymore."

"Right." I didn't need to use my key to enter the building, but I also couldn't find any other words to speak as we stepped inside. The living room and kitchen looked scorched, but still standing, the walls brown and singed and reeking of wet cardboard and soaked coals, but still more or less in place. I stopped in front of the couch, staring at the heat marks.

"It's—that's the outline of Steve's sleeping body," I managed, feeling sick to my stomach. I stared at the blackened cushions that stretched above the bumpy outline of what had been under my mom's afghan. "He should have been ashes. I thought you said she wasn't going to harm my friends because she didn't want to piss me off!"

He slanted me a glance. "Are you pissed off?"

"I mean—*yeah*. Fuck this bitch, he could have *died*." The other shoe dropped, and I turned to him, staring. "Unless this is some sort of flex. You're saying she *knew* Steve wouldn't be harmed? She's *so completely* plugged into the situation that went down in Volkov's club that she knew he had some sort of spectral armor against demon-based attacks? But that's insane."

He didn't answer and I swung away, heading for the stairs. "What am I saying?" I groaned. "All of this is insane."

I took the steps two at a time, cringing as I reached the second floor. My mom's room had the same kind of smoke damage as the first floor, and the bathroom was intact, but when I approached my own door, I grimaced at the blackened surface of it. "What the hell?"

"Delia." Lucian pushed past me, and it was a testament to how freaked out I was that I let him do it. He stepped inside and turned, reaching for my hand to help me over the scorched floorboards.

"Dude," I whispered, staring around the space. The closet wall was nothing but ashes, all the way down to the studs, the window had been blown out, and the other walls... "What *happened* in here?"

The white paint was gone, the words I'd painted over a thousand different times melted into a swirling mess, but the burn marks still looked almost like letters—like words— though written by the hand of a crazy person in twisting, slashing letters, and not representing any language I'd ever seen. "Is this a message of some sort? And Christ on a crutch, do we need to hide this from Mr. Graves and his contractors?"

Lucian reached out and knocked his fist on the wall, and the letters dropped like a spectral sheet, the thin layer of ash collapsing to the floor. Another rap, and the drywall completely disintegrated.

"We don't," he said, reasonably enough. "It was the most temporary of messages, and intended, as it turns out, for me."

"You?" I glanced at him. "Lucian you, or Palemerious you? I thought they decided you'd fled the city."

He tilted his head, as if genuinely considering the question. "Both, since we're one and the same. Lucian is an evolution of Palemerious."

"One no one was supposed to know about."

He nodded. "And they still may not, but I suspect we aren't the only ones who've been conducting some research these past few days. I was seen at Walsh's office, and there's no such thing as a completely unknown demon among the horde. Mirr certainly knows me well enough, and he's had some time to think about what happened to him and who might be responsible besides you. Asmodaea may not have known who I was when I showed up, but it wouldn't take that much effort to connect the dots, especially with the chatter of demons and their human sycophants. You've drawn attention, and by extension, so have I. And perhaps I've invited some of my own."

"You mean Jillian." I squinted at him. "Please tell me you two didn't hook up. I know she's your type."

He raised a brow at me. "Beautiful?"

"Possessed." I looked around the room, feeling...strangely lighter than I expected. Weirdly relieved. What did that say about me? "You know, when the fire first started, I thought for half a second that maybe you set it. That you'd decided I shouldn't live here anymore and that this would be the fastest way to get me out."

"Mm." He didn't seem concerned as he circled the room, systematically turning more of the scarred surface to ash. "And now?"

"Now, it's like you said. I'm pissed, but not despairing. I mean, sure, if I'd grown up with lots of loving memories of my mom and me spending Christmases in the living room, there would be tears. Losing this house would suck. But that wasn't the situation here. I mostly spent my days picking up bottles scattered around the house to get money from the recycling center and trying to find creative ways to make beans and rice last longer until Mom got paid again. And then when I got older, I basically stayed away completely if there were guys here, which there were. A lot."

"I'm aware."

I nodded, scanning the scorch marks on the ceiling. "So yeah, honestly, Demonella did me a favor. But she's still a fucking bitch."

He snorted, then moved to the closet. "There's nothing in here, I'm afraid. Your clothes didn't survive."

"Great." I shook my head. "Claire will be thrilled. She's already offered to take me shopping at a half-dozen stores this weekend. She insists my new wardrobe will be tax-deductible since my current one was destroyed in the line of duty."

"She makes a good point." He knocked his fist against the next wall, causing another layer of strange sigils and rambling script to shatter into dust.

I watched the smoke rise, then slanted him a look. "What is the message they sent you, anyway? It seems like a long one."

"It's not, really. It's more variations on the same theme. Demons aren't known for their creativity."

"Mm. And that theme?"

"We can get through to the Soos' side here. The wall is— well…"

He demonstrated by rapping a final time, and the drywall in the back of the closet completely dissolved, showing an open space on the other side. "Apparently, the Soos didn't use this closet much," he said, ducking beneath the closet shelving and pole and proceeding into the room. I followed, but he was right. Other than a few plastic hangers—which hadn't even been warped by the heat—the closet was empty. So was the room, save for piles of white dust that were barely visible on the carpet, spread out in vaguely arc-like patterns around the—

"Oh my God," I whispered, looking up to see Lucian studying me with a grim half-smile. "This is *salt*, isn't it? They laid down salt on the other side of my room." I felt the scowl stretch my face, but I couldn't seem to wipe it away. "They laid down salt to defend themselves against me!"

"Well, probably against me, to be fair," Lucian pointed out. He gestured above the doorway, where a small plaque was affixed, written in yet another language I didn't recognize. "This is a blessing in Vietnamese. Very simple and straightfor-ward. If the salt wasn't so specific, there'd be no reason for the landlord to suspect anything was amiss other than the Soos simply not needing this room."

"Yeah." Without giving it another thought, I shuffled around the room, disrupting the salt lines and scattering them into the carpet. "I don't think we need to give him any reason to have a conversation with them about this. Assuming the rest of the house isn't the same way."

"I don't think it is," he said, dropping his hand to the door-knob. "But it's easy to check."

Our recon of the Soos' side of the duplex was brief and impressive. They had converted the downstairs utility room into a second bedroom, while the laundry units were nowhere to be found. Maybe in the basement? Still, the rest of their home looked exactly like mine, only tidier and better decorated. The Soos appeared to be a simple couple with an enormous family. And I guess it wasn't too much of a problem that they had a demon next door, since they'd lasted in the house so long.

We went back upstairs and through my room, and I grabbed a tote bag from the closet and filled it with whatever toiletries I could scavenge from the bathroom. Then I stepped into my mom's room.

Lucian watched me from the hallway. "You never went into this room if you could avoid it. And you'd already cleaned out her belongings for Steve."

"I know," I said. He was right, of course. There really wasn't anything personal of my mom's in this room, not anymore. Other than her afghan, there was nothing left to remember her by. "She did her best, I guess."

"She prayed that she would miscarry," Lucian pointed out.

"I didn't say her best was all that great." Still, the observation gave me the boost I needed to walk out of the room for the last time.

Downstairs, I grabbed what I could find of Steve's belongings along with his slightly charred go-bag, and filled my tote bag with whatever schoolbooks and supplies I could find that had survived the fire. Lucian didn't even let me walk into the kitchen, declaring that he should have set that room on fire years ago, and we made it outside in another few minutes.

Mr. Graves, now off his phone, waved me over. "It's going to take some time to get it ready again. You'll be compensated for your rent for three months, though I'm hoping it'll take far less time than that."

"And the Soos? How long until they're able to get back in the house?"

He scratched his chin. "Probably about a month, all in. They'll also be compensated for their inconvenience, but the fire marshal says that their side of the house wasn't damaged much. Still need to rebuild the wall, paint, that sort of thing. They indicated they wanted to return. They asked about your side of the duplex, whether you would return. I guess they have family who were asking about it."

"Oh. Well, I mean I hadn't really thought about it, but I guess...if it's going to take three months or whatever, maybe I should um, find another place? I mean if you're going to have no problem renting it out again?"

He shrugged. "Up to you. Absolutely no pressure. Honestly, the place needed to be updated, but it was way down on the list of priorities. This all sort of came together like an act of God, you know? I mean, especially since nobody got seriously hurt. I am sorry about your stuff though. Smoke damage is a hell of a thing, even if the fire didn't get it."

"Yeah, well, you said that CG&E was going to pay to fix it up?"

"The amount they're giving me, I can fix up three or four places, yeah. And they said they'd pay you to replace all the contents inside—didn't even bat an eye." He shook his head, turning to look at the duplex with an expression of pure astonishment on his face. "Hell of a thing."

I joined him for a last, long look.

The duplex looked strangely small, shrunken in the late morning sun, the scorch marks radiating out from my side making it look like rotten fruit. I could almost imagine the flies buzzing around it, carrion feeders looking to pick over the remains of my childhood. I told myself I didn't care—and I didn't care. My mother had never wanted me, had resented me from the moment she'd realized she was carrying me in her belly. This house had sheltered me, sure, but it had also been the scene of the crime against my body, my spirit, the worn-out dwelling of a worn-out girl hauling a demon around. Maybe it was glad I was finally gone. Maybe it was tired too.

"It sure is," I agreed.

After I gave Mr. Graves the address of the office for any mail forwarding and worked through a few more details, I followed Lucian to the car. Not surprisingly, Sergei's truck had pulled up behind it, and the big man leaned against the passenger door, keeping watch. I waved to him as we approached.

"Give your boss a call, would you?"

NINETEEN

LUCIAN

Lucian slid a glance toward Delia, taking in the line of her jaw, the tight curve of her lips. Just watching her provided a simple joy he didn't know he was capable of. After so many years of seeing her in the mirror, watching her through her own eyes, to see her like this as a separate person, apart and away from him, was still unnerving.

If he were a human, or even a marginally less-depraved demon, he would seek to protect her. To keep her at that distance, and especially far away from the world he inhabited. Instead, he was driving with her to meet one of its darkest inhabitants.

Not a demon, of course. Nikolai Volkov was many things: a criminal, a murderer, a bastard drunk on his own power, money, and authority, but he wasn't a demon. Delia had managed to compartmentalize her activities in Volkov's club the night that she had rescued Steve from the creatures who had wanted to party with him.

Steve had been a tactical error on Lucian's part. He hadn't realized that she'd felt anything for her housemate other than reassurance that she wasn't in the duplex alone. He hadn't thought of her as having friends. She'd never made any attempt to have friends. He supposed that's what came of being possessed since you were ten years old, and the most adult person in the room until your mother died when you were seventeen.

A short, earthy curse drew him back to the present. Delia shifted beside him, shaking her head. "This is some bullshit," she muttered, glancing up from her phone as she felt his gaze. "It's not only ads now, it's articles. Articles that look pretty damn legitimate to me, about deaths over the past few days. All the Meadowbrook kids. Each one dying in more disgusting ways than the last. It can't be true. None of that can be true. But how is she even doing it? And am I the only one seeing these, or are their parents seeing them too?"

"That's an interesting idea," Lucian acknowledged as she scrolled to her message app and stabbed out a text, undoubtedly to Claire to ask her to find out if there was any truth to the stories of the children's untimely ends. "If this is a new ability that Asmodaea is exploring, it's entirely possible that you're one of a select few who are being fed this specific information. She can watch your reactions quite easily, anywhere there's a camera."

Delia made a face. "That's science fiction. Technology isn't to that level yet."

"Generally, publicly available technology is likely not so advanced, no. But cameras deployed for governmental purposes absolutely are. And there are more of them than you probably think. Regardless, we know that Asmodaea has eyes on you. It would not be difficult for her to track your reactions, especially if she has access to your phone—which she clearly does." He gestured to it. "You should probably get rid of that."

"It's my phone," she grumbled. "It's how people get a hold of me. And all she has to do is fuck with the next one and the one after that. Jesus. If she's got this kind of capability, could she download stuff to my devices? Like, could she put a whole bunch of porn on my laptop? How do you protect against a demon virus, anyway? This is some seriously fucked up shit if she's building this kind of power. Like, how is this even possible? She's a *demon,* not some kind of technological wunderkind."

"She doesn't have to be a wunderkind," he countered. "She only has to enter the minds of those who are. And deploy her lieutenants into their networks."

"Yeah, but we're not talking a dark entity shoving couches across the room here," Delia said. "We're talking computer networks, building security, hell—air traffic control. If she figures out how to do this on her own, which she clearly has, nobody's ever going to be safe again. How do you contain a demon?"

He glanced at her. "You don't. We've had this conversation before."

"Yes, we have. So you know that *killing* demons isn't actually part of the exorcism playbook. I get them out of things and send them on their way. That's how this works."

He shrugged. "It doesn't have to be how this works. I could kill them. I could also kill the humans they possess, which is sometimes even more effective."

She frowned, staring out the window. "Mordechai never killed. He said that wasn't something that any creature made by God should do."

"Mordechai is also dead," Lucian countered, the words

coming out a little harsher than he intended. But Delia needed to understand that the world she was now navigating was far more complicated than she realized. Far more complicated than he certainly had understood while he had been trapped within her.

And he *had* been trapped. He hadn't realized that until he'd read screed after screed of ancient script on Delia's walls, sneering at him, mocking him for what he'd refused to admit to himself. He'd been caught in a snare so completely, he hadn't even seen it snap shut.

The messages had been variations on a theme, as he'd told Delia. But he hadn't shared the theme itself: *Caught by a human child. Released by a mortal girl. Palemerious the Devourer, reduced to nursemaid and guardian.*

Crude, repetitive, meant to sting. Written in the oldest demon tongues so that any who saw them would know— seventh-level Palemerious had been trapped and exorcised by a human.

The horde knew that much. What they didn't know was how. They assumed she'd caught him in some brief possession, exorcised him, sent him on his way. Standard work. Humiliating for a commander of his rank, but not unthinkable.

They didn't know he'd been inside Delia for fifteen years. That she'd held him longer than any human should have been able to. That he'd seen through her eyes, touched with her hands, lived every moment of her life. That the shedim now guarding her wasn't some fourth-level servant—it was him, walking in flesh he'd helped forge from shadow and will.

The deception was already fraying. Volkov knew the truth. Mirr had felt his power at Walsh's office. Jillian's demon had circled him, sensing darkness she couldn't quite place. And Asmodaea—those messages on the walls were proof she was putting pieces together, even if she didn't have the full picture yet.

He would have to reveal himself. Soon. Not because he wanted to, but because Delia needed the horde to know. When the war came—and it was coming, Asmodaea's little stunt with the Warriors of Darkyn game proved that—Delia also needed every demon in Chicago to understand she wasn't just protected by some disposable shedim. She had *Palemerious* on her side. A seventh-level commander who would burn anyone foolish enough to touch her.

Let them mock him for being caught by a mortal. He'd spent fifteen years inside the one human who could stand against them all. And if that made him weak in their eyes, so be it.

He knew the truth. He'd been exactly where he needed to be.

That being said… There was quite a bit about ex-Rabbi Mordechai he still needed to learn.

"Seriously?" Delia leaned forward and squinted, craning her head as Lucian passed their destination and found parking on the street. "We're meeting him at another nightclub? Are these places even open during the day?"

The entryway to the Onyx was sandwiched between two high-end clothiers, its door set into a deep black swath of marble and its name appearing on a stainless steel placard.

"Steve hasn't been here?" Lucian asked. "He gave me the impression of wanting to try every club in the city."

"Steve probably *has* been here," she said. "But he's still heads down in the game, and I didn't want to distract him."

The door buzzed and slid open as they approached, allowing them into a vestibule with another security door on the other side. Through the glass, they could see a doorman click another button, and the second doorway slid open as well. Once they entered the foyer, Delia barked out a short laugh.

"They have full-time security at a club that's only open at night?" she asked, taking in the security officer's uniform as well as his desk, which was the club's hostess stand.

The guard, a heavily built man in his early thirties, merely grinned. "I go where the job takes me," he said, nodding to them. "Mr. Volkov will see you in the main bar."

They followed where he gestured, and within a few moments, they found Volkov sitting in a leather-tufted round banquette, a drink and some books sitting before him on the round table. He was dressed in a dark suit and a deep red shirt, his hair brushed back from his hard-angled face. He gestured them to sit, and his gaze met Lucian's briefly before sliding to Delia's—long enough for Lucian to confirm that no new demon writhed within him. Pity.

"Sergei said you were ready to learn more," Volkov began. "That's good. Things are moving too quickly for you to remain in the dark." His gaze flicked to Lucian. "And while I respect your desire to remain under the radar, the time for that has also passed."

"They know who I am."

"They do." Volkov nodded briefly.

"And by 'they', I assume you mean the demon horde?" Delia put her elbows on the table. "Or just our little corner of it?"

In response, Volkov sat back in his chair, a small smile playing about his mouth. His attitude toward Delia made every shedim-enhanced nerve quiver within Lucian, but the bastard didn't seem to realize how close he was to death. "It's dangerous for you to know these things, but more dangerous for you to remain ignorant. Still, not all of what I am going to say is going to be easy to hear."

"Cut to the chase, Volkov," Lucian said, fighting the urge to roll his eyes. Despite the human's usefulness, he could only endure so much.

Another nod. "I'll start with my role, then, and expand outward."

"Your role?" Delia asked. "What do you mean? You don't have a role. You're not a demon, and you're not possessed anymore."

"Both statements are patently true," Volkov said, lifting a glass to toast in an obvious salute to her part in that. "The more nuanced truth is that I should never have *been* possessed. I'm what's known as a Hallow, someone who can walk among the demon horde, but not be harmed by them. Most Hallows are born that way, but others are nearly taken, then rescued at the last minute."

"Like Steve," Delia said.

"Like your friend Steve, yes. He wasn't intended to be possessed that night, merely used as entertainment, but because he wasn't sanctified as off limits, he could have been taken. You ensured he wasn't, then and evermore."

"Entertainment," Delia muttered, but Volkov kept going.

"As a Hallow, I also should never have been possessed by Pithius, but as I mentioned, there were debts to be paid. While I won't put myself in that position again, it did prove instructive. And as I continue my work in the demon realm, it has already given me a certain understanding that I didn't previously possess. All things for a reason."

"Uh-huh." Delia narrowed her eyes at him. "What work are you doing with the demon realm?"

"In the course of my line of work, there are any number of syndicates one must navigate to achieve one's goals. Looked at with that lens, the demon world is simply another syndicate, and quite a lucrative one. They have needs for goods and services, much like any other organization, and they handsomely reward anyone who is able to provide them with what they want."

Delia made a face. "What they want. You mean like people?"

"Not as human cattle, no. Give me a little credit." Volkov's lips twisted. "But, when you're dealing with a society that's been trapped here since the Fall, entertainment is a premium they're willing to pay for."

He didn't look at Lucian when he said this. He could have. Lucian had trafficked more than his share of humans over the centuries, as Volkov undoubtedly knew. Yet he chose, in this moment, to hold that information back.

Interesting.

"Like the people in the club," Delia said. "You called Steve entertainment, but there's no way he signed up for that."

"Steve, I have come to understand, should never have been in the private salons. He came in with a scrum of performers who were well compensated for the night's activities. He would have been taken eventually, but you came in and saved him—saved me, as well."

"A debt you haven't repaid in full," Lucian pointed out.

Volkov smiled. "Far from it. And perhaps not one that I ever will." He matched Lucian's stare directly, but if Delia noticed the spike of energy between them, she gave no indication.

"What do you know about Finn Ashford?" she asked instead. "Anything at all?"

"Quite a bit, as it turns out. His story is one of those conspiracy theories that actually appears to have some merit. It's not only the gamers who believe that he didn't take his own life, and that he may not actually be dead. The demon courts do as well."

He glanced at Lucian. "Have you told her anything about the hierarchy? You're going to have to, eventually."

Lucian shrugged. "Her education isn't your concern."

"Give me the topline." Delia held her hand up. "And I don't want to get out graph paper right now, so try to keep it simple."

"Very well." Volkov's eyes went a little hooded as he thought. "There are seven major courts of demons. Within each court, there are seven levels of demons, which follow a distinct caste system. The lines go from exalted—seventh level, to base—first level. The fourth line, right in the middle, is the closest to humans. This level is where you'll find the shedim."

He shifted his gaze again to Lucian. "How are you enjoying your stint as a shedim, Palemerious? I understand the form is not as resilient as you might want."

Lucian bared his teeth. "On the contrary, I have found them to be suitable for even the most rigorous of activities. And it's Lucian now. Forget that at your peril."

"Why should I care about the fourth line being closest to humans?" Delia interrupted. "That feels important."

"It is," Volkov said. "We work a lot with the shedim. They serve as competent messengers and carriers into places humans shouldn't go. They are also avowed gamblers and gamers. The fourth level of every court loose in the city has long believed that Finn was taken by members of Samael's court, the Court of Ruin—no one knows why. But Mirr is spawn of that same court, and he's a fifth-level demon. And, of course, Asmodaea is its commander here in Chicago."

"Right." Delia made a face. "I'm going to need graph paper, aren't I?"

"No. You need only know that the Court of Ruin has long denied any involvement in Finn's disappearance until a few days ago. Several of their demons have been chattering these last few days, however. They're saying Finn is in Mirr's machine."

"Mirr's machine," Lucian echoed. "Not Asmodaea's?"

"Not Asmodaea's," Volkov said, tilting his glass to him. "Which you can bet she doesn't like."

"But they're both in service to the same guy, right?"

"Yes, but Asmodaea is seventh line, same as Pal—Lucian was, for all that he's currently borrowing a shedim's form." Volkov bared his teeth again. "They are a proud set, and don't take competition lightly. What's more, the shedim are now saying that Finn Ashford did not commit suicide five years ago. Instead, he discovered what Asmodaea was up to, and she learned that he was trying to shut down her efforts. She intervened, he disappeared, and Kieran Walsh has been playing catch-up ever since. According to the information that *someone* has leaked these past few days, she didn't kill Finn but somehow hooked him into the system as an organic processor, lending his neural patterns to make the AI seem more human in its interactions, and making the kind of split-second decisions that make Reflex so successful.

"Five years," Delia muttered. "Can he be saved, then? Can we get him out of there?"

Lucian glanced at her. "If there's anything left to be saved, yes."

"There has to be." Her statement left no room for argument.

"If he's still alive, Asmodaea won't let you take him," Volkov pointed out. "She needs him."

"Yeah, well, she doesn't get a vote." Delia glanced down at her phone as it buzzed. "Jesus." She turned the phone toward Lucian. It showed a news photo of a fire-consumed body bag. "This fucking had better not be real."

"You know it's not real."

"Yeah, well, it's starting to creep me out. I've gotta call Claire." She bit her lip as a new text arrived. "Like, right now."

She slid out of the booth and stalked away as they watched her. "You're playing a dangerous game, Lucian," Volkov said quietly.

"One could say the same for you," Lucian said. "You'd do well to remember—"

"*What?*" Delia's demand ripped across the room, and they both looked up to see her standing stock-still, one hand lifted as if to ward off an attacker as the other smashed her phone to her ear. "What do you mean she got a suicide note? Where—how?"

She whirled and stared at Lucian across the room. "*Fuck* that," she seethed. "Now they really are pissing me off. Tell Victoria we're on our way."

TWENTY

Lucian and I debriefed on the way back to the office, which turned into mostly me processing everything out loud. "We've got to take care of this right now," I said, for easily the fifteenth time. "If Reflex is allowed any more access, I don't know that we're going to be able to stop it from getting its hooks into the entire city's infrastructure. And if other cities start using Prometheus technology, how is that going to work? It's possessed! We can't have a demon-possessed AI getting plugged into every major network in the country. Like, what are they even doing? And why hasn't this been done already?"

I turned to him. "It hasn't, right? We're not currently being secretly manipulated by demon-infested infrastructure, are we?"

"It would explain a great deal of what we're seeing in the global news," Lucian pointed out.

"You're not serious. Are you serious?" I demanded, and he gave me a pitying smile.

"Delia, no. As much as humans would like to believe that

there is a method to the madness of demons, I assure you, there is not. Asmodaea is arguably different in that she has always been keen on creating structures to advance the penetration and influence of the horde. She's the one who has infiltrated the camps of generals. She has touched the minds behind some of history's most calculated wars and political coups. But she can only do so much. Volkov was correct in that there are seven levels of demons in each court, and the seventh is the last rung before overlord."

"Where you and Asmodaea hang out."

"Yes. But overlords do exist, a set of seven princes who control each court. Samael is the demon at the top of Asmodaea's order, and while he may be ultimately behind her actions, he also may not. She may be slowly gathering power so that she can knock him from his perch."

"She could do that?"

"If she's very strong, yes. But it's a treacherous risk. A demon who fails is sent to the lowest level and must begin the long process of crawling up through the ranks again, with every nasty, slithering creature knowing of her failure. Asmodaea would make the attempt at her peril."

We reached the office, and as we climbed the stairs, I thought about it. There was something about Lucian's explanation that didn't quite sync for me, but I couldn't pinpoint what. Then we walked into the office and my gaze leapt to the three giant computer monitors Steve had set up on his desk and Claire's, all of them playing different YouTube videos.

"What's this?" I asked as I entered, and Claire turned excitedly.

"Steve has gone above and beyond," she said. "Actually, they all have. You know how Reflex got its first big publicity, at least in the circles that count, with that Saint Patrick's Day bomb scare back in 2020? And how later it came out that there was no actual bomb, but hey, it didn't matter because it tested the system and everybody turned out okay? Well, come to find out, that wasn't the only false alarm."

Steve picked up the ball and ran with it. "Honestly, it was the fire at the house that really made me think about it." He switched the screens to other YouTube videos, and then still more, the flow of them too fast for me to track. "Sorry, I don't mean for you to watch these, I'm just grabbing them for analysis later. But bottom line, Chicago has had no less than three dozen flash fires in the last few years, all of them quickly resolved with the energy company assuming guilt and paying handsomely. What do you think the likelihood is that we could track the actual payments as originating straight out of Prometheus Solutions? They've been moving so fast, it would be easy to bury those kinds of outlays."

"It would make sense," Lucian said thoughtfully. "The system creates the crisis and then solves it, positioning Prometheus as the solution, quite literally. It's a win-win all around."

"Well, not really a win," Claire pointed out. "I mean, people were traumatized in those fires. They didn't know that they were manufactured, they thought they were the real deal. There's a lot of psychological cleanup that needs to happen after that—and why do I think that particular cost isn't reflected in the bottom line of these 'false alarms'?"

"But that's what's going to happen more and more," I said, staring at the screens. "The system has been proven to work. Hell, we pissed her off yesterday, and she had my duplex in ashes within twenty-four hours. How scary would it be if the system got into the wrong human hands? And would it be any scarier than it staying in demon hands?"

I turned to Lucian. "This is what has been bugging me. Are demons *actually* power-hungry for human power? Or do you guys just enjoy fighting amongst yourselves?"

Before he was able to answer, the sound of clicking heels in the outside corridor cut across the room. We fell silent as Victoria Ashford appeared in the doorway, looking exhausted. Her hair was no longer sprightly and coiffed but pressed to her head. Her suit was still professional, but wrinkled, and her face was haggard. She straightened, stepped forward, and handed me a sealed envelope.

"I couldn't look at it anymore. It was too difficult," she said. "And it's only part of the day's problems. I think you should know what's going on."

Claire and I exchanged a startled glance, but Victoria didn't wait for my acknowledgment to continue. "I've had a small internal team investigating irregularities in the Reflex system for the past few weeks. Our last stress test was a rousing success, yet the system has started to behave erratically. We've been seeing an uptick of grid disruptions, and we suspect that it's tied to Reflex."

"Did you know that the Saint Patrick's Day bomb was a hoax?" I asked her quietly.

She sighed, but she clearly knew what I was talking about. "Not at first, no. At first, we all believed what the data told us. There was a credible threat to attendees at the parade, we evacuated, and the threat was proven to be false. Eventually, it became clear that the communications generated to alert authorities to the threat had been fabricated by Reflex. The next step in its development was stress testing, so it simply had to create the stress. Walsh assured us that the AI had merely gotten out over its skis and that it wasn't a problem. It was a feature, not a bug, as he is fond of saying. We all heard what we wanted to hear, and nobody talked about it again. And then, of course, Finn died. After that, I deliberately didn't want to involve myself too much for fear of appearing to meddle, lost in my own grief. But I had my suspicions. Then, a few months ago, Walsh started behaving erratically at exactly the wrong time. That almost made me feel like things were normal, right? That the AI had simply been fallible in the hands of a man under extreme amounts of stress. But I don't think that's the situation."

She blew out a long breath. "As I said, my small team has credible data to support the idea of manufactured stress tests across multiple areas of exposure, from traffic lights to the airport to hospital networks and more. It's even tied into the financial sector. We were opening discussions on how to proceed when I received this new suicide note. And of course there's also this."

She reached into her bag and pulled out a second document, this one worn and folded.

"What's this?" I asked as she handed it over.

She smiled wearily. "This isn't the first suicide note that I received. And you'll notice the first one is handwritten, not typed."

I opened the document, and the few lines it hosted were brief and scrawled. I read it aloud. "I can't see myself anymore. The reflections won't stop watching me. Mom, I'm sorry. I tried to get out. I tried to stop it."

"Whoa, whoa, whoa…" Steve said abruptly. "Mei, you got that?"

"Dead on!" came Mei's excited voice over the speakers. Victoria looked startled.

"Who's that?" she demanded.

"Gamer team," Steve said proudly. "Best in the city. That

language in that letter? Finn may have written it to you, but we've also heard it in Warriors of Darkyn. 'I'm sorry, Mom' is practically his mantra."

"But...how?" she goggled. "How is that possible?"

"That, we can't help you with," Steve said, as I opened the more recent letter—the one Victoria had sealed into an envelope. I frowned.

"This isn't a suicide note as much as a confession," I said. "I can't face it anymore, it's gotten too big, and I can't manage the stress. I take full responsibility for the failed tests on Watkins Street, Mill Valley, and the Grammarcy nursing home. Thank God there was no harm done, but those surges were my fault. The system is too important to allow my weakness to undermine its success. I'm sorry, Mom. I love you."

I looked at Victoria. "I assume these are some of the failed tests from right around the time of the Saint Patrick's Day bomb?"

"That's the problem," she said, making a face. "There *were* no failed tests in those locations. Watkins Street is a million-dollar neighborhood of old stately homes, Mill Valley is a technology center on the outskirts of town, and the nursing home, well—it's a nursing home. We've scoured the system and the energy company's historical data. There's been no disruption of service to any of those locations at any time over the last five years."

"So it's a prediction," Rook said over the speakers, making Victoria jump again.

"How many people are online?" she asked sharply.

"Just three," Claire began, but Anya broke in excitedly from another speaker.

"Oh my gosh, I think you're right! What if he's warning us of tests that are going to fail? As a way of proving he's real?"

Victoria rubbed her forehead. "I can't—" she sighed. "If

Finn were here, he would think this all the grandest of games. These kinds of easter eggs were the things that he lived for."

I knew I shouldn't do it, but I couldn't help myself.

"We don't think Finn is dead, Victoria." I said the words quietly, but with absolute certainty. "We think he's alive, trapped in the system. And we think we can get him out."

"What?" She froze, her voice going breathy. "What are you talking about? I've heard all the conspiracy theories, Delia, and I've come to terms with his death."

"Well, maybe you should think about undoing some of those thoughts," Steve said. "We're hearing things, man, it's happening more and more. Check it, Mei?"

"Roger that," she said. A second later, a different voice came over the speakers, and Victoria went rigid. "The walls have eyes, man. Eyes and ears. Whoever's here is watching you—get out as fast as you can. No left, no right. Just out."

"That's—that's Finn's voice," she said. "But that can be digitized, can't it? What if the system—the game—is simply trying to trick you?"

"It's possible," Steve said, but I turned on Victoria.

"Even if you're right, Victoria, we can use this. We should use this. Between you getting an 'obviously faked' suicide note predicting future failures and gamers hearing Finn's voice in the system, in the game, it introduces a level of instability, right? Would that be enough for Prometheus Solutions to call off the rollout in a couple of days?"

"I don't see how," she said glumly. "There's so much money riding on this, and so many people in positions of power who want to see it move forward. A delay would be devastating to Prometheus Solutions, but it would be even more embarrassing to the people who are supporting the company."

"Unless they could come out smelling like a rose for being

super careful and wanting to protect their constituents, yeah?" Steve put in. "Check this out."

He pulled up another website, this one boldly announcing a new podcast from Dark Streets, which billed itself as "a true crime/conspiracy podcast, by Chicago for Chicago."

"What's this?" I asked. "You know these people?"

"Oh, I remember them," Victoria said, a tiny bit of color returning to her face. "I think there are some hardcore gamers in their group."

"You got that right," Steve said. He played several clips about Finn, each more strident than the last, but all carrying the same theme: no way had Finn Ashford taken his own life.

"These guys caused quite a stir back in 2020, and if we happen to bring them new evidence that maybe Finn is alive? That could get things rolling in a hurry," he continued. "This community is primed to believe, they have reach, and they're not controlled by Prometheus Solutions' PR department—at least not yet. If we move fast..."

"You would need to move fast," Lucian said. "While Reflex may be embedded in traditional channels, I suspect it's not established in these sorts of indie operations. The economies of scale simply aren't there."

"Bingo," Steve said. "So we can take everyone by surprise and blow it up. I bet I could get traction on this within the next twenty-four—maybe forty-eight hours, at the outside."

Victoria looked at him and smiled. "You remind me so much of him, you know? Finn would have loved working with you."

To my utter shock, Steve flushed to the roots of his hair. I was about to call this out when my own phone rang. I glanced down, then jolted. The caller ID read Officer Hernandez.

The police officer who'd investigated Mordechai's death... then stayed around long enough to help me exorcise a few demons at Max Graham's house. She was one of the good guys, but...damn, her timing sucked.

"I need to take this," I said, as Lucian's gaze moved to me.

I stepped out into the hallway and walked a few paces before answering. "This is Delia," I said, too brightly.

"Delia, hey. This call is not actually happening, but I wanted to give you a heads-up before anything becomes official, okay?"

I blinked, my voice going flat again. "Sure. Are you okay?"

She laughed. "Still the same old Delia, always worried about everything except for what you should be. I'm fine, but the department has received several videos and reports related to some seance or shit you did at Prometheus Solutions' head-quarters, jeopardizing their CEO Kieran Walsh, and threatening his events manager."

I stared at the phone in shock. "*What*?"

"Yeah, I figured that's how you would react, but you need to know from the people who are looking at it that so far, it looks legit. Obviously, in today's day and age, that's getting tougher to prove, but the department's got questions and I thought you might want to come up with some answers, right? A former partner of mine is on the case, Marcus Walsh."

My stomach spasmed. "Walsh? As in—"

"Yep, same family. Kieran's his nephew."

I stared at the wall, my mind stuttering with confusion. Walsh. Kieran's uncle. Coming here because Kieran—because Mirr—had called in a favor.

"But how..."

"How'd we end up with the family connection? Dunno, but Walsh is a stand-up guy. He's also kind of an asshat, but he means well. He works Special Investigations, the CPD unit that handles everything too strange for Patrol and too early for Homicide—missing executives, corporate threats, and the cases that look like something is about to go very, very wrong. Now he's pulled your ticket, and he'll be coming your way tonight. Again, just wanted to give you a heads-up. Unofficially."

She rang off without waiting for a reply, and I turned slowly back to the office, only to see Claire poking her head out the door.

"Everything okay?" she asked.

"Yeah, but we should get the office cleaned up," I told her. "I think the police are on their way."

TWENTY-ONE

Claire took over almost immediately after I told her what was going on. With the precision of a drill sergeant, she got Steve to take down the monitors and move them into my office, bullied Lucian and Steve out the door—never mind they both towered over her and one was a seventh-level commander of the Ravening Court—and even sent Victoria on her way with the warning that she would probably be next on the police's dance card.

By the time the police actually knocked on *our* door, Claire and I were chatting like two old friends, me with my shoulder against the door frame to the inner office, and her sitting at her desk. The loud, authoritative rap came after the heavy shuffle down the corridor, and she scooted around her desk and opened the door.

"Well, hello," she said, all pharmacist-cheer. "I'm sorry. Can I help you?"

The man, stocky in his fifties with a tired face and loose jowls, stared past her to me. "Delia Thompson?"

"Yes, of course," I said, making a show of noticing their officialness, though they weren't wearing uniforms. "Please come in. How can I help you?"

"And I'm Claire Bickwell," Claire put in. "I'm Delia's office manager and assistant. Can I get you anything to drink?"

"No, thank you," the man said. He held out his badge toward me, and I nodded quickly—*no need for me to confirm your credentials, sir!* "I'm Detective Marcus Walsh, Special Investigations, and this is Detective Ann Milo." The woman beside him —tall, angular, with sharp eyes that missed nothing—nodded briefly.

"Detective Walsh?" I blinked, all innocence.

He grimaced. "Before you ask—yes, Kieran Walsh is my nephew. My older brother's kid. Which is why I'm taking this particularly seriously. We're investigating an assault allegation at Prometheus Solutions, and we need to ask you some questions."

"*Assault,*" I echoed with credible surprise. "We were just there."

Marcus nodded. "I'm aware of that. And I'm aware that you were engaged as a…"

He glanced at his partner, who smiled at us. On closer inspection, I tagged her as being in her early thirties with what looked like a permanently skeptical edge to her expression. Probably something they taught her at the Academy.

"Wellness Consultant," she supplied. "Engaged to help ensure that Kieran Walsh was sufficiently prepared for his extremely stressful upcoming slot of meetings."

"That's right," Claire said. "Delia and I and a third associate, Lucian Gray, visited the offices of Prometheus Solutions two days ago. What's this about? I was there on site, so I'm happy to answer any questions you may have as well."

Walsh pulled out a tablet and set it on the desk between us.

"We received a formal complaint on behalf of Mr. Walsh alleging that you assaulted him during a wellness session."

"I most certainly did not," I said staunchly. "That's not at all what happened."

"Then what did happen?" Detective Milo asked.

I tightened my lips. I couldn't exactly say the truth in this particular situation—exorcists didn't tell tales out of school. "I think you understand that sessions are confidential, but I can assure you..."

"This might make things easier," Walsh said. He powered on the tablet and played the video. From the camera angle, it looked like standard security video footage of Walsh's meditation suite. Claire and I were clearly visible, but Lucian wasn't in the frame.

"I thought you said there was a third associate with you?" Milo asked.

"He was," I said slowly. "I'm not sure why he's not on the screen. He should be." The two of them exchanged a look, then the video started. In quick succession, Walsh stood back as if startled, and I lunged at him, forcing him down with Claire approaching from behind me, holding a syringe. She handed the syringe over to me and I plunged it into Walsh's chest. I gasped.

"What is *this*?" I asked, genuinely horrified.

"That's you, correct? And that's Ms. Bickwell with the syringe?"

I glanced over at Claire, and she was doing an incredible job of looking equally flabbergasted. "It's Dr. Bickwell, actually," she clarified. "When I'm not helping Delia, I'm a pharmacist at Reider's Pharmacy, and I can assure you a false video of me handing a loaded syringe to an untrained civilian isn't an accusation I take lightly. Who gave you this video?"

Finally, I noticed a smudge in the corner of the feed, vaguely manlike but distorted and rough. Lucian, it had to be, but was that what Lucian looked like on camera?

Fortunately, Claire remained focused on the issue at hand.

She leaned forward and studied the video carefully. "Can you play that again? Slow it down at the, ah, forty-seven-second mark?"

Detective Walsh scowled, but he complied, and Claire tapped the side of the tablet. "That syringe angle. You see how Delia is holding it? That's a direct plunge into Mr. Walsh's chest cavity."

Detective Milo nodded. "Which is exactly our concern."

"No, no. You don't understand. As I said, I'm a licensed pharmacist. You can check with Reider's for verification, but, bottom line, I know my way around syringes. If I'd handed her that one and she'd administered it that way, Kieran Walsh would be dead."

That got their attention. "Explain," said Detective Walsh.

Claire might not be wearing a doctor's jacket, but she had all the rest of the act down. She pointed authoritatively at the screen. "That trajectory? She's going through the intercostal space directly toward the heart. If that syringe contained anything—sedative, medication, even air—he'd have a cardiac tamponade or an embolism. That means dead or pretty near it, detective. He'd be in the ICU or the morgue, not sending you videos of his session. May I?"

Walsh gestured for her to proceed, and she leaned toward the iPad, zooming in on the syringe. "Also, look at my hand position here. I'm holding the syringe by the plunger, for God's sake. That's not the way you pass someone a loaded syringe. I know that's probably a very minor detail, but this video was fabricated, Detective Walsh. Even if I wanted to lose my license over a wellness session at Prometheus Solutions, which I assure you, I do not, there are certain things that I simply would never do. Handing off a syringe that way is one of them."

Milo exchanged a glance with Walsh, then Walsh pinned her with a glare. "You're saying Prometheus Solutions falsified security footage?"

"That I can't tell you," Claire said, straightening. "However, I can say that the video they sent to you is showing a scene that's medically impossible. Unless Walsh died and came back, this didn't happen the way it appears."

I struck while they were processing this. "Victoria Ashford hired me to perform a wellness session with Mr. Walsh. That much is absolutely true. He has a biohacking kit, which is the box that you see there, containing intravenous vitamins, adaptogens, and ketamine for therapeutic use, etcetera. That box was opened during the session, and Mr. Walsh became agitated, shoving the box to the side."

"Agitated, why?" Milo asked quickly.

"Well, it wasn't agitated-agitated, it was honestly more animated-agitated," I clarified. "He got very excited, and he wanted us to get excited with him. He wanted us to participate in a high-energy jumping practice which...wasn't exactly my thing."

"But he proceeded anyway," Claire said. She held up both hands. "Not my thing either, but he was the client. Is the client. Because he's not dead."

"What *is* your thing?" Marcus asked. "From the research we've done, you bill yourself as an exorcism consultant. That's a few steps above wellness guru, wouldn't you say?"

"Everyone's needs are different," I returned smoothly. "But Mr. Walsh *did* get injured, you're absolutely correct. He broke a vial and crushed it with his hand. He bled. And Claire, with her pharmaceutical knowledge, did inject him in his upper torso with a sedative. Not where this image is indicating, but I'm sure if you examine him, you'll see the syringe mark."

"Up here," Claire put in, tapping a point near her collarbone. "He was flailing, and I needed enough mass to inject without harming him."

"You injected him with his own sedative," Detective Milo said dubiously. "He gave you permission to do that?"

Claire waved that off. "He was a danger to himself and others. I felt I had no choice. And it was a commercially packaged sedative that I have used routinely in my own practice. I had no reason to think that it was anything other than what it was labeled."

"Uh-huh. And what happened then?"

"Then he stopped flailing," I said. "He collapsed on the ground, security showed up, and we cleared the room. From everything that I've heard from Mrs. Ashford, he recovered quite well. Apparently, he has been known to become... excitable. We hadn't been appropriately briefed."

The two of them exchanged glances, and Walsh closed the tablet. He leaned back on his scuffed heels. "We'll need to verify your credentials, Dr. Bickwell, and we'll need both of you to come down to the station for a formal statement, but tomorrow is fine for that."

"Are we under arrest?" I asked.

He gave me a thin smile. "If you were, then tomorrow would not be suitable for you to make a statement. Right now, we're gathering facts, and we're going to need to visit Mr. Walsh. I'm sure we'll find his statement extremely useful."

They were almost out the door when Walsh turned, looked back. "If the video is doctored, somebody went to an awful lot of trouble," he rumbled. "Why do you think someone would do that?"

I lifted my hands. "I don't know. Victoria Ashford hired me.

She's the one who arranged the session. I assume she's not the one who sent you the video footage? Walsh's events manager, Jillian Reeves, was the first person in the room after the session ended, and she saw everything."

Neither one of them reacted to the name of Jillian, but I knew in my bones that was where this video was coming from. I just didn't know why, precisely—other than, of course, to discredit me down to my toes.

They left, and Claire shut the door quietly, then turned back to me with wide eyes. "That video..." she whispered.

I waved her back to her desk and I sat at Steve's. "They may have eyes on this place for a little bit," I said, keeping my voice down. "We probably shouldn't leave right away. As far as they knew, we weren't simply hanging around waiting for them to show up. We had actual work to do."

"Yes, well, I think this work deserves some medicinal support," Claire said. She opened the door of the mini fridge by her desk and pulled out a box of white wine. "Join me?"

"Gladly." I waited until we both had glasses, then tilted mine toward her. "That was some impressive and highly authoritative bullshit you were spinning there. You're pretty good at this."

She grimaced a little sadly, staring down at her glass. "Well, this isn't my first rodeo with the police."

I blinked at her. Of all the things that could have come out of Claire's mouth, that was the last thing I expected. "What?"

She took a robust pull of her wine, then regarded her glass for a long minute. "I was a senior in high school, desperate for a scholarship. It was my only path to college. For whatever reason, I was chosen as the sacrificial lamb to the bullying practices of the local queen bee and her head sycophant. Their names don't matter, but they were horrible. Physical intimidation, blackmail, the whole nine yards. They forced me to do their homework, threatened me with violence if I refused, then threatened to rat me out once I finally helped them. I felt trapped. I could report them, but then I knew I was going to face more retaliation. I could just go along with it, but it was getting to the point where my own grades were starting to suffer. And I couldn't risk that. I needed to get out of that small town more than anything in the world."

By now I was staring. "What did you do?"

She looked up at me. "I drugged them with an untraceable knockout compound and exposed them to a lab pathogen we were experimenting with. It appeared, as it was later reported, a senior prank gone wrong with Petri dishes accidentally knocked over and spores released."

"Your senior prank?" I goggled.

"Oh, God no. No, I set it up so that it was their experiment and that I was to be the recipient of the spores. Instead, they got hit with the exposure early."

"Which you knew wouldn't kill them."

She shrugged. "I knew it shouldn't kill them, yeah. But it still did enough. They were quarantined at the hospital for four weeks, which took me to the end of the school year. I was able to take my finals, graduate valedictorian, and flee before they ever got out of the hospital. School officials decided nobody was to blame, and by the time they got out, their own recollection was pretty fuzzy. The knockout drugs I used were pretty good."

I was back to staring again. "That's freaking brilliant."

She snorted a little grimly. "Well, it was certainly felonious. And I didn't fight fair. I used my knowledge to harm, not to help, and it scared me. I was afraid to pursue straight-up science-science after that, in case this ever came back on me, so instead I went into pharmaceuticals, dedicating myself to controlling the substances that I had basically weaponized.

And, admittedly, boring the ever-loving shit out of myself in the process."

I laughed. "No wonder you were so interested in coming out on an exorcism with me."

She smiled back, seeming tentative for the first time since I'd met her. "Originally? I just wanted to help. I thought helping you would make me clean again. Like if I saved enough people, I'd stop being the girl who got back at her bullies by trying to kill them."

"Hey, knock that off." I shook my head. "You don't know what they would have done if you hadn't acted first. The way I see it, you did what you had to do. Push comes to shove, we all do. That's not cheating, and it's not cowardice. It's survival."

She took another long drink of her cheap wine. "You know, I've never told anybody that story. I often thought that I would, one day, but I never expected it to be like this."

"In an exorcist's front office? I'd say you could be excused for not planning that one out."

"I mean, fair," she said with a smile.

Claire's gaze drifted down to my hands, where I'd been unconsciously picking at my cuticles. She set her wine glass down with a soft *clink*.

"Delia." Her voice went quiet. Clinical. "How long have you been hurting yourself?"

I froze. "I'm not—"

She barreled over my protest. "Your nails are bitten bloody. You're wearing long sleeves in June. And I saw the scratches on your collarbone when you leaned forward." She didn't sound accusatory—simply concerned. Matter-of-fact. "I'm not judging, truly. But I do need to know if you're okay. Whether you are or you aren't, I can help."

I looked down at my hands. Raw cuticles. Ragged nails. The

cuffs of my borrowed shirt hiding the bruises that wouldn't fade, the scratches that kept appearing.

"It's not—" I started, then stopped. How did I explain this? *Holy objects still burn me. My body remembers being occupied. Sometimes I wake up bloody and don't know how I got that way.*

"It's complicated," I finally managed.

Claire leaned forward in her chair, both hands flat on her desk, as if she were grounding herself. Grounding both of us. "Delia. If you need help—if there's something going on that I should know about—"

"I'm handling it." The words came out sharper than I meant them to. I softened my voice. "I know it looks bad. And maybe it is bad. But it's...residual. From before."

"From Lucian." Not a question.

"From Palemerious," I corrected. "From fifteen years of—" I gestured vaguely at myself. "This. My body doesn't know how to be normal yet. It's still...figuring things out. And believe it or not, Lucian is trying to help with that." Not necessarily true, but I could tell by the easing of Claire's shoulders that it was the right thing to say.

She studied me for a long moment, then picked up her wine glass. "Okay. But if it gets worse, you tell me. I might not be able to exorcise demons, but I can prescribe something that'll at least let you sleep without clawing yourself open."

I managed a weak smile, her words hitting a little too close to home. "Deal."

She raised her glass to toast to it, and I lifted mine as well as she swiveled her chair a little, her eyes refocusing on the wall and her mind on our potential police problem.

"So...you think we're going to have problems with this detective? You think Jillian actually sent him that doctored video?"

"I certainly don't think Jillian Reeves was smart enough to

make that doctored video, I'll tell you that. And I didn't really feel like she had it out for me, so I vote for this having absolutely nothing to do with Kieran or Jillian, which doesn't necessarily make me feel any better."

"It's escalating," Claire said quietly. "The AI or demon or—whatever it is—is taking gambles and risks and seeing where things net out. It's adjusting on the fly."

"But it's screwing up too," I pointed out. "Like, this video? Total bullshit. I'm sure it was riddled with mistakes. So, who's really in control here? Because I'm beginning to wonder if some of these 'failed tests' are failures after all."

"Well, your house legitimately caught on fire," she pointed out.

"Caught on fire and nearly burned to the ground," I agreed. "But that *was* a mistake, yeah? It was too much, too over the top. It wasn't a warning to stand down; it was a call to outright war. Maybe that wasn't the demon pushing too far...but someone else taking advantage of them not paying attention."

"Someone like Finn Ashford?" Claire suggested. "Trying to get your attention the only way he knew how?"

I smiled and tilted my glass at her. "Got it in one."

TWENTY-TWO

LUCIAN

The light went off in Delia's office at 9 p.m., a solid hour after the detectives had left.

Lucian studied the building as he imagined them tracing their way to the exit, clicking along the wood-floored corridor, trotting down the steps. When they appeared in the doorway, a flicker of something warm and not especially pleasurable slid through him. Delia's shoulders were tight, her expression grim, but she was the one leaning protectively toward Claire, not the other way around. Her intrepid assistant had always been the most stalwart of presences, and yet now she seemed curiously vulnerable, lost.

He resisted the urge to reach out toward her energy, to test and probe the way he had done for millennia, able to sense at a touch the vulnerabilities of frail humans. Instead, he flexed his fingers. Occupying the form of a shedim had proven to be an unexpected delight. They were only fourth level, and yet because they were so close in form and function to their human hosts, they blended, they passed. And they had appetites and interests that sharpened in the midst of other humans. He hadn't expected that.

Delia saw him immediately, of course, and raised her hand, her smile doubling his internal confusion. She needed to be protected, but more than that, she needed to remember her own strength.

How long had he fought against that strength, never realizing that his mere presence had honed it to a diamond sharpness? She couldn't let it shatter now. He wouldn't allow it.

The two women hugged briefly, then Delia watched as Claire got into her car and pulled away. The serious blonde met his gaze as she drove past him, and he didn't need to use his demonic abilities to see the worry in her eyes. Worry, and a curious relief as well. Claire had divulged secrets this evening, he suspected. What secrets could the fiercely protective pharmacist-turned-exorcist-wrangler have? Once again, the thrill of discovery stirred within him, but she wasn't his focus tonight. He would leave her to her secrets, unless they harmed Delia. He didn't think they would.

"What are you doing here?" Delia asked as she approached him. "You didn't need to wait for me, and you certainly didn't need to wait outside. You could have practiced some of your yoga moves in the completely empty studio downstairs."

He smiled. "You haven't eaten in far too long, and you need rest. As it happens, I am uniquely capable of meeting both those needs."

"Oh yeah?" Still, she didn't object when he opened the door for her, and she slid into his vehicle with a noticeable tremor in her hands. How long had it been since she'd eaten a real meal? Too long. She needed to take better care of herself. He needed to take better care of her. He needed to control his asset.

They talked quietly on the drive, Delia showing no interest in their eventual destination, though he suspected she noted that they were heading away from his apartment, not toward it. Instead, she told him about Walsh's visit—the questions he and the female detective asked, the clearly doctored video. When they reached the Café Monroe, she squinted up at it, glancing at him as the valet approached them. "I've never been here," she said, taking in the warm, honey-colored stone façade, the discreet bronze plaque beside the door.

"I know," he said with a smile, not missing the shiver as she understood the full import of his words. Because, of course, he did know. He had walked with her every step from the age of ten. He knew where she'd gone to school, where she met the occasional friend, where she studied for her classes, and especially where she tried and failed to establish the normal routines of a normal girl. But Delia wasn't normal. He'd taken any chance of that away from her.

Though he was not the only one to blame for that, he was coming to understand.

The interior of the bistro boasted Edison bulb chandeliers, exposed brick, and copper accents that added warmth to its quiet, understated ambience. In the distance, an open kitchen flared with bursts of small flames, and Delia looked around with gratifying interest as the maître d' led them past tables spaced for privacy, conversation muted by the soft jazz undertone.

"Your table, Mr. Gray," he said with a welcoming smile as he turned, and Delia glanced between the two of them as they were seated. After the wine was poured and they were served an amuse-bouche of lavender honey, she narrowed her eyes.

"Do they actually know you here, or did they just do their homework?"

He lifted his own glass, sipped at the wine. It slid like a slurry of soaked ashes down his throat—one of the few downsides of the shedim form. When he'd occupied Delia's body, her pleasures had been his pleasures, and her pain had been his pleasure as well. Such was the virtue of being a demon. As a shedim, he was a reflection of humans, but not actually human. In fact, the only true pleasure that he had felt in this form had been when Delia had kissed him. That had been shockingly, arrestingly real and visceral.

He didn't need to be thinking about that right now.

The soup came and went, and Delia's patent pleasure also served to warm him as her smile finally reached her eyes, and she began to relax.

"That video today...it's a problem," she said. "It was quickly done, I think, almost crudely slapdash in a way that surprised me, but it shows you the potential of what she's capable of."

He nodded, pleased that she no longer attempted to name the demon out loud. She was a quick study. She needed to be. "Do you have any theories as to why it was so crudely presented?"

Delia grinned, and something twisted inside him at the sharp, devastatingly attractive expression. She didn't smile often enough. "I thought you'd never ask. Claire and I were having this same conversation, and we think—I mean, I don't know how this works—but we think that somehow Finn made that video and got it sent to the police. I'd be willing to bet that Jillian had no idea it went out. It was good enough, right, to cause a problem? But the moment you started looking at it more clinically, you could see that somebody dropped the ball. Except I don't think someone dropped the ball at all, I think that he made his own kind of power move."

"To draw the attention of the police? On the eve of Prometheus Solutions' big escalation?"

"Yes," she said as the main course arrived, a duck confit with blackberry gastrique and microgreens. She blinked down at it. "What am I even looking at?"

"Taste it. If you don't like it, we'll send it back."

Her almost visceral groan a few moments later indicated that there would be no need to alert the kitchen, and Lucian set his teeth, wondering at the reactions inside him. Volkov, for all his annoying insinuations, hadn't been completely wrong about the shortcomings of a shedim's form. Taste was one failing, senses were another. Because he was truly a seventh-level demon, Lucian's own sensitivity overrode the shedim's innate reactions, but it took focus. Watching Delia now, he was suddenly aware of an acute sharpening of those senses. He could smell her pleasure, taste the way she savored each bite of food, literally almost feel it slide down his own throat in a way that was nothing like the dusty paste of typical food.

Was this because he had shared so much more with Delia before?

Her words shook him out of his reverie. "...It's an AI with demonic power," she said. "If it works, if it's successful, it's not just going to expand, it's going to detonate, I think."

He refocused on her to catch up. "You think demons from other courts will notice?"

"I think if they're not idiots, they will, but even if they don't, it's a problem. What we're looking at is an escalation of, ah, the Big Bad of the Court of Ruin. He's going to get incredibly powerful in a ridiculously short period of time. If other demons aren't following suit already, they're going to quickly figure it out, or he could run a coup and, I don't know, take over other courts. Is that a thing in the demon world? Do you have coups?"

"Ultimately, all authority cedes to a single lord. There are certain things that even he cannot do. And a great deal that he could but chooses not to. The organization and rule of the horde beneath him used to be of paramount importance, but as millennia turned on millennia, the players changing but the game remaining constant, he lost interest."

She stared at him. "Lost interest. In ruling evil."

He shrugged. "There is an entire body of philosophy dedicated to the idea that humanity is only on this earth to have an adventure. Is it so surprising that perhaps the same truism extends to the angels who fell and the horde who serve them?"

"Sure, except that your idea of an adventure is to inflict horror, pain, isolation, and suffering on humans too weak to fight you off. How is that anyone's idea of a good time?"

Your pleasure is our pleasure. Your pain is even more our pleasure.

He didn't think that now was the best possible time for him to point out that truism of demonic existence, but his focus on the possibility made him miss Delia's next quiet words.

He blinked at her. "I'm sorry?"

She looked up at him, and the pain in her eyes took him by surprise. "I can't kill demons," she said simply. "I can't kill them and I can't be party to the killing of them. It was one of Mordechai's most sacred rules. This gift I have, this ability, which it seems like I still have even though you, I mean, we..." She waved off her own words. "I can't kill demons, Lucian. That's not what I do. They're still creatures of God. If I were to cause their deaths, then my own life would be forfeit. Certainly, my gift would."

"Then you allow me to do so," he said easily, but the words made his bones shimmer with an unexpected pain. No matter that he was operating as a free agent, and even though the devil ruled his domain with a loose hand, Belial was a different story. If Lucian killed another commander without Belial's sanction, there would be repercussions.

He pushed the thought out of his mind and instead reached into his jacket pocket, extracting a jet-black key card. He handed it to Delia.

"What's this?" she frowned, glancing down at it, then flipping it over for good measure. "There's nothing written on it."

"A stylistic indulgence of the management. The Hotel Palidor is less than three blocks away, and I've booked you into a suite for as long as you should like to have it."

"A suite!" She blinked at him. "Why?"

He smiled. "Because your duplex is no longer livable, and as much as I enjoy you sleeping within reach, you're entitled to your own space. I want to protect you, Delia, but I want you to know that you can protect yourself as well."

"Oh," she said with a quiet voice. "Thank you. That—I would like that very much. Thank you."

The rest of the dinner ended with that precious quiet blossoming between them, a growing comfort, the prickling of awareness that had not yet formed into anything that had to be addressed, but stayed quivering and uncertain, just below the surface. They exited the bistro and turned left, walking the three blocks through streets now lined with trees and Victorian streetlamps that cast warm pools of light. Delia didn't take his arm, but he remained acutely aware of how close she walked next to him, of every swish and rustle of her suit.

The Hotel Palidor was an art deco revival building, complete with marble floors and geometric inlays. Its lobby featured burgundy velvet seating, brass fixtures, and fresh orchid arrangements. He knew from his brief research that the hotel boasted fifty rooms total and that it was discreet and secure. The front desk attendant nodded to Lucian as they approached the elevator but made no move to speak to him. Delia kept her eyes on the elevator bay, her breath coming a little more fitfully as they stepped inside. Now he was careful not to stand too close, and he glanced at her as he pressed the button to the fifth floor. "Are you okay?"

"I'm okay," she agreed. But her gaze was fixed on the rising floor numbers that flashed in the digital display. "How did you find this place, anyway? Did you ask your, um, friends?"

He chuckled. "How charming that you think I have friends."

"Mm." Still, the deflection served to settle her nerves a bit, and she stopped worrying her lip with her teeth—a habit he'd noticed more and more that was proving damned distracting. When the doors opened on the fifth floor, they stepped out into a softly lit landing, with several screens in a line on the long buffet, each of them tastefully depicting images of the hotel's amenities.

The images jittered slightly as they stepped out, then changed completely.

"Oh my God!" Delia gasped, jolting to a stop. "That's me!"

"Delia, don't—" But even as he warned her away, Lucian found himself glancing toward the screens, and then staring, patently shocked. The elegant, tasteful images of hotel amenities had been replaced with four short-looped videos—all of them featuring a woman of Delia's description, and each enduring the most horrific trials imaginable. Falling from a rooftop, struck by a car, thrown into the water, set on fire—

He turned and barely caught Delia before she collapsed to the floor.

CHAPTER

TWENTY-THREE

I stared at the numbers flashing on the wall, rising with sinuous slowness to the fifth floor. The numbers were the only thing not seriously making me hyperventilate right now.

What was I doing here?

I mean, I understood the mechanics of it. After everything that had happened to me over the last few days, Lucian had correctly figured out that I needed space, and he'd arranged for me to have it. He'd waited until the police had left the office to make sure I was okay, he'd fed me gourmet food and then he'd slid the platinum card of hotel room keys over to me without making a big deal out of it. After that, he graciously and quite reasonably had walked me to my hotel and stood not too close to me while he made sure I got safely tucked into my room.

He wasn't going to do anything I didn't expressly permit, and he wasn't going to stay. So what was the problem?

The soft jazz at the Palidor was clearly sourced from the same streaming account as the restaurant. Maybe they had a bulk deal. "How did you find this place, anyway?" I asked abruptly, if only to override the quiet tune. "Did you ask your, um, friends?"

Lucian glanced at me with an amused glint in his eye. "How charming that you think I have friends."

"Mm." I didn't know what else to say. It'd been a dumb question. Lucian was a demon and demons didn't need hotel rooms to experience what they wanted from humans. They didn't need creepy old houses or dark clubs or deconsecrated churches for that matter. All they needed was the human; the rest was window dressing.

The doors opened, and I blinked with surprise at the modern-looking display of multiple screens on the ornately carved side table standing opposite the bank of elevators. They were flashing with images of the hotel's impressive breakfast room, fitness facility, meeting space—

I stopped short as the images suddenly morphed into four separate images of horrifying clarity—and shocking familiarity. "Oh, my God!" I gasped. "That's me!"

Lucian said—something, I was sure he said something, but I couldn't focus on anything but the images filling the screens. The first was quite definitely me on the rooftop of the building where we had our office. I'd noticed the widow's walk a dozen times as I'd driven up to the place, always wondering how in the world anybody would get up there, let alone a widow out on a walk. But now I watched myself standing up there, wind whipping through my hair, city lights spilling out on the street around me. It was nighttime, and it was beautiful, really. But a moment later somebody rushed up behind me, and I went tumbling over the ornate banister. The perspective on the screen changed and suddenly it looked like I was sliding down the roof, catapulting off the edge. I was heading for the concrete with the absolute knowledge that I was going to shatter into a pulverized pile of blood and bones—

The next image sparked and I jerked my gaze to it. I was on Michigan Avenue, distracted by my phone and beyond me I could see a black SUV with tinted windows speeding through a red light. I looked up and then once again the perspective changed. Headlights suddenly filled my vision and I was struck hard enough that my body went spinning, my phone flying. Distantly, I heard it shattering against the asphalt but then my turn came and I banged off another car and crashed into the concrete. This time I felt the blood in my mouth, heard the passersby screaming, as brakes screeched around me and glass broke—

"No!" Another image flashed, but this one on the third screen and my eyes widened to see me standing alone on the edge of Navy Pier. It was dark and deserted, more deserted than was possible in this city, but it didn't matter because someone was running toward me. Abruptly, I saw powerful hands grab my shoulders and lift me up, launching me over the railing. Once again, the perspective shifted, and I was the one looking at the lake, I was the one anticipating the cold shock of water, and somehow, I was wearing a heavy coat, heavier than anything I owned, and it dragged me down. I plunged into the lake and looked up, seeing wavering lights and feeling, literally *feeling* my lungs burning, the surface impossibly far away.

I convulsed, trying to jerk away, but then was frozen in place by the last screen, the last most horrible screen, where I was knocked to the floor and covered with a heavy, wet blanket. My nose crinkled up in shock—gasoline! And then there was the spark, and the entire blanket caught fire, and I was beneath it, I was burning! I—

I collapsed.

. . .

"Delia." Lucian's voice sounded far away and somewhere else, but I felt myself lifted, moved, heard his footfalls striding down the hallway, and the click of the door. I heard these things, and some part of my brain knew—*knew!*—that this was real, this was true. But my brain didn't seem to care, because I opened my eyes to a dozen different scenes, each playing new and brutal images that I couldn't tear my eyes away from.

Claire was now atop the widow's walk at the office while I watched helplessly from below, screaming but unable to be heard. Claire's body was the one plummeting, spraying blood as it crashed into the pavement.

I turned, and there was Lucian struck by a car as he sprinted across the street to try to reach me, his long, lithe body hurtling through the air.

Then Steve howled, and I whirled, horrified to see him back at the duplex, in front of the TV, only this time the fire didn't damage everything around him. It was Steve who had caught on fire, Steve who was wrapped up in my mother's afghan, reeking of gasoline, Steve—

"*Delia,*" Lucian shouted, and he was shaking me now, surrounding me, his voice growing more urgent as breath surged up, my throat constricting against the lake water, the fire, my lungs burning because I couldn't breathe—I couldn't breathe!

"Fire!" I gasped, and I struggled as he shoved me down, vaguely registering something soft and cushioned beneath as he leaned over me.

"Delia, open your eyes!" he commanded, but I couldn't open my eyes—I couldn't! The pavement had blackened them, the water was too cold, the fire had burned them to ash, and—

He snarled a curse unlike anything I had ever heard before, ancient and terrible. "You must consent!" he roared, and he shook me, hard, like I was a misbehaving doll.

"Yes!" I gasped. "Yes—" but the air rushed out of my lungs as he flung me back onto the couch and I sensed his body looming over me. I tried to twist and shrink away, but a moment later I felt a smear of liquid rubbed across one of my clenched eyelids, then the other, the sensation so foreign and viscerally wrong in a sea of other wrongness that it pierced through my haze of confusion.

I blinked my eyes open only to find him leaning over me, his black eyes so wild that the fiery red was clearly visible at the edges of his corneas, his mouth tight and his hair disheveled. He no longer wore his jacket, and his shirt was wrenched open at the collar—wrenched open and gripped in my hands, I realized belatedly.

We stared at each other a moment more, breathing heavily, and finally I gasped in a lungful of air, my lungs no longer scorched with acrid smoke, my body no longer weighted down with sodden clothes.

"Hi," I managed, and Lucian exhaled, his breath not smelling of cinder and death but dark spices and cool vanilla, sensual heat still radiating off him. For once, that scent wasn't chased with the odor of filth and decay.

"Hello, Delia," he murmured, and his hands came up to gently disengage mine from his shirt. "You're safe, now. You're okay."

"What..." I looked around wildly, but he still held my hands, preventing me from getting up.

"There was a transmitter in your bag," he said slowly, and I blinked at him, not understanding.

"What?"

"A transmitter. It was activated when we got close enough to closed-circuit screens. It would have eventually been triggered by the televisions in my apartment or the ones in this room, I think. It was mere chance that we encountered screens on the elevator landing."

"They were images of me dying—actual *images* of—"

"No." Lucian's calm denial surprised me, and I jerked my head back to glare at him. He held my gaze evenly.

"No, Delia. You saw images of your death on the very first screen. That one was by far the most compromised. Whatever you saw scrolled through once—twice—and then quit."

"It didn't," I said hotly, trying to shake him off me. He didn't move. "I know what I saw!"

"What you saw was a systematic visual disruption field that showed you a series of violent imagery and then triggered a highly focused and intense psychic break. It was a break that would affect everyone differently, but in your case, it activated regions of your brain that were specifically attenuated to violence and horror. You have a very active imagination, and it didn't take much to trigger you into a series of ever-worsening scenarios."

"But...how?" I asked weakly, slumping back into the cushions of the couch. Now Lucian did let me go, sitting back on his heels and dragging my feet off the couch to force me into a sitting position.

"You need to breathe, Delia. Deep breaths in, hold for a short count, deep breath out." He positioned me once more like I was a doll, but I let him. I couldn't do anything for that hot second but let him. What had just happened to me?

I breathed out, then choked on a short laugh. "Are you trying some of your yoga tricks on me now? Maybe we should have you host a class downstairs."

"Maybe so," he said, and the genuine relief in his voice made me look up.

I blinked. In that split second, watching me, Lucian looked genuinely haggard. Then the moment passed, and his impossibly gorgeous smile teased the corner of his perfect mouth. "Thank you for letting me help you through that," he said.

I made a face, more memories coming back to me. "Did you seriously lick my eyelids?"

"You were caught in a loop that you couldn't break out of on your own. This form allows me to have presence and function in the human realm, and that means I can touch you—affect you. I needed you to see what I could see, see the world for what it was, not in the way your overtaxed brain attempted to see it."

"So—was that a possession?" I asked. "Or was that AI?"

"It was both," he said, shocking me. "The program was fairly effective, but not *that* effective. But the second-level demon that was in it, a screaming wretch of a specter who clearly is regretting his undead choices right now, amplified its impact."

"You killed it."

His lips twisted. "It was second level. It was barely sentient to begin with, and as old as the Fall. Death to such a creature isn't so much death as a backwards slide into the primordial ooze. It'll slither its way out again eventually. It's only fourth line and above for whom death is a...more permanent inconvenience."

"It was that, um, low on the totem pole, and it still took me out?"

"It didn't take you out, no. It was like a battery that did the job it was plugged in to do. The code and your own mind did the rest."

"Right." I lifted a shaky hand to my face and felt the wetness in the crease of my eyelids as he glanced away. I blinked, and in my mind's eye, I saw me sitting on the couch as if I were staring at me from Lucian's perspective.

Only...I didn't look like I looked, or at least, not how I knew I looked. My face looked almost fragile in the soft light, my hair loose and tousled—not wildly manic. I looked smaller than I felt like I was, softer, and my eyes were huge and luminous, my mouth...

"Is this how you see me?" I managed, and Lucian looked back at me, startled. His gaze sharpened, and he leaned forward and lifted his hands, skating his thumbs over my eyes. I blinked, but of course I couldn't see myself anymore—only him.

And he was way too attractive for anyone's good.

"I needed you to see what I saw, instead of what you saw. The images on the screen were intended to shock your nervous system, but I don't have a nervous system, not really." He breathed out a soft chuckle that made me very aware of *my* nervous system. "I should have thought of it sooner, but your reaction made me realize something singular was going on. I dumped your bag and found the transmitter, and then I needed to dispose of it."

"My..." I looked past him and saw Claire's beautiful designer bag upended, papers and pens and my laptop scattered over the floor. Against the wall was a very definite scorch mark above a smoking electrical device. "Your cleaning bill is going to be a bitch."

"Good thing there's a future in exorcisms."

I couldn't help myself—I laughed, and I glanced up to find him looking at me oddly—too intently, too uneasily. I felt uneasy too, but not for the same reasons.

At least, I was pretty sure it wasn't the same reasons.

"Lucian..." I murmured, and his gaze dropped to my lips. He leaned forward without me asking him, almost as if he couldn't help himself, and I more than met him halfway.

His mouth touched mine with unexpected gentleness— once again, it was a question more than a demand. I felt the warmth of his breath, the slight hesitation as if he feared I might pull away. But I didn't. I couldn't. I wanted this more than he did, I thought. I definitely needed it more.

The kiss deepened slowly, exploratory, his lips soft against mine. One of his large, beautiful hands slid to cup my jaw, his thumb tracing the line of my cheekbone with devastating care. I felt the tremor in his fingers, the restraint he was exercising, and something stirred deep within me. A sensation that wasn't fear or compulsion or even residual trauma.

It was darker than any of that. Needier.

I shifted forward, lifting my right hand to his chest, my fingers once more dragging against the fine weave of his shirt. As I deepened the kiss, my tongue slipping between his teeth to taste, to savor, I slid my hand along the buttons of his shirt, grazing them with my knuckles.

"Would you..." I heard myself ask on a gusted-out sigh, the words slipping around us. This was how it had to be, of course. At least for now. Maybe forever. If he was going to take me, I would have to—

"*Yes*," he breathed sharply, not waiting for me to finish. And with a thrust so abrupt it almost bordered on violence, he pushed me back on the couch and pinned my arms back at the wrists.

He stared down at me, eyes dark and wild and sparking with red fire in their depths, and slowly—so slowly—never breaking eye contact until finally it was my eyes that closed, my breath that shuddered out raggedly, he dipped his head to brush my lips with his.

Then he bit down.

TWENTY-FOUR

LUCIAN

"Oh!" Delia's body convulsed beneath Lucian, but she didn't cry out in pain, didn't object—which was good, because he didn't know if he could have done anything to stop the maelstrom of fury and joy and savage, wracking pleasure that exploded through him even if he wanted to.

The taste of her on his lips arrowed through his body and set every nerve alight with a decadent, consuming fire. She was salt and heat and dark, rich wine, and he devoured the smell of her, the taste, the sound of her shuddering breath, the pounding of her heart. Her warmth arced up and surrounded him like a living flame, binding them together, raising the hairs on his arm and the cock between his legs with a pulsing, driving need that bordered on insanity.

He desperately wanted to taste all of her—her skin and sweat, her musk and heat, her blood—

Her blood—

Letting her lip go before he pierced her with his teeth, he

dragged his mouth over her cheek, her jaw, ducking his head into the hollow of her neck and inhaling her as he kissed and licked. Dimly, distantly, he realized he still pinned her down, and the thought of her beneath him, slim and shaking, this body he had experienced so intensely from within and now even more intensely from without, sent him spiraling into another shattering storm.

"Lucian—" she gasped, and, drawing in a wracking breath, he pulled his head up, his gaze filling with her impossible, staggeringly human beauty.

Her eyes were wide, her lips red with the friction of his brutal kiss. As he stared, a small orb of a tear formed at the corner of her eye, and he stared at it, trembling, wanting it more than all the riches he'd ever amassed, all the deaths he'd ever delivered to the darkened door.

This—this was terror and magic and horror at once. This was living, and this was death.

"It's okay," Delia said, her voice wobbling a bit, and he jolted his gaze to her. She stared back at him, not weak, not compliant with the dazed stare of the possessed, but hard and fierce. "I don't know what the hell is happening here, but it's okay. You're okay. I'm giving you—this. Me. You're not taking it."

She shifted beneath him, her body at once firm and pliant, and he shuddered, the smell of her rising heat intoxicating him. Slowly, carefully, he released her wrists, drawing a hand down to thread it through her hair. The strands were silken against his rough fingers, and it was all he could do not to close his fist around them, yank her head back.

Instead, he rode the sensation, savored it, gave himself over to it for another faltering breath. Need crested and simmered within him, the body he inhabited primed and hot, its cock thick with urgency. She might be giving herself willingly, but she had no fucking clue what she was giving herself to.

And she needed to know—he knew that. She needed to understand before he lost the ability to stop himself completely.

"This isn't normal, Delia." He leaned down and licked the nascent tear away, shivering as his tongue registered its salty sweetness. He continued to lick and stroke his way down her face as she groaned and arched beneath him. "I'm tasting you. Feeling you. I can feel *everything* about you."

"Well, not everything, I hope. Not yet." As he angled up to look at her, she lifted a hand and stroked the skin bared at his throat. He fought another shudder, and her eyes lit with pleasure and satisfaction. "I mean, I know you've been inside me already, but...this is different, right?"

Lucian's soft laugh spurred her to draw her hand down his shirt, unbuttoning as she went, baring his abs that to her, he knew, looked like any other human's abs, taut and now quivering beneath her gentle caress. She dropped her hand further, drawing a line along his straining cock, and he growled low in his throat.

"I've never met a shedim in the flesh," she murmured. "You guys should get out more."

His control frayed, and with a speed she clearly didn't expect, he grabbed her wrist and rolled them both off the couch, regaining his feet and yanking her close. He pulled her into his body, dragging her against him as he devoured her mouth again.

They pulled back, lungs heaving, and he glared down at her.

"This isn't *normal*, Delia," he repeated tightly. "None of this should be possible to a shedim. Not like this."

She blinked. "But—"

"But I don't fucking care." Hauling her close again, he lifted her in his arms and strode across the well-appointed room that he could barely see given the intensity of his need. He breached the bedroom door and in three more steps, he was at the bed, where he dumped her unceremoniously.

She scrambled backward and stared as he shed his clothes with several swift, brutal movements. Her gaze went to his cock and then to his feet as he climbed onto the bed, and his grin sharpened, even as she caught herself and blushed.

"Sorry," she managed, scooting away from him to shrug off her silky blouse. Her breasts swayed in the soft light, but he wasn't going to allow himself to be distracted by those, not yet.

"You thought my feet would be claws," he taunted as he watched her shimmy off her pants. "Leave those on," he said sharply as she reached for her silken panties. "Those are new."

She blushed again, and he smelled the embarrassment, the sensitivity. Of course, he would know what she wore next to her skin. He'd been inside her body for fifteen years. She'd never once paid for anything like this. "Claire is—thorough," she said.

She pulled back the cover and climbed back on the bed, not foolish enough to try to cover up—too hot, he thought, too keyed up. She practically crackled with electricity. "I did think your feet would be different, though."

Lucian smirked. "Cloven, you mean. A tell that would keep you safe from harm, even from the most deceitful of shedim." He moved toward her, noting how she pressed herself up against the pillows, the solidity of the headboard. She watched him with hunger, but still no fear.

Well, maybe some fear. Far less than she should. "Humans have a disarming way of othering anything that scares them," he murmured. "I thought you would have figured that out by now."

Her head snapped up, anger lighting her eyes, and now Lucian did take a precious second to revel in the beauty of her as she curled at the top of the bed, a cat not sure when to jump away—or if. Her small, round breasts, her slim torso, her sturdy, functional legs—legs that were no longer damaged. She could run hard when she needed to, he knew. He'd run with her more times than he could count.

She wasn't going to run tonight.

"Lie back," he murmured as he reached her, shifting to give her space to stretch out on the bed. Her gaze flickered to him, the heat rising in her face, along her ribcage, but he wasn't going to deny himself this. He wasn't going to deny himself anything. When she didn't move fast enough, he casually reached back and, with the slightest of movements, hooked his hands around her ankles and yanked her legs long and flat on the bed. Then he was between her legs, crouched like the beast that he was, their eyes meeting.

"Lucian," she whispered, but he turned from her gaze to graze the inside of her calf, licking and tasting his way up her leg, lingering in the hollow of her knee. When he reached the smooth flesh of her thigh, he gusted a sigh over the prickling skin, relishing her shiver. Then he stretched further, his lips brushing up against the hem of her panties, the scent of her like a drug. He drew his finger along the scrap of silk, hooking it and yanking it down—

It ripped in his hands.

"Lucian!" I barely had a sense of the tug on my underwear before he ripped it clean off me. I didn't know that was even a thing outside of movies, but then I'd also seen him move with startling speed and strength that didn't quite track for a human.

And of course, he wasn't human.

But my thoughts imploded as he threw the panties aside

and leaned forward again, his gaze tracking mine for a scorching-hot second before he refocused on the vee between my thighs and dipped down, his tongue sliding up in a slow, sinuous flick before it found my clitoris with unerring precision. He stroked, I gasped, and places in my brain that had been dormant my entire goddamned life suddenly roared awake. I clamped my hands down on his shoulders, tangling my fingers in his hair, but I didn't know if I wanted him to stop or keep going, to ease back or take me over the edge or—

"Not yet," he whispered, and I blinked my eyes open, then practically crossed them as he nuzzled me intimately, then turned to my inner thigh and traced a scorching hot trail over my hipbone and along my quivering belly. I held my breath as he reached my breasts, and I watched him watch them, as they lifted and fell in time to my erratic breathing.

"You didn't seek men out—or women," he murmured, his hot breath spilling over me. But it didn't smell like any part of me—it drifted around me with the aroma of jasmine and desert spices, of silk and darkness, and I felt carried away on the dream of it.

Lucian's words brought me back. "You barely even pleasured yourself."

I should stiffen at the intimate interrogation, but again—he knew all of this. He was the reason for all of this. I lifted a shoulder, dropped it, thrilled despite myself at how his gaze pinned to the movement, his eyes dilating with desire. "It was a little creepy with an audience."

"You didn't know you had an audience until the end," he murmured, and he leaned down then, taking one curled-tight nipple in his mouth and teasing with his teeth. An answering need triggered deep in my belly, and I hissed out a curse, which made him laugh. The soft chuckle vibrated against me, and I felt the liquid heat crest within me, the need spiraling tighter.

"Well, I knew enough to know sex wasn't anything I wanted. I didn't trust anyone enough for that. I didn't—*fuck*," I broke off as he nuzzled my other breast and his hand snaked down my body again, cupping against me intimately, probing, pushing.

"You like this?" he asked, punctuating the question with a deeper push, his finger stretching me as I arched. "There's no pain?"

I looked at him with hooded eyes. "Since when do you worry about causing me pain?"

His face darkened then, but not in shame or even anger. It was something worse, in its way, something more dangerous. Possessiveness, I would have said, except possession took on a whole new meaning here. And we'd already played that game. I'd won.

Sort of.

Still, I reveled in the naked need on his face, the volatile desire, and I didn't mind stoking that fire one bit. I had a lot of time to make up for.

I smirked. "I mean, if you want me to get geared up on some other guy's cock, I can—ah!"

I exhaled harshly as he pressed two fingers deeply into me, withdrew it, plunged in again. Our gazes met and locked, desire surging up like a living thing, and when I arched up against him, taking what he gave and giving it right back, I saw his eyes go fully black, the fire always at the edges surging to the fore.

In less than a blink, he shifted again and it was no longer his fingers pressing into me, exploring, dipping, but his fully erect cock, pushing into my liquid heat and damned near taking off my skull with the chain reaction of sensation that rocketed through me. I gasped, my hips tilting up, and I gloried in the guttural moan of pure astonishment that was practically wrenched out of Lucian. He drove into me, and I bucked right back, his hands clamped on my shoulders and mine gripping his wrists, and both of us staring, glaring, blasting fiery holes into the other's eye sockets as we rode the sensations jacking through us, lifting up, up, up—and then down again as he shifted, twisted, and rolled me on top of him.

My hands splayed over his broad chest, my fingers digging into his skin, and then I cried out as the sudden shift of movement sent me over the edge without warning. I shattered, my mind filling with the sound of pop rocks and my body vibrating violently as Lucian clapped his hands to my hips, steadying me, grounding me, his own muttered curse in a language I didn't know sending his body taut.

Heat seared through me where we touched, scorching and well beyond human levels, almost painful. His hands gripped me hard enough to bruise, trembling with barely controlled strength. I tasted more copper, smelling the char on my skin. It was both wrong and intoxicating, and somewhere in the haze, I felt my scratches burning like they were opening fresh— opening and searing shut in one agonizing rush. But I didn't pull away. I couldn't.

Then his whole body went rigid beneath me, and more ancient, guttural words spilled from his lips—cruel, needful, and filled with want. His eyes blazed gold and red now, and I felt the moment his restraint shattered completely.

My eyes flashed open—I didn't know I'd closed them—then I gaped in surprise as I stared down at his beautifully formed chest. There were words on his skin that hadn't been there before—words in foreign languages and archaic English, sigils and symbols and even complicated mathematical equations etched into the skin, gleaming below the surface. As he moaned out a breath in a long, toneless surge of formless sound, his eyes opened again and they were pure, undiluted flame. Twin points of burning gold that pierced me through as effectively as a bullet to my heart. Still braced on his chest, I held his gaze as he reached up to me, drawing a finger along my jaw, over my lips. It trembled slightly as I kissed it, and he blinked hard, his eyes returning to their habitual black.

"Impossible," he managed. Just that word, but it held the weight of millennia in it, a heaviness I couldn't understand, didn't want to understand.

Wasn't about to understand, right now.

"Hey there." I smiled as I rolled off him, then drew my hand down his long, lean torso. "Welcome back."

CHAPTER

TWENTY-FIVE

I woke with a start, disoriented by the quiet and the feel of different but still luxurious sheets, the smell of Lucian's skin and heat all around me, but—no Lucian.

No Lucian.

Staring at the ceiling, I let my eyes acclimate to the gloom of the hotel room. A clock glinted on the nightstand, betraying the time as 8:10 a.m. I couldn't remember the last time I'd slept so soundly. Then again, I couldn't remember the last time I'd slept with a full-on demon who wasn't still actively possessing me.

This was a lot to think about before coffee.

I rolled out of bed, naked but not cold, as if the burnt-ember and woodsmoke scent on my skin still carried the heat of the deep, consuming fire that had swept over, around, and through me for what had felt like hours but could have been mere moments. Time had ceased to have any meaning, never mind that the clock now read 8:13 a.m.

As I wobbled a little along the deep-pile carpet, I scanned my body. I felt better, for sure, but I still looked like I'd been dragged over concrete. That surprised me a little. What was the point of having sex with a demon if you didn't get a glow-up out of it?

My quiet snort of laughter sounded a little hysterical in the luxurious room, even to me.

Turning back to the bed, I saw the piece of hotel stationery perfectly placed on the corner. Stationery. As if people actually wrote things with their hands anymore. Still, I picked it up, my gaze lingering over Lucian's elegant script. Mordechai, not the Chicago Public School System, had taught me how to read cursive. He maintained there were too many family journals written in the before times that would be impossible for me to decipher without that skill, and he'd been right.

Now I read Lucian's note with a weird uncertainty in my gut. *Claire will collect you at 9. Read your phone messages.*

I frowned and glanced around, but my phone wasn't on the nightstand. A silky robe lay folded on the bed next to the note, so I shrugged it on, pit-stopped in the fully stocked bathroom, then padded out to the main room of the suite. My gaze fell immediately on the carafe of coffee on the table in front of the couch. It sat next to my phone and a small pile of croissants. I ignored the pastries and dove for the carafe, adding cream and sinking back on the couch with my phone and coffee in hand.

My message app had blown up.

Victoria's texts were the most relevant. The first was at 11 p.m.—just after we'd reached the hotel, I realized, when Asmodaea, Mirr, or one of their infernal minions had short-circuited my brain with their possessed hotel monitor trick. *Kieran moving Reflex announcement up to tomorrow at 3 p.m. Jillian already scheduling interviews. Won't budge.*

Another one had come through at midnight. *Pre-emptively contacted Detective Walsh. K's uncle! Walked him through medical analysis—video shows fatal injection angle, K would be dead.*

Walsh's forensics finally confirmed digital manipulation. Talked him down at least.

That made me curl my lip. Unless Victoria had demonic abilities of persuasion I didn't know about, I didn't think Uncle Marcus was giving up that easily. The next text confirmed it—and was even more terse.

Change of plans. Meeting at Prometheus, 9:30 a.m. System safety check. Asked Det. Walsh to be there in case K catches wind.

Then there were messages from Claire, tag-team texts from Claire and Steve, and a large group message that included Rook, Mei, and Anya. From all accounts, the system safety check was a ruse Steve suggested to let him get into Prometheus' servers—and an environment that was directly connected to the Warriors of Darkyn game that the rest of the team had remote access to. When the system went offline for reset, there'd be a window—thirty seconds, maybe a minute—where Steve could use the architect ability to find Finn's prison. That reset would also disrupt Mirr's control long enough for them to get Finn out...if he was still alive.

Steve's gaming cabal would stay offsite, but he would be operating from Prometheus' headquarters—if we could convince whatever passed as tech security to let him. Apparently, he thought his game knowledge would be a direct transfer to Prometheus Solutions' inner workings—that Finn had set up a back door for anyone who knew how to open it, and that anyone was Steve. Even through text I could hear him crowing at the idea.

As I scrolled through plans, timing, and fail-safes, the phone chirped with another text from Claire. *Will be there at 9 a.m. Please provide proof of life.*

I texted back and stood, looking around for my discarded suit and wondering if I should ask her to bring clothes. Then I saw the other gifts Lucian had left for me: a box on the countertop, opened, tissue paper spilling out, and a tailored black blazer and charcoal slacks draped over the chair, with a dove-gray silk blouse arranged over them. On the seat of the chair sat a pair of ankle boots and slim socks.

I bit my lip, staring for a second longer, then my gaze went back to the box as I registered the name on it. La Perla.

"No." I moved toward it, my mind leaping to the underwear Lucian had destroyed the night before—and sure enough, there was a set of black, sleek silk panties and a matching barely-nothing bra with a handwritten note tucked in from some underpaid staffer at the boutique that they were washed and ready to wear. My hand hovered over the scraps of material for another moment, feeling the whisper of possession that still swirled around them—his energy clinging to the silk like static. Lucian had chosen these. Handled them. And now I was going to put them on?

The clock now read 8:35 a.m. I set down my coffee cup with a thunk and grabbed the clothes.

Claire didn't bother coming into the hotel but waited a few car lengths down from the door. She had plenty to say the moment I slid into the car next to her.

"Coffee cup in the back is yours." She waved at the console as she pulled back onto the busy street. "And for starters, you look fabulous. One day, you'll wear makeup and look even more fabulous. You brushed your hair, though. You should do that more often. Those boots are everything. You should maybe wear something other than shades of gray."

I grimaced, glancing down at my attire. My entire ensemble had been chosen by a demon who went by the name Gray. Something to think about, but Claire wasn't done.

"Before we talk about how you spent last night, you should know that Victoria called me at 6:00 a.m., wound up. That was a lot of fun, but the upshot was that she and Walsh had been texting all night long and he is now on some kind of personal witch hunt thinking that someone is undermining his nephew at Prometheus Solutions. Apparently, she went all open kimono on Kieran's behavior, gave him some video of his erratic behavior and a list of all the drugs he's got rolling around his system, and even told him about Finn maybe possibly not being dead, and Kieran possibly not realizing it. That was a stretch, but she went for it—probably a good thing, considering."

I stared at her. "She told a *detective* all that? Why?" Then the rest of her words caught up to me. "And what do you mean, 'considering'?"

Claire's expression darkened. "Because Marcus's ex-wife was in a car accident this morning. 6:15 a.m., Michigan Avenue. Traffic light malfunctioned in a Reflex test zone. Green light, red light, back to green. The whole intersection went haywire. A delivery truck T-boned her sedan doing forty."

My stomach twisted. "Is she—"

"Alive. Airbags saved her. But given his level of access, Marcus got the traffic cam footage right away, and Victoria made sure he knew: that intersection's controlled by Reflex. No mechanical failure. No human error. Just the system...making a point."

I sat back, coffee forgotten. "The demon is threatening him."

"Looks like. And then Victoria sent him something else—an audio file with a timestamp from inside Prometheus' server logs, which she was sent in the middle of the night. Finn's voice." Claire glanced at me. "Marcus heard a dead man talking. A dead man saying his name, saying Kieran's not dirty, but that Prometheus is compromised and about to take the whole city down. So, yeah. He's taking this seriously now. Not because he believes in demons, but because people he cares about are getting hurt, and a missing person has somehow turned up alive inside a computer. Not that he can make any sense of that."

"Join the club." I exhaled a shallow sigh, tension tightening its hold on my guts. "I've got a bad feeling about this. Guns aren't exactly all that helpful against demons."

She slanted a glance at me. "Which raises an excellent question I should have asked before now. How *do* you kill a demon?"

"You don't," I said emphatically. "At least I don't. That's not the job. We get demons out of the thing that they're infesting and send them on their way. They're creatures..." I broke off my own words, hearing Mordechai's voice in my head. They were creatures of God, he would always say, with as much right to exist on this earth as every other creation. The only right that they didn't have was to control or bring harm to a human.

Claire didn't seem to notice the lapse. "Well, someone better give Detective Walsh that memo, because he doesn't strike me as the kind of guy to leave his gun at the door. But he'll be there and—even weirder—so will Kieran. According to Victoria, he's acting like he's had a full-on conversion since his exorcism, and he's willing to do anything to help us. She's not really buying it, but I think that's part of why she wants the detective there, maybe to talk some reason into Kieran. She says Kieran's amped up surveillance and security in the building, and he's jumpy as hell. Jillian has been attached to his side like Velcro, tossing out orders like she's queen of the world."

"Will she be onsite?"

"Only if God is cruel." She sent me a sidelong glance. "So... how was your night? You do realize you're going to have to tell me details. Not the icky details, but details. You get that, right?"

I took another long sip of coffee, then stared out the window for a beat. "I slept with him," I finally said.

"I figured that. Did your cooch fall off?"

"Claire!" I jerked my gaze to her as she dissolved into a peal of laughter, the sound bouncing around the car an unexpected balm.

"I'm serious! I did some reading last night after you guys went off in that ridiculous car of his, and if he's a shedim, he can do, like, all the things. Eat, drink, have sex—I mean, obviously—even freaking procreate. *Procreate*." She shot me another glance. "I do not want a sequel to Rosemary's Baby, okay? You don't pay me enough for that."

"That's not going to be a problem." I was pretty sure that wasn't going to be a problem, but it really hadn't been top of mind last night.

"So, was it great? I mean, it had to be great, right? Other than his feet being messed up?"

"His feet were not messed up," I confirmed. "And everything else...oh geez, what a pity. We're already here."

She barked another laugh as we arrived at Prometheus, driving straight up to the valet stand. "We are so circling back. Make a note."

We left the car with the valet parking staff and hit the lobby, taking the Prometheus Solutions elevator to the corporate level. This time, we weren't ushered all the way to the ends of the earth and Kieran's private enclave, but to a generic-looking corporate office on the twenty-first floor with great views of the city, a glass desk with minimal personal items on it, and a leather-clad conversational seating plan that screamed Zillow staging. The abstract art on the wall was so muted as to be wallpaper, and a scatter of plaques by the door featured a dozen different names. Other than the vase of fresh flowers on the sideboard, I didn't think anything in this office changed on a daily basis other than whoever sat at the desk.

Right now, that was Victoria, who typed busily on her laptop while Detective Walsh loomed behind her, his stocky build still comfortably swathed in a mid-grade gray suit. He smelled like weariness, antacids, and anger, and I wondered again at his insistence on being here.

"Oh, good, you're here," Victoria said, looking up. She glanced around the room. "We've lost your teammate to the server room, I think. He asked for a quick tour."

"Then he's where he should be," Claire said. She strode forward and held out a hand to Detective Walsh. "Good morning, Detective Walsh," she said brightly.

Bemused, he took her hand as Victoria pushed back from her desk. "I explained that today's activities would not cause any bodily threat to anyone. That it was nothing as much as eradicating a computer virus. But given the recent false allegations and falsified video that was sent from Prometheus Solutions portraying Kieran Walsh in a damaging light, and the ongoing questions around Finn, he wanted to be present, and I was happy to have him. Especially since Kieran changed his mind again about the announcement. It's on again, and I told him he had my full support."

She eyed me meaningfully. "I did tell Detective Walsh that I retained you after your work for the wellness center, and why."

I grimaced, but Walsh made a cutting motion with his hands. "Let me be clear," he harumphed. "I don't believe in demons or exorcisms. But I do believe in cover-ups and missing persons. I also believe in corporate espionage, and if Prometheus Solutions is engaged in hijacking city systems, with or without Kieran's knowledge, that's something that needs to be addressed by our cybercrimes unit. So, I'm here to see what needs to be seen."

He looked at Victoria. "For the record, I think this whole 'system reset' plan isn't going to knock any rats out of their cages, and if the mayor knew I was potentially holding up his golden goose reveal, he'd have my captain's head. But given what happened this morning"—his jaw tightened—"and given that your son's voice is on a message that shouldn't exist, I'm willing to watch this play out. You tamper with evidence, interfere with my investigation, or endanger anyone, I shut this down. Clear?"

"Crystal." Victoria smiled, her strain starting to show around her mouth. She turned as the door opened again and Steve burst through, followed by Lucian.

"The setup here is *excellent*," Steve announced, his eyes brightening as he took in Claire and me, and I focused on staring intently back at him instead of pinning my attention on the demon in the room. "It's kind of unreal how much their architecture mirrors some of Finn's earliest games, but that's exactly what I expected to find, so boom."

"And you are...?" Marcus asked once Steve took a breath, and I finally allowed myself to look as Lucian gave the detective a deferent nod. The erstwhile seventh-level commander of the Ravening Court had chosen a deep charcoal suit for today's confrontation, paired with a shirt of darkest crimson. Platinum glinted at his wrist, his dark eyes gleamed with anticipation, and his shoes were polished obsidian. If he was going to get taken by the horde today, he'd look damned fine doing it.

I waited for the revulsion to strike, the sensation of bugs crawling over my skin as I stared at Lucian—but it took a few beats too long to show up, and when it did, it was fainter, lighter. A chill skated over my skin at that realization, my body recognizing that its reaction was wrong, but not sure how to correct it. Something had changed between Lucian and me, and I didn't think I fully understood what yet.

"Lucian Gray, one of Delia's associates—and Steve Morrison, our tech consultant," he said. "I was also in the video you received from Prometheus Solutions, though only your digital forensics team may be able to find me."

Lucian gestured to me, forestalling Marcus's next question.

His eyes pinned me with defiance and possession, for all that his words were banal, even bored. "Delia told me about it. I just wanted to be transparent. I should be on that video—though not much of the footage was correct, from what she said."

"Yeah," Marcus said grimly. "We figured that out too." But he had his phone out, and he tapped away at it as Victoria squared her shoulders.

"The building has been largely cleared of all non-essential personnel," she said, while Lucian continued to stare at me. Did he sense a change in me, a shift? Did he know more about how he'd affected me than I did? "Kieran signed off on the reset this morning, but given his...instability, I thought it best he not be present during the actual procedure. The announcement's back to being scheduled for 3 p.m., so now he's preparing for that at a corporate offsite this morning. We've shuttled the entire team across town. We've passed it off as a well-earned pre-celebration, a thank you for everything they've done so far. That gives us four hours to reset the system and, well, see what we can learn. If it's nothing, then we button everything back up and can rest easy."

"And nothing will be destroyed?" Walsh asked abruptly. "This reset throws a wrench in the works for today, but all assets remain intact?"

"No problem there," Steve said with a grin. "There's a full backup of every scrap of code housed offsite. It hasn't been updated in the past month or so, which, you know, interesting timing, but—"

"Why interesting?" Walsh interrupted, and Steve offered him a shrug.

"Well, if Delia's right and there's been some, uh, unusual manipulation of the code this past month, then Kieran wouldn't want that necessarily mapped to the failsafe code. He'd keep it in the live environment, but not make it canon, you know? Especially if some part of him recognized that things weren't quite right."

Marcus thinned his lips. "Meaning, he suspected there was an outside influence."

"Maybe not consciously," I said. "In fact, probably not consciously. Otherwise, that update would have been made. And are we sure Jillian is offsite too?" I didn't know how powerful her squirrelly little infesting demon was, but I didn't want to take any chances.

Victoria frowned. "Well, yes, of course. But I can verify that."

"Do that." I turned to Steve. "How do you trigger a reinstatement of the backup?"

"It's easier than you think. All you need to do is take the system offline. Take out a circuit board without due process, and the whole thing shorts out. Reboot with a command to reinstall backup, and it overrides any existing programming." He grinned. "Shouldn't be a lot of fireworks with this one. Though if a computer's gonna start puking code, I'm here for it."

Victoria's calm voice overrode Marcus's next question. "Then let's go. The entire team will be back at 1 p.m. I'd like to be done well before then."

She strode out of the room, Claire and Steve on her heels, and I could tell that Marcus wasn't leaving until we did. Lucian stood deferentially by the door, and as I approached, I could feel the full-body flush swirling up from my belly, the perspiration pricking along my spine. He neatly followed me out, his low voice carrying only as far as my ears as Marcus humphed his way along behind us. "If I can contain Mirr, you can't stop me, Delia. Don't try. It's important."

I glanced up at him. "You can't kill him, Lucian."

"*You* can't kill him, according to rules that don't apply to me." He smirked. "I can do whatever needs doing."

"Not according to Volkov."

"Volkov doesn't know half of what he thinks he does. We can't let Mirr go—not with what he knows about manipulating infrastructure. And if he's already told Asmodaea...then she's got to go too."

I scowled. "No." Something about his self-assurance dug at me, and I thought again about his apartment, four floors below. He couldn't really care about the threat to humanity Mirr and Asmodaea represented, so what was he really after here? Was this some kind of coup he'd been planning while living rent-free in my mind? And for how long?

When we stepped into the elevator, he nudged me toward the back, then took my hand as everyone stared at the door in the time-honored way of elevator rides. He turned it palm up, and I stared as his own finger dropped to my skin, the cool touch making me jump. Without saying anything, he traced a series of lines and circles as we ascended to the twenty-first floor, my skin reddening with the contact, but the dark crimson lines sinking in almost as quickly as they were drawn.

I quirked him a glance as the doors opened again, and he folded my hand tight again, squeezed it.

"You aren't healing," he said quietly. "This will help."

He gestured me out as Marcus turned back toward us, and I dutifully followed the group, my hand stinging as I tried to place any of the symbols and sigils Lucian had traced. Had I seen them before, somewhere? Was this a language I could learn?

And why did Lucian's action feel faintly...precautionary? As if he might not be around to give me a booster sigil later?

A computer tech was still working inside the server room, and he looked up when Victoria entered. "Mrs. Ashford?" he asked, surprised, then smiled when he saw Steve and then the rest of us piling into the room behind. "What's going on? You need a second tour?"

"We don't, John, no. These associates are with an outside firm to ensure due diligence. Steve Morrison here was contracted due to his knowledge of the original architecture of Reflex. He worked with Finn on the original design, and as a third-party, white-hat consultant, he's been kept apprised of the original vision and its constraints, testing the system whenever needed."

That got John's attention. "You have?"

"He has." Victoria's voice hardened slightly to give the lie more weight. "So he knows what should be there, and what shouldn't. He has my full trust. As majority shareholder and founder, I'm authorizing a safety reset."

He blinked at her. "A what?"

"You heard me, John." She gestured to Marcus. "This is Detective Marcus Walsh, special investigations, with the Chicago Police Department."

John blinked. "Walsh?" he stammered, and Victoria smiled.

"Yes, he's related to Kieran, which is why he's taken a personal interest in our safety. You've been briefed on yesterday's video leak to them?"

The tech lifted his hands. "I told you, I don't know anything about that. I don't even know how it was generated."

"Understood," Victoria said. "But these irregularities are concerning. To make sure everything is safe for today's announcement, Kieran has agreed to reset to our most recent backup of approved code. I understand you can do that fairly easily?"

"Well, yes, but..." His mouth turned down as his mind churned through the ramifications. "But we've been implementing updates, running patches—none of that has been backed up, Mrs. Ashford. We can't just reset; it'll all get wiped out."

"Kieran is aware of that, but those updates are documented. They can be reinstated one by one—except for the one that resulted in the glitch that generated a false video and sent it to the police. If we're making this announcement today, then we're first going to back up." She held out a phone in a ballsy bluff. "You can call Kieran for verification."

"I..." He stared at the phone, then back at Victoria. "There's protocol to follow."

"I'm aware of the protocol." She smiled thinly. "I wrote it. As the primary shareholder and founder, I have full authority to make any changes at any time. Which you well know. You can document your objection in the incident report. Now please proceed."

John's jaw worked, but he turned back to the console. The moment he started navigating around the screen, I could feel the hair on my arms stand up as the temperature in the room dropped a good fifteen degrees.

"What the..." Marcus said as John squinted at the system panels.

"I don't know what's happening here. Temperature's hard-coded and nothing I'm doing should disrupt this. You guys feeling this?"

"Dude, this is like Space Station Six," Steve breathed. "Remember when we hit the deep freeze right before the aliens burst out of the computer main—"

The lights flickered, shadows seemed to rush in, and with a move so fast, I wouldn't have seen it except I was staring at the man, Lucian moved before I even registered the threat—barely a blur. One second Detective Walsh had a holstered weapon at his hip, the next, Lucian was in his space, hand on the grip, releasing the retention strap like he'd been born knowing how.

Walsh inhaled, maybe to shout, but Lucian already had the gun out and up. The shot cracked through the room, sharp as a bone splitting, and the round punched straight into the computer panel over John's shoulder. The whole console erupted—sparks, smoke, a hiss of frying circuits—like the machine had been holding its breath and finally exhaled. Screens went black. The lights flickered, then went to holy-shit red and blue.

Then the room started screaming.

CHAPTER

TWENTY-SIX

S parks exploded from the circuit board. Emergency red and blue lighting continued to strobe, and a hissing sound came from above us as multiple alarms started to cry out in protest. My ears rang, my sight blurred, and I gagged on the smell of fried circuits and melted plastic.

Multiple phones blared. Claire shouted something I couldn't quite make out, Steve hunched lower over his laptop, while Marcus went for his gun. That last automatic reflex caught my attention the most because Marcus shouldn't even still have his gun. Lucian had his gun.

Only Lucian didn't. He was now across the room, his arms spread wide, fingers twitching, searching the ceilings as if he had no idea what was going on.

A synthetic voice sounded over the speakers. "Security Breach Protocol Alpha engaged. Lockdown initiated."

The lights went off completely, then came on again, causing the tech to spin around, irritation and confusion warring for control of his face. "That's *Reflex,*" he snapped. "That's not supposed to happen. Reflex isn't installed inside Prometheus."

Victoria had her tablet out and was scrolling through something I couldn't see. "It's not supposed to be, no. But it has been, and now it's blocked me from access. My override codes aren't working either."

"Same. What the *hell*." The tech moved to another workstation and brought it to life with a few swipes of his hand. He keyed in a line of arcane-looking code, and my lips twitched as his screen exploded with about a billion more lines, all of which he read like a soothsayer. Apparently, magic took many forms in this world.

"Steve?" Claire asked over the bleating alarms.

"We're ready," he shouted from his command station. "And—"

"Got you!" The tech crowed as the alarms shut off. "Motherfucking fucking bunch of fucking bullshit *fuck*. But we should be good for another fifteen minutes before the code recycles and we get another symphony. Clearly, something in our code was fucked all to hell, so the reset was the right call." He pointed to Steve. "You need to take a look?"

"More than that," Steve shot back, one hand still smashed over his earbud, listening to his gamer group. "As of five minutes ago, we've got another building that's appeared in the game. This one's a monolithic tower where you enter at the top, and the treasure is located in the basement. Sound like anyplace you know?"

"What game?" The tech squinted at him. "What are you talking about?"

Rook's voice crackled over Steve's laptop speaker as Steve jerked his earbud out. "Let's hit it!" Rook shouted. Mei cheered through the connection, then Anya chimed in.

"I've got shields up!" she announced, as someone started pounding on the server room door.

Marcus turned, his gun on the door, but with a flurry of movement, Lucian was right by his side, reaching out. Marcus's eyes went a little wide and unfocused for a half-second as Lucian touched him, but he slid the gun back into the holster. A heartbeat later, Lucian was back on the other side of the room, standing near Steve.

My stomach cramped as I understood what I'd just witnessed. Lucian had done that. Lucian had pulled out a trained detective's gun and fired it point-blank at the server, then returned it and flashed to the other side of the room, all without the guy knowing what happened. He'd kept Marcus from following on his own instincts. He'd overridden a human, and he'd done it with no one the wiser.

Seventh-level demon, Commander of the Ravening Court. What exactly had I allowed back into the world when I'd set Lucian free at the Grahams? Should I have stopped him?

Could I have?

"Building is locking down, but—" the tech pointed to the door. "There shouldn't be anyone else here."

"Open up! We've got a breach!" the person outside yelled.

"Don't open that door," Victoria ordered. With Lucian no longer beside him, Marcus had his gun out again. Victoria turned to me.

"Shouldn't you be doing something?"

"I should, but I don't think you should be in here when I do." I jerked a thumb to the door. "Maybe deal with whoever's outside?"

"I can do that," Marcus said gruffly. He lumbered to the door, gun out again.

"Well, I'm not leaving," the tech announced. "Plus, you need me. Those alarms we just heard? They're like a digital dog. All bark and no bite. But they're designed to create enough of a distraction that, unless you've got noise-cancelling headphones you're never going to survive. That's the beauty of Reflex—uses the same kind of lo-fi weapons the military uses, right along with the high-fi stuff. We've got fifteen minutes before they kick on again. To stop it, I basically rebooted the security system, and it takes a minute to get online. So the good news is, you've got a break, but the bad news is, the reboot triggers a second-stage escalation. If we don't do a full reset with proper protocols—which includes a principal manning the controls—our redundant security measures *will* kick in."

He squinted around at us. "Again, what is it you think you're going to do?"

"Remove an obstruction," Lucian said calmly. He'd switched his attention from the ceiling to the main server terminal. "If Reflex's servers are offsite, what's this doing here?"

"Artifact," the tech shrugged. "It's plugged in, but we don't depend on it. It's meant as kind of a reverse backup in case the data center is compromised."

"Security, this is Detective Marcus Walsh of the Chicago Police Department," Marcus shouted, his hand on the door. "I am armed. Stand down." He opened the door and stepped outside as we all turned—then ducked back inside. "Nobody there," he said gruffly. "I'm going to check."

"Thank you," Victoria said, then returned her gaze to the tech. "But you said it's linked?"

The tech stared from the now-closed door back to her. "I mean, sure, but—"

"We're ready to go," Steve announced. "Give me five minutes before you start blowing things up, okay? Once we're in the tower, you can do whatever. Rook, Mei, Anya...who else do we have online? We're going to need shields. I can't lose you before we get to the bottom level."

"I've got my nephew's frat house locked and loaded," Mei announced cheerfully.

"But..." The tech flailed his hands, his gaze straying back to the screen.

"John, listen closely because I'm only going to tell you this once," Victoria said, turning on him. "Finn Ashford, my son, is embedded in the operating system of the company. Steve and his group are going to infiltrate a game he designed because we believe that whatever it is that is causing the system disruptions is also embedded within that same system. In the meantime, Delia and her partners are going to address the virus that's currently giving Reflex access to all of Prometheus Solutions' infrastructure."

He goggled at me, clearly skeptical. "You guys are coders?"

I gave him a grim smile. "No. But I can type."

"Oh, hell no," John said, turning back to the screen and lifting his fingers over the keyboard. "You can navigate all you want, but I'm going to drive—and what the hell are *you* doing?"

He directed this last demand at Lucian, who was tracing the outline of the server panel with his fingers. Lucian ignored him.

"We're in," Steve said, and I pointed to the screen.

"This is what I need you to type."

Above John, a movement caught my eye—the server's overhead camera shifting toward me, its red recording light blinking like a malevolent eye. I took a steadying breath and began to chant in Hebrew: *"Yitgadal v'yitkadash sh'mei raba b'alma di v'ra chirutei..."*

"What the fuck is that?" John protested as Claire rushed up.

"Here!" she snapped, pulling out a small, worn book from her supplies bag, a Jewish Siddur. "Type these letters as I say them, I don't think it matters if they're not a hundred percent correct."

"Yeah, it will," he muttered, but he bent and started typing as she recited.

The tech's fingers flew across his keyboard, lines of code streaming down his monitor, but it didn't take long for a reaction. "Holy shit," he muttered. "The system's fighting back harder now. Not error messages, either. It's completely rerouting me. Whatever you're doing, it's—"

"I see you, Mirr," I said, making direct eye contact with the camera lens. My voice carried over the alarms with an authority that surprised even me. "By the names of the Almighty—*Adonai, Elohim, Shaddai*—I call you to account."

A whining sound emerged from the speakers, high-pitched and petulant like a child's tantrum. "This is *my* place now," the voice crackled through the static. "This is *my* place now. They gave it to me!"

The tech's eyes widened, but he kept typing. "Jesus Christ, that thing is actually talking to—"

The whining shifted, becoming jubilant. "You think words can hurt me? I'm stronger now! Look what I can do!"

Every screen in the server room flickered violently. Sparks showered from an overhead panel, and the temperature dropped so suddenly that our breath became visible.

"Keep going," Lucian urged from the corner. "Switch to the Latin, hit it with—anything. Whatever tools you have."

Claire turned to me and shoved a small vial of holy water into my hands. I upended it over the nearest servers as I switched languages, mentally thanking Mordechai for these lessons for all that I didn't know what the hell I'd been saying at the time. "*Exorcizo te, immundissime spiritus, omnis incursio adversarii—*"

"Wrong faith, little girl," Mirr's voice flowed out of the server with greater strength now, losing its childlike quality. "Mordechai should have taught you better."

Hearing the rabbi's name in that stilted, crackling voice made my gorge rise, but I kept reciting the rite. The tech was typing frantically now, sweat beading on his forehead. "It's adapting to every command I send. This thing is learning our—"

A massive electrical surge erupted from his workstation. Lightning-blue energy arced across his keyboard and up his hands. He screamed, his body convulsing as the current ran through him, then he collapsed backward out of his chair, unconscious.

"Jesus!" Marcus shouted, but Claire was already there, pulling John away from the console. "He's breathing," she called over her shoulder. "Pulse is strong. He'll be okay."

I slid into his chair, my fingers finding the keyboard. The screen showed cascading errors, system failures spreading like digital wildfire. "What was he typing besides the rite?" I called out. "Because there's more than just Latin here."

"Containment protocols," Steve answered from across the room as Claire moved to my side. "Trying to isolate the infected sectors."

Not knowing what else to do, I copied the Latin prayer and pasted it everywhere—into log files, system messages, error outputs. If Mirr was in the code, I'd flood the code with prayers. *"Vade retro Satana! Nunquam suade mihi vana!"*

"It's working," Claire breathed, reading over my shoulder. "Or something is—the screens flicker every time you say it."

About a dozen lines in, the system offered up a new response—not a syntax error, but something more. The code began rewriting itself around my words, trying to block them, wall them off. But I kept typing, flooding every input field I could find. Another high whine emerged from the side panel, and Lucian moved up by my side as I kept typing the same line over and over.

"Are there other entities in there besides Mirr?" I demanded.

"No. But Mirr is a demon of deception and reflection. He can appear in several different places at once to several different people at once. He can act simultaneously."

"Dude, this is awesome!" Steve shouted suddenly, his attention on his screen. "We've got four straight-up armies of demons coming at us from all sides, but we are in the tower! Repeat, we are in the tower! Just have to get through the fucking trolls."

"I see you, demon scum!" Rook called through the speaker. "North side—wait, they're everywhere!"

"Guys!" I shouted. "It's not four armies—it's one singular demon. Only one. That means if you take any of them out, you take all of them out, or at least damage the shit out of them." I swung to Lucian. "Am I right?"

He blinked, his eyes glittering red in the strobing light. "You're right," he agreed.

"Excellent!" Steve announced. "New Mission. I'm going to get us to the basement of this tower. That's where the treasure is. Be ready for anything."

"Even demons jumping out of my screen?" Anya half-screamed through the monitor. "Fuck! What's with this graphics package?"

"Even that," Steve said grimly. "In WoD, you couldn't kill the demons for good, but rules are different here. You get a clear bead on 'em, keep hitting until you knock him down. But first, we've got your standard army of trolls guarding the door to the basement. Let's hit it."

"On you, Steve," Mei confirmed. "Anya, watch the rear. Rook, you're on point with me."

The team devolved into rapid-fire chatter, and I turned to Victoria. "Do you know anything about code?" I demanded. The tech still lay on the ground, breathing shallowly as Claire bent over him.

She waved her hands. "A little, yes. Enough to help Finn in the early days."

"How do you get rid of a virus?"

She blinked, then turned to the screen. "Well, if it's truly a virus, I would simply run a virus eradication protocol to identify and then get rid of it. But Reflex has completely taken over here. It's not going to let me run anything in case it's a malicious attack."

"Okay, so how do I get in?"

"Honestly, the fastest way is exactly what we were attempting—shut down the entire system as if there was a catastrophic attack. Reflex is backed up, and will revert to its former code, but—" she moved to a second terminal, leaned over it. "I should be able to trigger a catastrophic failure flag remotely. If I send it from my founder credentials, Reflex will think I'm authorizing an emergency shutdown. It'll reboot clean. I should still be able to—"

A second later, the server in the corner of the room exploded, sparks flying.

"Shit!" John convulsed on the floor, regaining consciousness with a scream before scrabbling away from Claire, his eyes wild. He stared at the smoking console, then at the screens still flickering with Mirr's presence, then at me typing prayers into the system. "What the fuck are you doing? We're all going to die!"

He bolted for the door, threw it open, and ran out.

"John!" Victoria shouted. She whirled from her computer station and raced after him.

I turned as smoke billowed out of the side server, my own eyes wide. "Lucian?" I called, choking on the acrid fumes.

But he was gone.

TWENTY-SEVEN

LUCIAN

Immersing himself in the circuitry of Prometheus Solutions should have felt more foreign than it did. The networks that humans had learned to cobble together to create their intricate computer circuitry and data clouds were not a construct that had come out of nowhere. Maps to the same energetic patterns had provided the webbing to the world since before the angels had fallen.

Lucian burst forward with an unexpected thrill, realizing for the first time exactly how constricted he had felt while embodying a shedim. As a seventh-level demon, he could move at the speed of a thought, and, freed from his human form, he raced through the elegantly constructed circuitry, following the sparking trail of Mirr.

"He is here! Here!" Mirr howled, the sound far ahead of him. "You told me to bring him and he is here!"

Lucian smiled. *I am here, Mirr, and Asmodaea is not. She is no fool.*

He reached out, sending his energy coursing through the circuits, painting the network in red.

Far ahead of him, Mirr's scream took on an entirely different tenor. "You have no power over me!" the reflection demon screeched. "She has elevated me to a higher order!"

"Even if she wanted to, which I assure you she does not, she doesn't have that kind of power," Lucian corrected him. "No demon has that kind of power, Mirr, without the blessing of Samael. Or do you think to rise above even him?"

"You don't know—You have been gone for too long! The courts are surging up—up! Power shifts, it grows. The humans will finally understand why we fell, and how we may rise again."

Lucian allowed that information to spear through him. He'd known there had been changes in the past fifteen years, indications on the periphery of his imagination. Mirr was a craven idiot, but he was also weak. He would not act on his own—not to do all this. Lucian could see that now, here in the reflection demon's domain. Asmodaea had planted him here to do her bidding. To draw him out.

A prickle of awareness snaked through him as Mirr finally stopped screaming and grew quiet. Lucian drew closer to see him flashing in the dark.

"I see you," whispered Mirr. "I see everyone...and I see her." His laughter swelled low and dangerous. "You walk a forbidden path, Palemerious."

Lucian stopped, turned, reaching out his awareness in the darkness. He needed Mirr to keep talking. "You toy with her, but you have condemned her. She deserves to know the truth, doesn't she?"

A shout erupted from the server room. "We're in!" Steve's voice rippled with excitement. "Down the stairs, down!"

"You're losing control, Mirr," Lucian pointed out. "You'll let them steal away the human who's making all this possible?"

"No human makes this possible," Mirr countered. "I control all. While you can't even control yourself...certainly not the human who practically vibrates with your energy now. Forbidden, Palemerious. She is forbidden to you. Humans aren't good for anything but *ruin*."

"No!" The voice that shouted through the circuits wasn't Steve's this time. It was Delia's and far off—too far off! She was trying to reach—what, who? He felt her panic like a clawing beast, scrabbling through his veins. She was running through the hallways of Prometheus Solutions, hallways that had now turned into mirrored, intersecting corridors.

"She'll never find him," Mirr cooed, before breaking off into a crazed cackle of sheer delight. "She'll never find him until she sees—sees what she has done, who she has hurt."

Despite himself, Lucian split his focus from the glinting specter in front of him to zip through the camera system, tracking Delia through the hallways. And then another image caught him, down a long corridor.

Detective Marcus stumbled away from Victoria and the crumpled body of the tech, only now the fifty-something detective looked dazed, confused. He crashed into one mirrored wall, then another, shattering glass with his gun. "What's with these walls?" he demanded. "Where did everyone go? That boy needs help—Security!"

He wheeled around another corner, and his gun came up— steadier now, resolute. "What the fuck is this?" He bristled, and Lucian watched his eyes widen with sudden recognition. "Barb?"

"Marcus!" wailed a woman's voice. "Help me!"

In an instant, Lucian knew what the detective was seeing,

what he was feeling. Even through the circuits, Walsh smelled of desperation and booze and long-ago baby bottles and sweet-smelling skin. Mirr roared with laughter as he showed the detective the figure of his bandaged ex-wife stumbling down the mirrored corridor, flashing from glass to glass.

Walsh had to know this was a trick, Lucian thought, but his mind refused to make the connection, and his iron-grip hold was slipping—slipping!

"Marcus!" Mirr screamed again.

Marcus unloaded his gun into the wall, and the sound of glass shattering barely covered his pounding footsteps.

"Don't kill him," Lucian snarled, "or I will ensure you never crawl out of the stain of your remains."

"Kill him...kill him? I can't kill a human, Lucian. Only a human can kill another human...or maybe a shedim. Plus, he's barely alive anymore anyway. You smelled the whiskey on him, the grease, the pain. Poor stalwart human in his tiny box of an apartment, putting on a brave face, while his ex-wife raises their little boy away from the fire and pain of the city. Only not today, hm? Today the city found her and...*push*! Poor Barbara, and Marcus couldn't stop it. Marcus couldn't keep the shadows from closing in. *Push*."

"I will end you, Mirr," whispered Lucian, and Mirr's laughter burbled out of him.

"You can't," the demon wheedled. "She has promised me power. Control. Cities and souls filled with light, so much light to *push*."

"I will." The words were there too, rich and full, written life-times, millennia ago. They rippled through him like veins through white marble.

"Marcus!" Delia screamed. "No!"

"He's clo-ose," Mirr chanted in a sing-song trill. "So clo-ose.

Should we give him a little push too? A push to be with sweet Barbara?"

Lucian's world was filled with running footsteps, gunfire as Marcus shattered more glass, and Delia's harsh, labored breathing. She needed to *stop*.

"Ohhhh..." Mirr's voice changed then, shifting to a mocking lilt. "Ohhhhh, I feel the power in this one, Palemerious. The knowledge. You did this, didn't you? That's where you were all this time? How much did you teach her, wearing her skin? There are rules, you know. Rules that don't break like...glass."

Another round of gunfire, more glass, and Mirr's laughter swelled. "Oh...this is rich, this is good. You didn't *know*. You didn't know what you had done—you still don't know what you have done. Delicious...and so tragic. Push."

Marcus wheeled around the corner, his eyes bulging, his mouth hanging open as he struggled to breathe. Delia was too far away—too far—and the images in front of her shifted—one Marcus went right, and another Marcus went left. She followed the wrong one.

He opened his mouth to speak, closed it. Marcus was too far ahead of her now, even if she turned and sprinted toward him. And Mirr was enjoying himself too much.

"I will end you, Mirr," he said, slipping forward through the circuits, drawing nearer to the fifth-level deception demon who was so enraptured with the stress and strain he was causing the futile human, a rat in a glittering trap, that he never realized Lucian was circling tight.

Lucian breathed in a long, deep, cleansing breath—he'd missed breathing in the demon way, the ingestion of so much more than mere air. The world had been created for his kind, after all, a playground to revel in the beauty and vibrancy of life, to aid the stunted blurts of existence that were the limits of most humans' experience on this plane. That they had fallen was no real surprise...that they enjoyed being Fallen was.

Perhaps that was why they had lasted so long, trapped amidst the mindless tide of humanity, seeking out every prurient vice, soaking up the darkness. Learning the limits of pleasure and pain.

But there was one pleasure doled out with restraints as exacting as shackles in a cell, or a noose above the open air—the snuffing out of a life granted by others' hands.

In all his millennia of service to the prince of Hell, he'd only been given this permission twice. In both cases, he hadn't sought out the commission, and he certainly hadn't sought it out now. But Mirr had gone too far in attacking Delia in her home. And in attacking Delia in her home, in peeling off the layers of paint, he'd seen too much. More than he probably knew, but Asmodaea was a discerning creature. Mirr needed only to stand before her, his eyes peeled wide with fear, and she would know the truth.

Distantly, Lucian tracked Marcus Walsh's path through the mirror-lined hallways, but he couldn't focus on the human and handle Mirr at the same time. Mirr was a fifth-level beast who'd gone fat on Asmodaea's indulgences, but in his case, fat did not mean indolent or thick. He swelled with power and privilege, and he finally turned to see Lucian closing in—and in his eyes, Lucian saw the thing he most feared.

"She'll know," Mirr hooted, his words curling around Lucian like a stinking tide. "She'll know you have been so close, and yet so far, buried deep inside a human whose keeper knew more about the horde than any human should. She'll know, and she'll find your precious Delia—" he said her name like a slur— "and she'll find her and take her apart, piece by pretty, pale piece. And if you're really lucky, she'll let you watch."

"You told her," Lucian said, matter-of-factly.

"I didn't have to," Mirr cackled, unable to lie, but willing to dress the truth in the pretty packaging of rebuke. "You're a fool to think she wouldn't find you, more the fool you didn't leave while you had the chance. But you couldn't give up the taste of it, could you? Couldn't keep from drinking the cup of darkness down. She'll know—and then she'll punish you. Belial will, too, if he's smart."

"Mirr..."

Lucian murmured the word from all sides, and Mirr, the distractible child that he was, looked up and around, allowing Lucian to edge forward the final few steps, to lift his hands like spiked manacles and fasten them around Mirr's reed-thin neck. The demon took form beneath him, all angles and edges, sharp as blades, but blades couldn't cut shadows.

"Stop!" Mirr spasmed beneath him, twisting, as he realized immediately that the hold that Lucian bore down with was not meant simply to subdue, but to crush. If he had any doubts, the rite of undoing flowed like smoke and ash over Lucian's lips, swirling around them both. "You cannot."

"I think we both know I can."

He'd been called on twice to perform this rite, after all. And such words as these were easy to remember.

"Stop," Mirr pleaded, beginning to writhe in earnest as Lucian's hold intensified, wrapping him with coils as dark as the abyss. "I can drop the walls, save the lump of a human, he won't die—won't die! And I won't die. I cannot, will not, could not face the *AllThatIsAndEverShallBe*. I cannot! I'll tell no one..."

Lucian almost laughed. *Tell no one?* As if Mirr could hide what he'd seen from Asmodaea's scrutiny. As if the moment she looked into his craven eyes, she wouldn't see Delia reflected there—her walls, her home, her deep and twisted connection to a seventh-level demon who'd spent fifteen years wrapped around her vital, beating heart, building her up, tearing her down.

And once Asmodaea knew, she would come for Delia. Not to kill her—no, Asmodaea would want to study Delia, to test her. To break her open to see what made her strong. And when she was done, there would be nothing left worth saving.

No. Mirr alive was a threat Lucian couldn't contain. Couldn't risk.

And Lucian was beyond stopping. He pressed down, seeing only the shadows of the fire that had swept through Delia's home, the mockery on her walls that she could never—would never see. The surprise in her eyes as she had seen herself die, over and over again, and the utter desolation when she'd seen the death of all those she had barely learned how to love.

"Be glad I give you this mercy, you miserable cur," Lucian breathed. With this rite, the demon wouldn't simply return to the muck and ooze of first-level status. He would be utterly eradicated—turned to dust and swept back to judgment before the all-seeing Creator, never to walk apart, to breathe apart again. Death was the ultimate abomination, the ultimate destruction.

"Nooo!" Mirr screamed, as Lucian bore down, then crushed his miserable rotted soul into oblivion with the last, char-scorched words of the ancient severance rite.

No sooner had Mirr's scream choked off than another one replaced it: Detective Walsh, unloading his gun yet again as he chased after the men he thought were hauling his ex-wife to her death.

This time, however, he didn't aim for the walls, but for the window he could not see at the end of the corridor. The tempered safety glass starred with impact craters, spidery cracks racing across its surface—but held. Held the way it was meant to, designed to stay intact even when shattered.

Until Marcus hit it.

Two-hundred-plus pounds of momentum struck the compromised pane, and Lucian watched—helpless now, too late to intervene—as the window tore free of its frame, glass, frame and man tumbling together through empty air. Twenty-one stories down to the street below.

Lucian gritted his teeth against the human's terrified scream, audible only to him and the Creator.

No one would survive that fall.

CHAPTER

TWENTY-EIGHT

I skidded around the corner, sure that I would see Marcus's large body pounding down the hallway ahead of me. But there was no Marcus; there were only mirrors and more mirrors reflecting me as I raced along hallways to nowhere. I knew this was only an illusion, knew I should be able to see past it—but it was a remarkably *effective* illusion, and my brain felt scrambled with every turn.

"We're in!" Steve howled, his voice echoing out over loudspeakers embedded God knew where, as if Prometheus Solutions really was a video game, created for the giggling amusement of its brilliant, broken founder. "Delia—Finn's on sublevel seven—seven! I didn't even know there could be a sublevel seven!"

A loud crash sounded in the distance, disorienting me, and at almost at the same time the mirrored walls flickered and disappeared, revealing flat painted drywall in their place. My eyes no longer tracking where I was going, I swerved and plowed right into one wall, bouncing off to crash on the other side of the hall, drunk, unable to keep my feet. A bay of eleva-

303

tors now stood at the end of the corridor. It'd probably always been there, but I would have raced right by it.

"Where's Detective Walsh?" I demanded.

"No clue," Steve shouted back. "But you've got elevators near you? We need to go down."

"Demons gone!" Rook shouted, his voice coming through the speakers as well, but tinnier, like he was speaking through Steve's laptop. "Disappeared like poof, but...whoops, check that, check that, demons back, what in the absolute..."

"We've got major horde action coming through the top of the tower! Whole new group!" confirmed Anya. "They're hitting us hard, harder than they should, like they suddenly woke up and realized what we were doing. I'm hit! Goddammit, I'm hit!"

"I've got you!" Mei yelled, but as I finally reached the elevators, Steve emerged from the server room down the hallway, his laptop in his hand. He stared around wildly, trotting my way as soon as he saw me. "Elevator?" he said hopefully.

I grimaced. "You trust it?"

"I mean...no, but twenty-one *flights*, man..."

"Stop!" Victoria emerged from the opposite direction, moving fast. She had her key card out and was brandishing it like a weapon, and she punched her fist toward us, then directed us to the right.

"Access stairs. No way would I trust the elevators right now, not even with my credentials. Worst case, we're locked down in a stairwell, but at least we're not going to fall to our deaths."

"Whoa," Steve offered, but we crashed in behind her, and she scrambled down the stairs, making good time in her high-heeled shoes. The shoes didn't last three flights before she kicked them off, but she barely missed a step.

"Did you see Marcus?" I demanded. "Or the tech guy?"

Victoria answered between short sprints down the stairs.

"John collapsed again—I left him with Claire," she huffed. "She promised to stay...there. Called 911, or she's trying to."

I glanced at Steve, still trying to run and follow his team in the game. "*He's* connected."

"Closed circuit, man," Steve huffed. "We might as well be in a black box. Lemme do this. I'll catch up."

He stopped in a stairwell as we continued to pound down the stairs. My legs burned, my lungs ached, but I felt that pain from a distance, like I was watching someone else race down those stairs, someone else doubling over with ragged breath. Adrenaline, fear, exhaustion—everything blurred together into a strange, acrid urgency.

Ahead of me, Victoria sucked in a deep breath. "Finn...Finn might be okay. He might. He was that biohack bro you...read about, always researching, always testing. If he... I mean if they..."

"He reached out...to us," I reminded her, my own breathing labored as we continued crashing down the stairs. Steve finally started moving again above us. "He might be okay."

"Yes." Victoria's hope was incandescent as we flew around the stairwells. The numbers on the doors blurred, running together, but eventually we reached a floor where there was more than one door. A second portal marked "Maintenance-No Ground Floor Access" stood beside the first, and Victoria didn't hesitate. She slammed her keycard on the reader. When it didn't react, she flipped it over and slid the card lengthwise into a slot at the reader's side.

The door clicked open.

"What the hell?" Steve asked as he came up behind us, but I couldn't tell if he was reacting to her ninja-level access or to something happening on the screen, which he somehow managed to keep tracking as we pushed through the doors.

"Finn again," she said grimly as we strode down a new

passageway. Lights flickered on, sweeping the utilitarian hallway in harsh blue-white light.

She stopped at another door and pushed it open.

"Not more stairs, man," Steve moaned, glancing up from his laptop. "The guys are down to the final level, but they're not seeing anything."

"No more stairs," Victoria agreed, gesturing to an elevator bay. "This attaches to the delivery bays. Only elevators. This far down—I mean, we'll have to risk it."

The elevator required no additional access code, and the doors opened almost immediately. Victoria and I exchanged a wary glance as we piled in, but she hit the S7 key and the doors snapped shut. "S7 is literally storage," she said. "I haven't been down here in years."

"We trust this?" I asked under my breath as the carriage started moving. Steve devolved into muttering curses at his screen.

"I don't think we have much choice," she said quietly. "And it's not stopping. Maybe we're...I mean, maybe..." She shook her head, lifting a hand to wipe the sweat from her eyes. "I don't know what's waiting for us down there."

"We've got movement," Steve said abruptly. "Rook, Mei? What's happening down there?"

"We're in the dungeon, but Steve, there's nothing here." Mei's voice vibrated with frustration. "It's a brick wall with no doors, no crevices. Totally flat rock."

"Rook, what's your strength score like?" Steve asked. "Can you take it down?"

"Not with my bare hands. But the wall isn't the only issue. This place is small, man. You couldn't even store six boxes in here and be able to turn around."

"Fake wall?" Anya offered. "Blow it up?"

Steve snorted, but the sound was grim. "Wrong game,

sister," he said. "There are no bombs in Darkyn. Strictly old-school."

The elevator pinged, the doors opened, and we piled out into a room that sounded eerily similar to the one that Rook and Mei had described. It was a shallow vestibule with a metal garage door spanning one side, cutting off access.

"A garage door," Victoria said, squinting to the sides. "So, deliveries, but...is this some sort of sealed-off bay?" She turned and surveyed the wall panel by the elevator and drew in a soft breath. "It's got another slot," she murmured. "Finn and his tricks." She slid the key in, and the wall opposite us lifted, curving up on its tracks...to reveal a nightmare.

A pod sat centered in a space bristling with electronics, a man clearly visible through the machine's window. His head was shaven, his eyes closed, and easily a dozen monitors surrounded him, buzzing and beeping.

"Finn," Victoria murmured, her hands frozen in a half-lift. I stared too. The pod looked—almost ordinary, like something you'd see at a high-end fitness club. Except for the tubes, anyway. I swallowed down the gorge punching up my throat.

"Is he alive?" Steve's voice was also hushed, and he was no longer staring at his laptop.

"I..." Victoria began, but she didn't finish. I understood that. Though monitors buzzed and beeped around the pod, a full schematic of brainwave readouts zipping across the screens, the man inside the pod looked like something from another planet —painfully thin, his face covered by a full breathing mask. Beneath his lids, his eyes jerked and twitched, but what did that mean, really?

As she visibly forced herself forward, another feeling of wrongness reverberated through the chaos—Lucian. I hadn't seen him since the server room, since the alarms and the cold and Mirr's mocking voice had crashed all around me. Where had he gone? My chest tightened, dread whispering through me. He was okay, of course—he had to be okay. I'd know it if he wasn't...right?

"Yo, we've got movement! Wall's going up!" Rook's voice startled us, and Steve dropped his gaze to the laptop again, then his eyes flared wide. He turned his computer around to display the same image that we were seeing, only on the screen, Finn was floating in a room surrounded by mist.

"Thing just slid up and dude's right there, man," Rook continued. "He's not waking up but, I mean, it kind of looks like he's smiling? Is that what you're seeing?"

Inside his pod, Finn didn't move, but a whoosh of crackling sounded over the speakers, making us all jolt. It sounded almost like words, but then the crackling stopped, and Victoria burst forward several steps.

"Finn!" she gasped.

Suddenly, steps pounded from a corridor I hadn't seen, and a moment later, Jillian Reeves dashed in, her body cloaked in scrubs, her hands covered, her face masked. "You can't be here!" she shouted. "This section is strictly—"

Something snapped within me. I didn't know if it was the stress of the server room attack, the fact that Lucian was gone and I didn't know where he disappeared to, the sigils that he had inked into me, or the memory of him still stretched over me, tasting, touching, demanding. But seeing Jillian made me flashback to her sultry smile, her liquid eyes, trained on Lucian like he was a morsel served up for her to take.

I didn't hesitate. I bolted forward, bearing toward her like a linebacker, no matter that she was easily six inches taller than me with curves to spare. The sheer fury of my assault took her by surprise, and we toppled over, me straddling her and grabbing her throat, squeezing hard as she pried at my fingers, her eyes flaring wide...

All I ever needed was to look deep into the eyes of the afflicted. I could help them.

And oh, Jillian needed my help.

I stared into the slithering mass of the demon inside her, identifying it as I had always been able to identify these miserable bastards.

"Alaria," I said silkily, ignoring the machines around us beeping and blurting with panic to rival Jillian's own. "Alaria, no longer trouble this child of the Creator. You cannot. You dare not disobey me."

"No!" Jillian's mouth parted in a rictus of a scream, her body convulsing. But she couldn't deny me. She wouldn't deny me. She wouldn't get her red-polished talons on Lucian ever again, in my dreams or anywhere else, and her despicable wretch of a second-level demon—

She vomited bile and filth, and the demon came out with it, its formless entity screaming with the need to escape. But I wouldn't let it escape unscathed, I would not.

"I banish you," I hissed, not knowing where my next words came from, but knowing what they meant—the utter desolation of a creature doomed to start anew in the filth of the first-level horde. "*Iterum. Ab initio.*"

The creature, broken and desperate, hissed away into the shadows.

Silence fell.

I stared at nothing and no one for a heartbeat, lost in a thrall of horror. I'd done this all wrong. Everything, wrong. I'd pushed harder, taken more from the demon than I should have. And I'd done it because I was *angry*. Because Jillian had looked at Lucian like he was hers to claim.

What did that make me? What had I become?

"Delia!" Steve was at my side, pulling me off Jillian, who

lurched away from us in a quaking pile, retching and heaving. "Delia, fuck…"

"Mom?" The voice crackled from the speakers—weak, uncertain, but unmistakably Finn's.

Victoria gasped. She scrambled toward the pod, stopping short to lift a hand tentatively, pressing it to the cool metal. A crackling hiss exhaled from the speakers, and the monitors jumped and buzzed, tracking new brainwaves gyrating with what looked, even to my shaky gaze, like waves of joy.

"Oh, Finn," she murmured, her breath catching as she peered through the glass. "Hi there, baby. I'm here."

Another burst of static, a hiss. And then a disembodied voice floated out from a speaker near the monitors. "It's about time," it said tonelessly.

My stomach clenched, and Victoria barked a strangled laugh. "Sweetheart, I—" she managed, her hand on the pod beginning to tremble. "Is that really you?"

For a long time, there was no response, only the hush and whirr of static. A tear trickled down her cheek as the answer finally came.

"I think so."

I winced. I mean…how could he know? How would any of us know, ever again?

Victoria didn't move from the pod for a long time. Her hand stayed pressed to the glass, tears starting, stopping, then flowing again. Jillian dissolved into her own flood of tears, and Steve went to her, cleaning her up as best he could, apparently more comfortable wiping away vomit than immersing himself in a mother's grief or…or dealing with whatever it was I'd become down here. Jillian finally curled up against the wall, weeping incoherently, her wails of confusion marking her as the victim.

She might even get away with that, I thought grimly.

We stayed in touch with Claire, informing her of what we found, waiting for the EMTs she summoned to arrive. When they did, Victoria coordinated with Claire to guide them down to Sub-Level 7 through the maintenance elevators. They burst like a hornet's nest around Finn's pod, shouting out monitor readings, assessing and strategizing whether—or even if—they could move him.

Finally, Victoria had enough. "Jillian," she snapped, with all the fury of a mother pushed to her limit. "If you don't want me to have you arrested right this instant, get up and tell these people what to do."

"What?" Jillian allowed Steve to help her to her feet and tried the innocent victim schtick for exactly five more seconds as Victoria's face reddened, her eyes going as flat and cold as a snake's. "Alright, of course. I was forced to monitor him, you understand. Forced! I only know what Kieran told me, and he—he—"

"I don't care about Kieran," Victoria snapped, waving to the pod. "Can he be released from this pod? Can we wake him up?"

"I..." she gaped at the pod, the monitors, and I didn't think she was lying, here. "I don't think so," she whispered.

The EMT turned to Victoria. "His vitals are tracking, but I wouldn't do anything too quickly, ma'am. Not until we under-stand what we're dealing with here."

"Of course. Of course." She nodded, accepting this, then turned to me with red-rimmed eyes as the EMTs' phones started blowing up all at once.

"Thank you," she said with a trembling smile. "For...finding him. Even though you said you couldn't conjure the dead."

I nodded, but my heart hurt as I stared at the man who'd been her son and was now...I didn't know. Finn was alive—sort of. Trapped and forever changed, but here. That had to count for something.

"Ma'am, we've summoned a medical team. We'll take good care of him," the lead EMT finally said to Victoria, his face steady and earnest. "But I need to be honest—I don't know if we can remove him from this system. Not without understanding what it's doing for him. If what you're saying is correct, his body's been sustained by these machines for years. We'll need specialists."

"I understand," Victoria said quietly. "Just—keep him alive."

She stepped to the pod again, resting her hand on the glass for a long, spellbound moment, staring down at her son. Then she let go.

Claire met us at the elevator in the lobby, her face drawn. The building was still closed to everyone but residents. Emergency personnel and police huddled in small knots, talking urgently. "They found Marcus," she said quietly.

My stomach dropped, and the lowkey dread I'd been fighting back for hours coalesced in a hard, gray lump in my gut. "Found him?" I asked, as Steve uttered a low groan. Unbidden, I thought of Joe Bell, back at the Graham estate. Joe Bell, whom I'd failed, who'd died because I was weak. And now, Detective Walsh...

"He—fell," Claire said tightly. "From the twenty-first floor. Tempered glass is strong but—yeah." She drew in a shaky breath. "Witnesses said he shot out the glass, then ran straight through it. He didn't have a chance."

The hallway tilted. Marcus—stalwart, determined Marcus, crashing down the hallway, calling out the name of his ex-wife, who was nowhere near here. I'd heard him, running, desperate, but couldn't reach him. I'd made the wrong turn—so many wrong turns! If I'd been faster, if I'd reached him—

I hadn't reached Joe either. I hadn't even tried.

"Hey." Claire's hand on my arm steadied me, and even Steve drew closer, though his eyes still looked haunted by what he'd witnessed in the basement. What he'd seen me do. "You okay?"

I wasn't, of course. Nowhere near it. But I nodded anyway.

"They're saying it's a mental break," she continued. "Stress, maybe drugs. Nobody can explain why he'd shoot out a window and run through it."

I grimaced. Nobody could. Nobody would. Because the truth—demon illusions, mirror mazes, a reflection demon tormenting him with visions of his injured ex-wife—would never be believed.

"It wasn't your fault," Claire murmured, reading something in my expression.

I didn't answer. Because I wasn't sure that was true.

And even if it wasn't my fault—even if there was nothing I could have done—Marcus was still dead. Another person I couldn't save. Another name to add to the list of people who'd died while I stood by and watched.

Claire's 911 call had reached first responders about the same time that emergency services received the panicked reports of the officer's death and the damage to multiple vehicles and pedestrians in the aftermath of the exploding window. Now I glanced around, clocking another absence.

"Lucian?" I asked her, but she shook her head.

"I haven't seen him."

My chest tightened. He'd gone somewhere from the server room—somewhere I couldn't follow. Now Marcus was dead. Finn was trapped in a pod. And Lucian—Lucian had abandoned us, or something had taken him. Mirr? Or was Mirr truly dead now—destroyed like the creature I'd banished or...or worse?

The sigils Lucian had drawn on my palm burned faintly, and

I rubbed my thumb across them. A goodbye, or a promise he'd return?

The shadows held no answers for me.

Steve wandered off, his focus back on his laptop, and additional information made its way to us as we waited to be released. The Reflex rollout had been postponed indefinitely. Kieran, barely coherent when found at the corporate offsite, was at Chicago General under observation. Jillian was in custody—and apparently professing her innocence of anything other than monitoring Finn, whom she insisted Kieran knew about—and I imagined Victoria would deep-six any implementation of anything remotely resembling Reflex for a very, very long time.

Finn Ashford, to all appearances, was in a medically induced coma but remarkably stable, all his vitals remaining steady. He hadn't spoken anything other than the four words to his mother, and she hadn't revealed to anyone he'd said even that—not yet. There was no trace of the medical team who'd actually kept him alive—monitoring the pod, ensuring the neuromuscular stimulation processes stayed running, the tubes stayed clear and functional. Nobody believed Jillian could have done all that, but the medical team who'd apparently been assigned to Finn had simply gone poof, like the demons in the Darkyn game.

Like Mirr, I realized distantly.

At least Finn was alive, though. He'd have a long, twisting journey to come out on the other side of this, but he had his life back.

Marcus, of course, didn't even have that.

I STARED at the lobby doors, half-expecting Lucian to walk through them. To explain where he'd been, why he'd left, what had happened with Mirr. But the doors stayed closed, my mind stayed quiet, and not even the still-tender bruises on my arms throbbed anymore.

Claire touched my arm. "Come on," she murmured. "Let's get you home."

Home. My lips twisted. My duplex was ash, the hotel no longer felt safe—nowhere felt safe. My office would do, I supposed. At least there, I could—

What? Wait for Lucian to come back? Pretend Marcus hadn't died? Ignore that I'd made a miserable demon's existence infinitely more miserable because I was a spiteful, jealous bitch?

"Yeah," I said quietly. "Let's go."

TWENTY-NINE

Claire pulled up to the curb outside my building as twilight settled over the street. The yoga studio's windows glowed warm against the gathering dark, and through the glass I could see people—actual people—rolling up mats, pulling on jackets, chatting like they'd just finished a perfectly normal Tuesday evening class.

I blinked. "Is that—?"

"Our yoga studio," Claire finished, equally stunned. "With... students?"

We'd left Prometheus Solutions only an hour earlier, the lobby finally empty of police and emergency personnel. It'd been a solid eight hours since the server room had filled with smoke and lights, and I still hadn't seen Lucian.

"I kind of want to—" I gestured vaguely at the studio. "Check it out. See if it's actually real."

Claire snorted. "You do that. I'm dragging my tired butt upstairs where there's wine."

I waited until she'd disappeared into the building before crossing to the studio entrance. The last student was leaving as

I reached the door—a middle-aged woman in expensive athleisure who gave me a bright, slightly dazed smile.

"*Amazing* class," she enthused. "Tonight's substitute instructor was something else. I've never felt so...centered."

"Oh, well, good!" I managed. "I'll have to check it out."

The studio was dim inside, lit only by the ambient glow from the street and a few strategically placed candles that were probably completely against the building's rules. Then again, tonight's yoga instructor wasn't much up on following procedure.

I somehow wasn't surprised to see Lucian standing at the far end of the room near the windows, his back to me as he adjusted something on the sound system. He wore dark pants and a fitted shirt, looking for all the world like any other yoga instructor cleaning up after a class. Except yoga instructors didn't typically move with the fluid, predatory grace of a seventh-level demon who'd just spent the afternoon killing one of his own kind.

"You seriously just taught a yoga class," I said abruptly.

He didn't startle—of course, he didn't—merely turned to face me with that unreadable expression I was beginning to recognize as his version of guilt. "The instructor failed to show up. The students did. I offered to teach, and more humans arrived. It often works like that."

"I bet it does." I stepped farther into the room, letting the door fall shut behind me. "You killed Mirr, watched Marcus die, and then came back here to teach downward dog to soccer moms?"

"Vinyasa flow, actually. And there was a retired accountant, a graduate student, and a man who I believe works in insurance." He paused. "The soccer moms were particularly enthusiastic, though."

I wanted to laugh. Or scream. Or possibly both. "Lucian..."

"Mirr is dead, yes," Lucian said quietly, all traces of humor vanishing. "I performed the rite of undoing when I got the chance, and he's gone. Completely."

"Banished, you mean—" I began, but Lucian cut me off with a glance. The temperature in the room seemed to drop several degrees, and I wrapped my arms around myself. "And Marcus?"

"I watched him fall." His voice was flat, matter-of-fact. "The window broke. Twenty-one stories. If it's any consolation, he didn't feel the impact."

It was, but I couldn't let him know that. "Could you have saved him?"

Silence. Then: "If I had chosen differently, yes. If I had let Mirr live and dropped the mirror walls, Marcus Walsh might have found his way to safety." He met my eyes. "I chose to kill Mirr instead."

The words hit like a physical blow. I'd known—of course I'd known—but hearing him say it out loud made it real in a way the past few hours of numb shock hadn't.

"Why?" My voice came out hoarse.

"Because he'd seen too much. Because he would have told Asmodaea what he'd witnessed in your home—the evidence of my fifteen years wrapped around you, the depth of our..." He gestured between us, frustrated. "Connection. She would have come for you, Delia. She would have taken you apart to understand what made you strong enough to hold a seventh-level demon for that long. And when she was finished, there would have been nothing left of you worth saving."

"So you killed him." I forced myself to hold his gaze. "Without permission. Breaking demon law."

"Yes."

"And now?"

Lucian moved to the window, staring out at the darkening street. "Now, there will be a tribunal. The courts will convene to hold me accountable for an unsanctioned kill. Belial will have to answer for my actions—I'm still technically under his command, even if I've been...absent." His jaw tightened. "Asmodaea will use it as leverage. The political implications are significant—and you might still be in danger."

I ignored that last part. "How significant?"

"Significant enough that every demon of note will be watching to see how this plays out. Significant enough that you, by extension, will also be watched." He turned back to me. "I'm sorry. I never intended to paint a target on your back."

"Well, you killed Mirr to protect me. That's what put the target there."

"I killed Mirr because he was a threat to you," Lucian corrected. "But also because he attacked your home, tormented you with visions of death, and violated the sanctity of the one place you should have felt safe. He also stood in my way. The strategic necessity and my personal desire happened to align in this case."

The candles flickered, casting shadows across his face. In the dim light, his eyes caught the glow—not quite red, but not quite human either.

"A tribunal," I repeated. "What does that mean? Punishment? Execution?"

"Potentially. Though it's more likely they'll use it as an opportunity for political maneuvering. Asmodaea will want concessions. Belial will want to minimize fallout. And I..." He exhaled slowly. "I will have to stand before them and justify my actions. Potentially claim you as my reason, which, again, would make our connection very public, very quickly."

"Will they come after me?"

"Not directly. Demon law is complex, but there are rules about harming humans under protection. And make no mistake, Delia—you are under my protection now, whether you want to be or not." His jaw tightened. "Which means every demon who wants leverage over me now knows exactly where to find it."

I thought about Marcus, about Finn trapped in his pod, about the bodies we'd left in our wake trying to stop Mirr and Asmodaea's plot. About the fact that I was standing in a darkened yoga studio having a conversation about demon tribunals with a creature who'd spent fifteen years living in my shadow... and millennia walking the earth.

"Everyone knows who we are now," I said. I moved toward him, and he watched me with hooded eyes. "What we are."

"Yes," he agreed. He didn't back away when I came right up to him, didn't flinch as I lifted my hand to place it on his chest. I felt the slow, steady thump of his shedim heart, and recalled an earlier, rougher cadence, when his body had been stretched over mine, when his mouth had taken, bitten, explored.

"And this is just the beginning," I said, holding his gaze with mine.

He leaned down and ghosted a kiss over my lips, the bare touch of him all the more intense for its whispering nearness. "Yes," he murmured. "A tangled knot that may never be untied."

I should have been terrified. Maybe I was. But mostly what I felt was a strange, settled certainty—the same certainty that had made me walk into the Grahams' house all those weeks ago, that had made me agree to hunt for Finn Ashford, that had made me start speaking the exorcism rites even when I wasn't sure they would work.

I pressed my lips to his, feeling his heat, his strength. Claiming it—for just this moment—as my own. A slow, rolling tide of pleasure swirled through me, filling up all the broken spaces, making me whole again. I rocked back on my heels and realized that the skin I could see beneath Lucian's tank top was no longer smooth and clear. Instead, strange symbols glowed, patterns etched in fire and blood. He held a hand to me. "You are not yet healed," he murmured, his eyes glowing red at the edges of his deep black irises. "I can help with that, finally. Fully, this time."

I swallowed, looking at his hand, the palm shifting and flickering with a song whose language I didn't know. Shouldn't know. Every touch would draw me deeper into Lucian's world, I knew. Whether he healed me or harmed me, I'd be marked, tainted. Changed. And one day...one day there'd be an accounting for that, I knew it in my bones.

I drew in a shaky breath, lifted my own hand—

"Delia? You in there?"

I jerked straight upright, and Lucian and I locked eyes. He lifted a long, elegant finger to his lips—then seemed to back into the shadows without moving, eventually disappearing completely. I blinked, and he was gone.

"Yes!" I answered, belatedly, turning as Officer Hernandez stepped into the room.

"Claire said I'd find you here," she said, squinting in the gloom. "You often hang out by yourself in an empty yoga studio?"

"Probably more often than I should, yeah." I walked over to her. "You heard what happened. I mean, how could you not?"

"I did." We stepped out into the hallway, where a few chairs stood at an angle, welcoming yoga students to sit and rest awhile. Neither of us sat. "You want to tell me what the hell happened in that tower?"

I met her gaze steadily. "Did you see the video?"

"Yeah, I saw the fucking video. They tagged me immediately because when a cop dies by suicide, it can fuck up the amount of money that his beneficiary gets. And his kid was his beneficiary—him and the boy's mother, who Marcus still loved, for all that she couldn't handle being a cop's wife anymore. He was a piece of shit partner, but he loved his kid and he loved his wife, and now they might not get the money they deserve because he fucking fell out of a fucking window because of you and the creepy-ass shit you're up to."

I winced, tracking the pain and anger in Hernandez's voice, and absorbing them like a body blow. But she wasn't wrong. Without me, Detective Walsh wouldn't have been on the twenty-first floor of Prometheus Solutions. He wouldn't have seen whatever Mirr had shown him that made him empty his gun into both walls and eventually the window that couldn't hold his weight when he crashed into it.

"Victoria gave a statement to the police," I told her, in the most even tones I could. "I was there when she did it and confirmed what she said. She demonstrated how the projection system at Prometheus Systems could be configured to play images that looked absolutely real. We couldn't see what the detective saw, but we confirmed that he called out the name Barb when he was running."

She stiffened. "That's his ex-wife. She'd been in an accident early this morning. She couldn't have been there. He knew that."

"Well, something he saw made him call out her name and assess a real threat to the people he was trying to protect," I said resolutely. "Victoria stated unequivocally that he'd drawn his weapon because of a threat he believed was real due to projections he was being shown."

"Yeah, I know all that," Hernandez said. "She also told the department that Prometheus Solutions would give two million dollars to his family over and above whatever insurance paid out. All of that's fucking great, and it's also not what I asked. I was there at the Graham house, Delia. I know the kind of work you do, and I know a tiny bit of the dark-assed shit you're rolling around in. So, I'm asking you again, what happened up there?"

I stared at her a moment more, taking in her hard gaze, set jaw, her slicked-back hair in a no-nonsense bun, and the shadows under her whiskey-brown eyes. She smelled like exhaustion and worn vinyl. I drew in a shaky breath and rolled the dice that I wasn't making a colossal mistake.

"Kieran Walsh was possessed by a higher-order demon that I successfully removed from him a few days ago, but did not destroy. Because I didn't destroy it, it entered the computer systems of Prometheus Solutions, specifically the Reflex architecture."

She frowned. "Reflex. That's the system they're using to run the transit system."

I gave her a tight smile. "It is, yes. It has a few more bells and whistles that weren't quite ironed out in time for the rollout that Kieran wanted to announce today. Adding a demon to the mix didn't improve things. The system...got a little volatile."

"The fire at your house," she said flatly.

"Yeah," I said, unsurprised that she knew about that. I suspected Officer Hernandez had made my file her number one focus today. "My attempt to exorcise the entity for the second time was successful, but while that was in process, it used the company's projection system to fatally disorient Detective Walsh. He died in the line of duty. He didn't kill himself."

"Uh-huh. What about the guy they found in the basement, this Finn Ashford? Is he possessed too?"

I lifted a hand, dropped it. "I don't know," I said honestly. "I don't think so."

She blew out a long breath. "You know, when I first started working with you, I thought you'd killed Mordecai Schneider. And I was kind of pissed that you hadn't, because that would've tied things up nice and neat. You hadn't, though, and you actually seemed to help the Grahams, so that was okay. But now we're looking at this, I'm thinking the real answer about Mordechai and Marcus is a little more nuanced, isn't it? I'm thinking maybe there is a little bit of blame to head your way. You may not have killed them with your own hands, but that doesn't mean you're not responsible for their deaths."

I didn't try to deny it. I couldn't. Mordechai had died because of demons he'd been fighting—demons that included the one inside me. Marcus had died chasing a demon I'd failed to destroy. I hadn't pulled the trigger, hadn't pushed them, but I'd set the wheels of their deaths in motion. And that weight would stay with me, whether Hernandez absolved me or not.

She waved around at the hallway, her lip curling. "And now you've hung out a shingle. You've got clients coming to your door, podcasts talking shit about you and people in high places checking you out—hell, I even got a call from a friend of mine in City Hall, and that's a person on the side of angels. There are people taking notice who are a hell of a lot more dangerous than I think you realize."

I opened my mouth to speak, but she held up a hand. "Only, wait, though. You're *also* a hell of a lot more dangerous, aren't you, Delia? By my count, two people have already died on your watch. Are there any more out there I should know about?"

"Not yet."

She smiled, the expression hard and a little grudging. "Probably one of the more honest responses I've gotten today. Certainly more honest than I was. Marcus was decent though, even if he wasn't a great cop. And now he's dead. That's going to garner you a lot more attention than I think you may be prepared for. I'm not saying you have a target on your back, but if you did, you may want to arrange for your own protection. Police protection may not be quick enough."

A target on my back. A lot of that seemed to be going around all of a sudden. "It's that bad?" I asked quietly. Who were these people in high places looking at me, and how did Hernandez know about them?

"Let's just say it's not great. And that's interesting, too, isn't it? A whole lot of interest swirling around you, questions that need answering. Better hope the answers, once they come out, don't end up with you in the morgue, yeah?"

She turned on her heel and walked out the door.

THIRTY

I stared at the journal in front of me, my eyes blurring from fatigue. It'd been three days since I'd seen Officer Hernandez. Three days since Lucian had disappeared into the shadows. Three days of phone calls we screened, podcasts we tried to avoid but couldn't, and three expensive nights at the Palidor Hotel because the duplex was still a charred mess...and would be for a while.

Something had to change, but what? I drew my finger along the heavily annotated journal—Mordechai's exorcism accounts, organized by year. This was the third journal I'd found from the year he and I had met—and so far, there'd been absolutely no mention of me. Which didn't make sense. I mean, eventually, sure, I could see him omitting mention, but the casual notation of the weird girl with the dogs who showed up during a child exorcism—that didn't rate at least a footnote?

A soft knock at the outer office door interrupted my brooding. Claire glanced up from her desk, then stood with a small smile. "Mrs. Ashford," she said warmly, opening the door.

Victoria stepped inside, looking softer, more at ease than I'd ever seen her. She wore a tailored suit, her hair swept back, but her eyes were red-rimmed in a way makeup couldn't quite hide. Still, they felt like happy tears, and she smiled as she approached my office door, smelling like fresh rain and mint tea.

"I hope I'm not interrupting," she said.

"Not at all." I stood, gesturing to the chair across from my desk. "How's Finn?"

"Stable. Improving, even." Her smile wobbled slightly as she sat. "He's communicating through the monitoring system—brainwave blips mostly, but a few words to me, when we're alone." She paused, swallowing hard. "It took them twelve hours to extract him safely from that pod and put him into life support we can actually understand. The technology Kieran used—no one's seen anything like it, at least not in standard medical care. We're bringing in specialists, but from our early exploration, no one is taking ownership, and they might not—ever."

I blew out a breath, wondering what kind of billionaire-funded labs demons had access to. Pretty good ones, it would seem. "Well, I'm pretty sure they know they'd be prosecuted, so I guess that makes sense. I assume Jillian's of no help?"

Victoria made a face. "No. She claims Kieran only asked her to monitor 'the body' as she referred to it within the last week. I don't like her, but I believe her. Kieran's finally coming out of sedation too. He's confused, though. Disoriented. The doctors think he'll make a full recovery, physically at least." Her expression hardened slightly. "Emotionally, psychologically—that's going to take longer. He doesn't remember much of the past few weeks. Jillian insists he must have known about Finn all along, but I don't believe that—not really. Kieran was...compromised. Like you said. It will take a while for him to come back from that. Both him and Finn."

"But they think Finn will be okay."

She nodded quickly at that, her smile returning and this time, reaching her eyes. "They do. He's weak, but he seems… intact. The doctors say it could be months before we know the full extent of his recovery, but he's *here*. He's with me again."

"I'm glad," I said, and meant it.

"I know you are. That's why I came to thank you properly." She pulled an envelope from her purse, setting it on my desk with slightly trembling hands. "The retainer we discussed, of course, plus a significant bonus. What you did—what all of you did—" Her voice caught. "You gave me my son back. However long it takes him to heal, I have him. That's everything."

"Of course." I watched her steadily, making no move for the envelope. "And Reflex?"

"Dead." The word was final, absolute. "I'm shutting down the entire project. Whatever that system became—or was always meant to be—it's over. We'll return to basic city infrastructure monitoring, the barest minimum to satisfy contracts already in place. Nothing more. Prometheus Solutions will continue expanding, but in ways we can monitor more effectively. With better guardrails." Her lips twitched. "And holy water, as necessary."

I nodded, allowing myself the tiniest exhale. Maybe I could find a new place to live, then. Maybe I wouldn't be looking over my shoulder all the time. Maybe.

Victoria stood, smoothing her skirt. "I won't keep you. I know you're busy. But if you ever need anything—anything at all—you have my number, Delia. And my gratitude."

She left as quietly as she'd arrived, murmuring her thanks to Claire as well, and I stared at the envelope for a long moment before Claire appeared in the doorway.

"That was nice of her," Claire said softly.

"Yeah," I agreed. "It was."

We both looked up as the door to the outer office opened again, and I blinked as Claire stiffened.

"Steve, hey! What's wrong?"

The sudden concern in Claire's voice had me out of my chair and rounding the desk. I entered the outer office to see Steve shutting the door to the hallway behind him, then turning around and sagging against it as if he were coming down off a very bad high. He was sweaty and pale, yet somehow managed to look chilled—quite a feat for the balmy June night.

"Are you okay?" I asked him sharply, and he looked up, his eyes wide enough that I could tell that they were dilated. What had happened to him?

"I'm good!" he said. "I'm good. But—I mean, something happened on the way over here, I got a text from a friend with an, um, dark sort of problem, and well—"

I held up a hand to cut him off. "I'm not sure if you've been paying attention, but now maybe isn't the best time for a new client. Did you see the promo for the next Dark Streets pod? 'Death from the sky, an exposé of the supernatural death of a Chicagoland detective.' Lying low may become our full-time job."

"Well, she isn't possessed, if that's what you mean. I mean, I don't think she is." He rubbed his hand through his hair. "None of the usual indicators apply, you know? She has a loving family, she's happy, like, all the time—she's a great person, you know? Nothing shitty has ever happened to her in her entire life."

My lips twisted, and I leaned against the doorframe. "Until recently, I take it?"

"Yeah, super recent." He nodded, then made a face. "But I don't think the shitty things are her fault, okay? I mean, I don't exactly have demon radar or anything, but she's not pinging anything weird—she never has. She just—she's having some bad things happen, like, around her. Weird things. Accident-like things, sicknesses—and before you ask, she hasn't gone to a witch or consulted a Ouija board or so much as stuck a pin in a corkboard, let alone a voodoo doll. Things just are, like... happening. So I was wondering if maybe you could talk to her?"

My hands came up again, and his words flowed even faster. "You wouldn't even have to do anything, I swear. Meet her and see if, I don't know, how she feels to you. It would mean a lot to me, and to her, too, of course. And to her family, because they're all super worried about her. She's really a great person, you'll see."

I scowled. "Steve, just because someone's nice doesn't mean they can't be possessed. I was possessed, and I was super nice."

"Were you, though?" Claire put in. "You were a child. All children are suspect."

"I was walking dogs!" I transferred my frown to her, and she shrugged.

"So maybe we should ask the dogs, is all I'm saying."

"Well, Grace is super nice, for sure," Steve said. "She's also maintained her contacts with all her family and friends, and she goes to church, like, a lot. She prays all the time and unlike some people, she can handle holy objects without burning her fingers off."

I dropped my hands to my side, then crossed my arms for good measure. "She sounds awesome."

"Has she tried therapy?" Claire asked. When I blinked at her, she waved off my surprise. "It helps! Don't act like you haven't considered it—you know, once your hands heal."

"Therapy's not the issue." Steve chuckled as I shot Claire a glare. "She's all in on that, has been since she hit puberty, I think. Like she's wayyyy down the Manifest Your Dreams path. Which is why none of this makes sense. But she texted me, and

I called her, and, I don't know, I told her maybe you guys could talk. Just, you know, talk."

"We're kind of new to be taking on pro bono cases," Claire pointed out. "Especially if we're going to have to start setting up a fund for personal protection."

"Oh, money's not a problem, either," Steve said quickly. "She's got a full ride at the U, and even if she didn't, with her parents…it's not a problem. And again, I don't think it's an exorcism situation, just, you know, she'd like you to make sure she doesn't have any bad juju on her."

"I'm not a witch," I reminded him. "Or a psychic. Or a shrink."

"But you can talk to her?" he asked hopefully, as if I hadn't spent the last five minutes telling him no. He'd seen what I'd done to Jillian—to Alaria. He should be careful what he wished for. Still…

I rubbed my brow, feeling a headache come on. "Fine. Sure. You can have her—"

"Great," Steve cut me off. He turned and pulled open the door, reaching out to drag in a young woman. "This is Grace!" he said in a rush, then shut the door again.

Grace was maybe twenty-three, with a sweet, open face and nervous hands. She wore a cross necklace that looked like she'd bought it at the same store that Claire had scored hers, and, true to Steve's description, could easily have passed for a Sunday school teacher. She smelled of sweet pea lotion and chewed-off fingernails and dragging, soul-killing guilt. Her eyes were the color of the sea.

"I'm so sorry for bothering you—I overheard. I don't mean to be any trouble," she began, pushing her red hair behind her ears in a two-handed, automatic motion.

"You're not a bother. Please, sit," I said, as Claire stood and bustled over, showing Grace to the small collection of chairs in the outer office. Clearly, Claire wasn't going to miss out on one moment of this meeting.

Once everyone had sat—Claire and Steve at their respective desks, Grace and I in chairs so I didn't feel like I was looming, Grace continued.

"I don't know what's wrong with me, honestly," she said, dropping her hands into her lap. "But for the past few months, people have started...they're getting hurt. First, my professor had a car accident—and I like him, really! He's fine! Then my ex-boyfriend—" She stopped, swallowing hard. "He cheated on me, which did make me mad, okay? I'm human. But the next day he fell down the stairs and broke his *leg*. And then my roommate ate food she would never have normally touched— like, spoiled food. Rotten food. She ended up in the hospital!"

By now her eyes were wide, her breathing coming fast. I leaned forward as gently as I could. "It could be a coincidence," I said. "These things aren't your fault."

"But it's happening so *much*!" Her eyes filled with tears. "And I'm starting to *feel* something, like when it happens, you know? Like there's something inside me, waiting for a shoe to drop. And I don't want that shoe!"

She gestured helplessly. "I don't want to hurt anyone. I'm not a bad person. I pray, I go to church, I try to be kind. But it's like—like I'm *cursed*. Or worse. Only I don't know what would be worse than that."

I do, I grimaced and glanced at Steve, who shrugged. "I've known Grace since high school. She's genuinely one of the nicest people I know. But three people around her have ended up in the hospital in the past few months. The odds of that—"

"Are astronomical," I finished. I eyed Grace, who gave the impression she'd melt if someone looked at her the wrong way. "You said you can feel it. What does it feel like?"

She opened her eyes wide. "It doesn't feel like anything

tangible," she said, the soul of earnestness. "Just, like—a waiting. A knowing. And it's not a knowing I want! Really—I want to go back to normal, not sit in judgment on—I mean, on anyone."

I heard the buzz of my phone in my inner office and stiffened. Claire did too. Without waiting for me to tell her, she stood and circled around her desk, then disappeared through the doorway.

Meanwhile, I focused on Grace. "And you said nothing like this has ever happened before? There've been no other, um, unusual experiences around you?"

"Other than me putting people in the hospital?" she asked bitterly. "No. That's it."

I snorted. Despite myself, I liked Grace. "Well, this isn't exactly our usual client need," I began, when Claire spoke up from behind me.

"The retainer is $500 a week for this level of work, three-week minimum," Claire said, stepping toward me and slipping my phone into my hand. "Delia will decide on a course of action, and if you agree, she can start the research work she'll need to do within the next few days."

"You can?" Grace asked, her eyes going wide. "You'll help me?"

"We'd be happy to—if you agree to the course Delia suggests. Which, of course, you're under no obligation to do, and we'll collect no fee until you do. As a courtesy to Steve."

Claire smiled at Steve, who was now staring at us both, looking a little gobsmacked. I understood the feeling. "I can draw up paperwork right now, if you'd like? To get things rolling," Claire said, and she gave me the meaningful eyeball as Grace started crying again, soft, pretty tears that made you want to wrap her up in cashmere.

"It'll be okay, Grace," I promised, not knowing what else to say, but that only made her cry harder. As Claire scooped Grace out of her chair to lead her over to her table, I finally glanced down at the phone.

It was Lucian, of course. Claire knew his text tone as well as I did. And his message was short, succinct, and undeniable.

Take the job, it said. *It's started.*

AUTHOR'S NOTE

This is a work of fiction featuring demons, possession, and exorcism practices pulled from multiple faith traditions—then thoroughly mixed, bent, and occasionally broken to serve the story.

I've taken creative liberties with theology. Many of them. On purpose. Nothing in this book should be taken as a fully accurate representation of any genuine faith tradition, religious practice, or theological belief system.

All characters, events, and circumstances are fictional. Any resemblance to actual persons, living or dead, or real events is coincidental. Any errors are mine—whether from research gaps or deliberate creative choice, it simply depends.

If you're looking for canonically accurate demonology, please consult a theologian. If you're here for a dark demon romance, welcome aboard.

ACKNOWLEDGMENTS

Summoning a book like this into life takes more than candles and questionable life choices. It takes people. Very good people.

To my publisher, Tanya Anne Crosby of Oliver Heber Books, thank you for your ongoing belief in this story and the tales these characters have to tell.

To my editor, Sally O'Keef: Thank you for challenging me to go further, dig deeper, and for not blinking when things got uncomfortable.

To my cover designer, Kim Killion: You somehow captured the essence of this story perfectly. I suspect arcane contracts were involved. Whatever magic you worked, I'm grateful.

To Judi Soderberg and Sabra Harp: Your feedback was invaluable, your insight sharp, and your support invaluable...as was your breathtaking speed to help me get the book out so quickly. I'm profoundly thankful for you both.

To my proofreader, Kesha Young: You caught what I swore wasn't there. If any typos remain, they crawled back in after you banished them. That's on me, not you.

To my readers: Thank you for walking willingly into the dark with me. For exploring the dangerous, the twisted, and the beautifully broken. You make stories like this possible.

And to Geoffrey: You made this story better. As you always do.

ALSO BY JENNIFER CHANCE

The Accidental Exorcist

Wicked As Sin

Sexy As Sin

Guilty As Sin

Fang & Fire

Court of Talons

Crown of Wings

Gatekeepers of the Gods

Courted

Captured

Claimed

Crowned

Boston Magic Academies

Touch of the Mage

Blood of the Mage

Heart of the Mage

Soul of the Mage

The Hunter's Call

The Hunter's Curse

The Hunter's Snare

The Hunter's Vow

Witchling Academy

Teaching the King

Tempting the King

Taming the King

About the Author

Jennifer Chance is an award-winning author of magical modern romance and romantic fantasy. She is also the urban fantasy and paranormal romance author Jenn Stark. For free reads, news, and a magical escape from the ordinary, connect with her at jenniferchance.com (linked).

link: https://www.jenniferchance.com

fb: https://www.facebook.com/authorJenniferChance/

OLIVERHEBERBOOKS